THE
MONARCH
ALLIANCE

I0835150

WHAT READERS SAY

Shades of Gray (Historical Fiction)

"This book has moved EVERY emotion in me, from page one to the end! I've laughed, cried, and often forgotten to breathe! EXCELLENT book!"

"Good enough to hold in my favorites for a reread down the road of time."

"I'm giving this to my wife to read and know she'll enjoy it as much as I did!"

Lacewood (Dual Era Fiction)

"My kind of ghost story." – BookBub Review

"Beautifully done." – Goodreads Review

"Strong storytelling prose." – The BookLife Prize, Publishers Weekly

"A lovely story of healing & hope." – BookBub Review

Deadline (Suspense/Thriller)

"Very engaging. Hard to put down." – Billy Allmon, Retired Navy SEAL

"A fast-paced and exciting read, and it's most highly recommended." – Readers' Favorite

"James's patriotic mystery features solid prose and moves at a rapid pace that will grab readers." – The BookLife Prize in Fiction

BOOKS BY JESSICA JAMES

Historical Fiction

Shades of Gray Trilogy

The Lion of the South

Liberty and Destiny

Above and Beyond

Noble Cause

(Alternative ending to Shades of Gray)

Suspense/Thrillers

The Monarch Alliance

Meant To Be

Deadline

Fine Line

Front Line

Presidential Advantage

Protecting Ashley

Holiday

Sleigh Bells Ring

Non-Fiction

The Patriot's Journey: 250 Sites To Visit For America 250

Award-Winning Author

JESSICA JAMES

www.JessicaJamesBooks.com

ISBN (Hardcover): 978-1-941020-51-7
ISBN (Softcover): 978-1-941020-55-5
ISBN (Ebook): 978-1-941020-50-0

Library of Congress Control Number 2025921928

Cover Art: *germancreative* - Lesia

1st edition April, 2026

To my dad—larger than life and
missed more than words can say.

*"The most dangerous secrets are
the ones you carry alone."*

— **Unknown**

Prologue

SHADOWS BLED ACROSS THE walls as thunder growled beyond the mountains—a warning disguised as nature itself.

A solitary figure stepped onto the balcony, fingers gripping the iron railing to steady herself against the wind. The lake below, usually calm and glassy, churned in a roiling mass of silver and slate. She shivered as she watched the squall approaching, coming fast.

Before she could move another gust swept through, tangling her dress around her legs like grasping hands. She stumbled backward into the room, just as the wind ripped the door from her grasp, slamming it shut with a deafening crack.

Once inside, she glanced at the mantel clock and realized more time had passed than she intended. The approaching storm—and the uneasy anticipation that came with it—had pulled her attention away. Storm or no storm, it was time to go.

Gripped by trepidation, she snatched the folded letter from her desk and moved with urgency into the hall. The wind outside howled like a chorus of lost voices, making it seem less like a storm—and more like an omen.

She made it down the stairs without incident and slid the heavy parlor door aside. The moment it opened, a blinding flash lit the room—followed by a thunderclap so violent it felt like the earth itself tore open.

Then came darkness, utter and complete.

Walking forward blindly, she found the back of a chair and grasped it, seeking the stability it offered until she could get her bearings. Using the fireplace as a landmark, she pulled the letter from her pocket with trembling fingers. She wanted to place it quickly and go back to the safety of her room.

At that moment the storm seemed to pause outside, as if the world itself was holding its breath. In the suffocating silence, she felt someone come up behind her.

"*Abigail.*"

The voice, low and close, sent a chill of fear up her spine, yet it was familiar enough to stop the scream rising in her throat.

Before she could respond, arms enveloped her from behind, pulling her into an embrace that was as powerful as it was unexpected. There was strength in the way he held her—an unspoken promise of safety—steady, comforting, and threaded with secrets.

Yet there was something else there, too. Risk. Ruin. A truth too heavy to carry.

"Why are you here?" she asked, her voice tremulous, as she turned around. "What if—"

When he laid a single finger on her lips, she felt him tremble—and *that*, more than anything, stilled her. She knew it wasn't from fear and it wasn't from weakness. He was stronger than anyone she knew.

It had to be the weight of what he carried—a truth too heavy, too sacred, to speak without care.

She remained motionless, breathless with anticipation, knowing whatever he shared next would matter more than she could yet understand.

"Not all things lost are truly gone." He took a deep, shaky breath. "And not all things hidden are beyond your reach."

She felt the words settle over her like the darkness—complete, impenetrable, and full of meaning she could not yet grasp.

One

BLEARY-EYED FROM THE LONG drive, Dani Vaughn jolted upright when her phone said 2.5 miles to go.

Thank Goodness. Almost there.

With her attention focused on the curvy road, she made the final left-hand turn into the entrance as instructed, then hit the brakes without thinking.

A gatehouse stood ahead, a postcard-perfect structure of stone and weathered wood, its entry softened by bursts of colorful flowers spilling from landscaped beds. Charming. Unthreatening...

Unless you weren't expecting it.

And unless you had something to hide.

Her fingers tightened on the steering wheel as she put her foot back on the gas and crawled forward, lowering her window near the bold red sign that commanded: STOP.

Like magic, an attendant appeared from the shadows of the overhang, clipboard in hand, his face unreadable beneath the brim of his hat.

"Hi... Danika H–Hunter," she said, forcing the name out almost the way she'd rehearsed.

If he noticed her hesitation, he gave no sign. But he studied her a moment longer than necessary before bowing his head over the clipboard, his vigilant eyes concentrating on the list.

A cold sweat prickled at the base of her neck, creeping upward like an icy whisper of doubt.

She hated using the fake name, but it was necessary if she wanted to stay under the radar. Anyway, it wasn't entirely phony. Hunter *was* part of her name—usually buried in the middle as a nod to a distant ancestor—but still legitimately hers.

The attendant's gaze moved over the sheet, then to another, as if verifying something. Danika's pulse quickened. What was taking so long? She shifted in her seat, spotting a police cruiser in a gravel lot to her right—tucked away, but visible. Concealed but not hiding.

Probably routine.

Probably.

Her eyes flicked to the center console, where the certified letter that brought her here rested. She didn't need to read it. The wording was etched in her mind, an official threat in careful disguise.

Press credentials "flagged pending review." The words were vague, but they cut deep. Not an accusation, yet effective enough to erode a decade of trust. "Pending further investigation, access to governmental buildings has been temporarily suspended."

Temporarily. That was the word they used. But reputations didn't pause. They unraveled.

That document had done more damage than a bullet ever could, dragging her name into watercooler gossip, twisting her work into something suspect, and transforming her own shadow into something she no longer trusted.

The paper on the clipboard rustled.

Danika swallowed hard and studied the landscape with a sweep of her eyes. She noted the gatehouse. The distance from town. The forest like a barrier on all sides.

If danger followed her here, it would have to work for it.

"Ah, here you are, Miss Hunter." The man spoke at last, pen scratching a checkmark next to her name. “One more moment.”

He circled to the back of her car and returned with a yellow tag.

“Take the road to the right and follow the signs. Enjoy your visit.”

Danika nodded, easing her foot onto the gas pedal. The hard part was over... yet relief didn’t come.

Instead, a flicker of unease sparked beneath her skin—like static in the air before a storm splits the sky. She turned right as instructed, passing a weathered wooden sign: Mohonk Mountain House – 2.3 miles.

So close. After hours on the road, after planning and re-planning every detail, she was nearly there. And yet, the nearness brought an unexpected weight. A quiet unease settled, threading through each breath like a warning she couldn’t name.

For a moment, she considered turning around. The thought flickered, then vanished. This place was perfect. Even the security gate felt like a blessing in disguise, offering an extra layer of protection.

As the road narrowed, winding through dense pines and hemlocks, she began to relax. *What could go wrong?*

This resort was secluded. Safe. A mountaintop haven above the noise and chaos of the world below. Perfect for digging into a story that demanded to be told. She’d come too far and uncovered too much to stop now.

The threats had rattled her, but they’d also confirmed what she already knew. This story was too big to ignore, too important to abandon, and undoubtedly too dangerous to chase—

Unless you had nothing left to lose.

Two

DANIKA REFOCUSED ON THE road just as a sign came into view: *No Guiderails for the Next 2 Miles*. Her knuckles whitened on the wheel as she steered carefully along the narrow, winding road clinging to the edge of the mountainside.

With every sharp curve, her tension crept higher—like the road wasn't just testing her driving, but her resolve. She leaned forward, scanning ahead with laser focus, and watched another sign slide by that read: *Slowly and Quietly*.

"Slowly and white-knuckily," she said under her breath, flexing her fingers to coax blood back into her knuckles.

A cool draft brushed her cheek, and Danika realized she'd left the window down after stopping at the gatehouse. She drew in the refreshing air—crisper, cleaner… *older*. The kind that made her breathe deeper without thinking.

Focusing on the road, she settled into the rhythm of the turns. Her nerves eased at the sight of white boulders lining the edge, blending into the landscape yet standing firm as a natural guardrail. It struck her how something so simple could mean the difference between calm and catastrophe.

As the road carried her higher, the forest began to change—the trees thinning, sky breaking through the canopy. A flicker of anticipation stirred in her chest as she wondered what lay beyond the next rise—and then, there it was.

Mohonk Mountain House emerged as if summoned, rising from the mountain with stunning majesty—part fairytale and part fortress. Towers jutted upward like exclamation points against the sky, their spires flashing glints of burnt red in the afternoon sun.

Not fragile. Not quaint.

Enduring.

The structure held a depth, a history—its beauty masking something far more permanent beneath.

Her head tilted back as she tried to take in the massive building that rose from the mountainside. It looked timeless, like it belonged here, nestled on the rocks in the middle of nowhere.

Following the signs, Danika eased her car through a stone archway marking the entrance. As she pulled to a stop near the front door, a valet appeared, dressed in a collared forest green shirt.

"Welcome to Mohonk," he said warmly as Danika stuffed a nearby leather satchel into a larger backpack and climbed from the driver's seat. His smile was polite and sincere, the kind of smile you'd expect from someone who enjoyed his job. "May we take your bags?"

"Yes, I have three," Danika said, handing him the yellow ticket she'd received at the gate. "Two of them are a bit heavy. Sorry."

"Not a problem at all, Miss Hunter," the valet replied smoothly, as he glanced at the ticket. "We'll have them to your room shortly." He wrote something down and then handed her a small valet stub. "Would you like me to take that one as well?" He motioned toward the oversized backpack slung over her shoulder.

Danika shook her head. "No, I've got it."

Inside was everything she didn't trust to leave behind—her laptop, notebooks, and a worn leather pouch filled with old letters she hadn't yet found the courage, or time, to read.

"Of course. Enjoy your stay."

As Danika stepped toward the lodge's heavy front doors, a low hum of an engine pulled her gaze back to a sleek black BMW gliding in beside her car.

She wasn't one to notice cars, but everyone else clearly did. Heads turned. The valet attendants stiffened, alert. Even a passing guest straightened his stance and adjusted his tie.

That's when Danika realized it wasn't the car that had caught their attention—it was whoever was inside. She waited for the driver's door to open, and within seconds it did.

The man who stepped out didn't rush. He moved with deliberate calm, as if the world would wait for him. Dressed in navy blue slacks and a white polo shirt, he carried the kind of quiet confidence that turned heads without trying to.

Danika wasn't the only one captivated.

"Hello, Mr. DuBois!" the young valet called, practically jogging over. "We didn't expect you until later in the week. Welcome back!"

The man gave a brief smile. "It's just Julian, remember?" His voice was low, sure. Controlled.

"Oh yes, sorry, Mr. DuBois... I mean, Julian," the valet stammered, laughing with nervous energy. "Do you have any bags?"

"In the back." Julian flipped his keys to the valet, already walking away.

No valet stub. No name tag. No further conversation.

Lingering near the doors, Danika scolded herself for the old habit of studying people—and assessing them. But there was something about this man that made turning away impossible. He didn't move like someone here to unwind and relax.

He moved like someone who belonged.

Not wanting to be caught staring, Danika turned back toward the entrance. The mountain air pressed against her back like the touch of an unseen presence, making her feel strangely at home.

The sense of belonging intensified when she passed through the first set of doors, only to be jarred by a sharp awakening of her senses. Not a shiver of intuition, but something tangible. A smell.

A vase of fresh lilacs stood on a side table inside the entryway. Pale purple like the ones her grandmother used to grow right outside the kitchen door. The scent wrapped around her, comforting and calming and rooted in memory.

The doors closed with a soft click, locking her in quiet. Not silence exactly, but the kind of hush that clings to old churches and cemeteries; a quiet that feels alive. She reached for the next set of doors as something stirred—appreciation, maybe. Or wonder.

Presidents had walked these halls. Diplomats and historical figures, too. And maybe, almost certainly, her great-grandmother. Every return address on the letters tucked in her backpack pointed here.

She knew almost nothing about the woman who received them—and secretly saved them. Not her age at the time, her status, or her story. Only that she must have once walked these halls—or knew someone who did.

Danika took a deep breath before stepping through. Instinct told her this was more than a doorway—it was a threshold between present and past, where time lingered and the walls held secrets waiting to be heard.

Three

DANIKA WALKED SLOWLY, UNSURE of which way to turn until she saw the spacious lobby to her left. Everything felt carefully preserved, steeped in tradition, and alive with history. It was impressive without being ostentatious, grand without being overbearing.

"May I help you?"

A receptionist waved from behind the long wooden registration counter.

Danika walked over, her steps muffled by the thick carpet. "Danika Hunter," she said. The name didn't feel natural yet, but it no longer caught in her throat as a lie—and that unsettled her.

The woman's smile never faltered. "One moment."

Clicking keys. A soft hum from the monitor. Then: "Ah, here we are. And it looks like you're affiliated with the conference through GEM-Co, is that right?"

Danika hesitated this time—not long—but enough to feel the heaviness of another half-truth settle over her. She gave a small nod. "Yes."

You're not lying, she reminded herself. *Technically...*

GEM-Co was the name she'd tossed out in desperation weeks ago when the reservation desk said the hotel was fully booked—unless she was tied to a conference group. She wasn't. She had no idea what the conference was about. But she'd been investigating GEM-Co for nearly two years and knew its influence reached everywhere. It was a gamble—but one she could defend if anyone started asking questions.

Somehow, it worked. She got the room.

"Good. You're early, which is ideal. Here's what to expect as security tightens closer to the event."

As the woman leaned toward the computer, focused on her task, a resort staff member hurried in and whispered something urgent in her ear.

Danika caught a single word: *DuBois.*

The receptionist's eyes flicked toward the lobby, then back. "You're all set," she said smoothly, giving no indication of anything amiss. "Enjoy your view of the lake, Miss Hunter."

Danika gave a quick smile. "Thanks," she said, turning in time to see the elevator doors standing open. She rushed in and reached for the sixth-floor button, her fingers brushing the hand of a man doing the same thing.

"Oh, excuse me," Danika said, as they both withdrew their hands. "I'm sorry."

He smiled, his dark eyes catching hers, and for a moment, the small space between them felt charged, as if the air itself had shifted.

It was the man she'd seen outside. Julian DuBois.

"No worries. What floor?" He looked directly into her eyes when he spoke, his voice smooth, like he was talking to someone he'd known for years.

"Sixth," Danika replied, a faint flush warming her cheeks. His eyes were a deep brown, almost black, framed by lashes too long to ignore. Just like outside, there was something about him she couldn't pin down. He had that easy, let's-be-friends smile and a magnetic pull that made it hard to look away... but beneath the charm, he felt too polished. Too practiced. Like someone playing a part.

He hit the button and stepped to the back. "You just arrived?"

She nodded, already regretting the obligatory elevator small talk. "Yes, looking forward to exploring after being stuck in a car all day. A loud beep signaled the second floor.

Oh, your first time?" He looked genuinely surprised to meet someone new to Mohonk.

Another beep as the elevator passed the third floor.

"You must be here for the conference." He leaned in, eyes locking on hers—liquid intensity, sharp and unwavering—the kind of eyes that don't just look at you, but through you.

"Yes, it's my first time." Danika ignored the question about the conference. She didn't want to entangle herself any more than she already had.

The elevator beeped again, and the door slid open, bringing Danika back to the present. She glanced up, surprised to see they were on the sixth floor.

"I'm Julian." He stepped forward and held the door with one hand while holding out the other. "Nice to meet you, um, ..." He tilted his head and paused, waiting for her to give her name.

"Danika." She took his hand and dismissed the feeling she was meeting royalty. Based on the reactions of people to his presence thus far, this was not just a regular visitor to Mohonk. "Nice to meet you."

"The pleasure is all mine." His voice, smooth and sincere, somewhat stilled Danika's pounding pulse. "What's your room number?" He nodded toward her key card. "Odd numbers have mountain views. Even ones have lake views."

Danika, alert and suspicious, answered without revealing the number. "The desk clerk said it's a lake view."

Julian's smile held, though a flicker crossed his eyes—as if her guardedness had caught him off balance. "Very nice. If you're a morning person, the sunrises are stunning." His voice was casual, but laced with something harder to place.

"That sounds perfect for me." Danika shifted the weight of her bag higher up her shoulder. "Nice meeting you."

"Thank you. Nice meeting you." Danika shifted the weight of her bag higher up her shoulder and turned to the left.

"Nice meeting you, too, Danika," Julian said, as he let go of the door. "You'll find there's a lot to see here." The elevator door began to close. "More than meets the eye."

What does he mean by that? Danika mulled over his answer as the door sealed with a soft thud. *Is he referring to the rich history of the place? Or something else entirely?*

She turned her head and looked back. *And why hadn't he gotten off the elevator? Wasn't this the top floor?*

Danika scolded herself. *Why do you assume everyone has ulterior motives?*

Still walking, she glanced at the key envelope, confirming she was at the right door: Room 670. As she tapped it, she made a mental note to do a better job of staying under the radar—like not taking the elevator anymore.

This conference everyone was talking about meant the place was going to be crawling with people. The last thing she needed was to have someone recognize her.

That would ruin everything.

Four

Danika stepped into the room and let the door whisper shut behind her. She paused, taking a slow turn as her eyes swept the space—absorbing, measuring, savoring. The smile that pulled at her lips came easily, surprising her with its sincerity.

She'd stayed in luxury hotels across the country and around the world, but this room was different. Not just elegant—intentional. Every detail hummed with quiet history, as though the room had been built not to impress, but to endure.

Victorian luxury and historic charm… that's what the website had promised. But the clever wording hadn't prepared her for the feeling that settled over her now. Like she'd stepped into a place her soul already knew. It wasn't merely classy and tasteful; it was a reflection of everything she loved—a quiet harmony of past and present that reached deep inside.

The carpet beneath her feet was a rich, muted mauve—plush and yielding, muffling her footsteps with velvety softness. She drew in a breath, letting it still the restlessness she'd carried up the mountain.

A fireplace commanded the far wall, flanked by two antique armchairs that appeared both dignified and inviting—quiet witnesses to decades of conversation. A sofa and low coffee table completed the seating area, understated but deliberate.

She crossed to the writing desk beneath the window, a slender-legged piece with a surface that bore the soft scuffs of long use. On the table sat a bouquet of fresh-cut flowers, vibrant against the dark wood, and a small gift bag bearing the resort's logo. She lifted the note nestled inside and opened it.

> *Dear Miss Hunter,Thank you for booking your extended 30-day stay with us. We hope you enjoy your upgraded suite as a small token of appreciation for your flexibility. Welcome to Mohonk.*
>
> Management

The handwriting was warm, personal. One more thoughtful detail in a room full of them. It made the stress of booking during a large conference feel distant, and the significant dent in her bank account worth every penny.

She turned the paper over and noticed the small line at the bottom: Smiley Brothers, Est. 1869—a quiet nod to the Quaker founders of Mohonk. She'd read all about the twin brothers, gentle visionaries who ran the hotel with strict values many had thought outdated.

Yet those very ideals became the reason it endured. No alcohol. No dancing. No card games in public areas.

Hard to reconcile that strict Quaker culture with the castle-like building she'd just walked into. But then again, this wasn't a place that had ever tried to fit expectations.

She lifted her gaze to the balcony doors, where the world beyond the glass shimmered with an unspoken promise. With a quiet push, she slipped through, the screen door giving a soft sigh as it closed behind her.

The view stole her breath. She pressed a hand to her heart, as if she could pin the moment in place before it slipped away.

Below, the lake lay like a shard of fallen sky, impossibly still and dark. Its surface mirrored the jagged cliffs above, their ancient stone faces aglow in the afternoon light. Shadows from puffy clouds moved leisurely across the water, revealing more than they concealed.

She leaned forward on the railing, drinking it all in and trying to remember what she'd read about the property. Hard to imagine this peaceful expanse being anything but grand, but its beginnings had been far more modest.

With the help of architects, stonemasons, carpenters, and gardeners, the Smiley brothers had added gardens, gazebos, landscaping, and more than 85 miles of carriage roads to the property that had started as a simple 10-room tavern.

Their work and vision had paid off. It was breathtaking.

For a few suspended moments, Danika forgot everything else—the reason she'd come, the story tugging at her conscience, the pressure that had driven her here. All of it began to dissolve into the hush. Not vanish entirely, but soften. As if the mountain had taken some of it from her without asking.

Turning back inside, Danika continued to explore, walking into the bedroom that had a matching door and balcony. Somehow her bags had been delivered and stood neatly stacked near the armoire.

Another fireplace greeted her here, too, no less elegant than the one in the living room. She ran her fingers across its smooth wood mantel, tracing the lines of craftsmanship that belonged to another era. Nothing mass-produced. Nothing rushed. She'd once interviewed a man who called this kind of work "soul-carving."

She understood that now.

Her gaze fell on the king-sized bed, its crisp white linens promising the kind of sleep she hadn't had in months. She pictured herself curled there, fire flickering at her feet, the hush of the mountains pressed close against the glass.

It wasn't cold at the moment, but spring clung to the air. She hoped for evenings cool enough to light a fire—the kind that crackled and filled the room with just a hint of woodsmoke, making the world feel safe.

Stepping back onto the balcony, Danika leaned against the rail, letting the sun warm her face. Below, the resort moved with quiet life: people strolling the trails, their laughter drifting down the hillside. Canoes glided across the lake in graceful arcs, oars dipping in rhythmic motion. Teenagers splashed one another playfully, their joy rising like birdsong.

She glanced over her shoulder at her bags waiting to be unpacked, and then back toward the lake.

No contest.

The trails were waiting.

Five

Hoping to avoid another unexpected encounter, Danika bypassed the elevator and found a slate stairway at the end of the hall. Her fingers trailed along the handrail, worn smooth by time and touch. She imagined the hands that had done the same—children, parents, grandparents—generations drawn to Mohonk seeking peace, connection with nature, or simple escape.

As she descended the final steps, that strange sense of belonging returned. It curled around her like mist: familiar, intimate, and just out of reach. There was something about this place that left her both unsettled and oddly at peace, like standing on the edge of a forgotten memory.

Heading back toward the lobby, she walked slowly, trying to take in everything at once. Paintings lined the walls in stately procession, each enclosed in a gilded frame that reflected the light like soft gold. Though she wasn't an expert, the brushstrokes, the layered colors, the cliffs rising above blue water—stopped her more than once. These weren't just decorations. They were echoes of the past.

She paused in front of one that featured a wild, windswept tree on the edge of a cliff. Its limbs appeared twisted in defiance, battered but still standing. Something about it struck her, sharp and sudden, like the wind in the painting had swept through the hall and curled straight into her chest.

The tree's resilience lingered in her thoughts as she walked on. Strength carved by time—a quality mirrored in the sight that awaited her next. Mohonk's Central Staircase appeared before her like a sculpture of wood and will. She hadn't noticed it earlier in her rush to the elevator, and now it revealed itself—elegant, precise, built to last.

Every stair and spindle showed the mark of skilled hands. She reached out, fingertips brushing the carved detail worn smooth by time. Each cut spoke of careful work and a commitment to making something that would endure.

It was more than a staircase. It was an unspoken tribute to the kind of craftsmanship that stands the test of time. Grand, but not imposing. Alive with a quiet kind of history.

"Amazing handiwork, isn't it?"

The voice slipped in like a breeze through a cracked window—soft, gentle, unexpected.

Danika turned to find an elderly woman in a wheelchair rolling in her direction. Her bearing was somehow regal, her silver hair swept into a loose, dignified twist. She smiled, her eyes bright with warmth and a glint of keen interest.

"It has a way of stealing your breath, doesn't it?" The woman's voice seemed familiar, as though they'd known each other in another life. "It's a shameless show-off." She laughed at her own joke, blue eyes sparkling.

"Yes, it's..." Danika struggled for the right word.

"Spectacular?" The woman offered.

Danika nodded. "Yes, spectacular."

"Well, there are 1,411 spindles, in case you're wondering." She paused a moment as if reflecting on a memory. "My Robert and I tried to count them once on a rainy afternoon. We got two different numbers and argued about it until the dinner bell rang."

Danika blinked, eyes flicking up the spiraling structure again. It towered above her now, a marvel of craft and artistry.

"One thousand four hundred and eleven?" she echoed, amazed at the number.

"Well, that's the number I came up with anyway. Each one crafted by hand. Can you imagine?" Her words felt heavy with history, as though she had seen generations come and go within these walls. "Sometimes I try to figure out how many people have walked up and down these stairs over the years." She paused, a hint of something wistful flickering in her eyes.

The woman's deep wisdom resonated in Danika's bones, stirring an unexpected connection. The silver-haired senior reminded her of her grandmother, who had taught her to cherish small beauties—the curve of a hand-carved spindle, the crackle of a fire.

"Places like this remind us that we're part of something bigger," the woman said, as if reading her mind. "Threads in a tapestry that started long before us."

Before Danika had time to respond, she extended a fragile hand. "You must be new here. I'm Mrs. Winslow."

"Nice to meet you." She took the delicate hand gently in hers. "I'm Danika."

"It's a pleasure to meet you." Mrs. Winslow's voice was as clear as a bell, filled with a quiet strength. "I do love to see people who appreciate the history and craftsmanship of this place. It's becoming rare these days."

"I love history." Danika took a step back and stared up the stairwell from a different angle. Then she turned toward Mrs. Winslow again. "Have you been visiting here a long time?"

"More than sixty years." She paused a moment. "In fact, I got engaged here... and spent every anniversary here." As she spoke of her husband, the light in her eyes seemed to soften, the way the sharp edges of the mountains dissolve at sunset. “My husband passed five years ago, but I still come for the summer.”

“Oh, I’m so sorry.” Danika knelt and touched the woman’s hand. “You must have so many dear memories here.”

Mrs. Winslow smiled and nodded. “Indeed, I do.” She leaned back in her chair and closed her eyes. “I swear, sometimes I can hear the rustle of paper and see him reading the newspaper in that armchair over there, waiting for me.”

Then she turned her head and waved at someone in the parlor. “Well, there’s Myrtle, now. Take care, dear.”

With a final smile, Mrs. Winslow glided away in her motorized chair, her presence lingering like a whisper of the past. Danika watched her disappear down the corridor, then turned toward the door and stepped outside.

Six

THE COOL MOUNTAIN AIR wrapped around Danika the moment she stepped outside—crisp and clean, like a first breath after rain.

She paused at the edge of the wraparound porch where wooden rocking chairs sat lined up like quiet sentries. Guests filled a few, their low voices and laughter too gentle to disturb the stillness. To her left, water trickled into a koi pond. The fish rose at her passing, mouths kissing the surface, bodies glinting like coins in a fountain.

At the massive stone archway, she slowed, trailing her fingers along the jagged facade that had once welcomed every guest to Mohonk. She didn't need to close her eyes to hear the echo of carriage wheels and rustling skirts, the excitement of travelers arriving with trunks full of clothing and expectations.

Traces of the past lingered beneath the surface, almost whispering through the stones.

The sound of a canoe oar slapping the water stirred her from the trance. The modern world tugged at her sleeve, insistent and loud, while history lingered like a whispered memory, asking not to be forgotten.

Passing the boat dock, she started up the steady incline toward the famous Sky Top Tower. Sunlight filtered through the trees, casting shifting patterns over the path and moss-covered stones, while to her right, the lake caught the light, sending it back in a scatter of fractured sparks.

When one of the many summerhouses came into view on her right, she paused. She'd seen this simple structure from her room, but hadn't fully appreciated its impressive simplicity until now. The gazebo-like structure was more than just a shelter or place to rest. It was a masterpiece of art and engineering, seamlessly blending handcrafted beauty with the rhythm of the natural world. Built of rough-hewn logs, it stood as a quiet gesture of stillness.

Not grand. Not ornamental. Just... present.

Danika stepped inside. The bench was worn smooth beneath her fingers, the air shaded and still. From this vantage, Mohonk Mountain House loomed large and imposing, the whole massive structure mirrored darkly in the still waters of the lake. From within the summerhouse, it looked like staring at a painting, the scene perfectly framed by its wooden beams.

Danika had read about these structures, first built in the 1870s by local craftsmen and farmers. But the descriptions hadn't done them justice. They weren't shelters.

They were sanctuaries.

She sat, letting the hush settle around her, and for a moment, she could almost see her great-grandmother here, skirts brushing the floor, gaze drawn to the same distant line of mountains. Had she felt this same calmness? The same sense of serenity?

A breeze stirred the trees, and goosebumps lifted along her arms. She turned quickly, expecting someone to be behind her.

The trail was empty.

She continued upward, the trail growing steeper as it wound past more of the quiet wooden shelters—each one blending into the landscape, built not to impress, but to *belong*.

Danika found the surroundings peaceful, though never truly still. Birds called from the trees, insects hummed in the brush, and the wind whispered through the leaves. The resort carried an aura of natural beauty that was constantly alive with sound, yet never loud.

Ahead, massive boulders jutted from the earth like ancient sentinels, unyielding and immovable, the kind of strength forged over centuries. Between them, narrow crevices yawned deep and dark, some bridged by slender wooden walkways that offered heart-pounding views straight into the shadows below.

She paused at one. The view down stole her breath, a dizzying vertical slice of shadow that sent a jolt through her boots and up her spine. So much obscured, layered with mystery, edged in danger. Just like the story she was chasing—riddled with gaps, shell companies, dead ends.

Danika shook off the thoughts pressing in and kept walking as the trail angled higher. Heat coiled in her calves, causing her to pause and take a deep drink of water from the resort's colorful water bottle. She contemplated detouring to her right to Whittier's Outlook, but decided to push on instead.

The climb was making something painfully clear: hours at a desk had left her unprepared for even a modest incline. Writing took discipline, but not the kind that built endurance. Chasing paper trails behind a screen hadn't prepared her for a mountain.

She continued her climb, thankful for the cover of trees and the slight breeze that stirred the leaves. The trail narrowed, then gave way to stairs—granite steps carved straight into the mountain. She leaned forward into the effort, every footfall its own promise: Keep going. Keep digging.

When she finally looked up, the tower was there, still above her, rising on the ridge like a medieval sentinel.

She hadn't yet reached the summit, but the structure appeared much larger than expected—sturdier, more imposing. Of course it is, she thought. The first tower, built of wood, had been toppled by wind not long after it rose in 1909. The second was claimed by fire. The third, too.

But this one, completed in 1923, had endured. Through storms, wars, and a century of change, it held its ground. Solid in a way that spoke of permanence.

Pushing up the final incline, she lifted her gaze and blinked at the sight. The tower loomed above her, massive and unyielding, as if it had risen straight from the mountain's bones. Its stone matched the cliffs around it, weathered and ancient, flanked by boulders so immense they looked placed by time itself. It wasn't just a structure. It was a monument. And it made her feel impossibly small.

She stood still, pulse pounding, taking it in. Then, without waiting to catch her breath, she walked up to the open iron doors and stepped into the cool hush within.

As her eyes adjusted, a massive fireplace emerged on the far wall—cold now, but the space still carried the scent of old smoke. To her left, a stairwell curled upward into shadow.

Still breathing hard, she started to climb.

Halfway up, she paused at one of the window slits carved into the thick wall—just wide enough to let in a blade of light. Through it, she caught a glimpse of the view waiting at the top. It was enough to make her keep going despite her protesting legs.

And then—light.

The stairs ended and a spectacle unfurled, almost like past and present colliding with the sky. Danika stepped to the edge and felt her hat start to lift in the wind. She held it with one hand, the other gripping the stone parapet.

Before her stretched valleys stitched with farmland, forests rolling like a rough green quilt, and mountains rising like waves frozen in place. The scale of the scene hit her—not with awe, but with weight. Turning slowly, she took in the sweep of fields and streams, the ridgelines shifting between shadow and light.

Her gaze drifted back toward the Mountain House. Even from this height and distance, the Victorian structure dominated the landscape, its reflection glimmering in the lake below. The building was immense, almost surreal in its grandeur, as though it had been plucked from another time and dropped here in the middle of the wilderness.

She closed her eyes for a beat, then opened them again as a shaft of sun broke through the clouds, striking the Mountain House in gold and sharpening its edges so that it looked less like a hotel than a fortress carved into the ridge.

She thought about the work and the willpower it had taken to build. Vision. Sweat. Stubborn defiance against everything and everyone that said it couldn't be done.

Kind of like her.

She had no blueprint. No team. Just a notebook, a laptop, and a web of secrets no one else dared follow.

But something had pulled her here.

Not comfort. Not relaxation.

Truth.

And no matter the cost, she wasn't leaving without it.

Seven

By the time Danika reached the base of Sky Top Tower, the wind had picked up and the light had shifted again—sinking lower, stretching long streaks of amber and gold across the valley.

She sank onto a weathered bench, propped her feet on a nearby boulder, and tilted her face upward. A hawk spiraled above, riding invisible currents with effortless grace. As she tracked its slow glide across the sky, her mind drifted. Time had that strange way of feeling both endless and fleeting—like the hawk itself, suspended on a current for a breath before floating onward.

It reminded her of how little control she had over the past—and over what came next.

Soon it would be tomorrow. Then August. Then the holidays… another year. Life didn't wait for clarity. It moved on, ready or not—even if she was still trying to catch her breath, still chasing answers that always seemed one step ahead.

She drew a deep breath and closed her eyes, letting the sun warm her shoulders. For one still moment, the ache of not knowing all of the answers ahead of time quieted.

When she opened them again, a movement caught her attention.

A man sat on one of the large boulders near her, alone, relaxed, wearing a denim shirt and faded jeans. He wasn't looking at her. Wasn't doing anything at all, really, other than soaking in the silence like she was. But there was something about the tilt of his head, the strong cut of his jaw that tugged at the edge of recognition.

Casually, she reached for her phone, fingers moving on instinct. She typed a name: *A. Dalton Rivers.*

Dozens of headlines and images filled the screen: a glossy movie poster, a sleek car ad, a grainy telephoto shot of him on a yacht. The stories ranged from the scandalous to the absurd, proof of a life dissected, distorted, and sold by the inch to anyone watching.

There was a time when he'd been impossible to miss: red carpets, magazine covers, late-night interviews. He'd been the action icon of a generation, playing a war hero one week, a leading man in a spy thriller the next.

Then nothing. Silence so complete it became its own story.

She studied her phone again. In the photos, he looked younger—no gray at his temples then. But it was unmistakably him: handsome, magnetic, captivating.

A giddy flutter rose in her chest—ridiculous, really, like she was sixteen again with his movie poster on her wall. She wasn't a teenager anymore, but the reaction betrayed her. If it really was him, he'd shown up like a plot twist—right when her story needed one.

She glanced at him again. His expression was unreadable from this angle, but there was a quiet confidence in his posture, like a man accustomed to attention. He sat scanning the trees, tilting his head at a songbird, as if trying to place the tune or remember where he'd heard it before.

He didn't look like a tourist. He looked like he belonged.

Yet his presence couldn't be a coincidence...

Could it?

Danika's thoughts spun. She'd been chasing a story for two years. A story with pieces that refused to fit, trails that vanished without warning. Now, one of the most elusive public figures of the last decade was sitting a few feet away, silent as a shadow.

He shifted.

She stiffened, trying to act natural, but her body tensed like it was bracing for impact.

Moments later he stood, slow and fluid. From the corner of her eye, she watched his gaze sweep the trail, not in a curious way, but tactical. Like someone trained to assess exits.

Danika forced herself to stay still, pretending to be engrossed in the landscape, but she couldn't help herself. When his boots scuffed the gravel near her bench, she looked up and made eye contact. His gaze lingered—not unfriendly—but not warm, either. Then, the faintest of smiles. Polite. Distant.

"Afternoon," he said.

His voice was low and smooth, with just enough of a drawl that she no longer doubted his identity.

Danika swallowed, willing herself to sound normal. "Hi."

Did he recognize her from that fleeting moment years ago when she'd asked for an interview? Doubtful. It had lasted all of ten seconds, and he'd dismissed a thousand just like it with the same effortless, *no*.

His contempt for journalists wasn't just known; it was practically legendary.

In the blink of an eye, he'd turned and walked away, moving with the smooth, deliberate ease of someone who had long been accustomed to attention but mastered the art of avoiding it. A man used to being seen, but never truly known.

She waited. Counted the seconds. *One. Two... Ten.*

Then she stood and followed. To do what, she didn't know, but she couldn't just let him go. Rounding the tower's base on the back side, she expected to catch sight of him on the next stretch of trail. A glimpse between trees. A footstep ahead.

But there was nothing.

No crunch of gravel. No figure in the distance.

Danika stood still, heart hammering. She didn't believe in coincidences. Not here. Not now. She'd spent two years chasing a story that never seemed to add up. She'd followed threads that disappeared into shadows—and Dalton Rivers lingered at the edges of them.

She continued to stare, expecting him to appear. But there was no sound. No movement. As if he'd never been there at all.

A ghost? A mirage? A figment of her imagination?

Her gut told her none of the above. This felt like a thread tugging at the edge of something buried deep. The pull was irresistible, but so was the sense that danger stood ready at the other end.

Eight

DANIKA RETURNED TO HER room, intent on digging deeper into Dalton Rivers. What connection did he have to Mohonk? And what had driven him to vanish from public view?

To some extent, his exit from the spotlight is what fascinated Danika the most.

Was it from regret? Humility? Burnout? No one knew for sure, but that didn't stop people from guessing. If anything, his departure only fanned the flames, causing tabloids to fabricate wild theories that caught fire on social media.

He'd worked hard to lay low, but in today's world, absence only sharpened the spotlight.

Danika's thoughts spun, reaching for connections she couldn't quite see. Her instincts told her he was connected to the story she was already chasing. There had been whispers, hints, pieces of the puzzle just out of reach, like someone was always one step ahead, erasing the trail.

She settled onto the couch and flipped open her laptop. As she waited for it to power on, her gaze fell on her backpack lying on the coffee table. A worn, tattered notebook lay beside it as if waiting to be opened.

Something about it made her pause, reminding her of the story still waiting to be written. Even as her fingers hovered over the keyboard, a different name surfaced, one wrapped in even more intrigue than Dalton Rivers.

Julian DuBois.

She'd seen him again in Lake Lounge while grabbing coffee. Running into him once might have been a coincidence, but twice felt like something else. He wasn't the kind of man you overlooked. Conversations stalled when he entered, and every gaze in the room seemed to trail him.

And yet, even as he conversed and laughed and shook hands, something about him felt... rehearsed.

Too polished. Too perfect.

Let's see. Danika pushed the spacebar and was greeted with the familiar blink of the cursor. Her fingers paused another moment before typing, as she considered the ramifications of typing in Julian's name. She was safe in her room in a remote mountain retreat using a VPN, but that didn't mean her online activity wasn't still being watched.

But what could it hurt? Julian had nothing to do with the political circles she was investigating. He was merely a guest at the same hotel.

As usual, curiosity and instinct outweighed her sense of caution. Her fingers settled onto the keys, and she typed his name.

The results filled the screen in an instant: articles, press releases, interviews. He was everywhere. A billionaire with a golden reputation, Julian was credited with funding orphanages, disaster relief efforts, and environmental initiatives across the globe. He was lauded as a humanitarian with vision and heart.

Danika continued to scroll, her skepticism mounting. *No one is this perfect.*

Her skimming stopped when a headline caught her eye: *Historic Return of International Peace Conference at Mohonk Mountain House.*

She clicked the link. The article detailed a World Summit on Peace and Reconciliation, made possible by funding from Julian H. DuBois III. His donation, described as "staggering," would help host global dignitaries and heads of state under the banner of unity.

Danika's gaze dropped to the date: three weeks away? She'd assumed it was past tense.

So that's the conference everyone's talking about.

No wonder the rooms were booked solid and security was tight. The requirement to be affiliated with the conference somehow, like through a Non-Governmental Organization (NGO), made perfect sense now. They didn't want just anyone on the grounds mingling with heads of state and public figures.

Leaning back, she exhaled. How had something this big escaped her radar? When they'd asked for an affiliation and accepted GEM-Co, she'd figured the event here was just another government retreat—an excuse for bureaucrats to escape D.C. for a few days. Nothing out of the ordinary.

The thought of world leaders descending on this resort filled her with a strange mix of anticipation and unease. For most journalists, this would be a dream come true; a once-in-a-lifetime chance to brush shoulders with power.

But Danika wasn't chasing a new story. She was trying to finish the one that had already consumed her.

She'd spent years asking dangerous questions, writing stories that didn't make friends. Dignitaries and diplomats didn't impress her anymore. If anything, being recognized felt more like a threat than an opportunity.

She wanted to stay in the background. Invisible.

Her eyes returned to the screen.

Julian DuBois. His name was everywhere with glowing profiles, curated quotes, and endless praise. Charming. Generous. Untouchable.

It all fit like an image built for headlines, not truth.

Danika tapped her fingers against the keyboard, unsure whether to dig deeper or back away. She didn't want to push her luck.

Just as she prepared to turn her attention to Dalton Rivers, a small headline from an obscure trade site caught her eye. The article was dry, heavy with bureaucratic language, but at the bottom was a hyperlink: Public Financial Disclosure Form (PDF).

She clicked and scrolled through the document, her eyes locked onto a single line item: *Global Emergency Management Council [GEM-Co] Allocation Recommendation Committee —Julian DuBois III, Chair.*

Her breath stilled. The cursor blinked. The walls suddenly felt too quiet.

A rush of memory surged unbidden—blistering sun, the stench of sewage and smoke thick in the air. A community hollowed out by loss, exhausted and angry people waiting for help that never came.

That had been the first time she'd questioned GEM-Co's narrative.

Her eyes went back to the screen. Julian wasn't merely a donor or figurehead. He was chair of the allocation committee. The person deciding where billions in taxpayer dollars were sent.

The man whose presence commanded a room, the one she'd first met in the elevator, was linked to the very thing she'd spent two years trying to expose.

Her fingers trembled. She closed the laptop like it might detonate and surveyed the room.

Everything around her changed. The soft lamplight, the inviting hearth, the serene view from the balcony—it all felt different now. A curated calm masking something deeper.

Danika stood and began to pace, memories flashing like newsreels of her first assignment covering GEM-Co's overseas relief work. The organization branded itself as a global savior: glossy brochures, smiling children, promises of aid in war zones and natural disaster sites.

But on the ground, the truth was impossible to ignore.

She'd gone to report a success story. Instead, she found rubble where schools were promised, families begging where food centers should have stood.

After filing a fully sourced exposé that stripped away the polish, her editor had replied within minutes: "Not the angle we're looking for. Drop it."

But she hadn't. She couldn't.

Danika squeezed her temples, trying to slow down the flood of rushing thoughts as she sat down on one of the chairs by the fireplace.

At first, she'd tried to rationalize the outlet's reluctance to publish her piece. Maybe the story was too big, too risky for them. But when she'd shopped it to others, the fallout came fast. Promised assignments vanished. Calls went unanswered. Emails ignored.

Was it fear? Complicity? Or something more orchestrated?

Not one to back down from a fight, Danika simply pushed harder and dug deeper. But the farther she went, the faster the walls closed in. Her name vanished from freelance rosters at major publications. Reliable sources stopped returning her texts. Most wouldn't take her calls.

The message became unmistakable: Stop digging or lose everything.

It wasn't just a story they'd cancelled.

It was her.

Nine

Restlessness gnawed at Danika, and she finally gave in. The moment the door swung open, a cool rush of air poured in, sweeping across her face and loosening the tightness in her chest. She stepped out, letting the breeze carry away the weight of her thoughts. Out here, with the lake stretching below her, she could breathe. She could think.

Two years.

That's how long she'd chased ghosts through digital paper trails—shell companies that vanished overnight, wire transfers to nowhere, names that led to dead ends.

At first, she believed it was incompetence. A failure of bureaucracy. Gross mismanagement.

But then she started thinking, what if it wasn't?

What if they weren't failing to *stop* the chaos—but *causing* it?

And if so, *why*?

She wandered back inside and dropped onto the couch, her gaze locking on the closed laptop. Somewhere in the maze of documents was a thread. She just had to find it.

But sometimes it felt like she was reading a political thriller, not governmental documents. GEM-Co had been linked to everything from rigged lawsuits and shady advocacy groups to diverting taxpayer dollars to shady organizations that seemed to operate above the law.

And yet, it was still being funded.

Still growing.

She leaned over and picked up the notebook, flipping to the dog-eared tab labeled GEM-Co. Three questions stared back:

Where is the money going?Who's benefiting from the chaos?Why isn't anyone asking questions?

The last question, at least, had an answer.

Two journalists had tried. One was smeared beyond repair, unemployable. The other disappeared from the industry. Addiction? Legal trouble? Nothing was ever confirmed.

Danika thumbed the edge of the page, her mind drifting.

Even now, after thousands of documents and endless nights cross-checking contracts, she had more questions than answers. It didn't make sense.

But maybe that was the point?

Corruption survived in the fine print. Paperwork so tedious, convoluted, and complex that no one had the patience to unravel it.

How could there be no oversight over billions of dollars siphoned into dead-end companies and to *consultants* with no last names? How could projects receive millions in publicly earmarked funds, yet provide no records to show where the money went?

No one seemed to notice.

Or maybe they did—and just didn't dare act.

Not with Senator Sebastian "Seb" Wiley at the center of it all. She'd heard the whispers... money laundering, voter manipulation, backroom deals that rewrote laws and destroyed lives.

No one questioned his power.

Then again, why would they? One call from Wiley could turn an aide into a senior advisor or destroy someone's livelihood before lunch. Even seasoned politicians tiptoed around him. Or groveled for his favor.

Danika rose and crossed to the window, the stillness of the lake offering a fragile balm to the churn inside her.

The scariest thing about Wiley wasn't what he said. It was what he didn't say. His power was quiet. Surgical. No bluster, no grandstanding. Just careers changed through committee reshuffles. Bills that never saw the floor. Legislation that bent legal lines.

Danika didn't have to imagine what he was capable of. She'd lived it.

Freedom of Information Act requests denied. Sources who went silent. Files marked public were suddenly sealed or reclassified. Wiley didn't just bury the truth. He made sure no one dared dig for it.

Danika rubbed the tension from her shoulders as she stared through the screen door. The scene below was almost idyllic—guests strolling, laughter drifting from the lake. But it suddenly felt too perfect, too calm. Like the hush before a storm breaks, when the sky pretends nothing is coming.

Taking a slow, deep breath, she weighed her choices... and her odds.

The decision wasn't hard.

Despite the danger, she couldn't walk away. Because deep down, beneath the fear, something sparked. She was getting close. An innate sense told her a breakthrough was near.

She kicked off her sandals as she walked back to the couch and reopened the laptop. Settling into a comfortable position, she nestled the computer on her lap, and instantly noticed the small asterisk beside Julian's name—missed earlier in the gut-punch of seeing it at all.

Skimming to the bottom of the document, she found a link for a footnote. *Probably a dead end*, she thought, but she clicked anyway.

* *Mr. Julian H. DuBois III appointed Chair of the GEM-Co Allocation Oversight Committee per directive issued by Senator S. Wiley, third day of June.*

Danika's stomach turned.

A recommendation from Wiley wasn't a suggestion—it was an order. And now Julian sat at the helm of GEM-Co's most powerful committee.

That kind of placement wasn't random.

It was strategy.

She just had to figure out what it meant.

Grabbing her notebook and a pen, she jotted down the date and wording of the appointment, her gaze shifting back and forth from the scrawled notes to the glowing laptop—until she noticed the screen flicker, then blink.

Once. Twice.

Then the computer went black.

"What the—?" She dropped the pen and tapped a few keys. Nothing. Dead.

Then, just as suddenly, it blinked back to life.

Kind of.

The document she'd been examining was no longer there. In its place, her browser homepage. She hit the back button. Nothing.

Danika stared, barely breathing. Slowly, she moved the cursor to check her browser history.

Blank.

She snapped the laptop shut and stood, crossing to the window to draw the blinds—more reflex than reason. The gesture offered no real protection, but it made the room feel less exposed.

"Okay," she whispered. "*Breathe.*"

The silence pressed in. She sat down, then stood and began to pace to work off the surge of adrenaline.

It could be a simple computer glitch, she told herself.

She stopped mid-step. *Highly unlikely.*

Or it could be a warning. She squeezed her temples. *Possibly probable.*

Danika paused long enough to gulp down some water from a glass on the coffee table, then mulled over the facts beginning to take shape.

She'd come here to disappear. To lie low. But instead, she'd walked straight into the eye of the storm.

Julian DuBois.

The name pulsed through her like a silent warning.

Philanthropist. Diplomat. Visionary.

And now, a major link between Wiley and GEM-Co.

She'd always known that taking on GEM-Co was dangerous; tying Wiley to anything illegal was a death wish. Now she had a single name linking them both.

Julian DuBois.

...Or maybe she had it all wrong.

She paced while twirling one strand of hair around her finger.

Maybe she was getting close. Or maybe she was playing straight into the story they wanted her to chase—just enough truth to bait her, just enough evidence to keep her busy.

She knew how easy it was to mistake a paper trail for progress. A few puzzle pieces could feel like the full picture if you wanted the story badly enough.

Still, she couldn't ignore the gut-deep certainty she was getting close.

She stared at the closed laptop. Every instinct whispered: Leave it for now.

And for once, she listened.

I'll pick it up in the morning, she thought to herself.

Then again... she wasn't sure how long it could wait.

Ten

Danika stood on the balcony, arms folded across the railing, her eyes tracing the quiet poetry of the landscape below. The lake shimmered beneath the soft illumination of the resort, reflecting the decorative glow of the summerhouses onto the glassy water.

She had to admit there was a calm here, a peace that seemed comforting and reassuring. The kind that creeps into your bones when you aren't looking.

Yet still, she couldn't settle.

The miles she'd driven, the climb to the tower, even the pressure of the story she was working on—none of it had worn her down. Restlessness hummed beneath her skin, a relentless nervous energy that never seemed to dull. It wasn't adrenaline, but something deeper, hardwired. Like her body didn't know how to stand still unless it was braced for impact.

Even as a child, she'd never been one for stillness. Her parents used to joke she was born with her engine running. But it wasn't just energy. It was survival.

Even now, when she was alone and everything around her was calm, her mind wouldn't stop scanning: what she'd missed, what she hadn't uncovered, what could go wrong. Stillness didn't soothe her. It sharpened her focus.

Well, that's why I'm here, she reminded herself. *To try to relax. Learn how... if that's even possible.*

She knew it wasn't going to be easy, because all she'd ever known was how to stay ready.

Walking back into the room, her gaze fell on the satchel sitting inside the door. The letters.

Perhaps they would provide some light reading and entertainment, allow her to chill. She hadn't meant to start reading them yet—there would be time. But curiosity tugged at her like a quiet invitation.

With a sigh, she picked up the bag, her fingers lingering on the worn leather before flipping open the flap. The scent of aged paper and dust rose instantly, transporting her back to her knees on a dirty floor, flashlight in hand, scraping her knuckles as she tugged it free from the shadows more than a year ago.

The attic had been empty, she thought. Her family had already packed and sold off what mattered to them. But the satchel, half-buried near the eaves, had escaped their notice. The way it had been tucked away in the darkest shadows of the attic suggested it had been lost long ago.

Or perhaps, wasn't ever meant to be found.

Inside, hundreds of letters rested in neat bundles, held by faded ribbons. Addressed to Miss Abigail Prescott in a neat, masculine hand, each one bore the return address: Noah Morrison, Mohonk Mountain House.

Abigail Prescott was her grandmother's mother. But Noah Morrison wasn't her great-grandfather.

That mystery alone would have drawn her in. But it was the sender's return address, this place, that made the pull irresistible.

She carefully untied the ribbon on the first bundle according to the stamped date and laid the letters on the coffee table. The paper was soft with age, the ink faded but still readable. She held one up to the light, fingers tracing the flowing script.

Who was Noah to Abigail?

Why had these letters been hidden so carefully?

She unfolded the first envelope with care, her breath catching with something close to anticipation. The date caught her eye immediately:

Ninth Month 10th, 1903
Dear Friend Abigail,

I trust thee will not think me too bold in writing, but I felt compelled to send these words. It has been on my mind to know that you arrived home safely, and I could not rest until I did so.

The air has turned cool here, a nip of autumn that speaks of what is to come. Yet my heart remains with the warmth of summer's end, and I hope you hold the same fond remembrances.

Your friend in faith,
Noah Morrison

Danika let the letter rest in her lap. The words were gentle. Friendly. But also restrained.

Who was this man who had written with such care?

And why had Abigail kept his letters, hidden away in a satchel no one was meant to find?

Her fingers ran over the edge of the paper. Would her great-grandmother have wanted this part of her life exposed? Or had she hidden it as a way to preserve it? Something too precious to destroy? Too private to share?

The house where her mother and grandmother had been raised, and where Danika had made her most cherished memories, was gone now. Sold without fanfare to strangers who didn't know the echo of laughter that once filled the kitchen. They didn't know the feel of sun-warmed floorboards under bare feet, or the scent of apples baking in the fall. To them, it was merely real estate. To her, it had been a living thing.

Finding the letters had felt like the last thing the past had to offer—as if the house had waited until the final moment to give up its secret.

She picked up the second letter. The same neat handwriting. A slightly darker ink.

Eleventh Month 16th, 1903
Dear Friend Abigail,

Your letter reached me this morning, and I must tell you how it lightened my spirit. I had not expected a reply, and so it came as a joyful surprise. It is a kindness I will not soon forget.

The mountains are quiet now, a stillness that permeates everything. The absence of guests leaves only the whisper of wind through the trees and the occasional call of hawks and owls. The stillness should bring peace, but my thoughts often wander to the summer.

If it is not a burden, I would welcome another letter. It would be a wonderful diversion to hear from you over the quiet winter months.

With all sincerity,
Noah Morrison

There was something in his tone, warmth, but also distance. A carefulness. As if the letters walked a line between propriety and something deeper.

Danika's thoughts turned to Mohonk. Guests had once arrived from New York, escaping the city heat for a few months in the mountains. Abigail's family had been one of them.

She flipped through the next letter, stopping when her eyes caught a particular line:

To me, it is a blessing that you stopped to talk to me at all, with my 'rough-hewn charm' as you call it. I had no way of knowing then that those first few words of introduction would lead to our future correspondence.

Your simple act of kindness transformed into something that is profound. Such are the workings of the Almighty.

Wishing you Holy Blessings,
Noah

Danika paused, letting the words settle. Something resonated with his tone, even more so than his words. This wasn't just the language of friendship, but it wasn't the language of courtship either. It seemed deeper, a connection that seemed to reach beyond time.

Sighing, Danika glanced at the clock. She felt like she was reading a novel and couldn't stop turning pages, but it was later than she'd expected. There were literally hundreds of letters, many years' worth. She would not be able to read them all tonight.

As she put the ones she'd read into one pile and began to put the others away, she decided to read just one more.

> *Do you remember how you used to say we were never truly alone when we sat near the fireplace watching the light from the flames dance on the walls? As I look over the mantel now, I see the same two souls looking on—one with a book, wisdom in his gaze, the other with a flower, her beauty ablaze.*
>
> *I wonder if they saw what we shared and have the same lovely memories?*

Danika's hand instinctively went to her chest, pressing over her heart. It ached at the tenderness in the words. Although she didn't really understand the meaning, there seemed to be a longing there—a quiet, gentle affection that felt real and intimate, even after all these years.

What had happened between Abigail and Noah? Why had these letters been hidden away, kept secret?

And why was this the first time she was hearing his name?

Danika sighed and tucked the letters back into the satchel. She wasn't ready to read more. Not yet.

There was too much to process, too many emotions pulling at her all at once. She felt like she was eavesdropping on a conversation never meant for her ears. Would her great-grandmother mind? Or had she saved these letters so this part of her story would someday be revealed?

Whatever secrets had been kept and for whatever reason, Danika hoped these letters were the key.

And she hoped she was ready for the answers they might hold.

Eleven

Danika caught the sound before the sight: the hush of rain, like gentle fingers drumming on glass. It echoed through the quiet as she brushed her hair, drawing her to the balcony door for a closer look.

Moments ago, the sun had been shining and she'd planned to head for the trails. Now, raindrops traced rivulets down the tall windows, turning the lake and the ridge beyond into a blurred watercolor landscape.

Plan B, she mused, exchanging her walking shoes for sandals. The trails could wait. This morning, she would explore what lay within.

Mohonk was a world unto itself, a labyrinth of rambling halls and hushed parlors beneath a roofline stretching nearly an eighth of a mile. A rainy day was perfect for roaming its seven stories of corridors, each lined with antiques, artwork, and architectural marvels.

Danika descended the slate stairs to the first floor, her footsteps softened by thick, patterned carpet. Along the way, she passed velvet-cushioned parlor chairs and sofas, their colors surprisingly vivid despite decades of quiet conversations.

Everywhere she looked, there was something to see. Tiffany lamps cast golden pools over antique desks. Clocks sat frozen on mantels, their brass hands stilled at forgotten hours. Everything felt touched—used, remembered, loved. As if the past hadn't vanished but merely stepped aside to make room.

At the Central Stairs, she paused, disoriented, thinking she should be in the lobby. Then she remembered Mohonk's main entrance sat one level down, part of its peculiar charm.

As she continued walking, she noticed a pair of closed old-fashioned pocket doors with a sign in front that read "Meeting in Progress." She glanced at her watch: seven fifteen. In a place where every room was open and inviting, this barrier felt strangely out of place... as though deliberately hiding something.

Danika almost walked past, but a flicker of curiosity stirred. *Maybe a quick peek.*

Curious, she slid her fingers into the ornate brass handle and pulled to the right to see if the door was locked. It was heavy, unwilling, but finally inched open; reluctant but yielding. The sound echoed, like the room beyond was being forced to awaken from a long slumber.

Danika lingered with her head poking through the doorway. Bathed in muted light, the room seemed to breathe with its own presence, harboring its own pulse.

Curiosity tugged at her. She stepped across the threshold and eased the door closed behind her, leaving a space wide enough to squeeze through.

The room seemed suspended in time, waiting for a gathering that hadn't yet begun. Neatly arranged rows of chairs faced a speaker's podium at the front, each placement deliberate and orderly.

Danika stepped further in, her gaze drawn to the right. A grand fireplace anchored the wall, flanked by tall vases. A bronze bust of a Native American chief stood to the side, his solemn expression conveying quiet strength as he stared out over the room.

To the right of that stood a towering grandfather clock, more cathedral than timepiece, its pendulum still swinging. The artistry of the piece drew the eye, not just its height, but the regal detail in every line, as if it were built to echo the room's heartbeat.

She moved slowly down the aisle, eyes drifting upward to the heavy beams that crossed the ceiling in dark symmetry. The craftsmanship whispered in every corner, needing no spotlight to be seen.

Danika paused, letting the room settle around her. There was a sense of permanence here, of beauty built to last. She could feel it in the quiet—the memory of hands that shaped wood, stone, and light into something meant to endure.

As she stepped closer to the massive fireplace, Danika's eyes drifted upward. Above the mantel, two portraits stared down at her. She recognized them instantly—Albert and Eliza Smiley—the resort's founders. Their faces were as familiar to her as family from the countless articles she'd read about the resort. But something about the paintings made her pause... almost like a flicker of memory, taunting her.

She continued staring, trying to understand the attraction, when the words from the letter she'd read burst into her mind, the passage so eloquent it was ingrained in her memory.

While above the hearth, two souls looked on. One with a book, wisdom in his gaze; the other with a flower, her beauty ablaze.

Her eyes darted from one figure to the other. Albert held a book on his lap, and Eliza clutched a flower. Whoever the man was who had written letters to her great-grandmother, he'd been talking about *this room.*

Danika's chest tightened with an emotion she couldn't explain. She hadn't thought much of the letters at first—old-fashioned musings from a time long gone. She'd rescued them from a dusty attic out of sentimentality, not because she believed they held any real importance. That's why they'd remained in the satchel, unread, all this time.

But now, standing here, those words felt alive, crashing down on her and shaking her to her core. Seemingly, little had changed in this room over the past one hundred years. She was looking at the same things Abigail had.

What had she felt? What secrets had she carried to her grave?

Danika blinked rapidly, her eyes stinging at the wish to know more. She wasn't the emotional type, but something about this moment cracked her open. She sank into one of the chairs by the fireplace, her breath uneven.

The connection to her own flesh and blood pressed down on her like a weight she hadn't realized she was carrying. She leaned forward, her face in her hands, when a voice cut through the silence.

"Miss..."

Danika shivered and looked at the paintings again, thinking she was hearing voices from long ago... ghosts, shadows, seemingly close enough to touch, but not really there. The room felt alive. Real.

The voice came again. Louder this time. More forceful. "Miss?"

Danika jolted upright, startled, and turned her head. A man stood sideways in the doorway, the light from the hall casting his face into shadow. He pushed the door open effortlessly to make room for his large frame and stepped inside, providing a better view.

He was tall and carried the kind of presence that commanded attention without saying a word. The black tie and crisp white shirt he wore lent him a certain professionalism—but the bronzed tone of his skin and the casual way he'd rolled his sleeves to the elbow suggested a man more at home outdoors than behind a desk. The tie, she suspected, was worn out of obligation, not preference.

"This area is off-limits to guests." His gaze swept the room guardedly as if looking for something hiding in the shadows.

When his attention returned to Danika, she took a fuller measure of him. His wavy dark hair wasn't exactly tousled, but neither was it neatly combed. His eyes, though, were what caught her attention and held her.

Stormy blue and unyielding, they were hard to look into—harder still to look away. They made him appear both approachable and untouchable, a man accustomed to being noticed but rarely, if ever, letting anyone close.

Danika stood, wiping her palms on her jeans. "I—I didn't know. The door wasn't locked."

The man's expression didn't change, though his brow creased slightly. He took a few steps closer, stopping near the fireplace.

"Are you a guest here?" he asked.

"Yes." She declined to offer her name since he hadn't asked for it. Her gaze dipped to his belt, where a laminated ID tag hinted at authority. "For a month," she added, hoping the fact that she had booked an extended stay might soften his view of her as an intruder.

He nodded once, slowly, as if running advanced mathematical equations in his mind while holding a conversation. "Well, this room is off limits to guests."

He didn't offer a reason why or an apology on behalf of the resort that it was unavailable. But he made it clear by his tone that he expected her to leave.

Danika swallowed, glancing back at the portraits. "I was j-just exploring and stumbled across it. And then..." Even though her voice cracked with emotion and she could feel a sudden rush of unwanted tears welling in her eyes, she decided to push right through. "I read a letter written to my great-grandmother." A sob choked her, but again she continued, "...and it mentioned this room."

She was hoping her obvious distress would soften his stance, but he simply crossed his arms and tilted his head. "It mentioned this room specifically?"

"Yes." Danika nodded, her voice steadier now. "It described the fireplace, the portraits. It's just—" She trailed off, glancing around the room again.

"It's strange to know she was here." She paused and allowed her gaze to roam. "*Right here.*"

The man followed her gaze to the portraits, and his expression turned suddenly thoughtful. "What year was the letter written?"

Danika hesitated. She wasn't sure she really wanted to share information with a stranger, but she could think of no reason not to. "The letters started in 1903. I haven't gone through them all yet."

The man nodded. "I see." Something flickered in his gaze—interest, maybe? She found it hard to tell. His eyes were mostly unreadable, but his stance reflected a calm authority, a kind of intensity that made her feel a mixture of curiosity and caution.

Even though she hadn't answered his question, he didn't press her for more. But his gaze lingered on her face as if trying to read her mind.

"Well, I'm going to have to ask you to leave. This room is closed for a private event."

"But it's early," Danika said, pushing back. "No one's here." She wasn't trying to break rules—but something about this room felt sacred. Personal. Stepping out now would sever a thread she hadn't finished following.

The man's expression cooled. He didn't look annoyed, just resolved. "We have high-profile guests meeting here. It needs to be secured."

The word hit harder than it should have. *Secured*.

She scanned the room again, more carefully this time. So this was where they planned to hold the peace conference. Her gaze drifted upward past the man's shoulder, and locked on a second floor she hadn't noticed before. A balcony extended overhead, lined with neat rows of wooden seats that were empty now, but watchful. Like a hidden gallery for ghosts.

Danika took a step back, goosebumps lifting on her arms. "You know what's strange?" she murmured, half to herself. "There were peace conferences in this room before, more than a hundred years ago."

She wasn't sure why she said it out loud—only that she suddenly realized she was standing in the parlor wing, the same place the Smiley brothers hosted international arbitration conferences from the late 19th to the early 20th century.

The man's gaze sharpened as he tilted his head inquiringly. "How do you know that? Was it in a letter?" His strong voice turned low as if they were discussing something secret or covert.

"I haven't read that many of them yet." Danika watched his face a she talked. "But they definitely cover some of the years conferences were held here."

The man apparently decided the conversation was over and that she needed to be shown the way out. He walked toward the door with a look of calm certainty and slid it open wide for her.

"The letters don't mention a peace pact that was signed here, do they?" His voice sounded like he was trying to be nonchalant, but Danika could hear the seriousness in his tone.

When she didn't answer right away, he turned his head back to her. "*Do they*?"

The gaze he shot her held the kind of intensity that made her almost forget the question. She swallowed before answering, not sure how much she should say.

Twelve

"What does a peace pact have to do with anything?" Danika answered his question with one of her own.

The man slid the door shut again with so much force, it shook. A new tension charged the air as he turned to face her.

Is there any mention of a pact?" His voice softened, but there was an unsteady undertone, a tremor that hinted at the emotions he was struggling to keep under control. And those intriguing blue eyes now sent a very strong you'd-better-take-me-seriously message.

"I don't know." Danika shrugged.

"You mean you won't tell." He stood up straighter and crossed his arms.

"I mean I don't know," she repeated firmly. "Like I said, I haven't read them all. I brought them along so I could read them while I'm here."

He remained silent, but his gaze was unwavering as he weighed her words. "What years did your great-grandmother come here?"

"Why is this all so important?" Danika tried to mirror his strength by crossing her arms. "I don't even know your name. Why should I tell you about personal family matters?"

He hesitated, then gave a curt nod, as if conceding her point. Taking a step toward her, he extended his hand. "Cole."

Danika eyed his hand warily before reaching out. His grip was strong, steady, just as she assumed it would be. "Danika," she replied, her tone cautious. She didn't give her last name since he hadn't offered his. "Nice to meet you. Do you work at Mohonk?"

"I help with security," he said, his voice steady but with that same vagueness that seemed to be a part of his demeanor.

Danika bit her lip, feeling her irritation flare up again. "Everyone's talking about this big conference coming up. Is that why you're *helping with security*?"

"It's less than three weeks away." He surprised her by providing a direct answer this time.

Progress, she thought, raising an eyebrow. "I guess that means a lot of moving parts for you," she mused aloud, as though thinking it through. "You'll have regular guests, the conference attendees, visitors, media..."

"No regular guests," he cut in. "Only those tied to the conference."

Before Danika could respond, a foot appeared in the doorway, and it slid open even wider. The movement was followed by a man with a stack of boxes precariously balanced in his arms, held in place by his chin. The moment broke the tension like a snap of fingers, and Danika took the opportunity to take a deep breath.

"Hey, bro, a little help?" The man's voice was muffled by the boxes.

Cole stepped in, lifting a box with ease. The newcomer dumped the rest onto a chair. He was young and broad-shouldered, with a happy-go-lucky kind of smile.

"That's a long walk," the man grumbled. "Thanks for the help."

"You're on the wrong floor," Cole said. "We're using the Cliff View room on the third floor.

The man looked surprised at first. Then angry. Then dejected.

"You can use the elevator," Cole suggested. "The computers will be heavy."

The man stood and stared for a moment as if thinking, or *hoping*, that Cole was kidding. "I think I'll save them for tomorrow," he said, wiping a bead of sweat from his brow.

Turning, he spotted Danika for the first time. "Sorry, I didn't see you." He looked back at Cole. "I didn't mean to interrupt."

"I'm Danika." She stepped forward and extended her hand.

"Rudy," he replied, grasping her hand firmly. "Nice to meet you."

Danika knew she would have no trouble remembering the man's name. His cheeks were red, and so was his hair.

"Likewise," she said, offering him a smile.

"I guess I'll haul these upstairs." Rudy began lifting the boxes again. "Sorry again for the interruption."

"No worries," Danika replied, still trying to piece together the dynamic between the two men. Rudy's light-heartedness was a stark contrast to Cole's brooding intensity, that was for sure.

As she listened to the sound of Rudy's footsteps fading, she turned back to Cole. "I guess I'll be going too."

"Is there a possibility I could see those letters?" Cole's voice was careful, measured, but there was something underneath—a hint of urgency that she hadn't heard before.

Danika turned, studying him. "Why?" she asked, tilting her head, her curiosity piqued again. "Do you think they're important?"

"They could be." He placed his hands on the back of a nearby chair, leaning forward as if to emphasize his point. "I'm not going to get my hopes up, but there's no harm in looking... if it would be okay with you."

Danika's mind raced, weighing her options. There was something about Cole that made her wary—his evasiveness, the way he kept his cards close to his chest. But at the same time, there was something that intrigued her. And the mention of the pact tugged at her journalistic curiosity in a way she couldn't ignore.

"I can't tomorrow," she said after a moment. She had made plans to work on GEM-Co in the morning and do some more exploring in the afternoon. Plus, she'd only just started reading them. "Maybe Wednesday?"

"Is seven too early for you?" Cole asked. "We can meet right upstairs in the Cliff View Room."

"In the *morning*?" Danika was an early riser, but she wondered about the urgency of having a meeting at seven in the morning.

"Yes, in the morning." Cole's tone hinted at frustration. "Is that too early? It's the only time I can squeeze it in."

"No. That's fine." Danika frowned. "What room did you say?"

"Cliff View. It's straight up above this room, two stories," Cole said, noticing her confusion. "At the end of a short hallway."

As she turned for the door, Cole spoke again, his voice quiet but firm. "By the way, Danika..."

She turned to face him, raising an eyebrow in question.

"Don't tell anyone else about this." His eyes locked onto hers with a seriousness that made her pulse quicken.

"About what? Our meeting?"

"About anything."

"You mean that I have letters from the 1900s?" Danika asked, her tone skeptical.

Cole's lips pressed into a thin line, his jaw tightening slightly. "Anything."

The weight of his request hung in the air. Danika searched his face for a hint that would explain his reasons. His features were stony, unreadable, but there was something about the way his eyes drilled into hers that told her this was more than a casual request.

He wasn't daring her to challenge him. He was warning her not to try.

"Okay, but only if you promise to tell me *why* when we meet on Wednesday."

Cole hesitated, his lips pursing as if he wasn't used to negotiating. But after a long pause, he gave a curt nod, his gaze never leaving hers.

Then he stepped aside, allowing Danika to pass. She hesitated at the threshold, casting one last glance into the room.

Something about it clung to her, like it might hold answers. The question was—answers to what?

Thirteen

DANIKA STOOD ON THE balcony, cradling her coffee as the first light of dawn crept over the horizon. The sky blushed with soft gold and pale rose, casting a warm glow over the treetops and painting the lake below in shimmering strokes of light and color. Day three, it seemed, was set to redeem itself. The storm-washed world lay still, and not a single cloud marred the morning sky.

The sound of footsteps and a bobbing light caught her attention as someone emerged from the trees near the lake path. It was a jogger, moving effortlessly, his rhythm uninterrupted despite the rough, uneven terrain.

Danika wasn't a jogger, but admired those who got up before dawn to get their morning exercise in before most people were even getting out of bed—especially if they were on vacation.

As the jogger grew closer, his form became more recognizable. It wasn't someone on vacation. It was Cole, the security guy, wearing a pair of navy blue sweatpants and a T-shirt with the sleeves cut off.

She watched him jump effortlessly from rock to rock before hitting the footbridge, never breaking his stride, and seemingly not even breathing hard. As he hit the wooden planks, he reached up and pulled his headlamp off, as if it were second nature, and continued until he veered out of her sight. He reappeared again seconds later near the dock and headed up the trail to Sky Top Tower.

Danika's gaze scanned the path where he'd emerged, trying to calculate the distance. She'd been out of breath walking up the Sky Top Trail, and he was apparently going to jog up after having already completed one of the other trails before dawn.

She took a slow sip of coffee and shook her head. *No thanks.*

Lowering herself into one of the dark green rocking chairs, she rocked as the morning unfolded. The sky shifted from lavender to flame, gold spilling over the cliffs like a secret being revealed.

But answers didn't come.

She tried to be still and savor the sanctity of her favorite time of day—that in-between time when the world feels both awake and gently suspended, not yet morning but no longer night.

Instead, restless thoughts crowded in. She sighed, checked her phone, and went inside to dress. If peace of mind wouldn't come, perhaps answers would. The research waiting at Oak Cottage promised a welcome distraction.

***

After a brief walk from the main hotel, Danika reached Oak Cottage, tucked among the trees across from the riding stable. Its yellow siding and green trim made it look more like a residence than a keeper of historic secrets. Unlike the musty, cluttered research rooms she was used to, this archive appeared comfortable, warm, and orderly.

Having arranged the meeting in advance, Danika was greeted by the archivist as soon as she arrived. "Good morning, I'm Nadine," she said, shaking her hand. "I pulled the guest books for the summers you mentioned," but let me know if you want to go deeper."

Looking around, Danika recognized how rare this was—a business still in the same family since 1869. Even better, someone along the line had the foresight to preserve every artifact, as if they'd known it would all matter someday. Guest ledgers, architectural plans, inventories—each relic carefully labeled and guarded. To her, it felt less like a research space and more like stepping into a memory house.

She ran her fingertips over the stack of records, her heart thudding with quiet anticipation. *Noah*. The name had been looping through her mind ever since she'd read the first letter. It was there in careful script, at the bottom of each page, carrying a warmth that had somehow reached across a century.

But who was he? And why had her great-grandmother, a girl from an elite New York family, been corresponding with him?

She'd always believed her great-grandmother's trips to Mohonk were about leisure: carriage rides and teas, a retreat from the heat of New York. But the letters hinted at something more intimate. Something deeper.

"Here's a chair with good light from the window," Nadine said, pointing with a nod of the head. "The ink has faded on a lot of these documents, so let me know if you want a magnifying glass."

"Thank you." Danika glanced over the ledgers and sat down, pulling one that was marked 1903, the date of the earliest letter. The cover was worn, the pages yellowed at the edges, making her handle the historic record with care.

Tracing the names with her finger, Danika scanned for Abigail Prescott and Noah Morrison. She slowed down when the names began to run together, afraid she would miss them. Just as hope began to fade, Abigail's name appeared—listed with her parents, an aunt, and several unfamiliar names from New York City, all arriving the first week of June.

The sight of her great-grandmother's signature filled her with a quiet awe. Elegant and flowing, the penmanship belonged to a time when mastery of the pen still mattered. Abigail Prescott, 16. The ink had faded to a soft sepia, yet each loop and line still carried unshakable confidence. It was more than a name—it was the imprint of a girl standing at the edge of the unknown.

She turned another page, excitedly scanning the list of names for Noah. Page after page, she studied until her eyes burned from the concentration. He had to be here!

As she flipped to the final page, her breath caught. *Please, please be here.*

Barely breathing, she ran her finger down the list, name by name, careful not to miss any. The paper crackled faintly under her touch. But when she reached the bottom, her hand stilled.

Noah's name wasn't there.

She stared silently out the window, trying to recall the content of the letters. The earliest ones were dated 1903—that was the year they met. She looked at the volume again to make sure she had the right one. Embossed gold letters stood out against the black leather cover: 1903 Guest Register.

Her heart sank, heavy and hollow, as silence pressed in around her.

"Hit a roadblock?"

Danika jumped at Nadine's voice and then nodded. "Yes. I'm looking for a Noah Morrison. He was apparently here in 1903."

"And he's not in the Register?" Nadine questioned.

"No." Danika thought back to the letters. "And it's strange because according to the letters I have, he was here well into the autumn and winter."

"That's odd," Nadine said. "Mohonk wasn't open that time of year back then. Are you sure he was a guest?"

Danika looked up at her. "Well, no. I guess I just assumed he was."

"Hmm." Nadine put a finger on her chin. "Well, I have some records that might include staff and workers, let me pull them."

"OK, it's worth a look."

As Nadine disappeared, Danika sat in silence, her thoughts racing. She hadn't considered the possibility that Noah was anything but a guest. But now, that assumption felt flimsy.

His words were polished and sophisticated, yet he'd spoken of long days and rough-hewn charm. Perhaps she had it all wrong.

The idea shifted everything.

"Here you go," Nadine said. "Hope you get lucky."

Danika opened the document and began reading. Her gaze skimmed over the names, heart ticking faster with each line. She didn't want to get her hopes up, not after striking out in the guest register, but a quiet urgency pushed her forward.

She turned a page and then another—and there it was. *Morrison, Noah. Age 17. Hired as an apprentice carpenter.*

A hollow ache opened, a space for a story she'd never known existed. Noah hadn't been a guest. He'd helped build this place.

Danika flipped ahead, anxiously scanning the pages. His name reappeared in later years, but the apprentice title changed to journeyman—and then to master carpenter.

She sat still, the room hushed around her.

No wonder for all of the secrecy between her great-grandmother and Noah. He had been here, not as a guest, but a local craftsman, working beneath the towering peaks of Mohonk's architecture. The realization sent a shiver down her spine.

Danika sat back in her chair, fingers resting lightly against the open pages.

So this was the man who had written those letters.

The word Quaker stood beside his name. It fit—the tone of his letters, the quiet wisdom, the humility. *Morrison*, a name with deep roots in the Hudson Valley.

The connection between Noah and Abigail was a little clearer now. She could picture her great-grandmother, a girl of sixteen, stepping into Mohonk's grand lobby for the first time, her world of glittering ballrooms and societal expectations colliding with something simpler. *Something real.*

Danika closed the ledger and stared at the dusty light filtering through the windows.

These tiny tidbits of new information filled her with excitement—and a sense of frustration. In some ways, this newfound information created more questions. Deep down, something else stirred. A quiet recognition she couldn't quite name. A story her family had never told.

Or perhaps they didn't know.

Perhaps Abigail kept it a secret, not because it was forbidden, but because it was cherished. Too private. Too sacred. Too revered to be revealed in a mortal way.

Maybe it was never meant to be spoken aloud, but a story destined to be found—quietly, in its own time, by someone chosen to remember.

Danika glanced at the worn volumes spread before her, the scent of paper and time thick in the air. The past didn't feel buried here, only veiled, lingering just beyond the surface, patiently waiting.

Fourteen

DANIKA ZIPPED THE LIGHTWEIGHT backpack shut, her fingers pausing on the flap as if sealing away something sacred. After discovering that Noah had been a carpenter here, she hadn't been able to stop thinking about him.

Her great-grandmother's letters seemed more significant now, filled not just with words but with meaning, the quiet echo of a story never told aloud. It would have been easy to stay inside, to curl up with the letters and read by lamplight. But the spring sun was too warm and the sky too blue. After spending hours in the archives, she needed to move and explore the same paths Abigail once had.

She tucked the next few letters into her pack and headed outside.

Lake Mohonk caught her attention as it always did, the water still and glassy today, except for a pair of canoes slicing through and causing small wakes near the far shore. Two elderly gentlemen stood on the dock, hands in their pockets, staring into the blue, as if they might find some answers there.

The lake had been here long before any of them, formed by glacial ice that carved a serpentine basin into the mountain. Its quiet permanence reminded her of Noah—not a guest, but a man who helped shape this place with his hands, then disappeared into its history.

She followed a sign onto a path enclosed by interlacing branches that dappled the ground in shifting light. The trail rose and dipped, narrowed and curved, each bend revealing tangled limbs, lichen-stained rocks, and the occasional shaft of gold slanting across her way."

Her breath came quicker now, but she didn't mind.

A boulder ahead caught her eye, and she slowed. Split in two, the massive rock straddled the path, half on one side, half on the other. Walking between, she ran her fingertips along its rough, cool surface, wondering if Abigail had once done the same.

After a few more twists and turns, and wondering if perhaps she was lost, there it was. Nestled in a quiet hollow and ringed by weathered stones, the Mohonk Spring trickled steadily into a timeworn trough.

The round stone columns built around the spring gave the scene the look of something built to last—part temple, part ruin. A place meant for secrets. For stillness.

Danika lowered herself onto the low stone wall, the cool surface firm beneath her. She shifted, leaning back against one of the rounded pillars, and then stretched her legs out, resting her sneakers on the massive boulder that was one with the spring.

The hush of the forest wrapped around her like a blanket, broken only by the soft trickle of water and the distant rustle of leaves. Here, where guests had once gathered for refreshment over the span of centuries, she felt at ease and comfortable, half in shadow, half in sun, wrapped in stillness.

The past didn't feel distant out here. It felt close. Watching.

Danika unfolded one of the letters, the paper delicate beneath her fingers, and began to read. The ink had faded with time, but the voice in the words still felt vivid—alive somehow, in this place that seemed untouched by time.

As the lines unfurled, she rested her head back against the rough stone behind her, lost in a world that no longer existed, yet somehow still lingered here.

> *Dear Abigail,*
> *I saw you this morning walking toward the Spring, though I don't expect you noticed. You were with friends, so I didn't dare interrupt. Still, just seeing you brought a bit of light to my day. It's a strange comfort, knowing we share this place—even if from a distance.*

A breeze stirred, lifting the hair from her neck, and the fine hairs on her arms rose in response. She hadn't picked this letter for any reason; it was simply the next one in the pile—but here she was. *At the Spring.*

Coincidence?

Or fate?

She pressed the page to her chest, trying to remember what silent urge had led her to this particular trail on this particular day. In her mind, it was purely chance, a trail she hadn't yet explored.

But then again, the coincidence seemed too precise—like something or someone had quietly guided her steps.

She put that letter away and reached for the next. It was short and sweet.

> *Dear Miss Abigail,*
> *You asked me why I read poetry. I might ask in return—how can one live without it? Wordsworth once wrote, "Fill your paper with the breathings of your heart."*
>
> *I suppose in that way, poetry is much like faith—both require*

belief in something greater than oneself. And perhaps, like prayer, poetry is simply the soul reaching for something eternal.

With Blessings – Noah

Danika rested the letter across her knees and gazed into the trees where dappled light danced across the moss like shifting lace. A carpenter—quoting Wordsworth. The thought settled deep in her chest like a breath she hadn't meant to hold. No wonder Abigail kept writing to him.

She closed her eyes, trying to picture them—a young woman in gloves and lace and a young man with calloused hands, perhaps sitting beneath these very branches, trading thoughts on life and literature. He seemed fluent in both poetry and world affairs, a man grounded by his hands yet stirred by words. And still, their lives couldn't have been more different.

Without a photograph to help fuel her imagination, the image faded, and she turned to the next letter."

I thought of you today as I worked, as I often do. There is a rhythm in shaping wood, much like the rhythm of poetry—a quiet order, a hidden meaning beneath the surface.

It's odd how lines of verse stay with me even as I work. As I hammered today, a poem rose unbidden: "She was a Phantom of delight / When first she gleamed upon my sight..."

The words lingered longer than they should have. I won't pretend to explain why—some things are best left between the lines.

Danika took a deep breath and let it out slowly. What would it feel like to be the inspiration for such words? Not fantasy or flattery, but something deeper—something rooted in emotion and high regard.

She reached for another letter, only to find the bag empty. A sigh slipped from her lips. She'd been in such a hurry to get outside, she'd only grabbed a couple.

Disappointed, but content, she sat a while longer, letting the mountain's tranquility surround her like a breath held in reverence.

Then, rising stiffly, she stepped toward the spring. Kneeling by the pool, she ignored the sign—*Drink at your own risk*—and cupped her hands beneath the icy flow. Drinking deeply of the water that trickled out of the mountain felt, somehow, like a shared memory passed down through stone, stream, and time.

As she turned to go, a new feeling stirred—not curiosity, but purpose. She no longer felt like an outsider chasing the past, but part of it, guided as though Abigail had left a trail for her to follow.

Fifteen

Danika stepped outside, pulling her sweater tighter around her shoulders as the chilly evening air whispered against her skin. The sun seemed to be resting on the top of the distant mountain range, casting the Sunset Porch of Mohonk in a warm, rosy light.

The long row of rocking chairs stirred with quiet silhouettes—some hunched in thought, others murmuring in pairs—while the faint clink of glassware drifted on the breeze. The boards beneath kept time with the steady rhythm of rocking, a lullaby for wandering thoughts.

She scanned the line of rockers. Near the far end, one chair sat apart from the others, angled slightly, like it didn't want company. *Perfect.* She made her way over, brushing a tendril of loose hair from her face, as she lowered herself onto the wide wooden seat.

The chair groaned under her as she sat, its armrests polished smooth by generations of hands. The sky had shifted to lavender and rose, the lingering light feathering across the peaks like paint brushed on a canvas.

Despite the magnificent view, her thoughts lay tangled in her great-grandmother's letters. It was uncanny how alive the past felt here, like the place remembered.

Danika let her head fall back and closed her eyes. A friendship between a teenage girl and a local craftsman—improbable, maybe even scandalous, back then. She could almost hear the disapproval echoing from another century.

A slow, even creak broke her reverie as someone shifted in the chair beside her. She turned a little, enough to see the back of a man's head, his chair positioned slightly to the side and in front of hers as he faced the horizon. He hadn't been there when she sat down, had he? She'd thought she'd taken the last chair, but perhaps, tucked so far in the shadows, it had escaped her notice.

Even from this angle, she could see his attention was focused on the sky with an intensity that bordered on reverence, a concentration so deep it made her feel like an intruder for noticing.

Danika turned her gaze back to the setting sun, too, and watched the violent beauty of the sky as it flared with a wash of orange and red. People oohed and aahed as the sun took its final dip beyond the horizon, but mostly they were captivated and reverent. Someone clapped when it blazed one final time before sinking into indigo, leaving the pink and pearly afterglow to linger.

After a few moments, the clouds caught fire at the edges, a sight so breathtaking it drew an involuntary sigh of awe from her lips.

"Breathtaking, isn't it?" The man beside her responded to her unintended display of emotion.

He spoke without turning his head, like someone used to quiet company. His voice held the trace of a Southern accent that had mostly worn off, but still lingered around the edges.

Something inside her stumbled, then raced. *Dalton Rivers.*

"The best free show in town." She said the words sincerely as she watched the sun's majestic departure.

"No matter how many times you see it," he added.

His tone was careful, measured, but not unfriendly. Still, she wasn't sure how much she should push.

They sat in silence for a few minutes, listening to the soft wind stirring the trees, the hush of dusk settling over the mountains.

"I think I was lucky to get a seat," Danika said after a pause, not wanting to let this moment get away.

He gave a small chuckle. "Timing's everything."

A flutter stirred, part nerves, part disbelief. Dalton Rivers, the movie star who'd disappeared from public life years ago, was sitting ten feet away, watching the sun set like any regular guest. No entourage. No camera crew. Just... here.

Danika had fallen in love with his on-screen persona years ago, back when she still believed movie stars were as heroic as the roles they played. Of course, she'd been in her late teens, and he was perhaps ten years older. But he wasn't just famous at the time—he was the action icon of a generation.

They sat without speaking for a while, the silence companionable, not awkward.

Danika wanted to ask a thousand things, but said nothing. Instead she remained silent, eyes fixed on the pewter-colored clouds as they dissolved in the deepening twilight.

Finally, Dalton spoke again, breaking the silence as he gestured with his hand toward the long row of rocking chairs and the people enthusiastically watching the darkness deepen. "I always wonder what people are thinking when they sit out here."

Danika closed her eyes for a moment. "Well, I was thinking about how life never turns out the way you think it will. And then, you find out that's okay."

Dalton turned his head toward her. His voice was gentle. "That's a good thought."

"How about you?" She tilted her head inquiringly.

Dalton hesitated. Then, without looking at her, he said, "I was thinking that sometimes you need places like this to remember who you are."

She wanted to study his face to find the reason behind the words, but it was still out of view.

"I like that," she said.

A breath of silence stretched between them as Danika wondered how Dalton remained under the radar. No one taking pictures. No one asking for autographs. *Perhaps that's why he chose Mohonk*, she mused. The resort was beloved by power players and the wealthy. Fame didn't really matter here—discretion did. Even those who recognized him seemed willing to respect his space.

She heard the chair creak as Dalton stood. "Time to call it a day," he said as he turned to leave.

Danika's heart sank. "Good night. Maybe I'll see you around."

He looked back at her, making eye contact for the first time.

"Maybe," he said, as a deep purple blanket of darkness descended and thickened around them.

She listened as he made his way across the porch to the door, heard it open and close behind her. And just like that, he was gone again, leaving her with a single word and a thousand questions. *Maybe*.

Sixteen

The other guests had trickled off the porch one by one, their voices fading into the night. At last, Danika followed, the evening air cool against her skin as she slipped inside and made her way back to her room.

When the door clicked shut behind her, the world outside quieted, yet her thoughts remained restless, tangled in the day's revelations. New discoveries. Hidden truths. And letters that read like whispers from a not-so-distant past.

She crossed to the lamp and switched it on, bathing the room in a warm, amber glow. Without hesitation, she reached for the next bundle of letters and sank onto the couch. Closing her eyes, she tried to picture her great-grandmother as a young woman, walking the same trail she had walked hours earlier.

What had she felt reading Noah's words for the first time?

Danika touched the envelope, amazed at the graceful penmanship and the words that read like poetry. There was something in them, a quiet ache, a reverence, that felt deeper than simple friendship—a kind of yearning that was both beautiful and heartbreaking.

She leaned back, settling into the couch, and let her gaze rest on the small pile of letters she'd already read. They reminded her of her grandmother's house, now gone, offering echoes of a world that no longer existed.

And maybe that's why these letters mattered so much. They were all that remained, fragile pieces of a story nearly lost. Had they been discarded in haste?

Or had someone hidden them there because they were too precious to let go?

She opened the letter in her hand and began to read.

Dear Abigail,

I have often wondered if my hands were meant only for crafting with hammer and nail, or if, by some miracle, they were meant to shape something more lasting. Every piece of wood I work, every cut I make in a freshly milled board, is a quiet act of faith. To build something strong, something meant to endure—it is not so different from the foundation of one's soul.

A knot tightened in Danika's chest, a surprising ache for a man she'd never met, but whose voice on the page felt painfully real. She put the letter down and stared toward the window at the darkness beyond. Noah's way with words was so profound, it made her want to understand his meaning and motivations. He seemed to be exposing his very thoughts and soul to her great-grandmother.

She continued on to the next without stopping.

You asked if I remember the first time I saw you. I did not answer you honestly then, but I will now.

I remember the day vividly—two summers ago, in the garden near the lake. You were very young, but even then, you carried yourself with a grace that left me breathless. I was but a boy with sawdust on his hands, unworthy of speaking to you. And yet, fate is a strange thing, is it not?

I do not know what force allowed our paths to cross beyond mere pleasantries, but I am grateful for it.

As she read, Danika began tracing the arc between the letters—the greetings growing warmer, the information more personal. It was a paper trail of a quiet love taking root, and the journalist in her enjoyed piecing it together just as much as the woman in her was falling under its spell.

She stood and stretched, muscles stiff from sitting too long. Making her way into the small kitchen, she grabbed an iced tea, then went back to the couch and reached for the next letter.

My dearest Abigail,

The season turns again, and with it, the return of familiar faces. Today, as I worked near the garden, I saw you step from the carriage, poised as ever, your eyes shining with the delight of homecoming. I do not think you noticed me, but I saw you, just as I did years ago when I was a boy of seventeen, and you even younger.

That first day, I thought you must be the daughter of a king—so regal, so beyond my reach. Little did I know then that the years would grant me the privilege of knowing you, speaking with you, and sharing thoughts I have spoken to no one else.

Danika looked at the dates of the letters. In the beginning, they had been separated by months... that had eventually turned into weeks. Now, she looked at the date of the next letter she was about to read, and realized it was the next day.

She flicked through the envelopes and noticed that during the summer, they weren't stamped with a postmark. They were made out to Miss Abigail Prescott with Noah at Mohonk written in the corner.

Danika stared at the empty fireplace as she put herself in her great-grandmother's place. Of course, Noah would have been busy with his duties as a carpenter, and Abigail would have been under the watchful eye of her father. They must have developed a way to communicate every day—through letters if they could not find a way to meet in person.

She picked up the next letter.

My dear Abigail,

My future is not one of grand houses and gilded rooms. It is made of wood and labor, of sweat and quiet pride. But, if I were allowed to dream—if I dared—I would dream of an evening like the one we spent by the lake. Of words spoken freely, of your laughter unburdened by expectation.

But I am a practical man, and dreams, for men like me, are dangerous things. They can lead a man to hope for what he cannot have.

And yet, here I am, writing to you.

A frustrating heat burned behind her eyes at the mention of the reality of their situation. It wasn't just his class-bound heartache; it was the raw injustice of a story silenced. She knew that kind of frustration.

She hurriedly moved onto the next letter.

If I were another man, I would tell you that I have thought of you every summer since that first one. That the moment you step from the carriage each June, I feel my heart rise like the sun cresting the lake. But I am not another man. I am simply Noah. And so, I will only say this—if dreams are to be shared, then I will entrust mine to you.

Danika could not stop reading now. The letters created a story she could not shake from her mind. They conveyed happiness and heartache, love and longing, the pulse of something that went straight into her soul.

Your words are like gifts. Your gazes, sweet rewards. Every minute spent in your company is a rare treasure—moments for which I have no words. I cannot pretend I do not feel it. And I do not believe you can either.

She replaced the letter and rubbed her temples, trying to clear her head. It was all too much, too tangled, too overwhelming. But she couldn't turn away now. What if these letters contained something important? Something that could help the security guy, Cole?

A glance at the clock made her blink. Nearly midnight. She rarely stayed up past nine. She'd been reading for hours, lost in ink and memory, and though her eyes burned with exhaustion, her mind was wide awake. The past no longer felt distant. It was pressing in—alive, unfinished.

She stood and crossed to the window. Except for the lights reflecting from the summerhouses, the lake stretched out in shadow, still and endless, like it was holding its breath.

Back at the table, her gaze fell on the scattered letters. She would read a few more and see if she could find any mention of a pact. She didn't want to go to her meeting with Cole tomorrow and share only intimate details of her great-grandmother's summertime love.

She had come here chasing a story—corruption, power, hidden agendas. But this? This felt bigger. Older. Like she'd stumbled onto a thread that ran straight through her bloodline and into something she didn't yet understand.

She kept reading until the words became too blurry to see. The writer spoke of hidden truths and secrets that could not be spoken aloud, of a world on the brink of change. Every letter wove the threads of a tapestry, a story full of meaning and emotion. Yet Noah's words seemed to hide as much as they told, as if he were trying to convey something elusive before it slipped through his fingers.

The problem was, she had no idea what it was.

Seventeen

Ding. Ding. Ding. Danika sat straight up in bed, unaccustomed to the sound of the alarm on her phone. It had been a long time since she'd needed it. But staying up late reading, followed by a night of wild dreams… of looking for something she was unable to find, left her exhausted.

Glancing at the clock, she hurried out of bed and dressed, still half-groggy. With no time to spend on her hair, she pulled the long locks back into a quick, loose braid, pulled on a ball cap, and then headed to the room where she was to meet with the security guy.

She took the slate steps to the third floor, then walked down the hall toward the central staircase. When she turned the corner, she saw the hallway Cole had mentioned and the double doors at the end that said "Cliff View." As she walked toward the entrance, a man dressed in a black T-shirt and khaki pants appeared out of the shadows.

"Excuse me, Miss. This room isn't open to the public."

Danika looked at the tall, broad-shouldered man and saw he was wearing an identification badge like Cole had. Her eyes drifted to the small closet-like room behind him that held a chair and a small desk she hadn't even seen.

Wow. *Security is really tightening,* she thought.

"I have a meeting—"

"Name." He didn't even let her finish as he glanced down at a small notebook in his hand.

"Danika Hunter."

He nodded and stepped aside without saying another word.

Danika walked down the steps confidently, but hesitated when she got to the closed door, doubt pooling in her chest. Was this a good idea? What if..."

Her grandmother's words of wisdom surfaced gently, yet forcefully. "You don't have to know the ending to take the next step."

She eased the door open and stepped into what looked like a makeshift command center. An elegant event space had been carved into sections with temporary partitions, its overhead light fixtures overshadowed by the glow of monitors. A low hum filled the air—servers buzzed, keys clacked, voices murmured in concentrated tones.

Her eyes followed the sound and found Cole and Rudy sitting behind a desk, both leaning toward the computer screen with such concentration they didn't notice her enter. The way the two were deep in their work, it appeared they'd been at it for hours. She glanced at her watch. It was 6:56.

"Good morning," Danika said, trying to project her voice.

Rudy looked up and waved. "Hey. Come on in. Be with you in a sec."

Danika nodded, feeling slightly out of place among the technology and tension. She sat down at a small table in the corner and pulled out some notes from her satchel, sorting through them with care.

A moment later, she heard the scrape of a chair beside her and looked up to see Cole sitting down. His presence seemed to fill the space, creating a subtle tension, though his expression was calm. "Thanks for coming." He placed a cup of coffee and a small tablet on the table in front of him as he folded his large frame into the seat. His blue eyes, a bit softened from their earlier intensity, flicked from the Mohonk cap on her head to the letters in her hands. "There's plenty of coffee if you want any."

"No, thanks," Danika said.

"Okay. What did you find?"

Danika dared not look directly into those deep blue eyes. "I think we agreed that you'd tell me what's going on first." She wasn't going to let him steer the conversation this time. "Why is this so important?"

Cole leaned back, his eyes narrowing. "Are you a lawyer or something?" He tilted his head, but his gaze didn't leave hers.

"No," Danika replied firmly, leaning forward, matching his intensity. "But I'm not going to show personal letters of a family member to some-one for no reason."

"She's been gone for three quarters of a century," Cole pointed out, a trace of impatience edging his voice. His one hand clasped a pen, and Danika watched his fingers tighten.

"They're still personal," she countered, sliding the pages of notes she'd brought closer to her chest.

She wanted to trust him, and she wanted to protect herself. Unfortunately, the gap between the two felt impossibly wide.

Cole glanced up at the ceiling, a long breath escaping through his nose, as if working hard to keep himself in check. He leaned forward, resting his forearms on the table. His voice wasn't loud, but there was a definite edge of hostility to his tone.

"Okay. There's a major international peace conference here in seventeen days."

Danika stopped an eye roll before it got too dramatic and nodded. "Yes, I already know that much from our earlier conversation. And you're here helping with security."

There was a short pause before Rudy leaned out around his nearby desk. "He's *head* of security."

Danika cocked her head and eyed him accusingly. "*Head* of security? I could have sworn you told me you were *helping* with security."

"I'm *helping* with security... as *head* of security," Cole said indifferently as he shot a sharp glance toward Rudy.

"I see." Danika's distrustful instincts kicked into high gear. "So what else are you *not* telling me about this peace conference? I mean, it's about peace, right? How much security does a place need?"

Cole's posture, although seemingly relaxed, radiated an intensity that made her stomach tighten. There was something about the way he looked at her, focused and unyielding, that told her he *was* holding back something significant. That was confirmed even more when he took a moment to speak, choosing his words carefully. "Unfortunately, a lot more than you might think."

"Why? Don't a bunch of dignitaries get together, discuss world affairs, and sing *Kumbaya*?

Cole snorted. "Not quite."

Danika leaned back in her chair and crossed her arms, a signal to him that she wasn't budging until he explained what was going on.

He took another deep breath and held it for a moment, as if trying to find the right words without telling her too much. "There are several opposing factions involved."

"*Opposing* factions? You mean people who don't want peace?" Danika had a sudden sense that she had timed her visit to coincide with something much bigger than she had imagined.

Cole nodded. "Yes. Factions that don't want peace." He didn't elaborate.

"That sounds strange." Danika tapped her fingers on the table, her mind racing to absorb what he was telling her. "And that doesn't explain your interest in the letters and why you're looking for the mention of a pact."

Cole's gaze flicked to the stack of papers she'd brought, as he drew in his breath. It was obvious that providing background information to someone he didn't know was painful to him. "Mohonk was instrumental in hosting peace and arbitration conferences in the late nineteenth and early twentieth centuries," he explained.

"Yes, I read about that." Danika nodded. "The owners were Quakers, committed to peace. The gatherings were so highly regarded, they inspired the formation of the Hague Tribunal in the Netherlands."

"Correct." Cole continued, his voice steady. "In 1906, tensions were high between several world powers, and Mohonk was meant to be a neutral ground for negotiations. Everyone had high hopes that the conference would provide a way forward."

"Okay?" Danika made it clear she still didn't see the connection. "Did it?"

"Not anything recorded." Cole paused to take a sip of coffee and became more deliberative with his words. "But in the early 1930s, a small newspaper published an article about a letter discovered among a deceased professor's papers. The letter made vague reference to a 'pact for enduring peace' that was signed in secret by the delegates at the 1906 arbitration gathering."

"Then where is it?"

"No one knows. People have been looking for the document for years... generations even. But it's nowhere to be found."

Danika began analyzing the information. "Who wrote that letter that was discovered? Where is that? Can I see it?"

"No one knows that either." Cole pushed his chair out and stood as if he'd reached his limit of sitting still.

"Wait. What?" Danika shook her head disbelievingly. "Both the letter and the pact are missing?"

Cole nodded from where he stood staring out the window at the lake, and then turned to face her. "A newspaper article was written about the existence of the letter, but that's the only source. Whether or not a letter ever existed—and whether or not a pact ever existed—is really speculation."

"How could that be?" Danika tilted her head toward him quizzically. "They're so important. How could they be lost?"

"Once the letter was published, lots of theories about the pact began to surface." Cole shrugged. "Some say it was hidden and accidentally destroyed during a rehabilitation project. Others say it was proposed but never signed. Still others say there was a disagreement among the signers at the last minute, and it never came to be."

"But wouldn't there be an official record of that?"

"That's the strange part," Cole said, walking back to the table. "There's no other mention of it, except the conference minutes include a vote for secrecy about an unknown matter. The vote was unanimous. That's where the trail goes cold."

Danika blinked, the mystery slowly unraveling before her. "A unanimous vote for secrecy with no details." She shook her head. "What a mystery."

This was exactly the kind of story she loved digging into, no matter how long it took to find the answers. Unfortunately she was only here for a month, and the clock was ticking on the other story she had to write.

Cole nodded. "Most historians think it's a legend at this point—they call it the Mohonk Myth. Others chalk it up to a journalist fabricating a story to get a headline." He pulled his chair out and sat down again. "When I heard you had letters from that time period... Well, you never know."

Danika's eyes flicked down to the letters, the weight of their importance settling on her. "And this pact... it's connected to the upcoming conference?"

"This conference will involve many of the same players, or at least their modern counterparts. If we could find evidence of an actual written pact, signed by representatives of these nations, it might calm things down by proving that nations were once seriously committed to peace." He picked up his cup and took another sip of coffee. "At the very least, it could take the edge off the tensions that exist between some of the warring nations today."

The room seemed to grow quieter as Danika absorbed his words. The idea that a hidden document from more than a century ago could still have an impact on today's global politics was almost too much to comprehend.

"That pact could have changed the course of history," she murmured.

Cole met her gaze, his expression serious. "Actually, it still could. The world has never been in such disarray as it is now."

Eighteen

As Danika sat silently and absorbed the words, a palpable barrier of distrust re-emerged. A line from one of Noah's letters echoed in her mind: *Be cautious of those who try to befriend you. Remember that deceptive paths often lie beneath the veil of misdirection.*

She wondered why it had come back to her so clearly when she'd been half-asleep when reading it. *Had it been written for Abigail?*

Or for me?

Her eyes lifted to Cole. She didn't know this man—nothing beyond his name and clipped professionalism. And yet, she was about to hand him letters, a connection to the history of this place that no one else knew about.

Yes, he seemed capable. Commanding. Direct. But were those reasons to *trust* him?

She studied his face, but his expression gave nothing away. His gaze was steady, sharp with confidence—and something more. A watchfulness. A vigilance. As if he were always assessing, always calculating.

Her mind began to churn, and her imagination to run wild. He could be a spy for all she knew, working for the government, or worse, for Julian.

What if he were a mole for a foreign agency looking to unearth the pact for their own ends? Ridiculous, maybe. But not impossible. Not *here*.

Her pulse quickened. She had no one to ask. No way to explain the situation without exposing something she wasn't ready to share. The deeper she got, the less she could trust anyone.

Cole's voice cut through her spiraling thoughts, low and firm.

"Now that I've fulfilled my part of the obligation," he said, "it's time for you to fulfill yours."

Danika met his gaze and found herself caught there, held by the intensity in those unflinching blue eyes. She cleared her throat, hoping her voice would remain steady. "Okay, but first, can you give me a business card? Or something that proves you are who you say you are?"

"No," was the reply, quick and direct. He punctuated the bluntness with a dismissive shrug, implying the request was pointless and inconsequential. "I don't have a business card."

"You run a security business and you don't have a card?"

"I work for a firm that runs a security business and operates by word of mouth," he said. "We don't need business cards."

"Really?" Danika rolled her eyes skeptically. "You expect me to believe that?"

Cole moved a little closer and spoke in a hushed tone. "The company I work for performs a level of security that most people don't need. The ones that do, know how to find us."

Danika wasn't sure what he meant by that, but it sounded somewhat reasonable. He was, after all, sitting in a command post at Mohonk, and appeared to be in charge.

Her gaze drifted over to Rudy, who looked up from his computer and nodded. "He's legit," he said, nodding toward Cole. "Show her your security ID."

Cole unclipped the ID from his belt and tossed it onto the table. "Here."

Danika leaned over and read:

> Title: OPERATIONS COMMANDER – SECURITY
> Name: Coleman J. McCain
> Clearance: Level 1 – Full Access
> Affiliation: Phantom Force Tactical
> Event: Mohonk World Peace Summit
> ID #: 7KX9-TAL-1505

"Okay." She met the steady weight of his gaze and wished she hadn't. In the depths of blue, a storm brewed—an unspoken warning that she had pressed too far.

She watched him lean back in his chair and cross his arms, tilting his head to better study her. "Since you're so interested in my background, let me ask you something about yours."

Danika shrugged. "Sure. I have nothing to hide."

"Really?" He raised his eyes inquiringly. "Then, why are you using a fake name?"

The question floored Danika so soundly that she sat speechless, unable to form words or come up with a response—or even to breathe. She merely stared at him and blinked, and could feel, rather than see, Rudy look up from his computer, waiting to see what would happen next.

"You ran a background check on me?" She kept her expression neutral, but her heart thudded painfully against her ribs.

"I checked you out, if that's what you're asking." Cole rested his tanned forearms on the table. "That's what I do." He leaned a little closer and held her gaze. "As head of security."

The shock of his words yielded quickly to anger. Danika threw her pen onto the table. "You have no right—!"

"You have that wrong." He interrupted her with his hand. "It's my job."

Danika let out a humorless laugh, more out of nerves than amusement. "That doesn't give you the right to pry into my life. I'm not a threat to your conference, and I'm certainly not part of whatever secret international conspiracy you think is going on here."

Cole's accusing gaze didn't waver. "You're not exactly making it easy to believe that."

Danika bristled. "I have reasons for using a different name, which by the way, is not *fake*."

"*O-k-a-y*." He drew the word out as if he were trying to make sense of her statement. "Not fake, but not the one you go by. Do I have that right now?"

"I shouldn't have to explain anything to you." Danika realized as she was speaking that even her defense of her actions sounded a bit suspicious. "And if you're trying to intimidate me, it's not working."

"I'm not trying to intimidate you. I'm trying to figure out if you're a problem I need to deal with. The fact that you lied to get a room—"

"I didn't lie!" Danika leaned forward, slapping the table with her hand. Then she leaned back and exhaled in exasperation. "Okay, I *may* have walked a fine line of mixing half-truths with vague facts, but..."

"In my business," Cole said, his eyes locked on hers, "a half-truth is a whole lie."

When she had no immediate reply, he continued, "So as I was saying, I need to figure out if you're a problem I need to deal with, or someone who just got caught in the wrong place at the wrong time."

"I'm neither," Danika responded. "I'm simply here to... relax, take a break. That's all."

"*R-i-g-h-t*." He made an exaggerated circular nodding motion with his head. "And you just happen to show up at the same time as a high-security international peace conference, using a fake name, with no agenda except to... umm, *relax*."

In the silence that followed, he glanced down at the tablet he'd strategically placed by his coffee cup and then went back to scrutinizing her. "You told the front desk you were affiliated with a certain organization attending the conference. Is that right?"

Danika's eyes darted down to the tablet as well, unable to believe that this man actually had *notes* on her. He may not have been sure this subject would come up, but he was nonetheless prepared for it. The level of professionalism struck a new shock of fear through her.

Her jaw clenched as she sat back in her chair and crossed her arms over her chest, angry at the way he was able to twist her own words to make her sound like she was guilty of an offense that didn't even exist. "I guess it's your right to believe whatever you want, but stay out of my business."

"I'll stay out of your business when I'm sure it's not a threat to mine." He tipped his head slightly as he glanced at his notes again. "Let's walk through this, shall we? You show up here three weeks before a peace conference that will involve high-level officials from across the globe. I could probably let that slide as a coincidence, but the fact that you're staying an entire month—"

"That wasn't my idea," Danika interrupted, trying to defend herself, angry how he made her presence and her actions sound suspicious. "I had to agree to that to make sure I could get a room."

"Of course you did," he continued without pausing, "Then, I find you wandering around in a room that's off-limits..." He held up three fingers. "In my business, that's what we like to call, *Strike Three*."

Danika sat staring straight ahead, biting the inside of her cheek, trying to figure out what to say next. She had to give him credit. He was thorough.

"What else did you find out about me?" she asked, shifting her gaze from somewhere over his shoulder to his eyes. "Besides my name?"

He didn't answer at first, which forced Danika to scrutinize his expression and try to decipher what he was thinking. All she saw was a quiet arrogance, an irritatingly calm confidence that both aggravated and captivated her. This was a man who didn't need words to remind her who held the upper hand.

After a few awkward moments, she asked again more forcefully. "*What else*?"

"Nothing of interest." He never removed his icy blue eyes from hers now. "Except you're a journalist."

"That's not against the law. Right?"

"Not as long as you follow the rules."

"What rules?"

"*My* rules."

Danika sighed deeply. This meeting was not going the way she had thought it would. "Which *are*?"

"Let's start with, stay out of rooms that are off limits."

"Fair enough." Danika raised her chin, assuming all of the dignity she could muster. "I'll certainly respect any rooms that are clearly marked *off limits*."

Cole frowned and paused as if weighing the benefits of arguing the point. He apparently decided it wasn't in his best interest. "Let's get back to the business at hand. Did you find anything about a pact?"

Nineteen

Danika looked down at the notes she had brought, unsure of what to do. This whole thing had suddenly gotten way more complicated than she'd anticipated. If she had known the letters were this important, she would have stayed up and read all night.

She still wasn't sure if she could trust him—maybe she never would. But for now, the letters were still in her possession. And as long as she held them, she held the edge.

"I only brought a couple," she said. "Ones that sounded like they were talking about something important."

"Really?" Cole looked disappointed.

Danika slid a letter over to him. "I transcribed them rather than bring the originals. This passage caught my eye." She waited for him to start reading. "Most of the letters I've read so far discuss things he and my great-grandmother did while she visited. This one was different, mysterious."

She watched as Cole read the words:

Though the nature of my work is humble, the hands of fate have seen fit to place me at the crossroads of history. My current labors bear the weight of many hopes... and perhaps the future of nations. I can say little more until I see you again and we can talk in person.

The next excerpt Danika handed him was even more revealing:

Dear Abigail - I probably said too much in my last communication—not too little—as you observantly pointed out.

As Mr. Smiley told me once, great orators have their speeches, but their words rely on memory to recall them. On the other hand, craftsmen have the advantage—their creations in wood will last as long as the elements allow.

Cole slowly raised his eyes to meet hers. "So this guy, Noah. What's his story?"

"He was a carpenter here," Danika said. "He started as an apprentice and worked his way up to master carpenter."

He raised his eyebrows as he stared at the paper, obviously understanding that, as a carpenter, he would have access to lots of hidden nooks and crannies in Mohonk.

"And this was written in 1905?" He glanced up again. "He writes in riddles, doesn't he?"

Danika noticed that Cole's eyes had turned from blue to a dark, deep pewter. "Yes. March."

"That's a year before the peace conference," Cole murmured, almost to himself.

"So is this." Danika slid a piece of paper toward him, her eyes drifting over briefly to Rudy when she noticed that the background noise of his typing had stopped.

> *There is something gratifying in laboring with purpose, especially in a place where even a humble carpenter is welcomed not just for what he can build, but for who he is.*
>
> *Mr. and Mrs. Smiley have shown me a kindness I did not expect. Though my station is modest, they treat me as one they trust. It is a strange thing—at least in my station—to be seen not only for my skills, but for my heart and mind.*

Cole put that one to the side and went on to the next one.

> *You say you understand Mr. Smiley's respect for me, but it isn't only as a craftsman. He speaks to me of more than tasks and timetables—but often of ideas—and sometimes even my thoughts on peace. I am not sure what I have done to earn such regard, but I carry it with quiet gratitude. It is true that respect, like a well-built beam, is shaped over time with steady hands.*

Danika waited until she was sure Cole had finished reading. "Don't you think it sounds like Noah is almost in the inner circle here? I can see why my great-grandmother would have been smitten with him."

"What do you mean?"

Danika sighed dreamily. "A mere carpenter by trade, yet it appears he was treated as an equal by some of the most powerful men of his time." She stared out over his shoulder. "He probably had no formal education, but in his letters he recites poetry and the Bible like a gifted writer." Her gaze came back to meet his. "He must have been a truly remarkable man."

Judging from the look on Cole's face, he was not impressed by her romantic notions of Noah. Instead, he appeared to be mulling over the man's acceptance into the Smiley's inner circle.

He crossed his arms and pushed back on his chair until it teetered on the two back legs. "Unusual for the time period," he said, nodding thoughtfully. "But with the Smileys being Quakers... and the fact that they're in the hospitality business... it isn't that hard to conceive that they would trust him so completely."

He rubbed his jaw as if that would help him put the pieces of the puzzle together. "Which means he would possibly have access to everything they had access to."

Danika looked over at him at the tone of his voice. "What are you thinking?"

Cole shook his head. "Just thinking out loud. If there was an official pact and it was hidden, Albert Smiley's office would be a logical place."

"Which is where? Does it still exist?"

"It still exists, but it's not private. His original office faces the lake and is connected to Lake Lounge."

Danika's heart sank. That room was a very public space. Hundreds of people passed through every day. It was probably one of the busiest spaces in the hotel besides the dining room.

"How much renovation work was done in there, I wonder."

"As far as I know, only cosmetic things," Cole said. "The infrastructure, including fireplaces, is all the same." He brought the front of the chair back to the floor with a bang. "Can you think of any letters that talk about the office?"

Danika shook her head. "He mentions stopping by to see Albert in his office, or having a meeting in the office, but I don't remember anything specific. I'll have to re-read them."

"Okay. It's just a thought."

"So you think Noah might have known about the pact—and might even have been involved in hiding it?"

"I'm not saying that at all." Cole looked up from writing something down on his notepad. "I'm saying these letters are the only connection we have to the past. And since Noah is the author of the letters, it might be worth investigating."

"Well, it would make sense." Danika stood and began to pace. "When you think about it, that space would have been very private back then." She turned around and looked at Cole, excitement growing inside her. "It's a place the Smileys would have felt comfortable in. The number of people who had access would have been limited. It's the perfect place to hide an important document—I want to start looking!"

"Whoa. Slow down." Cole shook his head. "There is absolutely nothing in the letters that indicates that. I was going over in my head the possibilities and how things have changed since back then. That room came to mind."

Danika sighed. "It would be hard to be discreet and look for something in there." She glanced over at Cole hopefully. "Would the staff close it down for you to look around?"

"I'm sure they would, but I don't want to ask." He scribbled more notes. "It would be too obvious. I don't want anyone to know I'm looking, let alone *where* I'm looking."

Danika nodded, feeling the unease settle in her bones. What had started as a fun project to read her great-grandmother's letters had spiraled into something far more important. And now, they were possibly competing with those who had the power to destroy everything and everyone who got in their way.

"Well, maybe there are more clues. I'm not even a third of the way through yet."

Cole looked up, obviously surprised. "Really?"

"Yes. It's time-consuming." She looked over at him. "If you are ever bored in the evening, you're welcome to help."

He seemed to ignore the invitation, but stared at the words on the paper in front of him as if trying to read between the lines.

"Oh, here's the rest of that last letter." Danika pulled two pages that had been stuck together apart. It's just another paragraph, but it seemed intriguing."

> *I look at these hands, covered in sawdust and dirt. Yes, I have built many things in my life, but how can I help build something as fragile—and as complex—as peace?*

An inquisitive, determined expression gleamed in Cole's eyes. Even though she'd only just met him, she could tell he was making swift calculations, taking silent notes. Finally, he spoke. "If a pact exists, we have to find it," he said, "before anyone else does."

"Why? What do you think they would do with it?" Danika asked, her voice barely above a whisper, as the weight of it settled over her.

"Destroy it," Cole replied without hesitation. "Erase it from history."

He looked toward the window, jaw tight. "And if they can't find it themselves, they'll bury anyone who tries to bring it to light."

Danika said nothing. There was nothing left to say. But a quiet unease tugged at her, an instinct that the letters held more than sentiment. More than love.

Maybe something that was meant to stay hidden.

"Thanks for sharing these," Cole said as he helped gather the letters for her. "You know where to find me if you find anything else."

He walked her to the door and paused, hand resting on the knob. "I don't think I need to tell you the necessity for discretion."

Danika nodded. "I've kept bigger secrets."

She regretted the words the moment they left her mouth, but it was too late to take them back.

His gaze flicked to hers, impassive and calm, but obviously filing the comment away for later.

She stepped through the doorway, resisting the urge to glance over her shoulder.

The last thing she needed was for him to think she had more to hide—because to be honest, she wasn't sure what he might find.

Danika's breath caught. Her heart lurched. She hadn't used that—hadn't even touched it. She would have remembered seeing it with the door open.

Someone had been looking for something.

Her thoughts shot back to the man in the hallway. The way he moved—stealthily—not like a guest just leaving their room. It was as if he'd been warned she was coming and was trying to get away.

She should have paid attention. Should have been more aware of her surroundings.

Too late now.

She sank onto the edge of the bed, her mind focused on the intruder. What had he been after? The only thing of value she carried was information—the story she was chasing... *or the letters.*

She'd gone to great lengths to stay under the radar. No one at Mohonk was supposed to know her real name.

Or that she was a journalist.

Or that she'd brought with her a bundle of century-old letters that could change everything.

Only one person knew all of it.

Cole McCain.

Twenty-Two

Danika hurried across Lake Porch, hoping to make it inside before the next gust of wind struck. Taking the final steps, she lunged for the door, one hand outstretched while the other fought the strands tearing loose from her ponytail. The rebellious locks lashed her cheeks and tangled against her lashes until she could barely see.

She hadn't thought to grab a hat, foolishly trusting the morning's bright sun and clear sky. Looking down as the door opened, she hurriedly took the last remaining steps. "*Whew.*" She exhaled in relief once the door slammed shut behind her.

As she raised her gaze, she noticed Cole coming from the opposite direction. She thought she saw a glimmer of humor cross his eyes at the sight of her hair in such disarray, but it was gone in a flash, if indeed it was there at all.

"Windy out there?" he asked innocently.

"Just a little." Danika pushed the runaway strands from her face, regretting that she hadn't worn a ball cap to keep her hair in place.

"Storms blow up fast around here." Cole never stopped walking.

"Do you have a minute?" Danika cocked her head toward him as the memory of the intruder came rushing back into her mind. "It's important."

"Is it about the letters? Did you find something?" Cole stopped and glanced at his watch.

"No, I haven't had time to read anything new. But I need to talk to you."

She saw a noticeable shift in Cole's sense of urgency. "I have to check on something on the trail, and then I have a meeting." He closed one eye as if trying to remember his schedule. "Maybe around..."

Before he could finish, a man Danika had met earlier in the breakfast line opened the door and walked in. He noticed her and smiled. "Hey, how ya doing?"

Then he saw Cole. "Hey, brother. What's up?"

He didn't wait for an answer, but kept walking into the hotel.

"You know him?" Cole turned to Danika, his demeanor turning suddenly searching and cold.

"I've *talked* to him. I wouldn't say I know him." Danika answered, apprehensive at the sudden change.

"Don't talk to him." The words were spoken in a way that didn't allow debate.

Danika jerked her head toward him. "Excuse me? What did you say?"

Cole wrapped his fingers around her arm—not tightly, but firmly—and led her to a quiet corner of the room.

"He's a PMC and he..."

"A what?"

Cole took a deep breath, as if exasperated that he needed to explain. "A private military contractor."

"So *you* know him? Danika tilted her head, showing her confusion.

"Yes, I've worked with him before."

"And you don't like him?"

"I like him fine. He's good at his job."

"Then why do you want me to stay away from him?"

Cole glanced at his watch. "It's not something I can really discuss right here." He looked around. "Can we meet somewhere?"

Danika blinked her eyes a few times. "I just asked you to do that, and you didn't have time."

"I'll make time."

"Okay. Where?" she asked. "The library?"

"Too crowded."

"Eagle Cliff?"

"Too far."

Cole glanced toward the door again. "Give me twenty minutes, and then meet me in SecHQ."

"*Where*?"

"Security Headquarters… you know, third floor."

"I thought you were too busy?"

"I am." He started walking. "I'll see you in twenty."

Danika stared after him, frustration mounting. "Why do you have to be so impossible?" she muttered—not loud, but apparently loud enough.

He paused at the door, glanced back over his shoulder, and offered a faint shrug, exuding the cool indifference of someone used to being in control and not caring what anyone else thought about it.

* * *

Danika quickened her step to get to the meeting room on time after throwing her hair back into a ponytail in her room. She arrived at the same time as Cole was approaching from the opposite direction.

The area was now marked with *No Access. Staff Only* signs, and a man who looked every bit the Secret Service type sat in a chair off to the side in a small alcove. Dressed in black, with a somber expression and a barely-noticeable earpiece, he lacked only a pair of dark sunglasses to complete the picture.

Cole gave a curt nod toward the man, which was returned, and said to Danika, "Follow me."

As soon as they entered the room, he threw the notebook he was carrying onto a table and walked to the corner of the room. "Want some coffee?"

"No thanks." Danika sat down at the same small table and glanced around the space. There was no Rudy this time. The room was empty except for the two of them. She tried to quiet her foot that was tapping nervously against the floor as she waited for Cole, who finally placed a cup of coffee on the table and sat down.

Sitting across from her, he leaned back in his chair and stretched his legs out in front of him. After studying her for a moment, he broke the silence. "Sorry to be so direct down there, but Trent's not here to make friends."

"If you say so." Danika shrugged. "He seemed friendly enough in the breakfast line."

"Being friendly is a ploy—it gets you access faster than force." He took a slow sip of coffee. "People let their guard down around nice people."

"Interesting assessment." Danika raised an eyebrow. "So you think he's dangerous?"

"Not to you directly. PMC's are hired to protect assets—oil rigs, VIPs, whatever—." He paused a moment and studied her. "In other words, they thrive in conflict zones."

The fog in Danika's mind began to lift, the pieces clicking into place. She leaned forward, elbows on the table. "So he's one of the people you referred to that aren't here for peace."

"One of the many... Defense contractors. Arms manufacturers. Dealers." He clasped his hands together on the table. "The people who profit from instability aren't clamoring for the end of conflicts."

Danika's mind raced—names, corporations, politicians—all of the entities with something to lose if war dried up. There was no shortage of them.

GEM-Co surged to the front, unspoken but blaring. She didn't say it out loud, but the implication twisted in her chest, tightening with each breath. No wonder their name had unlocked her reservation. They were here... shaking hands, making deals that shifted lives and fattened pocketbooks. Quiet power disguised as diplomacy.

"So the more conflict in the world, the more money they make." She squeezed her temples to relieve the tension her thoughts caused. "Basically, peace doesn't pay."

Cole sat back, a flicker of something unreadable crossing his face. "You figured all that out pretty fast."

Before she could say more, a soft buzz broke the moment. Cole turned a little to the side, concentrating, his attention focused.

"Copy that," he said, barely louder than a whisper into the mic clipped on his shirt. "Go ahead and check it out."

Danika watched the change ripple through him—the poised readiness in his shoulders, the calculation behind his eyes. "What is it?"

"Nothing to worry about." He stood and crossed to the console near the wall, fingers flying over a keypad. A series of black-and-white surveillance feeds blinked onto the screen, and he scanned them rapidly.

He spoke into his mic again, so low, Danika couldn't hear, then returned to the table and sat down as if there had been no interruption.

"Like I told you earlier, most people think the peace pact is a myth. But if it's real—and if it surfaces—it could lead to major de-escalation in conflict zones."

Danika thought of Trent—his easy smile, the casual way he'd slipped into the breakfast line, disarming and friendly. "So they don't use threats these days," she murmured. "They use charm."

"There's no such thing as an innocent conversation," he added matter-of-factly before taking a sip of coffee so dark it looked like dirty oil.

"Yes," she said, trying to hide the sarcasm from her tone. "I'm learning that."

Her eyes lifted to meet his, and a flicker of unease passed through her. She wasn't sure who he was really working for—and the calm in his voice made her wonder if he belonged to the same world Trent did.

She had come in ready to confront him, to demand answers. But now that the scope of what they were dealing with had widened—now that she saw the danger—she chose to hold back. There were too many layers. Too many masks. For the first time, she felt the true gravity of what she was up against... alone.

Masking her suspicion with a careless shrug, she shifted tactics. Better to stop pressing for answers and simply play along. A sweet smile and a touch of innocence might be all it took to make him underestimate her.

"You must have your hands full, figuring out who's actually here for peace... and who's not."

Cole gave a dry, humorless chuckle. "You don't bring in someone like Trent for the view. He's here because someone's expecting trouble—or planning to cause it."

That caused her mind to race. "So, I guess the list of questionable attendees is long," she said in a casual voice. "Energy, tech, construction... stability threatens profit in all of those sectors."

He nodded once. "Most of them are here to make sure nothing changes. And they'll do whatever it takes to keep it that way."

Danika studied him. For the first time, she wasn't sure what unsettled her more—what he was saying or how calmly he said it. He seemed genuine, even protective. But the truth was, she still didn't know who he really was.

"I never realized profit and chaos were so closely intertwined."

Another lie. She'd known it the moment she began digging into GEM-Co. But this wasn't just about exposing corruption anymore; it was about survival. Trusting Cole might be the biggest mistake she could make.

She exhaled slowly, the air thick with the weight of everything she now knew. She said the words she was thinking out loud. "This is getting complicated."

Cole gave a weary nod, then looked her square in the eyes. "Now that we've got that out of the way—what did you want to see me about?" He glanced at his watch, as if he had somewhere else he needed to be.

Twenty-Three

DANIKA FROZE. SHE'D COME to confront him—about the man outside her door, the open safe, Julian's cryptic tone. But the words caught in her throat. Something about the way Cole watched her—quiet, steady, unreadable—tilted the balance of power before she even began.

Was he acting? Or was he sincere? If she confronted him, what would he do with that information? She opened her mouth to say one thing—but pivoted and said something else. Not the smooth redirect she was hoping for, but his eyes—those steady, watchful eyes—rattled her.

"I—uh—just had a question about the day-pass policy," she blurted.

The moment it left her lips, she wanted to snatch it back.

Surprise flashed in Cole's eyes, but his gaze didn't waver. He picked up his coffee and took a sip, watching her over the rim of the paper cup. "Day-pass policy?"

Yes. I overheard two women on the trail yesterday," Danika said. "They weren't overnight guests but planned to head up to the resort after their hike. Made me wonder how that works."

He placed the cup down on the table with slow, deliberate care. "And you're concerned because...?"

Danika shrugged, trying to act casual. "Well, if people can just wander into the building off the trails, that's a potential security gap, right?" Her voice was steady, but she was sure he could see her pulse hammering in her throat.

His expression didn't change. "So basically, you're asking me how I do my job?"

"No, of course not," she said quickly, the denial too fast, too sharp. "I just meant... it made me wonder how you keep track of who's actually on the property."

He leaned back, arms folded loosely across his chest. "And that's suddenly important to you, *because...*?"

Danika hesitated. *Why is he making this so hard*?

"Because I like to know who's around me," she said. Another shrug—flimsy, forced. "Old reporter habit. I notice patterns. Inconsistencies."

"That so?" He tilted his head, expression unreadable. "Even though you're here to... relax?" He leaned his chair back on two legs, watching her like a man with all the time in the world.

She hated how easily he turned her own words into weapons. But ending the conversation now would feel like retreat—and she wasn't ready to concede.

"Noticing things doesn't just shut off when you're on vacation," she said, her voice sharper than she intended. "And that got me thinking about credentials during the conference. You know—access levels, restricted areas... that sort of thing."

Cole's chair landed hard on all four legs, and he leaned forward, as if he wanted to make sure he'd heard correctly. "Credentials?"

His voice stayed even, but something shifted in his expression. A new flicker of doubt. Caution. "So you urgently wanted to see me about *credentials*."

"I mean... I never said it was *urgent*, exactly." She met his gaze and held it, and found it to be one of the hardest things she'd ever done.

"Oh, you're right, Danika," Cole stared into her eyes. "You said it was *important*. Sorry, I stand corrected."

"I'm just thinking ahead." Danika forced herself to sound calm. "You never know when something newsworthy might happen at a place like this."

"Oh, so you'd need *PRESS* credentials," he said mildly. The way his arms were folded over his chest caused his biceps to tighten just enough to remind her he was not, by nature, relaxed. He tilted his head to signal his confusion. "Again, I thought you were here for a break."

His gaze—cool, appraising—stripped away whatever explanation she'd rehearsed in her head. Words fluttered, disjointed and useless.

"I was... I am... But—" She should have stopped and let the silence do the talking, but the pause stretched, and her mind raced to find a way to fill it.

Cole said nothing. Just waited. No interruptions. No reassurances. Instead, letting her twist in the silence she'd created.

"Don't go getting all defensive," she finally said. "I was just... curious."

"Curious," he echoed, a flicker of amusement in his voice, like there was a hidden joke there she wasn't privy to. He reached for his cup and gave his coffee a slow swirl as he stared at it. "Curiosity does seem to be a habit of yours."

Danika stiffened. "I ask questions. It's what I do."

"Of course." He nodded slowly, one eye narrowing as he raised his gaze and studied her face. "But they're oddly specific questions... about security protocols, no less."

She let out a breath, louder than she intended. "Let me guess—asking questions is now a red flag."

"No." He studied her as he talked, like a man cataloging evidence. "But asking the wrong ones... in the wrong tone, is."

She didn't respond right away as her mind flipped through options—humor, deflection, retreat. No, she was already in too deep. Whatever this was between them, it had long since passed the point of friendly conversation.

"I'm just confused," she said finally, throwing up her hands. "I had no idea what I was walking into when I booked my room. That's all."

He stared at her in silence. "Uh-huh." He lifted the cup again—but he didn't drink. He just scrutinized her over the rim. "Remind me," he said, his voice smooth and quiet, "who exactly you're here with."

Danika looked away, staring vacantly out the window—half from frustration and half from fear. "I'm not here with anybody."

She turned back to him, pulse racing. She'd dug the hole, and now it was clear he wasn't going to reach down to help her out. No. He was going to watch and see how far she'd fall—or how much deeper she'd dig.

"I'm not asking where your cameras are or how to bypass security," she said, tone edged with brittle humor. "I just asked about credentials. How people are vetted. That's it."

She forced a weak smile then, wishing she could erase the last five minutes from her life. Somewhere along the way, she'd lost control of the conversation. She could see it in his eyes—not just skeptical. Suspicious. The kind of stare that makes the air feel heavier. Harder to breathe.

Her pulse ticked up, and a lump formed in her throat as she realized this man was trained to spot deception. The thought of it pressed down on her like a slow-building storm—thick, electric, and impossible to ignore.

Cole took another sip. Slower this time. Measured. As if casually waiting for her to make another mistake.

"So, let me get this straight." He set the cup down and stared at it for a few seconds before raising his steel blue eyes to meet hers. "You're concerned about people with unauthorized access, is that right?"

Danika nodded, taking the bait and falling into his trap. "Yes! I'm concerned about the people who don't belong here—but somehow are. That's correct."

Another pause. Another calculation behind his eyes. "Funny," he said. "That's exactly what I'm concerned about..."

Silence. Thick. Calculating. Suffocating.

She stiffened. "What's that supposed to mean?"

He didn't flinch. "Why don't *you* tell *me?*"

The part of her that had been trained to dig, to probe, to press for the truth—collided with the part that was supposed to lie low and relax.

And still, somehow, she met his gaze. Even if every nerve in her body told her not to.

As he stared at her intently, she could almost see him replaying every conversation they'd had since her arrival, scanning it all for inconsistencies. His eyes didn't just reflect suspicion now—they flared with a silent warning.

"Tell you what," he said in a tone that indicated dismissal. "I'll see what I can do."

Then his eyes drifted to somewhere over her shoulder as if he were concentrating on a separate conversation, and apparently he was. He lifted the mic on the corner of his shirt to his mouth and said, "*Stryker 1-1. Copy that. I'll be there in five.*"

Danika took his nod toward her as a cue to leave and headed out the door. She didn't breathe until she was back in the hallway.

She'd come to confront him—to demand answers, to gauge whether he could be trusted. But instead, she'd sidestepped the truth, stumbled over her own deflection—and handed him every reason to doubt her.

He was the consummate professional: calm, measured, always a step ahead. She hadn't rattled him—or even unsettled his composure.

All she'd done was raise his guard and lose his trust.

And for some reason... that stung more than she expected.

Twenty-Four

DANIKA MOVED DOWN THE hallway, her steps slow, her thoughts a tangle of confusion, mixed with just enough regret to sting.

She paused in her room long enough to braid her hair into two pigtails and tug on a ball cap, then headed for the trail that circled the lake. So far, it was her favorite—quiet, shaded, winding enough to make her feel like she was going somewhere, even if she wasn't. She needed that now. Movement. Air. Space to think.

She counted back. Five days. That's all it had been.

And yet already the lines between instinct and emotion, truth and manipulation, had begun to blur. What started as an escape was unraveling into something far more complicated—and far more dangerous.

And now, instead of answers, she had only more questions. Questions that left her uncertain whether the truth was something she wanted to find at all.

She stepped through the side door—the same one she'd crossed earlier when she ran into Cole—and welcomed the soft breeze that brushed against her skin. The wind had faded, but she was grateful for the cap. She lowered her head as the sun caught her face and walked toward the old stone archway where guests had once arrived and departed.

As she descended the steps, movement on the porch above caught her eye.

Cole...

Or was it?

It definitely didn't resemble the detached, tight-lipped head of security with the ever-watchful eyes and interrogation-style conversations. This man looked... different. His posture was relaxed; his smile unguarded.

Danika's gaze drifted to the woman beside him. Wearing sweatpants, with her brown hair pulled back in a casual ponytail, she looked up at him and laughed—a genuine, effortless display of mirth as she adjusted his tie for him.

Beneath Danika's surprise, something twisted—a flicker of doubt, maybe even hurt. It wasn't jealousy. More like the uneasy sting of realizing she might have misread him—or worse, misjudged him entirely.

Sensing her stare, Cole glanced down.

Their eyes met.

His smile vanished. His posture straightened. Face shuttered. The warmth vanished, locked behind the same professional distance she'd come to expect.

She got the message.

Without breaking stride, she turned her head and kept walking, as if she hadn't seen a thing.

The trail welcomed her with open silence. Shaded and familiar, it steadied her breath, dulled the noise in her mind. Sunlight splintered across the lake like scattered glass, and birdsong fluttered from the canopy above.

She focused on the rhythm of her steps. One, two, three. Keep moving.

She needed space. To relax. To unwind.

And she needed time to figure out who was telling the truth—and who was merely better at pretending.

She had just made it to the far end of the lake when she heard the sound of steady footsteps behind her. She stepped aside to let the jogger pass and noticed it was the woman Cole had been talking to earlier.

The jogger kept moving, but when she got to the point of the lake marking the halfway point, she stopped and bent over, panting.

"This jogging stuff is for the birds," Danika heard her say as she put her hands on her knees and gasped for air. "I'm too old for this."

She looked up when she saw Danika approaching. "Don't mind me. Had to stop and catch my breath."

Danika smiled as she approached. "Trying to get into shape or just running for the joy of it?"

The woman looked up and grinned, still breathing hard, but seeming to get her joke. "Can't say I've ever found the joy in it."

"Me neither," Danika said. "I've tried, but I prefer walking. I get joy out of this." She lifted her hands toward the lake and the sky.

"Smart woman." She straightened up and pulled a water bottle from her side pouch. "I'm Peggy, by the way," she said between gulps.

"Danika. Nice to meet you."

Peggy nodded as she returned the water bottle. "You walk this trail often?"

"It's only my second time."

"I love this loop," Peggy said. "Especially in the morning, before everything wakes up."

"I'll have to try that." Danika started walking again, and Peggy fell into step beside her. "Morning is my favorite time."

"Me too. It's the perfect time to hit the reset button and start over."

Something in the woman's tone—the ease, the shared rhythm of the trail—put Danika at ease. No probing, no pretense. Just two women walking.

"You here on vacation?" Peggy asked after a while. "Or... the conference, I guess."

"A little of both," Danika said after hesitating a beat. "A little work, a little personal."

Peggy nodded, not pushing. "Mohonk has a way of giving you what you need, right when you need it."

Danika glanced at her. "Is that what brought you here? The conference?"

"No. I work here," Peggy said. "Twenty years this July."

Danika's eyebrows lifted. "You don't look old enough to have worked anywhere that long."

"Bless you." She laughed. "But I'm older than I look."

"Keep doing what you're doing," Danika said. "It's working."

"Thanks. It probably has a lot to do with enjoying my job." Peggy paused as she thought about the details. "I've done everything from waitressing to reservations—and even the stables for a while."

"Oh, that sounds like fun," Danika said. "Riding every day would be a dream job."

"Yeah. That was my favorite." Peggy glanced sideways at her. "Horses are easier to wrangle than guests."

"I'm sure," Danika agreed. "I need to put a trail ride on my to-do list while I'm here."

"Oh, you're a horse person? We should go riding sometime. It's been too long since I've been in the saddle."

"I'd love to." Danika felt like she'd known Peggy a lot longer than a few minutes. "It sounds like you never have a boring moment around here."

Oh, believe me." Peggy crouched to retie her shoe, then stood again. "I was just talking with someone earlier—one of the guys who's been around almost as long as I have. We were reminiscing about the good old days." She paused. "Otherwise known as our *wild days*."

Danika raised a brow, wondering if she was talking about Cole. "*Wild* days?"

Peggy's laugh held something softer beneath it. "Let's just say we weren't model citizens back then." She glanced over at Danika. "You know how teenagers are. Midnight swims. Late-night meetings by the firepit. Secret meetings in the garden summerhouse. Nothing too terrible, but we gave the managers plenty of headaches."

Danika nodded. "And you both still work here?"

"Well, I never left. But he did—joined the service after graduation. Gone a long time..." She paused, took a breath, then added with a faint, wistful smile, "Twelve years, to be exact... Not that I was counting."

The quiet weight in her voice told Danika she'd counted every minute.

"So this guy came back to work because of the conference?" Danika asked, becoming more sure she was talking about Cole.

"Yes, not sure that was the original plan but..." Peggy's voice trailed off, then she shrugged. "Julian requested him."

The crunch of gravel underfoot was the only thing filling the silence as the words hit Danika like a kick in the gut. She forced herself to keep walking. *Julian requested him*. Her mind raced as she weighed the chances that Cole was not just working *for* Julian—but *with* him. It didn't seem possible. Then again, she didn't know him. Maybe he was so practiced in the art of deception that he knew how to gain her trust and manipulate what she thought about him.

It had worked, because she'd actually started to feel bad for not trusting him.

Why is this all so confusing and complex?

When Peggy didn't elaborate, she pushed for more.

"Julian DuBois? Wow. He's a pretty big figure around here from what I've seen." Danika kept her tone as casual as she could as she probed for more information. "Your friend must be pretty impressive to be requested by him."

Peggy's voice took on a new sense of wistfulness. "Oh, he is... *Impressive.*" She glanced over at Danika. "I mean, that's a good word for him."

Danika didn't want to intrude, but she also didn't want this moment to pass by without finding out a little bit more.

"How did Julian get him to come back if he was in the service?" Danika kept her voice light. "I know he's good at pulling strings, but that's not an easy task."

"Oh, Julian didn't pull him out of the service or anything." Peggy shook her head at the misunderstanding. "He was injured during a covert operation... severely, so he'd been discharged. He works for a security firm now with other veterans."

Now Danika knew she was talking about Cole. She remembered the name on his badge, Phantom Force Tactical. So that part of his story was true.

Peggy talked while staring straight ahead. "He has a reputation for being the guy you call when you're praying for a miracle... so of course, that's why Julian wanted him."

Danika decided to change the conversation now that she'd confirmed her suspicion. The conversation was getting a little too personal. "Since you've been here forever, what's your favorite place on the property?"

Peggy laughed. "Oh, there are so many. Have you found the little cave under the footbridge by the Lake View porch?"

"No. That sounds interesting. Where is it, exactly?"

"When you go over the bridge, look to the right," Peggy said. "You'll see steps going down. You'll only notice them if you're looking. Just follow the path."

"Any others?" Danika realized what a treasure it was to talk to someone who knew the resort so thoroughly.

"Well, my personal favorite is the two-story summerhouse in the garden." She sighed as if recalling pleasant memories. "We used to hang out there a lot." Her voice turned wistful, and she blinked away the moisture that came with the memories. "It was kind of a secret meeting place for the summer help."

"I'll have to check that one out." Danika tried to recall her walk in the garden. She didn't remember seeing a summerhouse there.

"It's kind of camouflaged because it's covered with vines, but you can't miss it."

They came to a fork in the road, and Peggy pointed to the right. "I need to go check on something. Sorry if I talked your ear off."

"Not at all," Danika said, smiling. "It made my walk fly by." She gave a final wave and turned back to the trail, but her mind was focused on only three words that Peggy had said: "*Julian requested Cole.*"

And just like that, the thread of doubt tugged again.

Was Cole another piece on Julian's board?

Or was he playing his own game?

Twenty-Five

THE DINING ROOM AT Mohonk shimmered in golden light, the ornate light fixtures casting soft reflections across the tables. The low hum of laughter drifted through the air—refined, unhurried—the kind exchanged by people with nothing to fear and nowhere else to be.

Danika had settled into her seat, the evening's menu still in her hands, when movement in the doorway caught her eye. There, perched at the threshold of the dining room, was Mrs. Winslow—the sweet, sharp-witted woman she'd met on her first day at Mohonk.

Danika had seen her a few times since their first meeting, always engaged in conversation, always wearing that smile, equal parts warm and knowing. She didn't feel like just another guest; she seemed part of the very fabric of the resort, seamlessly entwined with staff and visitors alike.

What caught Danika's eye wasn't just Mrs. Winslow—it was Cole, kneeling beside her. His broad frame leaned forward, both hands gently cradling one of hers. The two were deep in conversation, their voices low and lively. Even from across the room, Danika could see the flush in Mrs. Winslow's cheeks and the warmth of her smile—authentic, unguarded. Whatever Cole had said, it had earned the kind of affection and respect that can't be faked. The kind that's built slowly, over time.

A quiet weight settled in Danika's chest—a mix of surprise and something harder to name. Whatever it was, it landed with unexpected force.

Mrs. Winslow's laughter rang out once more as she nodded at Cole's reply. He gave her hand a final pat before rising with effort, a grimace tightening his jaw as he pushed to his feet, the deliberate motion betraying pain.

A quiet exhale slipped from Danika when he rested a hand on Mrs. Winslow's shoulder for a parting squeeze. It looked genuine, and her reaction confirmed it—so much so that Danika couldn't take her eyes off the doorway until he exited the room.

Turning her attention back to her menu, Danika tried to concentrate on deciding what to eat, but the scene she'd just witnessed was hard to erase from her memory.

She scanned the dinner choices, letting her eyes linger on the cleverly worded descriptions, each dish more tempting than the last. After a quiet moment, she made her choice and set the menu aside, reaching for her glass of water.

As her gaze lifted, another scene grabbed her attention, causing the smile to slip from her lips.

There, just a few tables away, sat Dalton Rivers. But it wasn't Dalton that caused the creeping unease to take root—it was the man sitting across from him: *Julian DuBois.*

The sight was a sudden, sour note in the room's symphony. The fragile sense of peace she'd felt just moments before evaporated.

Dalton? With Julian?

A cloud of disappointment settled over Danika. She'd been starting to like Dalton—quiet and withdrawn as he was. There was something unpretentious beneath his aloofness, something she'd glimpsed in the few words they'd shared.

He seemed like someone who valued solitude, who had no interest in the spotlight—and to her, that felt honest. Even admirable.

She began to defend him in her thoughts, searching for logic to steady the uneasy feeling rippling through her. Of course he and Julian knew each other. People in those circles always did. Eating together didn't mean Dalton was part of Julian's web of deception... *necessarily*.

Danika picked up her menu again, mostly to give her hands something to do. But her gaze kept drifting.

Julian sat like a man used to being watched, his fingers drumming lightly on the tablecloth. To his left and Dalton's right, two impeccably dressed women laughed at something he said, their smiles as polished as their diamond-studded earrings.

Danika's stomach tightened. They looked more like props than guests.

Strategically placed distractions, perhaps?

Then her thoughts turned darker. Maybe they were enticements, a little extra incentive in case a deal needed sweetening. She'd seen this kind of theater before in D.C.—too polished to be real. Everything about it screamed coordination, not coincidence.

This was no simple dinner. It was a negotiation.

She'd heard the whispers about Dalton Rivers—tax irregularities, offshore accounts, a quiet federal probe that never quite surfaced. They were the kind of stories that could destroy a career... or be conveniently extinguished with the right ally.

Was this dinner about clearing his name? Or a warning that the price of silence was rising? Was Dalton being courted? Recruited? Or was the message more pointed—delivered not in whispers behind closed doors, but in plain sight?

She'd never believed the rumors about Dalton's alleged crimes, but what if he was tangled up with Julian? What if she'd underestimated how deep this went?

She stared out the window, thoughts churning. Fame opened doors. Dalton's celebrity gave him instant credibility—something Julian could use, and likely had been eyeing for a long time.

Was this dinner meant for conversation—or calculation?

A reward for Dalton? Or a warning?

It was impossible to tell if he was walking into something—or trying to walk away.

Danika exhaled and dropped her gaze to the menu, forcing herself to focus. Maybe she was reading too much into it. Overthinking. Assuming more than she had a right to.

And yet—her eyes lifted again, almost involuntarily. Julian was speaking now, his smile smooth, effortless, the kind that could win a surrender before the first shot was fired. He was good at this. Too good.

One of the women leaned in then, fingers brushing Dalton's sleeve. A casual touch? Or a silent message? Coincidence? Or confirmation? Then, as if to cap the moment, she pressed a painted nail to a phone and handed it to him.

Dalton glanced down, his smile twitching...tightening. His jaw went rigid.

Then, almost imperceptibly, he nodded at Julian.

Danika's pulse stuttered.

It could be nothing.

But what if it wasn't?

Danika took a sip of her water, her pulse thrumming in her ears, as she realized she needed to include Dalton Rivers in the tangled web of power, money, and influence. Watching him now—at ease, charming, yet undeniably guarded—she realized something else.

This was not a man easily figured out.

And that made him dangerous.

Twenty-Six

DANIKA SANK INTO THE rocking chair, hoodie drawn tight against the encroaching chill. The evening had settled in with a sharpness that felt out of season. From her perch above the lake, the summerhouses glowed along the water's edge, their amber reflections dancing on the glassy surface like flickering candlelight.

It should have soothed her. But her thoughts, like the wind-stirred branches, refused to rest.

Her laptop rested on her knees, open yet forgotten. The blinking cursor on the blank page reflected the standstill in her thoughts. She hunted through memory, sifting for patterns, trying to unravel five days of observations that refused to make sense.

Dalton Rivers was the thread she couldn't place.

She hadn't expected him here. She hadn't expected him anywhere. The man had vanished from public life with the kind of precision that suggested intention, not accident. So why now? Why *here*?

She rocked slowly, her gaze trained on the lake while her mind replayed the scene from earlier: Dalton seated across from Julian in the dining room, his posture guarded behind a practiced smile. Julian—charming, magnetic, radiating the kind of confidence that wielded power and demanded control.

To anyone else, it might have looked like camaraderie. To her, it looked like pressure. Or was that just her imagination?

Could Dalton be the opposite of what everyone thought—a reluctant player in someone else's game? Her instincts whispered yes. But her training warned her not to jump to conclusions.

What if Dalton wasn't dining with Julian in support of him, but was *forced* by him? What if his presence was meant to distract—to confuse anyone watching and make them believe that Dalton was part of the conspiracy?

The thought came uninvited and landed heavier than expected. She turned it over, tracing possibilities she hadn't considered.

It looked to her as though Julian was dragging him back into the spotlight, determined to use him. That's what Julian did. He was a master of manipulation—shaping people's lives, leaving them to realize only afterward that every choice had been his, not theirs.

She tapped her finger against the laptop's edge, restless.

Her earlier conversation with Dalton echoed in her mind—his words about the peace of Mohonk, the solace found in silence. Maybe this wasn't merely a retreat. Maybe it was a refuge.

Danika exhaled hard and opened a new tab. The quiet click of keys was the only sound on the balcony as her fingers picked up speed.

She started with Dalton's early work—film credits, interviews, long-forgotten articles. The usual press clippings painted the picture of a rising star: charming, camera-friendly, the kind of man the public wanted to believe in.

She skipped past the polished profiles and sensational headlines, diving instead into archives, review forums, and obscure blog posts that were buried deep.

That's when she found the flops—two early indies, poorly received. One reviewer wrote: "Pretty face, empty delivery." Another film never made it past the festival circuit.

And then—nothing.

For eighteen months, there was only digital silence. Then a slick, polished op-ed appeared in The Atlantic, praising Dalton as a breakout humanitarian voice after a "transformative role" in a political drama.

The film had apparently launched his career. But who funded it?

She followed the studio trail to a shell LLC based in D.C., dissolved within a year. *Typical.*

Danika dug deeper, combing through archived business records until she uncovered a financial disclosure. Several names appeared on the list, most of them unfamiliar. But halfway down, one froze her in place: S. Wiley Holdings.

Her pulse skipped.

She followed the trail of the D.C. address and found it was tied to a consulting firm known for shaping campaigns and culture—rarely seen, yet always pulling strings.

Could it be that Wiley?

She dug further, cross-referencing names with donor lists and FEC filings. And then she found it: Sebastian Wiley, now a senator, but once the shadow behind media companies, entertainment ventures, and viral advocacy campaigns.

A chill traced her spine, sharp and unwelcome.

The man who funded broadcast news and cultural campaigns had helped build Dalton's public image. And he hadn't done it alone.

She scanned deeper into corporate records and campaign ties. Wiley's firm had collaborated multiple times with Julian's nonprofits. The overlap was too obvious to be a coincidence.

Danika sat back and rocked a few times, the unease crawling across her skin.

They hadn't just supported Dalton's rise—they'd scripted it. Bought the narrative, lit the stage, and sent him out to perform.

And there was a good chance he didn't know it was happening... at the time.

Danika's fingers hovered over the trackpad, then typed another query. Tax evasion charges had once been whispered—never confirmed, never denied. Buried, perhaps?

She knew enough about Senator Wiley to understand one thing clearly: He had the power to bring those charges forward. And just as easily, the power to make them disappear.

Was tonight's dinner an invitation?

Or a warning?

Even out of the spotlight, Dalton remained a valuable asset. His familiar, trusted face could sell a failing policy or dress disinformation as truth, making him indispensable to men like Julian and Senator Wiley.

It also made him dangerous to them—if he ever stopped playing along.

Danika leaned back slowly, the chair creaking beneath her. The night air suddenly felt even colder.

Senator Wiley and Julian hadn't just supported Dalton's rise—they'd *orchestrated* it. Funded the project, spun the narrative, built the myth.

Maybe Dalton hadn't walked away from the fame, but fled the architects who built it. He'd figured out the invitations he was getting to speak, the roles he was being offered, were all part of a deceitful scheme.

Danika stared into the dark line of trees, the implications spiraling. She'd been tracking the threads of something similar through GEM-Co—an alliance between government, media, and entertainment. Three industries, one script.

Maybe Dalton was being drawn into the latest phase of the propaganda machine, creating programming designed—not to entertain—but to erode.

Sex, drugs, and violence were carefully staged to appear ordinary. Scripts were crafted to blur the lines, and programs were engineered to make society's worst vices look like good choices. A familiar face could shift public opinion faster than any legislation or a thousand lobbyists.

Danika rose abruptly, the rocker creaking at the change in weight. She paced the narrow balcony, rubbing her arms against the cool air. The lake shimmered silently below, but inside her, the storm gathered.

Why had he come here? Why now?

And why had he accepted an invitation to dinner with Julian?

Did he agree to one last performance? One final role?

If he did, it meant that Julian had something on him. Something that would force his hand.

But maybe this time, Dalton wasn't interested in reading from their script. Maybe there was a chance for her to get his side of the story. She had to at least try.

But how?

Her heart sank.

Because he probably wasn't going to give her a chance.

Twenty-Seven

THE GENTLE HUM OF conversation in Lake Lounge during Afternoon Tea Hour was a comforting backdrop to the soft clinking of teacups meeting saucers.

Danika sat in one of the plush chairs in the far corner, her gaze drifting between the lake outside and Albert Smiley's office just a few yards away. People wandered through the room without a second glance, unaware of the history that took place there.

From that very room, Albert Smiley would have heard the clatter of horses' hooves crossing the wooden bridge—his cue to scan the guest list one last time before stepping out to greet each arrival by name.

Danika tried to picture the conversations that had once unfolded inside this room—the quiet deals, the veiled negotiations, the peace talks weighted enough to ripple across continents. She imagined the crackle of wood in the fireplace, the rustle of papers, the tension that often settled in before history was made.

She was still chasing that image when movement at the main doorway drew her eye.

Cole stood in the threshold, framed by soft lamplight and shadow. He wasn't a man to fidget—but there was something about him that never fully stilled. Like a coiled wire.

His gaze swept the room—sharp, deliberate, calculating. Then he spoke quietly into his mic, checked his watch, and disappeared into the lobby without a glance back.

Danika took a sip of her now-cold coffee and looked back at the lake, allowing the scene to settle deeper.

She wasn't sure which hit her first, the piercing alarm that split the air or the smell—burnt plastic and something unpleasant. Not woodsmoke. Not kitchen grease. Something synthetic and wrong.

Guests jumped. Tea cups rattled. The hum of conversation was replaced by a sharp intake of breath across the room.

Staff moved in quickly, calm but urgent. "Please evacuate." They waved people toward the exits at the lake doors and into the lobby area, where they directed them out the main doors.

Danika stood with the others, heart pounding now. She glanced toward the room on the other side of Albert's office and saw a light haze, low and rolling, like fog with intent. A woman coughed. A man covered his nose with a napkin.

Since most of the smoke seemed to be billowing toward the lake doors, she moved toward the lobby exit, her journalist's instinct flaring.

A loud voice cut through the room, citing an electrical malfunction and directing everyone to evacuate at once in an orderly fashion.

Danika's mind spun. She'd never smelled anything quite like this. Her gut twisted.

Since she was in the back of the room, she was among the last to exit. Just as she hit the doorway, the small haze began to billow. People began coughing and moving a little faster, as staff helped round up stragglers and kept everyone moving.

Danika held her hand over her mouth and noticed one figure moving against the current, toward Lake Lounge and the smoke. It was Cole. "Is everyone out?"

She nodded. "I think I'm one of the last." She coughed.

"Good. Keep moving." His gaze lifted as he tried to penetrate the thick haze in front of him. Cole didn't move. His jaw flexed, his shoulders tensed.

"Did you see Mrs. Winslow leave? She was sitting in Laurel Lounge a few minutes ago."

Danika tried to think. She'd seen Mrs. Winslow in her usual place by the window in the Lounge, but that was out of her line of sight. She didn't remember seeing her leave.

"No... I..." More smoke billowed out the door. "Keep moving," Cole said. "Get outside. The fire department is on the way."

Danika grabbed his arm as he moved toward the smoke, startled by the strength beneath her hand—lean, solid muscle—like steel wrapped in cotton. "Cole, wait for the firemen."

He didn't pause. "Okay. Keep moving."

That was all she heard before he disappeared into the smoke.

Heart pounding, she pushed through the main doors just as the first fire trucks pulled to a stop. Outside, the sunlight hit like a slap—too bright, too sharp after the dim chaos inside.

As firefighters jumped down from the trucks, pulling hoses and gear with practiced urgency, she ran to one of them.

"There's still someone inside," she said.

The firefighters didn't hesitate—and the mood shifted instantly. Gear was passed. Helmets buckled. But seconds ticked by, dragging into minutes, as Danika stood rooted, eyes locked on the smoke-filled doorway.

Waiting.

She tried holding her breath to see how long she could last, but gave in with a sharp gasp. The smoke, though thin, curled from the building like something alive, pulsing with a sinister rhythm. Every second stretched and snapped. Her reporter's mind flashed to every story she'd written about how smoke steals lives faster than flames.

What if they didn't make it?

What if there wasn't a happy ending?

What if—

Her eyes scanned the doorway, but nothing emerged. Just smoke—sometimes thin and drifting, sometimes dense and roiling, as if the building was exhaling long-held secrets.

Just as the first firefighter stepped forward—

Movement. A shadow.

For a beat, she thought it was a trick of the haze. But then the shape solidified, forged from grit and haze, blackened at the edges but upright.

Cole carried Mrs. Winslow in his arms, her head pressed to his chest, a napkin clutched to her face. His face was black with soot, his eyes red, chest rising and falling in sharp, ragged gasps.

Danika stood rooted as the medics moved. She couldn't make out any words, but saw the grip of Mrs. Winslow's frail fingers on Cole's wrist as they lifted her away.

As soon as she was out of sight, Cole dropped to his knees, coughing hard, one hand braced on the ground as he tried to clear his lungs.

"Here, dude." A firefighter slipped an oxygen mask over his face. "Sit down."

Another firefighter, the one who'd spoken earlier, gave a low whistle. "Heck of a job, man."

Cole inhaled a few times through the mask, then pulled it off, swiping a soot-covered hand down his face. "Water?" he rasped, nodding toward a discarded bottle lying on the ground.

Danika grabbed it and handed it over, only to watch him dump it over his head, the water streaking black down his face.

She opened her mouth to speak, but nothing came. Her heart was pounding too hard, her throat too tight. For all the times she'd seen him steady, sharp, and resolute—this shook her.

He looked up at her, eyes red and glassy from the smoke. "Why are you staring at me like that?"

She looked at him accusingly, suddenly angry that he could almost give her a heart attack, and then act so nonchalant. "Why did you do *that*?" Her voice was loud and screechy.

He looked genuinely confused. "Do *what*?"

"Go back in after Mrs. Winslow."

"Because she would have died." His expression indicated he didn't understand her point.

Danika crouched in front of him, locking eyes with his soot-smudged face. "So could you."

He gave a slight shrug, then lifted the oxygen mask back to his face.

A firefighter approached and clapped a hand on Cole's shoulder. "Let's get you checked out. That much smoke isn't something to mess with."

Cole took another gulp of the oxygen and then stood as if he was going to comply. But in one fluid motion, he removed the mask and handed it to the fireman. "Thanks, but I've got work to do."

Then he turned and walked away.

Twenty-Eight

As Danika walked toward Lake Lounge later that evening, the scent of smoke reached her, a lingering ghost of something that could have been much worse. The only damage from the fire had been contained to a small storage alcove—a few blackened ceiling tiles that looked more like a warning than a casualty.

But the area was now wrapped with yellow CAUTION tape, while cleanup crews worked to remove the soot and smell. Large fans hummed in the background, pushing fresh air through the area. Already, the sharp odor had thinned to little more than a trace.

Despite the lateness of the hour, people continued to gather outside the tape, telling each other how glad they were that the fire hadn't been worse. As Danika moved sideways around the crowd, she noticed a man entering the cordoned-off area wearing a safety vest and a hard hat.

She did a double-take when she recognized Trent, the man she'd met in the breakfast line. The PMC, as Cole had called him.

His presence made Danika stop in her tracks. At first it surprised her, but then it made her mad. What would *he* be doing in there?

Suddenly, it all became clear.

The fire was just a diversion, a way to lock down the area so no one could get in to see what was going on. They were in there right now looking for the pact!

Her mind immediately went to Cole as she thought about the conversation they'd had over her letters. *He* was the one who had mentioned Lake Lounge. *He* was the one who had said it was too obvious to just close down the room!

The fact that she'd trusted him—maybe even started to like him—ignited a storm in her mind. This was all the proof she needed. Furious, she yanked out her phone before remembering she didn't have his number. Her hand curled around it anyway, trembling with the urge to act.

She almost ducked under the tape to search the room herself, but stopped. No—if he was behind this, he'd be smart enough to be somewhere else. Not look like he was involved.

Bypassing the crowd, Danika took the steps two at a time to the third floor. She was getting ready to head down the hallway when someone grabbed her arm from behind. "Sorry. Staff only," the man said.

"I'm here to see Cole!" Her voice came out louder than she expected, thanks to her adrenaline and anger.

"I'll have to check and see if he's here."

"If he's not here, get on your radio and *find*—"

Before she could finish her sentence, the door at the end of the hallway swung open.

"What's the problem out here?" Cole stood in the doorway, strong and imposing, his expression sharp with irritation.

"I need to talk to you." Danika didn't wait for permission—just stepped down the short staircase and marched past him into the room. She heard Cole exhale loudly and the door close behind her with a bang.

"There's a proper way to find and meet with me—and this isn't it," he said from behind her. She thought it was anger that lowered his voice until he paused and turned away, coughing deeply—a harsh, raw sound that reminded her just how much smoke he'd inhaled earlier.

"I have to admit," Danika said, turning toward him, "I'm a little surprised you're not down there with Trent... helping search for the pact."

Cole's gaze jerked toward her. "What are you talking about?"

"Lake Lounge. The fire this afternoon. It was all just a diversion, wasn't it?"

He cocked his head and stared at her. "Can you please explain what you're trying to say?"

"Don't pretend you don't know that Trent is down there right now searching for the pact."

"What would make you think that?"

"Because I *saw* him! Does he do post-fire cleanups as part of his PMC duties, do you think?"

Cole raised both hands in the air. "Slow down. Tell me what's going on."

"You're head of security, right?" Danika asked. "You're the one who decides who goes in and out of that room. Correct?"

"No. The cleanup is being handled as a maintenance issue—not security. The hotel didn't want me to divert resources to that, since it's just a matter of taping off the perimeter while they work."

He planted his feet, arms crossed—his usual stance when he was either losing patience or holding something back. The atmosphere between them thickened, heavy with tension and judgment.

"Tell me what you think is going on." His calm voice infuriated her even more.

"What I *think* is going on?" Danika's voice grew shrill. "How about what I *know*? I *know* that we sat right here in this room and discussed the possibility of the pact being hidden in *that room*." She stood face-to-face with him, refusing to back down despite his intimidating size and strength. "Am I supposed to believe it's just a coincidence that it's now closed down to the public, and a known private military contractor is part of the cleanup team?"

"So you think *I'm* behind this?" Cole shook his head incredulously. "Why would I set a fire at the time of day that I know Mrs. Winslow is sitting by the window—and then risk my life to get her out?"

That reply stumped Danika completely. She began pacing, brushing a stray tendril of hair from her face, before stopping and stabbing her finger into the top of the table. "All I know is that we sat right *here*, just the two of us, and discussed the possibility of the pact being hidden in that particular ro..."

Her voice trailed off toward the end as the thought struck her that they *hadn't* been alone. Cole seemed to come to the same conclusion at the same time. Both of their heads turned toward Rudy's desk, which was not occupied at the moment.

"How well do you know him?" Danika asked, seeing that he was thinking the same thing. Her anger evaporated immediately, leaving only confusion—and regret.

"He's the only member of my team who was assigned to me. My guys do security, not administrative work. I'd never met him until a few weeks ago."

Danika pulled out a chair and sat down hard. "Then someone else really is looking... and now they know everything we talked about."

Cole sat down across from her and squeezed his temples. "Okay. Calm down. We just need to reassess."

Danika put her head in her hands and shook her head back and forth. "Sorry. I thought..."

She faltered before finishing, but he accepted—or perhaps, dismissed—the apology with a curt nod, seemingly unwilling to linger on what couldn't be undone.

Danika should have left it at that, but pressed on with an explanation. "When I heard Julian specifically requested you for security, I guess I assumed—"

Cole's head jerked toward her. "I don't know where you heard that, but Julian hired the company I work for and selected me because I know the property. End of story."

Danika hit her head with the palm of her hand. "It's all making sense now. That's why Julian seemed to know so much... because of Rudy. Not *you*."

Cole tilted his head. "Wait. You talked to Julian?"

"I ran into him on the path by the lake." Danika shrugged.

"You just *ran into each other*? What did he say? What did he know?"

"It wasn't so much anything he said but *how* he said it." Danika stared over his shoulder as she thought about the conversation. "It was like he wanted me to think he knew something. I couldn't put my finger on it."

Cole nodded, but she could see he was completely lost in thought now, planning his next move.

"You're going to confront Rudy, right?" Danika looked up at him.

His gaze landed on her thoughtfully. "Not sure."

"You're not *sure*?" Danika threw her hands in the air. "Could it be any clearer?"

Cole held his hand up. "Hold on. Hear me out." He leaned forward and talked in a low tone as if there were someone else in the room.

"If I confront him and get rid of him, we'll never find out who he's working for and what they know."

"Okay, true, but—"

"He also knows the ins and outs of the overall security plan," Cole said, interrupting her. "I can't jeopardize that getting handed over or sabotaged by a disgruntled employee. We're too close to the conference."

Danika exhaled sharply, frustration tangled with reluctant respect. She hated to admit it, but he was right. Instead of rushing to do something rash, as she would have no doubt done, he'd analyzed the situation from all sides... and all in mere seconds.

As always, he hadn't reacted. He'd calculated. While she was still reeling from the shock of learning Rudy was leaking information, Cole had already sized up the perimeter, assessed the threat, and started mentally reshuffling the pieces. He always moved with unshakable calm, untouched by the chaos around him. That composure unsettled her—his control a sharp contrast to her own mind, which was always spinning in a thousand directions.

She leaned back in her chair, the silence stretching between them. "So, what now?"

Cole's gaze swept across the room. "First, I'm locking this place down. Computers, physical files—access goes on a strict need-to-know basis."

"Don't you think Rudy will notice?"

"No. I'll still give him plenty of access—to the things I want him to see."

Danika turned toward him, brow creased. "What does *that* mean?"

He paused, long enough that Danika thought he'd said all he intended to say on the matter. But then he spoke again.

"It means, sometimes giving a man rope is the only way to know what he's planning to do with it."

She narrowed her eyes. "So you're going to give him false information and see what he does with it."

"I didn't say that," he said evenly.

"But that's what you meant."

He didn't confirm or deny, just let the silence answer for him. The way he set his jaw told her his thoughts had already moved six steps ahead. Under normal circumstances, it would have irritated her—but this time it didn't.

This time, it steadied her.

She leaned forward, arms crossed on the table, studying him. He wasn't just calculating—he was sensible and insightful and frustratingly logical. She exhaled and shook her head. "You kind of infuriate me when you're right."

He glanced up, the faintest spark in his eyes. "I've noticed."

Danika smiled, hoping her cheeks weren't as red as they felt at the look. "I thought you were going to say that I kind of infuriate you when I'm wrong."

"I don't have time for that."

She wasn't sure if he meant he was too busy, or if she was wrong so much that he didn't want to waste his time, but she didn't press the issue. "If I'd have found out about Rudy, I would've confronted him. Demanded answers."

"Yeah." His voice softened just a bit. "That's a normal reaction, I guess."

The quiet between them shifted. It wasn't the strained silence of suspicion anymore, or the brittle distance between two people questioning each other's motives. It was something else now. Something more honest.

"You're not very good at trusting people, are you?" Cole turned toward her fully, his eyes locking onto hers with a quiet intensity.

"Should I be?"

He shrugged. "I guess in your line of work, that's not a bad thing." He leaned forward. "But we're on the same side now, right?"

Danika tilted her head questioningly.

"If you have a problem, you can confront me about it. But we both need to be on the same page and agree we're after the same thing."

There was something in his voice that stopped her—not just the words, but the weight behind them. It wasn't a challenge. It wasn't even a demand.

It was an offer. A hand extended. A truce declared.

The shift caught her off guard. She nodded, slow and cautious. "Yes. Agreed."

Something flickered in his expression then, gone almost before she could name it, tucked behind that detached, impenetrable calm. She knew what it was. Trust—hard-won. Fragile.

Easily lost.

Maybe this wasn't the safest step she could take, but it felt steady, solid in a way that made her breath catch, just for a second.

Danika's mind drifted back to earlier that day, to the smoke, the chaos, and the moment Cole had emerged from the shadows.

"Have you heard anything about Mrs. Winslow?"

"They're keeping her overnight, but she should be released tomorrow," he answered. "She's a trooper. She'll be okay."

Danika leaned in closer and spoke in a hushed voice as she changed the subject back to the one at hand. "Do you think they found anything?"

Cole stared thoughtfully into the distance. "I don't know. But I think it will become obvious in the near future."

The sound of the door opening interrupted them, and they both turned their heads. Rudy walked in, looking dejected and glum.

"Oh, hey." He looked up and planted a big smile on his face. "Sorry, didn't mean to interrupt. You going over more letters?"

"No. Just chatting." Danika stood. "Actually, I was just leaving."

She walked toward the door and was glad when she heard Cole follow.

"Okay, see ya, Danika." Rudy's tone was back to being cheerful, but it didn't ring true.

"See ya, Rudy." She managed to keep her face impartial, and as she looked back at Cole, not surprisingly, so did he.

Twenty-Nine

DANIKA WASN'T SURE WHAT compelled her to sign up for a tomahawk-throwing class. Maybe it was curiosity. Maybe it was a subconscious rebellion against everything else filling her head—treaties, secrets, and a web of lies she couldn't seem to untangle.

Or maybe she just wanted to feel like someone else for an hour and celebrate her anniversary. She'd been at Mohonk for one full week.

Whatever the reason, she now stood on a woodchip-covered range, clutching a hatchet-like object and wondering what she'd gotten herself into. The instructor, a lean, athletic guy with boundless energy and a slightly mischievous grin, made it all look easy—like throwing a tomahawk was as natural as tossing a softball.

He breezed through safety instructions with the casual flair of a bartender reciting a drink menu, completely unbothered by the nervous expressions of half the group.

Danika turned the weapon over in her hands, not entirely convinced it belonged there.

"First time?" a voice said beside her.

She turned and nearly dropped the tomahawk.

Dalton Rivers stood just a few feet away, dressed down in jeans and a black Henley, the sleeves pushed up, and a ball cap pulled low over his eyes. Somehow, even incognito, he was unmistakable.

A jolt went through her, sharp and electric—her reporter's mind cataloging the details even as the rest of her simply stared.

She had been wanting to talk to this man for years, and now he stood just feet away. It wasn't the excitement of meeting a celebrity that unsettled her—it was the weight of everything she wanted to know.

"Is it that obvious?" she managed.

He smiled. "Only to those of us equally clueless."

She looked at him fully for the first time in clear daylight and saw the leading-man appeal. It wasn't just the way he stood, or the quiet confidence in his expression—it was the ease he carried, the kind of masculinity that didn't need to announce itself. His features were sharp but softened by age and experience, the kind of handsomeness that stayed with you.

What struck her most were his eyes—deep, warm brown with a flicker of mischief, as if he knew more than he'd ever say.

She gave him a wink. "Come on. You look like the type of guy who throws tomahawks for a living." As he turned to answer her, the sunlight caught on the silver threaded through the edges of his hair. *Premature*, she thought. He couldn't be more than forty-five.

"Hardly." He cracked a half-smile. "But thanks for the endorsement."

Danika shifted the instrument from her left hand to her right and back again.

"I don't know much about tomahawks," Dalton said, watching her movements, "but I'm pretty sure they don't bite." His easy tone and amused eyes pulled a reluctant smile from her.

"I know... but I can't figure out which arm to use."

"Excuse me?"

"I'm left-handed."

"Oh." Dalton nodded. "You're one of *those*."

She moved the tomahawk again from her left hand to her right and raised her arm. "I shoot right-handed, so I'm thinking I'll go with my right."

"Interesting." Dalton raised his eyebrows. "I'm right-handed, and I'd be downright dangerous with my left." He glanced over at her. "Probably dangerous either way, honestly."

They stood in easy silence through the first few throws. Her first attempt missed completely. The second hit the target's edge with the wrong end of the blade. Dalton didn't fare much better.

But then something clicked. She adjusted her stance, focused on what the instructor had said—use your whole body, not just your arm. The next tomahawk landed squarely in the wooden target with a satisfying *thunk*.

"Nice," Dalton said, eyebrows raised. "You sure you never did this before?"

She laughed, surprised by how natural it felt—and by the unguarded, unrehearsed sound of his laugh in response.

He wasn't performing for anyone now. He was just a man at ease in the quiet, as if he'd traded the spotlight for something real.

His next throw hit just to the left of the bullseye.

"Beginner's luck?" she teased.

"I'm competitive," he replied, stepping back. "And possibly showing off." There was something warm and soft in his humor. Even his eyes seemed lit with amusement.

It didn't take long for Danika to realize this sport demanded every ounce of her attention. By the fourth throw, the hidden pacts and secrets had faded, replaced by the simple rhythm of aim and release—and by the surprising discovery that hurling sharp objects at a wooden target could be as addictive as it was fun.

At the end of the session, the instructor patted Dalton's back. "If there's ever a celebrity lumberjack tournament, you're a shoo-in."

Dalton grinned, then looked at Danika. “Only if she’s on my team.”

She felt a flicker of warmth in her cheeks, but wasn’t sure if it was from his words or the way he said them.

“Well,” she said, over her shoulder as she returned her tomahawk, “that was unexpectedly exhilarating.”

“Agreed. And thanks for not laughing when I almost threw mine backward.”

“I’ll save that for next time.”

“Next time?” he echoed, the corner of his mouth lifting. “You’re going to do this again?”

“Maybe.” She smiled. “It’s a skill that may come in handy someday... You never know.”

“Remind me to never get on your bad side.”

Danika’s mind raced. She might not get this chance again. She held out her hand. “I’m Danika, by the way.”

He hesitated, the kind of pause that spoke of a man used to keeping his name to himself, then took her hand. “Andrew. Nice to meet you.”

Her mind snagged on the name. Andrew. The “A” in A. Dalton Rivers. The quiet offering of a real name felt like a crack in the armor—small, but real.

As the group drifted toward the resort, Danika moved quietly into step beside him. They walked in companionable silence for a few minutes before Danika spoke again. "Okay, I’ll admit it—that was actually a lot more fun than I expected."

Dalton smiled. "Anything that lets you throw sharp objects at something without consequences? Hard to beat."

She smiled. “Honestly, I was nervous at the thought of being somewhere with no TVs. But this? Way better than the evening news.”

“By a long shot.” His tone dropped—low, grave, and abruptly stripped of all humor. “Much better for your mental health, too.”

She glanced over at the sudden shift in him. "You sound like someone who's thought about this topic a lot."

He shrugged. "The effects of mass media on your brain? Probably more than I should."

He kept walking, hands in his pockets. A breeze kicked up, scattering dry leaves across their path. "Places like this? No TVs, no noise—they're good for the soul. It's too bad more people don't try it."

"I have a confession to make," Danika said lightly, trying to keep the conversation going. "I kind of miss the nightly news. I feel like I've lost touch."

Her words made him stop walking. "I hate to break it to you," he said, his tone shifting, "but there's no such thing as news anymore. It's all theater."

"Theater?" she asked, as he began walking again. "All of it? You really believe that?"

"Yes, I do," he said, his voice edged now. "Journalists—the people who love to preach about truth—are the first ones to trade it in for a state dinner invitation or a juicy tell-all book deal."

He kept walking, but Danika slowed—his words hitting a little too close, causing her to regret bringing up the subject.

"I agree there's corruption in the industry, but I don't think they're *all* like that." She tried to keep her voice neutral. Light. *Did he know her profession? Was he prodding her? Or was he just letting off steam*? "I'm sure *some* of them have integrity."

She tried to sound persuasive, but she knew her tone was not very convincing.

Dalton cocked his head. "I guess I just haven't met one like that yet."

They walked a few more steps in silence. Danika wanted to push back, defend her profession.

But she couldn't.

She'd seen it firsthand. The traded favors, the silent compromises. The way truth got shaped, softened, packaged, spun... until it fit.

The road split, and Dalton turned to the right and nodded toward her. "Have a good afternoon."

"Nice meeting you, Andrew," Danika replied in return. "See ya."

She glanced back and watched him walk away, kicking rocks out of his path and shaking his head.

The late afternoon sun was warm, but a chill needled beneath her skin. Getting Dalton to talk to her was going to be even harder than she thought—especially if he found out who she was.

Thirty

STILL RIDING THE RUSH from the tomahawk class, Danika wasn't ready to go back inside. Adrenaline hummed, thoughts knotted, and without noticing, she drifted past the resort's edge into the garden. The first cool drop of rain on her skin made her look up, startled by how far she'd wandered.

Far from any shelter, she kept walking. Blue sky ahead promised the shower would be brief, but Peggy's mention of a summerhouse in the garden tugged at her curiosity.

Where was it?

She paused on the path, glancing left, then right, until her gaze snagged on a dense tangle of vegetation amassed near a pair of old stone columns. Moving closer, she realized what she'd taken for shadow was a structure—half-hidden, half-swallowed. It didn't seem built so much as claimed, as though the earth had decided to take it back.

Danika approached slowly, like it was a living thing—half-wild, half-shy, retreating from the polished charm of the surrounding garden. The building rose from the garden like a secret planted there, its weathered two-story frame wrapped in cascading vines. Clusters of purple flowers, remnants of spring, still clung to the wood like memories unwilling to let go.

Whatever waited inside, it pulled her forward—out of the rain and into something she couldn't quite name.

Five worn steps led upward, and the railings, crooked and half-swallowed by new growth, curved inward like an invitation. The whole structure felt alive, with leaves stirring softly in the breeze and bees drifting lazily through clusters of lightly swaying blossoms.

From a distance, the summerhouse looked ready to collapse—but up close, it felt solid, as if it might outlast everything else.

At the first landing, Danika paused, taking in the wide circular bench that wrapped around the inner edge of the platform. She remembered Peggy saying it was once a favorite gathering place for the young workers, half-hidden from the rest of the world.

Looking around now, she could see why. There was seating enough for half a dozen down here, with another level waiting above her.

She drew a steady breath, taking in the rough-hewn railings and vine-draped walls. This wasn't just a summerhouse—it was a place that invited secrets. A hideaway. A lookout. A fairytale left unfinished.

With one hand braced on the center post for balance, Danika began to climb the narrow spiral stairway, her steps slow, her anticipation quiet but sharp.

At the top, she stepped into the shelter of the upper level. Vines ran rampant over the railings, curling thick and wild, forming a tangled veil of green that cloaked the world beyond in mystery.

Peeking through the maze, she could see the stone summerhouse to her right—the only one not made of wood. Straight ahead, the castle-like structure of Mohonk rose in quiet majesty, its turrets softened by mist.

And below her, the gardens stretched with stately precision, the quiet paths meandering through beds that burst with 30,000 tulips each spring. Even now, between seasons, the symmetry and care were evident—a place built to impress, but also to endure.

Danika turned slowly, taking in the view, trying to picture the people who once climbed these same steps. Built in the late 1800s, this summerhouse had likely hosted everything from stolen kisses to whispered proposals.

She lowered herself onto the bench, the staircase curling beneath her like a ribbon of time. A soft hum floated through the vines—bees drifting through blooms, unbothered by past or present.

This was the only two-story summerhouse on the property and among the oldest. But even half-swallowed by vines and softened by time, it still carried the quiet gravity of memory. Danika could almost see them—ladies with parasols, men in tailored coats—meeting in defiance of expectation, their gloved hands brushing in passing, hearts beating faster in the hush between footsteps.

Closing her eyes, she let the sound pull her deeper, and tried to picture them—Noah and Abigail—meeting here in secret, their words hushed, the world outside held at bay.

She wondered if Abigail had once waited in a place like this—hands folded in her lap, listening for Noah's footsteps on the path below, knowing that a mere stolen minute together might come at a cost.

Although the original summerhouse was long gone—rebuilt, reshaped, its very bones replaced—something lingered. Maybe it wasn't the structure that remembered, but the space itself. The air still held the weight of risk and the thrill of defiance, as if certain kinds of love left echoes strong enough to outlast wood and stone.

Danika leaned back against the bench, fingertips tracing a heart etched into the wood. She could picture Noah and Abigail here, and almost hear their whispers. Every caress or glance they exchanged must have spoken volumes.

Looking around, she imagined the summerhouse in a modern light too. Peggy, her co-workers... and Cole.

She could almost see him here—years younger, unburdened, slipping up the narrow stairs after a long shift. Maybe for a break from the noise. Maybe to meet someone.

She wondered what he was like before his time in the service. Before whatever happened that carved that distance into his eyes. Did this place remember him, too? His footsteps on the stairs, his voice echoing between the rafters, his laughter carried on the breeze?

She hesitated, her hand resting on the rail as she tried to imagine the young, rebellious teenager. She could imagine him taking those stairs two at a time, leaning over this same railing, all swagger and steel, as he laughed with his coworkers.

Maybe this was where he came to be alone. To breathe.

Her gaze lingered on the far corner of the upper platform, where vines spilled over the rail like a green waterfall. Then again, perhaps in his *wild* years he'd waited here, heart pounding, for someone to arrive. She pictured whispered promises, a first kiss—an unrecorded summer, left out of the pages of his story.

Hard to imagine... but even Cole had a beginning.

A breeze stirred the wisteria around her, rustling leaves and petals like a whisper too faint to catch. The moment broke, her thoughts slipping through her fingers before she could hold onto them.

Her eyes drifted past the tangled vines to the Mountain House beyond—and with it, her thoughts shifted, unbidden, to Dalton Rivers.

A different kind of mystery. Not bound to this place by memory, but by questions. He'd given her a few glimpses—just enough to prove he knew more than he was willing to reveal.

And now she didn't know what unsettled her more: what he might know...

Or the possibility that he'd never tell her.

She turned back to the bench, her palm brushing the timeworn wood. Maybe that was the hardest part—trying to untangle two threads at once. Two men she'd just met, each carrying his own history behind eyes that revealed almost nothing.

Leaning back, she let the hush of the garden settle around her. For a moment, it wasn't just the past she felt here—it was something still alive. Like the story was still unfolding, and somehow, she'd become a part of it.

Maybe that's what stories did—looped and spiraled, pulling people into their orbit across years, decades... lifetimes.

And now, somehow, she was part of one. Not as a witness. But as a thread.

Thirty-One

THE LETTERS HAD KEPT Danika company for the better part of an hour, their fading ink and careful script pulling her deeper into a world that felt both distant and strangely near. She had read and re-read certain lines, searching between the words for meanings not yet clear. Now, the pages lay scattered across the coffee table, her thoughts too restless to continue.

Leaning forward, she reached for the velvet pouch beside the stack. The letters carried emotion, stories pressed into paper and ink. But the piece of vintage jewelry she tipped into her palm from the pouch held something else entirely—*mystery*.

The butterfly brooch gleamed in the low light, its wings richly colored in shades of deep orange, red, and black. Intricate flecks of gold created a textured, mosaic-like effect that added a layer of elegance and mystique. The coloring mimicked the delicate and vivid markings of a real monarch, but with an almost stained-glass brilliance.

She hadn't meant to bring the brooch. It was priceless—a family heirloom that could never be replaced. If she lost it, she'd lose the last tangible link to her great-grandmother's story. But in the end, she couldn't resist the pull. It was more than jewelry—it was a thread to the past.

She stared at the vintage piece for the thousandth time, admiring the workmanship... how the light glittered and sparkled off the wings. It looked delicate, yes—but also defiant. Like it had something to say.

Just as she turned back to continue reading, a sharp knock broke the silence, shooting a spark of fear through her. It wasn't late, but late enough that visitors felt unexpected. Coupled with the fact that she'd placed the "Do Not Disturb" tag on her door after seeing the mystery man, made it seem out of place.

When she opened the door, Cole stood there, hands on his hips, sleeves rolled up, tie loosened—as casual as she'd ever seen him, though his air of quiet intensity was still very much intact.

"Thought I'd take you up on that offer about reading those letters," he said. "Unless you're too busy."

Danika arched a brow. "I thought *you* were too busy."

She didn't bother asking how he knew what room she was in. She didn't want to think about what he might know about her.

He tapped the radio clipped to his belt. "Everything's quiet—for now. And if it's not, they'll find me."

She stepped aside, gesturing him in. "Well, if reading old love letters is how you want to spend a Friday night..."

He walked toward the coffee table without waiting for an invitation, talking over his shoulder. "You really shouldn't open your door like that."

"What do you mean?" Danika walked over and tried to organize the ones she'd read and the ones not yet opened.

"You should have asked me for identification, or—."

"Or a code word or something?" She looked at him over her shoulder.

"Wouldn't hurt." Cole sat down on the couch and leaned over the coffee table, looking at the stack of letters. "But I mean, seriously, don't just open the door."

"Well, it's not like a code word would have kept that man from entering my room the other day," Danika said, plopping onto the couch beside him.

Cole's head turned toward her. "What?"

"A man. In my room. At least I *think* so. I thought I saw him coming out."

"Wait." He stood and tilted his head to the side. "Did you report it?"

"N-n-o. Nothing was missing... so I couldn't be sure."

"You're *sure* nothing was missing?"

She nodded. "All I found was the door to the safe hanging open."

"And everything was still in there?" Cole raked a hand through his hair, clearly agitated by the news that her room had been breached.

"I didn't have anything in there."

He tilted his head. "Where were the letters at the time?"

He had already started walking back toward the door.

"The wood box," she said casually.

He turned, his gaze shifting toward the hearth. "Did you say the wood box?"His eyes landed on the rustic container beside the fireplace, where a supply of wood was furnished to each guest.

Danika gave a small shrug. "I figured no one would bother checking where the firewood goes." She paused, then added, "And apparently... they didn't."

He stared at her for a beat—silent, unreadable. Then the corner of his mouth lifted into a half-smile, unexpected, authentic... and brief. "Nice work."

The smile—and the approval—caught her off guard, landing with more weight than she expected. It left her speechless.

Cole turned back to the door, opened it, and slid his hand up and down along the side.

"I'm going to fix this." He lifted his lapel mic to his lips and had a brief conversation with someone named Trapper as he opened and closed the door, answering questions in a low voice.

At last, he closed the door and turned toward her again. "Will you be here tomorrow morning?"

She nodded, and he said, "10-4," to whoever he was talking to.

"What's going on?" she asked when he walked toward her.

"A couple of my guys will be here in the morning to fix that. They'll explain everything."

He made it sound like that was the end of the conversation, but Danika questioned him. "You can't just add another lock. Julian will get suspicious."

"Don't worry, Julian won't know—and neither will anyone else. We're just going to add another layer of security."

Danika had no idea how they were going to do that, but decided to get back to the business at hand. She sat down on the couch and pulled a few letters out of a pile she had put to the side. "I've been trying to piece together some kind of timeline."

Cole sat down beside her on the couch and pulled the coffee table closer. "What's this?" he asked, pointing toward the vintage piece of jewelry.

"It's a brooch." She pointed to a letter on the table. "I was just reading about it. Noah made it... with his own two hands."

"What?" He leaned closer. "Has anyone else seen it? Does anyone else know about it?"

"No. I've never really had it out until now." She pushed the letter toward him. "Read this."

My Dearest Abigail,

To hear that the Monarch pleased you warms me more than

I can say. I only hope you will forgive its imperfections, for I crafted it with my own clumsy hands—hands accustomed to shaping wood and stone, not fine metalwork.

Cole lowered the letter after reading it and stared into space for a few moments. "Where did you get the brooch exactly?"

"It was in the attic, tucked away with the letters," Danika said. "I thought it was beautiful, but it holds even more meaning now."

Cole nodded in such a way that she could tell he was analyzing and scrutinizing every facet of this new discovery.

"I mean, just think... Noah created this with his own two hands." Danika placed that brooch in her flat hand and stared at it as she spoke. "It's one thing to receive a piece of jewelry, but to know it was handmade by someone who loved you?" Her voice caught, emotion rising before she could stop it. "I can't believe I have something so..." She trailed off, searching for the right words, but unable to capture the depth of the revelation.

"Romantic?" Cole's voice broke the silence, but his expression wasn't soft—it was focused. Sharp. She could see it in his eyes: the wheels were turning as he searched for clues.

Romance was the last thing on his mind.

"Read the second page," she urged. "It's even more mysterious." She'd been reading the letters as if they were fragments of a romance, not clues to the larger peace pact. Yet the more she read, the more the words seemed to hint at something beyond affection—vague, elusive, but carrying the shape of clues.

As you learned that stormy night, the care with which it was made extends beyond mere sentiment.

Cole exhaled slowly, rubbing a hand across his jaw. "That's interesting."

Danika reread the passage, her brow furrowing. "He seems to be saying it's more than just a romantic piece, but it's pretty vague. What happened on that stormy night?"

Cole read the letter again, his lips moving as he concentrated.

"Don't you think it's strange how he mentions a Monarch?" Cole glanced over at her.

"No." Danika shook her head as she picked up the brooch. "He's talking about the brooch."

"But wouldn't you call it a butterfly if you were describing it?"

"I don't know." Danika picked up the brooch and studied it thoughtfully. "It's orangish. So it's a monarch."

"But he also capitalized the word Monarch," Cole mused. "I wonder if that was intentional," Cole mused.

"Why? What do you mean?"

"Maybe he's not really talking about a butterfly. Maybe it's a symbol? A title?"

Danika nodded and closed her eyes. "Monarch... it makes me think of royalty. A king."

"Or it could be a codename for something entirely unrelated." Cole shook his head with exasperation. "Darn these riddles."

"If you think that's interesting, listen to this one," Danika said before reading a passage from the next letter.

The Monarch was chosen, not for its beauty alone, but for its quiet strength.

In love, as in history, it is steadiness that endures. When strength is veiled in beauty, its true purpose often goes unnoticed.

Silence settled between them, thick and weighty, as Cole took the letter and read it again to himself.

Danika leaned in, reading it with him. She could feel the truth hovering just out of reach, its shape becoming clearer, its edges sharpening. But it wasn't whole. Not yet.

Cole finally broke the silence. "Maybe I'm overthinking it, but it sounds like he's trying to convey something important here."

Danika shook her head. "No, you're not overthinking it. Now that I'm reading it again, I agree. But what does he mean by *true purpose*?"

"He could be referring to something specific that we haven't yet found." He looked up and stared into space. "Or frankly, he could just be writing in general terms. Beauty *can* veil just about anything." He glanced at Danika thoughtfully, his gaze lingering. "Sometimes it's the beautiful things that hide the most..." He stopped himself, jaw tightening, as he turned away. "Or maybe I'm reading too much into it."

"What does any of it mean?" Danika threw her hands up in frustration. "Is there a pact or isn't there?"

Cole straightened, rubbing his jaw again. His frustration was evident, but so was his determination. "I think the pact is still here somewhere," he said, as if speaking it aloud made it real.

"Really?"

He nodded. "Just a feeling."

Danika sighed in exasperation. "Maybe you're right. But that doesn't mean we're any closer to actually *finding* it. It feels like we're missing something."

"Something small, but important." Cole studied the letter he had in his hand. "But the only Monarch that comes to mind for me is the NGO that operates out of D.C.—and I doubt that has anything to do with a brooch made more than a century ago.

Silence filled the room for a second, and then Danika jumped up off the couch, snapping her fingers at the same time. "Oh my gosh!"

Thirty-Two

COLE JERKED HIS HEAD up to eye her questioningly. "What?"

Danika smacked her forehead with the palm of her hand. "I can't believe I forgot about this." She walked over to the small desk and picked up a piece of paper. "I laid it aside so it wouldn't get lost. I wanted to read it again."

Cole took the paper she handed him. "What is it?"

"It's a newspaper clipping." Danika sat down beside him and leaned in. "It was mixed up with the letters. I thought it was there by mistake, but it makes sense now."

A PACT FOR PEACE

In what attendees are calling a "monumental moment for mankind," a group of distinguished leaders convened this week at the Mohonk Summit for Global Understanding to lay the foundation for a new international fellowship rooted in peace, prosperity, and moral conviction.

Dubbed the Monarch Alliance by one of its members, the group

> *aims to promote nonviolent conflict resolution and foster global cooperation. Guided by Quaker values of harmony, peace, and integrity, they pledge to serve as a beacon of hope and a catalyst for lasting change.*

Cole stood abruptly and began pacing before he stopped at the window and stared out into the distance. "The Monarch Alliance," he murmured, almost to himself. "Then they *are* related."

"Does that mean something?" Danika asked.

He looked back at her. "You've never heard of the *Monarch Alliance*?"

She frowned. "The humanitarian organization? They sponsor peace tours, disaster relief—"

Cole turned to face her, his expression harder than she'd ever seen it. "That's the story they want people to believe. But they fund chaos. Monarch doesn't clean up messes. They create them... to keep entire countries dependent."

A chill swept through her. "Like GEM-Co."

"It's exactly like GEM-Co, but that's just one tentacle of Monarch's reach."

Cole turned, hands on his hips. "While we're on the subject, what's your actual connection to GEM-Co anyway?"

"Just doing research," Danika said carefully, watching his face. She'd learned the hard way not to overshare what she knew about that organization.

Still, his words shook her. She'd thought exposing GEM-Co's corruption would be like slaying a dragon. But it was apparently only a small part of the beast.

Cole accepted her vague response and began to pace. "So the Monarch Alliance started here—probably with good intentions—as a way to broker peace. They managed to get a pact signed by international powers." He stopped and turned. "So why was it buried?"

"The peace philosophy went off the rails at some point," Danika said, sinking back onto the couch. "The mission changed, I guess."

"That's putting it mildly." He pressed a hand to his thigh, as if calming an old injury. "They claim peace, but they profit from war. Fund both sides, no matter the consequences."

Danika waited for more, but it appeared Cole had stated all he intended to on the subject. The distant look in his eyes spoke of both anger and anguish—a silent testament to just how deep and personal his connection to the Monarch Alliance truly was.

She stood again, unable to relax. "So what do we do with this? Just pretend we don't know?

"We don't do anything." Cole looked at her, eyes flaring a warning. "Not yet. This isn't a scoop. It's a red flag exposing danger."

"Are you saying you want me to sit on this?" She stopped and turned. "If the Monarch Alliance started here—if this place is ground zero—I have to follow it."

"Why?" he asked, tilting his head. "Do you understand how serious—and deadly—this game is?"

Danika's jaw clenched. "If I back off now, then what was the point of everything I've done? Everything I've lost? Why did I bother coming here?"

The fire in her voice faltered, just a little, but enough for her to recognize the truth. It wasn't defiance driving her. It was desperation. For the first time, she realized her greatest fear wasn't danger or exposure—it was getting this close and failing.

Cole watched her carefully, his tone softer now. "I'm not telling you to walk away," he said calmly. "I'm saying maybe—just maybe—slow down."

"Slow down?" The words hit hard. He might as well have told her to jump off a cliff. She turned toward him, eyes sharp. "While people are probably out there right now destroying evidence and rewriting the truth?"

He nodded, calm as ever. "Believe me, I understand the urge to rush." He let the silence stretch for a beat. "But sometimes it makes more sense to listen to the guy you've already admitted is always right."

Her gaze snapped to his, fury flickering—only to catch the faintest trace of humor in those dark blue eyes.

"I never said always," she shot back, folding her arms as she stalked across the room. "Anyway, you can't hold that over my head for the rest of my life."

"Why not?" he said, shrugging with infuriating ease. "What's the point of always being right if you can't enjoy it?"

She rolled her eyes, but the edge had softened. The tone of his voice calmed her. Steady, not argumentative. Insistent, yet gentle.

"You might be used to working alone," he continued, "but this isn't a solo mission. I don't override you to be difficult. I do it to keep you safe."

She let out a long breath and sank into the couch, tension lifting from her shoulders. She hated to admit it, but he was right... again. Not *always*. But this time, undeniably.

Her gaze drifted to the stack of letters on the table, their edges yellowed and worn. She reached for the top one but didn't open it.

"I wonder how many people know the Monarch Alliance began here," she mused.

"It was formed more than a century ago," Cole said, sitting down beside her. "No one would want to be connected to what it is now. The question is, what happened?"

"And *when*," Danika added. She leaned back in exasperation. "You'd think with a new administration coming into D.C. every four or eight years, someone would put a stop to this," Danika mused. "Everyone knows about it, but no one does anything?"

"It's been going on for so long and it's so well organized that it isn't just one agency, one administration—or even one ideology anymore," Cole said. "That's not an excuse, but it's the reality."

Danika nodded. She'd been trying to unravel the maze of entities involved in GEM-Co, but each had its own public mission. Each provided just enough plausible deniability to remain under the radar.

Cole picked the newspaper clipping off the coffee table to read it again, causing a separate piece of paper to flutter to the floor.

"What's that?"

Cole picked up the paper, his fingers careful not to tear the fragile edges. He studied it briefly before handing it to her. "Looks like it was stuck to the back of that. I guess someone wanted to keep the letter and the newspaper clipping together."

Danika took the sheet, her heart quickening as she recognized Noah's familiar, slanted handwriting. Her great-grandmother's letters had always carried a weight of mystery, but this one felt different.

Cole leaned in close, shoulder-to-shoulder, so they could read it at the same time.

> *I never imagined I'd be seated among such men—diplomats and world leaders—discussing matters far beyond the reach of my hands. I felt like a rough plank beside polished mahogany. Yet when it came time to name the Alliance, they turned to me, as if my simple voice held some wisdom.*

Danika glanced up at Cole.

> *I cannot say with certainty where the name first arose—only that it came to me with the clarity of conviction: the Monarch*

butterfly, drifting through the gardens at Mohonk.

It seemed the perfect symbol for what this group must become. Like the Monarch, we are destined to navigate uncertainty with quiet strength. Majestic not because of power, but because of purpose...

Danika lowered the letter. "The Monarch Alliance," she whispered. "It was Noah. He *named them*!"

Thirty-Three

THE TWO OF THEM sat leaning over the coffee table, just staring at the pile of letters.

"I don't think we're reading too much into this now," Cole said. "I think the answers are here; we just need to figure out Noah's riddles."

"It's almost like he wants to make sure the truth is told, but doesn't want to tell too much." Danika drew her legs up under her and repositioned herself to get comfortable. "Sometimes I think every letter we find gives us more questions than answers. Even the newspaper clipping makes everything more mysterious."

"But it does tell us one thing." Cole leaned back with a confident expression on his face.

"What's that?"

"It shows why some people want to make sure the document stays hidden."

Danika still didn't connect the dots. "Meaning?"

"If there really is an international peace pact, it would prove that foreign powers were once united in their quest for peace." He stood and walked to the window, staring out with his hands in his pockets, before turning back. "The last thing they want is for Monarch's true origins to be revealed."

"Who's *they*?" Danika asked. "Do you know who's behind Monarch now?"

He shrugged. "Hard to say. There's high-level governmental involvement for sure, but it's hard to put a finger on."

"That would make sense from my experience," she mused. "Documents that disappear. Reports that are suddenly 'classified.'" She paused and stared into the empty fireplace. "It's almost like a shadow government pulling the strings."

Cole returned to the couch and sat. "They realized how easy it is a long time ago," he said. "Put the right people in the right places, and suddenly you've got lawmakers ignoring the Constitution, intelligence agencies silencing whistleblowers, and wealthy financiers pulling the strings on funding and media."

His words brought a wave of emotions to Danika as she stared at the pile of letters. She hadn't grasped the historic significance they carried before. But now, they felt like a key—a dangerous one that could unlock truths far darker than she'd anticipated.

"This may be getting too dangerous for you..."

The words hit hard, pulling Danika's gaze to Cole. She opened her mouth to respond—but froze. It was exactly what she'd just been thinking. Had he read her mind? Or was he simply one step ahead?

"The people hunting the pact... they don't see it as just paper," he said, voice low and steady. "It's a threat—a symbol of everything they've spent decades trying to bury."

He leaned forward and looked straight into her eyes to make sure she understood. "If it's found, it will crack the foundation of their power."

"Believe me, I understand the ramifications." Danika stood, circling the room with her hands on her hips, thinking about other journalists who had dared try to expose some of Washington's inner workings. She knew the stakes.

She stopped in front of Cole. "But it's hard for me to comprehend the lengths these people will go for money."

"It's about more than profit." Cole kicked his legs out and crossed his arms. "They engineer instability... create a never-ending military presence so they can fuel their political and corporate machine for generations."

"In other words, they break things just so they can profit from rebuilding." Danika turned around and faced him as more of the puzzle pieces began to fall into place. "It's not corruption, per se... It's a strategy."

"Exactly. The money isn't being wasted or stolen in the traditional sense," Cole said. "It's being funneled, redirected, shifted into private firms and political entities."

Danika rubbed her temple, frustration pressing against her skull like a vice. None of it made sense. Or maybe it made too much sense, which was somehow worse.

The upcoming summit was being hailed as a landmark event—a global peace initiative that would increase transparency and expand humanitarian outreach. On the surface, it appeared to be a noble endeavor. But with Julian at the helm, Danika knew it was nothing but a cleverly curated illusion.

"It's still mind-boggling that they just keep getting away with it year after year." She walked back toward the couch. "Why don't people see the truth?"

"For one thing, the Alliance isn't officially part of the government, so it operates outside of normal checks and balances." Cole loosened his tie a little more as he talked. "For another, they're masters at manipulating the media. They *leak* a story to the media—completely bogus or only partially true—and then use the story that journalist writes as proof that the entire fabrication was factual."

Danika sat down mechanically on the couch beside him as bits and pieces of her own career began appearing in front of her eyes, like a movie playing that she didn't want to see.

Her thoughts drifted to her exposé on illegal arms smuggling five years ago that had led to numerous awards. She'd actually been *proud* when her article had been used by congressional intelligence committees as "independent verification" that a problem existed.

Her writing had been used to justify funding requests and policy shifts.

She put her hands over her face in shame as she remembered a committee member shaking her hand, saying, "*Your story makes the story real.*"

She'd thought it was a compliment, but now she remembered the laughter the comment elicited from other members. He was admitting out loud that they had used her story to make the story *appear* real. No wonder it had resulted in so many smiles!

She began rocking back and forth, trying to stop the images and the memories.

But they didn't stop.

All of her hard work, notoriety, and accolades were built on lies.

She hadn't been breaking news. She'd been making it—for them.

"Are you okay?"

She felt Cole's hand on her shoulder, steady and grounding, but she had no words. All she could do was nod. He gave her a squeeze and then let his hand fall away.

"They are master manipulators," he said, as if he somehow knew what was causing her turmoil. "They've successfully swayed public policy and engineered influence all over the world."

She didn't answer. Her throat was tight, the knowledge of everything she hadn't seen pressing heavily on her heart.

"I've been there," Cole said, hands clasped, elbows resting on his knees. "Thought I was doing something that mattered. But I was just another piece on a big chessboard."

He looked over at her, his expression softer now. "We can't change the past, but we can decide what we do next."

Danika remained silent for a few long moments, mulling over his words before glancing up at him. "So that's your nice way of telling me to '*suck it up and stop feeling sorry for myself*,' right?"

A genuine smile tugged at one corner of his mouth—slow, unguarded—a quiet kind of approval that hinted at a shift both disarming and dangerous.

"No one's ever accused me of trying to be nice before, but... *yes*."

Danika dragged her eyes away and squeezed her temples hard, so she could focus on the task at hand. Cole was right... *again*. Now wasn't the time to dwell on mistakes. What good would that do?

Her mind drifted to GEM-Co and the Monarch Alliance—and the ripple effect a peace document would cause in the highest circles of Washington. This wasn't just about foreign powers. There were men right here who would do anything to keep certain truths buried.

Like Cole said, if a pact had been signed—and it was found—it would upend everything.

"Okay. Back to business," she said. "Is there anyone coming to the conference that you're sure is involved in all of this?" She looked up at Cole. "Besides Julian, of course. Do you know any names?"

"Only one name comes to mind, and I don't have any proof." Cole raked a hand through his hair. "But if I were a betting man, I'd say Senator Sebastian Wiley."

Danika didn't need a mirror to know that all the blood drained from her face at the mention of Wiley's name. "He's *here*?" Her voice cracked even though she'd only spoken two words.

Cole looked at her curiously. "Not yet, but he's attending. Are you okay?"

Danika bit her bottom lip as a way of suppressing the tumult raging inside her body. "Yes... I-I just..."

"You've been threatened by Wiley." Cole said it as a statement, not a question, his blue eyes gleaming with something like concern.

Danika dragged in a deep breath and tried to keep her hands from shaking. "He's got a lot of power," is all she said, while trying to decide if she should stay or leave. She was inclined to run into her bedroom and start packing her bags until she felt Cole's large hand on top of hers.

"He's not coming in until the afternoon before the conference starts and only staying two nights."

Danika swallowed hard and nodded as she tried to understand her visceral reaction to Wiley's visit. She was wary of him, yes. But this deep-seated fear—verging on terror—surprised even her.

"Okay." She didn't say anymore because she couldn't.

Cole removed his hand, but not before their eyes locked. For a fleeting moment, Danika felt something unspoken pass between them—a glint of understanding, of shared goals, even if neither of them fully grasped the weight of what lay ahead.

Then his phone vibrated. She heard it, but also felt the shift in him as he pulled it from his pocket. Whatever he read made him grow still, the only movement a slow blink, like his mind was racing to catch up.

"Bad news?" she asked, watching him closely.

He raised just his eyes from his phone, his jaw tightening noticeably, and didn't say anything. Then his gaze scanned the room as if looking for something.

"Did you ask for this particular room?" His tone didn't seem ominous, just curious.

"What?"

"Did you request a suite?"

Danika shook her head. "No, it was an upgrade. I was surprised because I had so much trouble getting a room to begin with... Why" She leaned closer and locked eyes with him. "What's wrong?"

"I just got a text," he said, "that Senator Wiley is coming in two days earlier than planned."

"*Just now*? Right when we were talking about him?" Danika began to look around, the room seeming to close in around her. Her skin began to crawl. "Do you think this room is bugged?"

"No," he said calmly, rising to his feet. "I think it's just a coincidence."

"That's a pretty big coincidence, if you ask me," Danika said, not even trying to disguise the fear in her voice.

"Not really." He crossed the room, slipping a small, matte-black device from his pocket—no larger than a deck of cards—and turning it on with a quiet click. "I set up my notifications to get a text any time there's a change to a VIP's schedule."

"And it just happened to come in while we're talking about him?" Danika shook her head and then watched him curiously. "What are you doing?"

"Proving to you that this room isn't bugged," he said. "So you can sleep at night."

The red LED light lit up, blinking once, to show it was on. He swept it across the room with practiced movements—subtle, controlled—pausing near the smoke detector and again by the desk lamp.

Danika held her breath. The device gave a faint pulse of static near the wall vent, then went quiet. Cole angled it again, slowly, methodically. Nothing.

After a few more passes, he switched it off. "See? All clean."

She let out a breath she didn't realize she'd been holding. "And if it hadn't been?"

"I'd have pulled you out of here whether you wanted to go or not."

There was no bravado in his voice—just quiet certainty, like someone who'd done it before. Someone who knew how the world really worked and knew what to do about it.

"You always prepared like that?" she asked, nodding toward the instrument in his hand. "Expecting the worst?"

He met her gaze. "Let's just say I stopped being surprised a long time ago."

The moment stretched, the air heavy between them. She wondered how many times he'd done this before—swept rooms, tracked threats, calculated exits. The calm in his expression suggested this was routine, easy for him.

Danika looked up at him. "But now what do we do?"

Thirty-Four

Cole didn't answer right away. He didn't need to. Danika already knew what they needed to do next. They needed to get back to work. Not just for clues, but for clarity. For something to hold onto in a world that was shifting under their feet.

She scooted down to sit on the floor, her legs folding beneath her, and began to sift through the letters. Somewhere in this stack of fading paper was the truth they needed. And she wasn't stopping until she found it.

They couldn't fix what had already happened—but maybe, just maybe, they could stop it from happening again.

Danika needed to stay focused—now more than ever. If these letters held clues, she needed to find them and atone for the mistakes she'd made in the past.

"This is so frustrating," she said, after a few minutes of reading. "There are hints of something here. I just can't quite put my finger on what it is."

Cole took one of the pages she handed him, his brow furrowing as he read. "His phrasing," he murmured, "it's careful. Always like he didn't want to say too much."

She nodded. "Yes. It's subtle, especially if you're just reading one letter. But when you put them all together, there's definitely a pattern." She reached over and began reading the next letter.

> *I spent the morning making repairs in the garden, the same place we spoke last spring beneath the lilac sky. I can still hear your laugh in the wind if I close my eyes long enough. I know I don't belong in your world, not truly. And yet, each word from you makes me forget all that.*
>
> *You once said that the heart doesn't care what a man earns or his status in society, and I've carried those words with me ever since.*

"I'm so glad we don't live in those days." Danika rubbed her temples. "Do you think the pact could be hidden in a summerhouse?"

"They've all been repaired and replaced over the years—some as many as five or six times," Cole said. He paused as he read a letter. "Except for this one." He handed the letter he'd been reading to Danika.

> *The circle of stone has kept our secrets well, but I fear our visits there may be too visible to wandering eyes. Perhaps it's time we found a place less exposed—and closer at hand. Do you agree?*

"He's talking about the stone summerhouse by the garden." Danika put her hand on her heart. "I wondered why there were so many letters... sometimes more than one a day during the summer months. They must have left letters for each other there instead of meeting in person."

"That summerhouse was built in the late 1800s, so it definitely would have been here," Cole said.

Danika looked down and read the letter again. "But it looks like they were getting ready to find a new hiding place." She threw her hands up in the air. "We're always one step behind."

"I remember another letter that talked about the two-story summer-house." Cole shuffled through the letters.

"That's an old one too, but like you said, the wooden ones aren't original structures." Danika leaned over the letters. "I think I read something about that one being completely rebuilt in 1999."

"Here's the one." Cole opened it with cautious care.

> *Every time I feel the hush of a warm summer evening, I think of the way the vines wrapped us in silence, like they knew how precious that hour was. Two stories above the world, and yet it felt like only you and I existed.*

"That's definitely referring to that summerhouse," Danika said. "I was just there today. Isn't that strange?" She leaned back against the couch and exhaled. "It almost feels like I'm being led around to places that were important to Abigail."

"There are so many hints, but nothing concrete." Cole rubbed his jaw. "Let's write this all down so we don't forget anything." He pulled a small notebook out of his pocket and drew a line down the center of the page. He wrote at the top of the two columns: "Noah" on one side and "Abigail" on the other.

What do we know about Noah?

"He was a Quaker," Danika said. "Very religious."

Cole nodded. “And a carpenter. A craftsman. A man who works with his hands.” He wrote down some notes and then looked up again. “How old was he?”

Danika stared at the ceiling as if it held the answer as she did calculations in her head. “I think he mentions that he’s seventeen in 1903.”

“So he’s twenty or twenty-one in 1906 when the conference is held.”

“Why would that matter?” Danika looked at Cole questioningly.

“Probably doesn’t, but I like to have the facts in front of me when I need them. If he were seventy-six, it would mean that he probably wouldn’t be able to scramble up a rocky path or hide something where it required climbing a ladder.”

Danika looked around. That doesn’t rule much out.”

“No, not yet. Let’s keep going.”

“What else do we know about him?”

“He was connected to my great-grandmother somehow.”

Cole nodded and drew an arrow to Abigail’s name.

“He was kind-hearted and generous,” Danika said. “That is clear from his letters.

“And he was very close to the Smileys.”

“Yes,” Danika said. “He was trusted and respected by the family.”

“Which gave him access to the office and other parts of the building that may have been off-limits to some.”

Cole continued to write down notes as Danika shuffled through the letters. The room remained quiet for a time, save for the rustle of paper and the occasional creak of the couch as they shifted positions.

Finally, Danika leaned back with a sigh, staring at the ceiling as frustration bubbled to the surface. “Maybe we’re chasing ghosts,” she muttered. “This pact could have been destroyed decades ago. If it ever even existed.”

Cole didn’t look up from the letter he was reading. His eyes scanned the page intently, his brow furrowed in concentration. “Maybe,” he said after a pause, "but if it does exist, these letters are the best chance we have of finding it. There's a reason that others are looking."

He set the letter aside and reached for another, moving with a deliberate precision that contrasted with Danika's more haphazard approach. She went back to reading the letter she held in her hand, which began to tremble as she read the poignant words.

> *You once asked me what I would build if I could build anything. I never answered you then. I think maybe I was afraid. But the truth is—I would have built a life. One with you in it.*
>
> *Not grand. Not gilded. Just honest.*

She swallowed hard, a frustrating heat burning behind her eyes. It wasn't just the class-bound heartache that affected her so deeply. It was the raw injustice of a story silenced—the very thing she was now fighting.

"Anything important?" Cole asked.

"No." She tried to keep her voice from shaking as she continued to read.

> *I cannot fault your father for wanting to protect you. I am not the future he imagines for his daughter. My hands are too rough, my name too plain, and the world I know doesn't come with inheritance or power.*
>
> *But love—true love—doesn't wait for permission... It can't.*

Danika put the letter down and stared into space.

"You sure there was nothing in that one?" Cole studied her reaction.

"Yes. Nothing about the pact." She bit her lower lip. "Just heartbreak."

Cole nodded and went back to his stack of letters.

After another hour, Danika stood up and stretched, rolling her head from side to side. It was late, and it was getting hard to keep her eyes open. "Are you officially off duty?" she asked out of the blue.

Cole glanced up, obviously surprised, and put down the pencil he'd been holding. "Excuse me?"

"Are you off duty? I have a cold beer if you want one."

He leaned back on the couch and cocked his head. "Sure."

When she returned from her kitchenette, she handed him a chilled bottle and gestured toward the balcony. "Come on. Let's get some fresh air."

Cole followed and eased himself into one of the rocking chairs. "I have to admit I didn't take you for a beer drinker," he said as he twisted off the cap.

"Wow." Danika looked over at him. "That sounds a bit judgmental. I'm almost afraid to ask what you think I drink."

He brought the bottle to his lips and took a swig. "To tell you the truth, it's not something I've given much thought to, but beer is not the first thing that would come to mind."

Danika smiled. "If we're being honest, I don't really consider myself a beer drinker either. I only like beer when it's ice-cold on a warm night."

Something flickered in Cole's expression when she glanced over at him—amusement, maybe. Something else, too. Something she couldn't quite name.

"Can't argue with that," he said.

The water stretched out before them, a dark mirror reflecting the lights on the summerhouses and even the pinpricks of light from the stars. Although it was only June, the air was thick with summer, the distant hum of insects filling the quiet spaces between them.

Cole kicked his feet out in front of him and took another sip from the bottle. "Ice-cold beer on a warm night. That is perfection." He looked over at her. "You might just get off my troublemaker list with this."

Danika laughed. "Really? I'm still on your troublemaker list? Is that a lifelong sentence without the offer of cold beer?"

"Might be." His tone turned business-like again, as if he didn't like the fact that they were feeling comfortable in each other's company.

"Well, I hope the bad guys don't hear this conversation and give you a beer. It's a quick way to get off your list."

"I don't think it will work for anyone else." He spoke the words while staring straight ahead, and Danika wasn't sure what he meant by them.

Silence stretched between them as they stared out over the water. Clouds swept across the moon now and again so that light and shadows appeared to be playing on the cliffs. Danika was lost in her own thoughts when Cole broke the quiet and ended the peaceful solitude they had shared for a few minutes.

"What are you really doing here?"

It was a question that, once again, took Danika by surprise. She let out a long breath, trying to decide how much to tell him. It didn't sound like he was just making small talk. It sounded like he really wanted to know.

"The *truth*," he said, emphasizing the point, his eyes still glued to the water in front of him.

"Come on." Danika shifted uncomfortably in her chair. "You probably have an entire file on me." She lifted the beer to her lips and tried not to gulp. "If not, just call the FBI."

Cole's head jerked over toward her. "What did you do to warrant having an FBI file?"

Danika stared into his wise, understanding eyes and suppressed the urge to actually confide in him. Instead, she stood and leaned out over the railing, stalling for time. "It's kind of a long story, to tell you the truth—"

Another couple came out on their balcony close by, prompting Danika to stop in mid-sentence and Cole to nod in understanding.

When Danika sat back down, they remained silent, but it was the easy kind, the kind that didn't demand filling.

Then, almost absently, Cole lifted his bottle. "A toast," he said.

Danika smiled with surprise and raised hers in response. "To what?"

Cole was quiet for a beat, his gaze drifting to the horizon where the lake met the inky sky. "To cold beers on warm nights."

They clinked their bottles together softly, the sound barely more than a whisper against the night.

"Hopefully, Albert Smiley won't hold this against me," Danika quipped, referring to the resort founder's strict rules about alcohol. "But I'll drink to that."

She felt the impact of Cole's gaze before he spoke again. "That's the first time I ever saw you smile," he said.

"Excuse me?" She cocked her head to the side.

"I mean... I guess you smiled before, but it never really reached your eyes."

Danika shook her head. So he saw her the same way she saw him—serious, guarded, always on edge from too much thinking and too little peace. They both lived like they were walking on fragile ice, one misstep away from everything shattering.

The moment she turned her attention back to the night sky, a flash of light caught her eye—a split second of brilliance slicing through the inky blackness like a mysterious secret from the universe.

Her breath caught, and without thinking, she grabbed Cole's arm—solid and unyielding beneath her fingers.

"Did you see that?"

From the look on his face, he had. His gaze remained skyward, eyes catching the last trace of light. Danika couldn't help but wonder—how often do two people get to share a moment so rare? And what did it mean?

Maybe it was a silent message, etched in stardust from her great-grandmother. Not a coincidence, but a sign. A memory reaching across time.

Or perhaps it was a promise of what was still to come.

Not the type to dwell on signs or chase after meaning, Cole downed the last of his beer and stood. "It's late," he said. "Thanks for the cold one."

But as he turned to head inside, his gaze lifted—just for a moment—back to the sky, making her wonder if he'd felt it too... this mystic secret meant only for them.

"Thanks for the help with the letters." Danika rose to her feet. "There's another whole stack I haven't taken out of my satchel yet."

That made Cole stop. "There is?"

Danika nodded. "We're a little over halfway now."

Cole nodded slowly, as if thinking—or hoping—there was still a chance of finding something of significance.

"I'm not sure how much time I'll have to read tomorrow," Danika added. "I'm going to spend some time in the archives and see if I can dig up any other mentions of a pact."

Cole turned around. "You are? What time?"

"Around ten? I'll probably be there a couple of hours, if you want to stop by."

"I might do that," he said, turning back to the door. "I'll try anyway."

It wasn't the words that he said so much as the way he said them that gave Danika pause. Not quite friendship, not quite casual camaraderie—something in between.

"Great. See you then." She pulled a business card out of her wallet as she walked toward the door. "Here, take this."

Cole glanced at the card and nodded before shoving it into his pocket. "Thanks again for the beer, Dani."

In a moment the door closed behind him, leaving Danika to wonder about the casual use of her real name on his lips.

And why it felt so intimate coming from him.

She was halfway to the bedroom when her phone vibrated with a one-word text that let her know Cole understood she'd given him her cell number and wanted his in return. It simply said: "Cole."

Thirty-Five

THE MORNING SUN APPEARED slow to rise—or was at least reluctant to shake off the haze of night. Mist curled along the lake's edge, softening the world in shades of pewter and ash. Everything felt suspended—like the day itself was holding its breath.

Danika stood on the balcony, barefoot, a mug of coffee warming her hands, waiting for the sun to peep over the cliffs beyond. It had become part of her morning ritual—this silent vigil above the sleeping world—waiting for the steady rhythm of footsteps to round the far side of the lake trail. Always his footsteps. Always that measured, confident cadence she now knew as his.

But this morning, the familiar sound never came.

Frowning, she glanced at her watch. Still early. Maybe he was just running late, especially since he'd been here until almost midnight. She leaned against the railing, eyes scanning the trail that curved like a ribbon through shadow and mist.

A soft murmur broke the stillness—a low whisper of voices carried on the breeze like a secret. She peered down and caught sight of movement along the edge of the lake by the dock... a dozen or so men half-shrouded by darkness, their figures barely distinguishable from the trees behind them.

As her focus tightened, she saw they were standing in a loose circle around a single figure—Cole.

Her heartbeat throbbed in her ears.

He wore cargo pants and a fitted olive shirt, clipboard under one arm, his voice too low for her to hear but commanding enough that every man around him leaned in to catch every word. Even from this distance, his presence was magnetic. Riveting.

Danika's gaze lingered on him. There was something about the way he stood—steady, assured, slightly apart—that gave her pause. He projected strength without needing to prove it. Displayed authority without really needing to say a word.

After a few minutes, Cole slid the clipboard into the large backpack slung across his back without bothering to unshoulder it. Just before turning away, his head tilted, and she could have sworn he looked straight up at her.

She stepped back, heart thudding. Could he see her cloaked by the shadows of the balcony? Did he know she watched each morning, coffee in hand, searching for something she couldn't quite name? The breath she didn't know she was holding caught painfully in her throat.

Below, Cole nodded to his men and turned toward Lake Shore Road. His first steps faltered, a subtle hitch in his stride; a slight limp. But then it smoothed out, absorbed by momentum—or by will. Had the pain loosened its grip as he moved? Or had he just pushed through it? She imagined him gritting his teeth and driving himself forward by sheer force of will—the way, she suspected, he had done with most of the battles life had thrown his way.

The others followed—dark shadows moving like a swarm of quiet bees.

She tightened her grip on the coffee cup and stood there long after they disappeared. Eventually, she sank into one of the rockers and watched the sun rise in full brilliance, wondering what new questions, and, hopefully, answers, the day might bring.

A part of her wanted to linger longer and let the morning drift by untouched, but she wanted to go back to the archives today. A string of unanswered emails pulled her back inside.

She dressed quickly in jeans and a white T-shirt, and twisted her hair up into a loose bun. She'd just placed a big hair clip to hold it in place when a knock echoed through the room. Sharp. Precise.

Checking her watch... seven on the dot, she put her eye to the peephole. Two men in dark polos waited patiently, tool bags in hand.

"Morning, ma'am," the taller one said when she opened the door. "We're here for the new security install."

Danika blinked. *Right.* She'd forgotten about the conversation concerning the door. She stepped aside.

They moved with efficient precision, unpacking parts and small devices that looked more suited to a lab than a cozy hotel room.

"May we borrow your key card?" one asked.

After handing over the key card, she sat on the edge of the couch, laptop open on her knees. She tried to concentrate, but her focus drifted. The soft clink of tools, the muted beeps of scanners, and the repeated sound of the door locking and unlocking filled the space like a metronome for her nerves. Every now and then, one of them muttered something technical—or an expletive—she didn't quite catch.

Danika tried to answer emails, but a memory kept flashing back—of returning to her room with the safe's door ajar. Someone had been there. The upgrade being installed wasn't just a precaution. It was necessary.

She glanced over her shoulder after about two hours and noticed one of the men touching up the paint with a small brush... a small detail to make sure the work wasn't noticeable.

"All set, ma'am," the taller of the two said, offering her a reassuring smile. "The paint will dry in a few minutes. Stryker will be by to explain how it works."

"Stryker?"

"Oh, sorry, ma'am. Cole," he said, returning the key card to her.

As if summoned by his own name, Cole appeared in the open doorway behind them, his presence filling the room without a word of announcement. His hair was still damp from an apparent shower after his run, and he now wore navy blue trousers and a matching tie with a white cotton shirt.

"Any issues?" he asked, running his hand along the door, carefully avoiding the paint.

"No, sir. Smooth install."

The men packed up and slipped out. Danika turned to the door.

"I don't see any difference."

Hopefully no one else will either," Cole replied, his gaze drifting to her hair before becoming all business. He held up a blank white card. "This disengages the magnetic lock. Your hotel key still operates the regular lock."

"Okay... but how does it work?"

Cole touched the paint to test that it was dry, and then motioned for her to follow him into the hallway, closing the door behind them.

Danika swiped her hotel card and heard the familiar click, but the door didn't open."

"Now swipe this card right here," Cole said.

Danika looked at the official-looking plaque to the left of her door that said *Room 670: Lake View Suite*. She couldn't remember if it had always been there or if it was new. In any case, it looked like it belonged.

After swiping the card, she heard another click, and this time the door opened.

"That's easy enough," she said as they stepped back inside.

Cole glanced around. "I still wouldn't leave anything important out. But the door's solid now."

Danika exhaled. "Thanks. For setting this up. For sending your guys."

"That's why we're here." He turned to go, but paused in the doorway, looking over his shoulder. "Any questions?"

She hesitated a moment as she thought about it. "Yes. One."

"Shoot."

"What if I forget this key card... or lose it?"

Cole stopped, his hand resting on the door frame, and took a deep breath before answering. "I have a backup."

He turned, facing her fully. "Are you okay with that?"

The way he asked—not casually, not authoritatively, but with noticeable concern and consideration—caught her off guard. This wasn't just protocol; it was trust, being asked and offered in equal measure.

His eyes held hers—clear, unflinching, steady—almost like he needed her permission for more than just a security measure.

She tightened her fingers around the card and gave a small nod. "Yes. I'm okay with that."

Something eased across his face, subtle enough that she doubted anyone else would have noticed. He stepped back, putting distance between them again, retreating to the safer ground of professionalism.

"Good," he said. "If you run into a problem with it, shoot me a text and I'll send someone over.

He ran his hand down the door frame one more time as if admiring his men's work, before speaking into the mic on his lapel. "Stryker 1-1. Copy that. On my way."

Danika opened her mouth to tell him she was heading to the archives—but he was already gone.

Thirty-Six

DANIKA SAT WITH HER head bent over yet another letter, scanning the contents for any mention of a pact. The archivist had been helpful over the past hour, bringing box after box of documents that didn't appear to have been disturbed for decades.

Around eleven, the door swung open and Cole stepped in, much to Nadine's delight.

"Cole!" she said, hurrying from around her desk to give him a warm hug. "You never stop by."

"Been a little busy," he replied, returning the squeeze.

"I know... the conference. Everyone's busy," she said, looking up at him over her glasses. "I can't wait until it's over."

"I'll be glad too," he said, noticing Danika for the first time and nodding in her direction.

"I guess you're here for the same thing as Miss Danika." Nadine noticed the exchange. "Anything to do with the peace conference of 1906, right?"

"That's right." Cole walked over and pulled out a chair. "Sorry, I'm late. Had a meeting and...." He glanced at his watch as he talked. "I have another in thirty."

"That's okay." Danika slid some letters toward him. "I'm just skimming these for any mention of the conference. Nothing promising yet."

"I wish I could help more," Nadine said as she clicked through a list of records on her screen. "Far as I know, the conference was announced, held… and then silence. No major revelations."

"Don't you find that strange?" Danika asked. "Three hundred delegates and almost no follow-up?"

Nadine blinked. "Now that you mention it, yes."

"I did find this with some background information." Danika pushed a piece of paper toward Cole and proceeded to summarize it for him. "The International Arbitration Conference of 1906."

"It was a pretty big deal," Nadine said. "Congressmen, clergymen, diplomats—all pressing for world order through arbitration and justice instead of warfare."

"So do the clippings mention anything specific?"

"Actually, yes," Danika said. "One of them says that three-fourths of the attendees were in favor of a new accord they were working on."

"But?" Cole looked from one to the other.

"But a small minority opposed it so strongly, they decided not to force it through," Nadine added.

"Even with that much support?"

"It was bold. Radical. Possibly dangerous," Nadine said. "Some of the delegates feared reprisal."

"Why?" Cole asked.

"It would have exposed corruption and undermined the growing arms industry," Danika said. "The delegates decided the world just wasn't ready."

Cole raked a hand through his hair. "So the vocal minority hijacked the narrative. Sounds familiar."

"I'm sure the vote to bury it was driven by real fear," Nadine added. "The pact wouldn't have been legally binding, but it still would have carried political weight."

Cole leaned forward. "So there had to be something in writing, right? You don't take a vote on a vague idea. They must've had a draft—something in black and white."

Danika and Nadine exchanged a glance. Neither had thought of that.

"True," Danika murmured.

Cole's eyes narrowed. "Then where is it?"

Nadine shrugged. "I'm sorry. Other than the fire, I can't think of anything else written about that conference."

"Excuse me?" Danika tilted her head toward Nadine as if she couldn't possibly have heard her correctly. "The fire?"

Cole turned his head toward Nadine, too, with the sharp, deliberate attention of a man who had just heard something he knew was important, but didn't know how.

Nadine blinked at their sudden shift in energy and let out a small laugh. "Oh! I assumed you knew about that."

Danika shook her head, pulse quickening. "What fire?"

Nadine gave a dismissive wave. "Nothing catastrophic. Just a small fire in Albert's office, the last day of the conference. It was contained quickly, but some documents were lost."

"Do you have anything on that?" Danika's voice stayed calm with effort.

"Of course." Nadine rose and rifled through a cabinet.

Just as she pulled a file, she chuckled. "Funny how everyone's suddenly interested in that fire."

Danika froze. "Excuse me?"

Nadine turned, setting a small stack of newspaper clippings on the table. "Oh, I just mean—no one's asked about it in decades, and now, all of a sudden, it's come up twice in the past month."

Cole met Danika's gaze, his jaw tightening.

Twice.

In the past month.

"Who else asked about it?" Cole asked, his voice calm but serious.

Nadine hesitated, her eyes flicking toward the door. "One man came in person—young, polished, dark hair. The other emailed. Both asked about the fire and documents."

Danika kept her voice steady. "Did they take anything?"

"I sent scans to the one who emailed. The other read through the file. He was insistent—asked for an exact inventory of what was lost."

Danika fought to keep her face neutral, but her pulse hammered in her ears as she reached for the top clipping. The paper crinkled beneath her fingers, brittle and yellowed with age.

The headline read: "*Small Fire in Mohonk House Office – Historical Papers Lost.*"

Cole's jaw set—controlled, deliberate, as he leaned over her shoulder and skimmed the main points: "last day of conference," "documents unrecoverable," "minor damage."

"The timing," Danika said, "during the last day of the conference..." She glanced at Cole. "A little too convenient, don't you think?"

He turned to Nadine. "Do you keep a log of archive visitors?"

Nadine shook her head. "I got his first name when he made the appointment. Bruce, I think it was."

Danika pressed. "Did anything strike you as odd?"

Nadine closed her eyes as if trying to picture the encounter. "He said he was researching resort history... asked about the fire's timing." She opened her eyes and shrugged. "He was really persistent, I remember that. Wanted to know what exactly was destroyed. He had a look in his eye I didn't like, to tell you the truth."

Cole stood, hands in his pockets. "May I take photos?"

"Of course." Nadine handed over the clippings. "Just be careful with them. They're fragile."

They both photographed the articles and thanked her.

Outside, Cole exhaled. "Well, we can look at the bright side."

Danika blinked. "There's a bright side?"

"Whoever's hunting the pact probably thinks it's gone. Destroyed by the fire."

"But you don't?"

"After reading Noah's letters, not really. He was just crafty enough to have done something like that as a diversion, or to have hidden the pact somewhere else before it happened."

Danika stopped walking, unable to concentrate on two things at once. "So let's say the pact was signed and put away for safekeeping in Albert's office. Noah suspected something might happen and moved it?"

"Possibly. The clipping said that a small number of the attendees were adamantly against it. And whoever set the fire did not want that document to see the light of day."

"Which means they believed the pact had enough punch to fear it," Danika said, her voice barely above a whisper. "They knew it could change everything."

"Someone wanted it erased, that's for sure. That fire wasn't random."

"This makes one thing perfectly clear." Cole stared down at her with a look of determination on his face. "We need to read those letters a little faster."

Danika nodded in agreement.

Because now, it wasn't just a mystery.

It was a race.

Thirty-Seven

DANIKA PLACED HER FEET carefully as she walked over the uneven surface of boulders near the resort's spa and paused long enough to look over the edge. Below, the sandy beach of the lake stretched in an unbroken ribbon against the blue water, undisturbed by beachgoers at this early hour. The morning light cast long rays of light across the rocks, tinting them with a rosy hue and softening the stark edges of the cliffs.

But it wasn't the beauty of the moment that caught her attention—it was the two figures partially hidden in the shade of the craggy outcrop.

Cole and Peggy.

Even from this distance, Danika could feel the tension radiating between them. Cole's hands moved with sharp, punctuated gestures, his broad shoulders taut with frustration. Peggy, in contrast, stood rigid, her arms locked tightly across her chest. Whatever he was saying, she wasn't having it. After a beat, she turned her back to him, her body language indicating a barricade.

Danika swallowed, feeling a flicker of guilt for intruding, even unintentionally. She wasn't close enough to hear their words, but she didn't need to. The emotions on display—anger, defiance, something deep and unresolved—spoke loudly enough.

Not wanting to eavesdrop any longer, she shifted her footing and continued her walk, heading toward the main path that would take her by The Granary. She stepped onto the wooden planks of a footbridge when hurried footsteps echoed up the stairway from the beach.

Danika kept walking, head down, when she nearly collided with Peggy. The anger in Peggy's eyes was unmistakable, but it wasn't anger alone. Pain lived there too, raw and unmistakable, about to overflow.

"Peggy," Danika greeted cautiously. "Hey."

Peggy inhaled deeply as if trying to compose herself, but the effort was in vain. Her lower lip quivered for just a second before she turned away, crossing her arms in the same stubborn gesture Danika had seen moments ago.

"You okay?" Danika asked.

"Yeah. Great." The words came out clipped, tight with emotion.

"Want to talk about it?"

Peggy let out a sharp breath and dropped onto the edge of a picnic table, eyes on the swaying canopy of leaves above them. "Not really." A beat passed, then a short, humorless laugh. "Turns out I have a big brother I didn't know I had."

Danika blinked. "Big brother?"

"A friend of mine. At least, I thought he was a friend." Peggy's voice was tight with frustration. "Now he thinks he gets to decide who I can see—like he's suddenly in charge of my life."

"Maybe he's just being a good friend—trying to protect you," Danika offered.

"Protect me?" Peggy huffed. "What kind of friend tells you to stay away from someone—like it's an order?" She shook her head, anger brimming. "And to think I waited all these years for him to figure out his feelings." Her eyes snapped to Danika. "Honestly—the sheer gall of that man!"

Danika fought to keep her face neutral, though something about Peggy's tone—and who she meant—sent a ripple of discomfort through her. She focused on the first part instead. "I guess it depends on who that *someone* is that he doesn't want you to see."

"That someone is Julian DuBois. Can you imagine? Telling me to stay away from one of the richest, most eligible men at the resort?"

A chill ran down Danika's spine. "Julian?" she repeated.

Peggy turned, her expression shifting from frustration to suspicion. "Yes. Why?"

Danika hesitated, choosing her words with care. "Because I think your friend might have your best interest at heart."

Peggy's expression hardened. "I'm not a child, Danika. I can take care of myself."

"Of course you can." Danika sat beside her, lowering her voice to something softer, steadier. "But maybe there's more to Julian DuBois than meets the eye. He's charming, yes. But he's also manipulative. Dangerous."

"You've got to be kidding." Peggy scoffed and stood abruptly. "You sound just like *him*."

Danika worked to keep her expression neutral. "Well, maybe we've both seen what Julian's capable of."

Peggy's eyes flashed with defiance. "Well, Julian asked me to accompany him to a dinner, and I'm going."

She stood and walked away, kicking imaginary stones out of her way as she walked.

Danika watched her go, unease tightening in her gut. Peggy was attractive and intelligent, but that probably wasn't why Julian was interested. She was one of the most genuine, honest women Danika had ever met—and far too trusting to see the danger he posed.

But if neither she nor Cole could talk her out of it, they'd just have to wait and see how it played out.

Danika glanced at her watch. She needed to move if she was going to reach her assigned spot along the trail in time. Her gaze drifted toward the beach—Cole would need to hustle, too.

Thirty-Eight

Danika paced a few steps, then sat down on a rock, straining her ears for the sound of footsteps. Just when she'd checked her phone for the fiftieth time to make sure they were still on schedule, she heard them.

She paused, waiting to make sure they'd made it to the designated point, and then started walking with a light step. She stared at the ground as if concentrating hard on the uneven path, until she rounded a bend and saw two figures appear in her peripheral vision.

"Well, look at this," she said, with a look of surprise on her face. Rudy stood in front with a clipboard tucked under one arm and a cheerful smile on his face. Behind him stood Cole with a pair of binoculars slung around his neck and an old, creased trail map open in his hands.

As usual, he didn't really stop. His eyes shifted from tree line to treetops, pausing occasionally to study something unseen.

"I didn't expect to see you two out for a hike."

Cole's jaw ticked, just slightly. "We're not *out for a hike*."

"We're just double-checking trail markers," Rudy chimed. "Updating the resort's maps for the security teams."

"Cool." Danika turned toward the left and studied an overgrown path with casual interest. "I never saw this trail before. Mind if I tag along?"

She didn't wait for a response, but noticed that Rudy shot an uncertain glance back at Cole, who offered nothing more than a brief exhalation and a disapproving glance.

"Trail's a mess," Danika said conversationally. "More like a deer path than a walking trail."

They followed her single-file for a time as the path narrowed beneath a canopy of gnarled branches. Danika, a few feet ahead, half-turned to ask something over her shoulder—and her boot slipped.

As she pitched forward, Cole reacted instantly—grabbing her arm with one hand while bracing them both against a large boulder with the other. His grip was steady, a silent touchstone that reminded her of their unspoken partnership.

"Whoa." A laugh burst from her, a beat too loud. She fought to make it sound like surprise, not a calculated performance, but the strength in his grasp caught her off guard. Not just the firmness of it, but the calm steadiness beneath. It wasn't just reflex. It was reassurance. An unexpected jolt that was far more intimate than she'd planned for.

Quickly recovering, she placed her hand against the rock for added balance, then followed Cole's gaze as he stared at the boulder.

It was massive, ancient-looking, and unmistakably split down the center, like it had been cracked by the blade of a giant's sword. Time and weather had smoothed the break, but the division was sharp enough to catch the eye.

Danika's eyes widened, and she took a half-step back from the rock, her hand flying to her mouth. "Wait a second." She reached into her back pocket and unfolded a small slip of paper, reading it aloud in a voice just above a whisper: *"That day of sunshine and a sky of blue beside the rock that was split in two."*

She looked up. "It's a rock split in two," she murmured, as if saying it aloud would confirm what she saw.

Rudy stepped forward, peering at it. "Is that from a letter? That's pretty neat."

"It really makes it all real, doesn't it?" Cole brushed his hand over the timeworn surface before giving her an almost imperceptible glance that said, "Don't overdo it."

Then he paused, fingers lingering on something just beneath a thin layer of moss. "I wonder if there are any other secrets hidden here."

"What do you mean?" Danika put her hand on the rock beside his.

"If Noah had something to hide, this would be the kind of place," he replied. "Secluded, but memorable. Somewhere only he and she would know."

He leaned in, squinting. "Doesn't this look like an arrow?"

Danika stepped closer and followed his gesture. A faint groove ran diagonally across the face of the stone—subtle, worn by time. It could have been anything: natural erosion, a trick of shadow, or something more deliberate.

"Could be," she said, her voice softer now, cautious.

Rudy moved beside them and used his fingertips to clear away more moss. "I see it too... kind of. Could be an arrow." He ran his finger along the groove, brow furrowed. His curiosity was genuine.

"It's probably just runoff," Cole said after a moment, stepping back and brushing his hands together with his characteristic cynicism. "Water finds its way through everything eventually."

"Maybe?" Danika echoed. But her eyes lingered on the groove.

Cole straightened and turned his back on the rock with an air of finality as if it were not worthy of a second glance. "Funny how our minds play tricks. See a shadow and call it a sign. Let's keep going."

Danika nodded, though none of them moved right away. The split boulder sat in quiet dignity, wrapped in moss and shadow, appearing to guard some long-buried truth.

"It's amazing to think they stood right here," she said. "All those years ago, looking at the same rocks, the same sky."

She glanced beyond the boulder, up the incline where the sun caught on a patch of wildflowers. Her eyes narrowed. "That's kind of strange," she murmured.

Cole and Rudy turned their heads simultaneously to follow her gaze.

"What is it?" Rudy asked.

"Those rocks up there." She tilted her head. "They look... arranged."

Just off the trail, about thirty feet ahead, two smaller stones leaned together to form a near-perfect triangle.

Cole laughed in a way that almost sounded natural. "I think you've been reading too many old letters."

"You're probably right," she admitted, shrugging her shoulders. "But it's kind of the perfect spot to hide something."

"We could spend all day chasing shadows if we're not careful." Cole started walking again. "Come on, let's go."

As the trail curved and the trees thickened, Danika glanced over her shoulder, a shiver of anticipation—or maybe fear—tracing a line down her spine. She caught one last glimpse of the boulder, gray and silent, bathed in the dappled light of the woods, and wondered, just for a moment, if what they'd uncovered had brought them closer to the truth—or, as intended, uncovered the ones trying to keep it buried.

Time would tell.

Thirty-Nine

By late afternoon, the pre-arranged walk in the woods still lingered in Danika's thoughts—sharp, unsettled, impossible to set aside. She hoped they'd succeeded in steering attention where it didn't belong, but doubt clawed at her.

Had it worked? And if it had, how would they even know? The uncertainty pressed closer with every passing hour, leaving her too restless to focus on the screen any longer. She pushed back from the desk and stood, her legs stiff, her thoughts tangled.

She needed to walk, she decided—just a quick stretch to shake off the tension and refocus her mind. With no particular destination in mind, she ended up in Lake Lounge. Pouring a cup of strong coffee, she stepped outside.

The sky hovered in that uncertain space between sun and storm—patches of blue fighting through a veil of silver clouds. The lake mirrored the mood, its surface shifting from still to stirred with every subtle gust.

Danika stood at the edge of the wrap-around porch, the scent of her coffee mingling with the faint dampness of a short afternoon shower. Somewhere across the lawn, birds chattered in short, energetic bursts, as if unsure whether to continue the day or take cover. The air felt heavy, like it was holding its breath. She stayed there a moment longer, absorbing the quiet, the calm before... something.

With her coffee nearly gone, she turned to go back inside—then froze. Just outside the lodge doors stood Cole and Peggy. Talking. Laughing.

Looks like they made up, she thought to herself as she approached from the other direction. They appeared comfortable and relaxed as they chatted.

Danika approached slowly, schooling her features into something neutral.

"Hey, guys," she said, lifting a hand.

Peggy turned with a bright smile. "Danika! Afternoon!"

Cole's reaction was slower. His brow furrowed as his gaze bounced between the two of them. "You two know each other?"

"Yeah, we've run into each other before," Peggy said. "Do you know, Cole?" Peggy asked. "This is Dan—."

"We've met," Cole interrupted, looking none too pleased, as if two separate worlds were colliding and he had no control over it.

Peggy blinked at him before she gave Danika a big smile. "Okay, then. Small world, right?"

"*Tiny*," Cole muttered.

Peggy didn't notice the edge in his voice—or chose to ignore it. "We were just talking about going riding tomorrow," she said, turning to Danika. "Didn't you mention you liked to ride?"

Danika nodded before she caught Cole's subtle warning look—a flash of steel in his eyes that screamed "*don't you dare ask her*."

Peggy—either not noticing or choosing to ignore it—barreled on.

"Six a.m.," she said cheerfully. "Can you go? I'll ask Laurie to find you a mount."

"I'd love to," Danika said. "If it's okay with you, Cole." She decided to be nice and give him the opportunity to offer a legitimate security reason for her not to go—something concrete. Not just that it was her.

Cole sighed. "To tell you the truth, it's not a leisurely trail ride."

"Oh, the more the merrier," Peggy said with a wave of her hand. "I'm just going so he isn't out in the mountains alone while he's doing his thing. It will be nice to have some company."

"I'll stay out of your way," Danika offered. Her tone was even, but her eyes challenged his. "Promise."

Cole looked as though he were balancing two live grenades in his hands, before giving her a hard stare. "You sure you've ridden before?"

"Stop being so combative," Peggy said, shaking her head. "How many times do I have to remind you—I'm older and wiser? Just be nice and play along for a change."

Danika wasn't sure whether to laugh or back away. It sounded like another sparring match was about to break out between the two old friends.

Cole straightened, arms crossing over his chest in that unmistakable stance of someone bracing for impact. "Not sure 'older' translates to 'wiser' here," he said, his blue eyes drilling into Peggy's big brown ones. "Because when it comes down to you talking me into something, it's usually right before things go sideways."

"Ha. Very funny." Peggy gave an exaggerated shake of her head. "You know that's not true."

Danika couldn't resist stealing a glance at Cole. From the look in his eyes, it probably was.

"I grew up around horses," Danika said to reassure him and defuse the situation. "Worked my way through college in stables."

"Fine," he said at last in a tone that indicated quiet defeat more so than reluctant approval. "Don't be late. I leave the barn at six."

"Great. I'll see you in the morning."

***

Danika hurried down to the barn, knowing Cole meant business when he said he was leaving promptly at six.

She found two horses in the aisle already saddled, with Cole pacing up and down with his phone in his ear. He put the phone on his thigh for a minute and pointed. "The big gray is yours."

He brought the phone back up and said. "Okay, got it. I gotta go."

"Where's Peggy?" Danika stood in front of a gray gelding that was lifting its head up and down as if ready to get moving.

"Not coming," he said as he moved over to a large bay horse that was built like a tank.

"Why not?"

"She said she's not feeling well."

"Oh, that's too bad." Danika couldn't tell from the tone of his voice if he believed Peggy's excuse or not, but it was definitely tinged with something—frustration, maybe.

"Yeah," Cole muttered, tightening the cinch strap on his horse with practiced ease, though the sharp snap of the leather betrayed his irritation.

One of the barn workers unhooked Danika's horse from the ties and handed her the reins. "This is Titan. He'll need to be checked up a bit tight at first, but he'll settle down once you're away from the barn. Don't let him get away with anything."

She saw Cole glance over at her as if expecting her to ask questions, but she just nodded. "Sounds good."

"There's a saddle bag here for your stuff." Danika nodded and put the water and snacks she'd brought, along with her phone, into the bag and then walked Titan over to the mounting block and climbed on.

As soon as she hit the saddle, Titan started following Cole, who was already mounted and heading out of the barnyard.

She let the horse trot to catch up before pulling him down to a walk. "Thanks for waiting," she said.

Cole just looked at his watch. "Sorry. I have a strict timeline. I told you this wasn't a pleasure ride."

Danika had about a million questions, but knowing what little she did about Cole, decided it was best not to ask them. Instead, she asked him about his horse.

"He looks like he has some draft horse in him," she said in a casual tone. Cole sat tall and deep in the saddle on the massive horse as it pranced and sidestepped along the path.

"Yeah, a draft and thoroughbred cross. He was used for foxhunting before he came here, so he's not ready for guests yet." Cole talked while staring straight ahead. "He'll settle down."

Danika nodded and concentrated on her own horse for a few minutes as he pulled and tested her skill before relaxing down to a walk.

After their initial brief conversation, they rode in silence to Eagle Cliff, where the rising sun hung like a huge suspended ball over the mountains. Cole stopped his horse and grabbed something out of his saddlebag before dismounting and handing the reins to Danika. "I'll just be a minute."

He appeared to limp a few steps before getting back to his regular gait as he walked over to the edge of the trail. Then he pulled his phone from his pocket, sent a text, and appeared to be waiting for an answer as he stared into the distance.

Within seconds, Danika heard his phone give a quiet ding. He glanced at it, looked at the ground, and then moved five steps to his right before waving his hand in the air. His phone dinged again, and after reading the message. He pulled a small notebook out of his back pocket and began taking down notes, looking around as if noting landmarks and measuring steps from one to another.

Danika strained her eyes to see a figure on the faraway mountainside, but saw nothing.

Satisfied with the location, he pulled a small red flag from his back pocket and planted it discreetly. Then he walked over, took the reins from her, and swung back into the saddle. The motion was fluid, but Danika caught the quick grimace—and the way his hand pressed against his thigh, easing some unseen ache.

"On to the next one," is all he said.

"On to the next *what*?"

"Signal point." He glanced over at her. "Part of the hoping-for-the-best and preparing-for-the-worst plan."

"What do you need to signal?"

"Hopefully, nothing." He pulled back on the reins to slow down. "I just want to be ready for the worst-case scenario... which would mean losing all communication with the outside world."

Danika's eyes opened wide, both at the thought of such a thing occurring and the wisdom of having a backup plan in case it did. This would be a last resort if the hotel complex were compromised. An old-fashioned way to alert authorities for help.

She looked over at him with a new sense of respect. "So you're setting up your lines of sight?"

"Exactly. I studied drone footage to set up the preliminary watch points. Today, we're making sure we have clear sight lines. And tomorrow other agencies will arrive to go through some scenarios and drills to make sure we're all on the same page."

Danika realized how daunting a task it would be to protect everyone at the peace conference. And how lucky they were to have someone as organized and dedicated as Cole to do it. She looked over at him. "When do you sleep?"

He frowned. "When this thing is over." She didn't think he was going to say anything more, but then he added. "Julian is making it harder than it needs to be."

"Julian? How?"

"He nixed this part of the security plan. Said it was overkill. That's why I'm doing it so early. So he doesn't know."

"What about Rudy. Does he know you're out here?"

Cole shook his head. "No. I told him I might be a little late today, but didn't give a reason why."

He slowed his horse and turned in the saddle, resting one hand on the rump of his horse so he could look at her. His expression remained unreadable, but his tone had shifted—measured, serious. "Since it's question time, I've got one for you, too."

The air shifted—subtle but sharp. This wasn't idle conversation. And he definitely wasn't about to ask her if she was having a good time.

Danika braced herself. Something about the way he looked at her, steady and unblinking, made her feel exposed, like she was standing beneath a spotlight.

"Are you focused on finding the pact?" he asked. "Or are you still just chasing a story?"

She blinked, caught off guard. "What do you mean?"

"I mean, if it comes down to one or the other—truth or a headline—I need to know which one you'll pick."

"I'm not going to leak information to someone if that's what you're asking. I—"

He cut in, his voice more gentle. "No, that's not what I'm asking. The people we're dealing with... they don't bluff. I just want to make sure you understand, someone could get hurt."

He didn't say it as a threat. He said it like someone who'd already seen the cost and was trying to protect her.

"Do you have new intelligence I don't know about?" Danika asked, wondering why this was coming up all of a sudden. She'd thought they'd put it behind them.

He shook his head as his horse started moving again. "No. It's just been on my mind. I don't want you taking chances—especially not for a headline."

They rounded a corner of the carriage road and could see the side of the hill where they'd mapped out the trail the day before. Both of them drew their horses to a stop simultaneously, ending the conversation.

"Wow. That didn't take long."

A crew of four men wearing orange vests and appearing to carry clippers and weed trimmers moved slowly up the path.

Danika stared silently, her mind trying to accept what she was seeing. The trail they were clearing wasn't one designated on any map. In fact, it hadn't been a trail at all until she'd discovered the unusual split rock a few days ago and mentioned to Cole how cool it was.

"Julian said something about clearing some trails for more accessible views," Cole said, as if not surprised by the scene. His tone was neutral, but his jaw had that familiar set to it.

"That path isn't good for viewing anything but rocks," Danika said, with a touch of disdain in her voice.

"Especially rocks split in two." Cole urged his horse forward and then turned in his saddle. "Let's go take a look."

As Cole and Danika approached, the entire crew, one by one, stopped working. Every head turned to watch them, tools held loosely, movement suspended. The silence was instant and complete—and unnerving.

Danika felt the hairs rise on the back of her neck.

Cole pulled his horse to a stop beside one of the men. "Mind if I ask what you're doing?"

The foreman smiled thinly, his eyes unreadable. "Mr. DuBois is interested in the, um, historical features of this area. He asked us to make it more accessible."

His tone was polite, but the words landed with an edge that made Danika uneasy.

Cole sighed and pulled out his badge. "I'm head of security, and didn't receive any advanced notice about a crew being up here."

The man didn't flinch. "You'll have to talk to Mr. DuBois about that. He's the one who sent us."

With one hand on the reins and the other casually on his thigh, Cole nodded toward the second rock formation where one of the men was standing, hedge trimmers in hand.

"You're cleaning everything out, clear up there?" he questioned, as if making casual conversation.

"That's the plan," the foreman said. "Now, if you don't mind, we need to get back to work."

As Cole spoke, Danika scanned the workers' faces. One of them looked familiar. It took a moment before she placed him because he usually wore a suit, not an orange vest.

A member of Julian's personal security team, now posing as part of a landscaping crew.

He caught her staring and quickly looked away.

Knowing they weren't going to get any more information, Cole and Danika turned their horses in unison and rode for a while in silence.

"Nice touch pointing out that second rock formation yesterday," Cole said.

"Spur of the moment decision," Danika replied. "When you pointed out that arrow, I decided it needed a follow-up."

She held out her fist, and he leaned back and tapped it with his.

"I love it when a plan comes together," she said. "Leak confirmed."

The steady clop of hooves filled the pause until Cole finally spoke. "Yep. And it just made everything a lot more complicated."

Forty

Twilight bled into the lake like spilled ink as the porch fell silent. A few guests lingered, mere shadows in suits and shawls. Danika hadn't planned to stop, but the quiet drew her in. She sank into a rocking chair and exhaled.

Here, she could think. No letters. No secrets. No suspicious glances or hidden agendas. Just the lake. The sky. The hush of evening settling in.

Her thoughts ran wild. Rudy's easy smile and unbridled enthusiasm—all a lie. The weight of it settled over her, dull and heavy. She folded her arms and rocked, the chair's creak the only sound as she tried to grasp the scope of what they'd uncovered.

How far did Julian's reach go? Was Rudy just the start? For all she knew, every soft voice on the porch belonged to someone who'd already chosen a side. Maybe the whole resort was wired. Every face a mask.

The chair beside her creaked.

She turned at the exact moment he did. *Dalton Rivers.*

His expression mirrored hers: surprise. They both offered a faint, almost sheepish smile.

"Didn't see you there," she said.

"I was here first." He tilted his head. "I think you're stalking me."

She raised an eyebrow. "You don't strike me as someone who gets snuck up on."

"You'd be surprised. Some people will go to great lengths to sneak around."

Danika smiled even though the way he said it made her think he intended a double meaning.

"The sunset is on the other side of the resort," Dalton said, interrupting her thoughts. "In case you're confused."

"It's too crowded out there tonight." Danika inhaled and let the crisp evening air seep through her. "This side is more peaceful."

Dalton seemed to take the statement as a hint and didn't talk. The lack of conversation that followed wasn't awkward, just quiet, like the lull between waves. But in that stillness, the air changed, as though waiting for someone to break the silence.

Dalton finally did. "I have to admit I was surprised… and impressed," he said, with a slight smile on his face. "With the tomahawk, I mean. I think you're dangerous."

Danika shrugged. "You're the famous action hero, not me." The words spilled out unintentionally, but she didn't regret them. The clock was ticking. She couldn't wait forever to make a move.

Dalton looked over at her, his eyes unreadable. "So you do know who I am." It wasn't a question—more a confirmation of something he'd been pondering.

"I never said I didn't."

He considered that before replying. "But you never brought it up before."

"Neither did you." Danika looked at him sideways and smiled. "I figured you are probably here to get away from autograph seekers, so I didn't want to pry."

He nodded. "Good guess."

Based on his usual aloofness, Danika figured that would probably be the end of the conversation, but he spoke again. "Which film is your favorite?"

Danika remained quiet, weighing her options as her heart pounded in her ears. "Sorry," she said at last, giving him a sheepish smile. "I haven't actually seen any."

That seemed to dishearten—or confuse—him more than offend. "Not even one? And here I thought you were a fan."

She offered him a warm glance, trying to steer the moment away from tension. "Just because I know who you are doesn't mean I've binge-watched your entire career." She hoped he didn't notice the redness she could feel rising in her cheeks. In truth, her teenage bedroom wall once displayed three of his movie posters, and she could quote half the lines from his early military action roles. But that wasn't something you said to a man like him—especially not when you were trying to keep him at arm's length and project neutrality.

"You know who I am, but haven't seen any of my movies." He didn't say it as a question, but as a statement to be analyzed. He remained silent for a few moments before speaking again. "Unfortunately, that would back up what Julian told me about you."

The mention of Julian's name was like a draft of cold air seeping through a crack in the door. Danika suppressed a shiver, tried to keep her tone light. "Julian? I didn't know he knew me well enough to talk about me behind my back."

"Julian knows everybody." Dalton's tone was no longer light or even particularly friendly.

"I'm not sure I want to ask what he told you." Danika forced a laugh.

"Just that you're a journalist." Dalton stared straight ahead. His posture was still relaxed, leaning against the back of the chair, but there was something in the way his hand gripped the top of the armrest—tightly, as if he were grounding himself, trying to hold back whatever was simmering just beneath the surface.

"Oh? And you're still talking to me?"

That cracked something in him, just slightly. He looked over with a crooked smile. "Only because you asked the right questions."

Danika blinked in surprise. "I didn't ask you any questions."

Dalton nodded but didn't look at her this time. "Exactly."

Sitting back in her chair and rocking a few times, Danika tried to keep the conversation going. "What happens when someone asks the wrong questions?"

The only sound that followed was the slow, rhythmic creak of their chairs, each rock charging the air with the kind of tension that made her uneasy.

"I answer something else."

She swallowed hard and decided to take another chance. "Honestly, I've been trying to figure out how to tell you myself. I didn't want... whatever this is... to end." She hesitated. "In fact, I was starting to kind of like you."

Dalton stilled. Her words clearly caught him off guard. His brows lifted, and for a beat, he just looked at her, searching and uncertain. Then a cautious smile tugged at the corner of his mouth. "Well," he said quietly, "that's... unexpected." There was something warm in his eyes now—something she hadn't seen before.

Danika felt the air shift and quickly reached for a lighter subject.

"Is there one you recommend? I'm not much of a movie person, but I could give it a try."

He paused, clearly weighing whether or not to re-engage. "If you're curious, try Iron Valor. It's an old war film I did. A bit tragic, but one of the few I'm proud of."

She smiled. "I like those kinds of movies."

"It's long," he admitted. "And frankly, a little depressing."

"I'll keep that in mind next time I have three hours and a glass of wine."

He looked over at her, something softer in his expression now. "Make it a bottle and you'll be good to go."

Their chairs creaked in a slow, calming rhythm. She let her eyes drift closed, just for a second, as her thoughts roamed. "Is that the movie that had a last-minute script change? I remember there being controversy over the politics in that one... new world order, global agenda."

Dalton turned his head. "That was Iron Verdict, not Iron Valor," he said, his tone as sharp as his gaze. "Different movie. Entirely different message."

"Oh," she said quickly. "Sorry. Easy to mix up."

"Not if you've seen them." He stopped rocking. "For someone who doesn't know anything about movies—or me—you seem to know a lot more than the average person."

She winced. "Oh well, I think that came up when I was looking for something else," she said, being completely honest. "It's funny how that happens sometimes."

A few seconds of silence followed, and then the chair beside her creaked as he stood.

"Yes, it's funny how that happens, isn't it?" The tone was sharp and carried no humor.

Danika looked over, regretting that she'd been so interested in keeping the conversation going that she'd overstepped her bounds. Dalton stood beside his chair, looking down at her, the moment of ease between them slipping away like mist in the morning sun.

"Let me give you a little advice, free of charge."

Danika braced herself, unsure if she should apologize or stay silent.

"Finding the wrong thing at the right time?" He stared straight into her eyes. "That's not luck. It's strategy."

She blinked. "What's that supposed to mean?"

Just then, she heard an exclamation from a woman behind her.

"Oh my goodness," she whispered. "Is that...?"

Danika turned her head as the woman took a hesitant step toward Dalton.

"Excuse me," she said. "I don't mean to bother you, but are you who I think you are?"

Dalton looked up. A pause. A soft smile that didn't quite reach his eyes. "I used to be," he said.

The woman laughed in a way that revealed her nervousness. "I told my husband—I *knew* it. We loved *Shadow Protocol.* We still quote it."

"Thank you," Dalton answered in a polite but preoccupied way. "That's one of my favorites, too."

The woman beamed. "Would you mind if—"

"Of course not," he said, already reaching for her phone and taking the selfie before she could ask. His movements were fluid, gracious. "It's nice to meet people who have seen my films."

Danika knew the comment was directed at her, not them.

A few moments later, the couple moved on, still buzzing. Dalton turned back with one last glance at Danika and then walked away.

And with that, he left her there, the empty chair beside her still swaying, like the echo of a conversation that had pushed just one question too far.

Forty-One

Danika stood on the lake porch, gaze drawn to the cliffs beyond, where Sky Top Tower pierced the hazy blue. The water shimmered in the afternoon light—calm and reflective—but the air felt charged now, laced with a silent undercurrent of anticipation.

It wasn't just the atmosphere that had shifted. Beneath the familiar sounds of laughter, clinking glasses, and soft footfalls was something quieter—more alert. The porch, once a retreat for readers and napping guests, now buzzed with restrained energy, as if everyone was waiting for something to begin.

The security presence wasn't obvious. And it wasn't overbearing. It was just... present. Intentional. Measured.

She noticed it first in the lanyards. Guests who once roamed freely now wore color-coded badges. A simple security protocol on the surface, but Danika had been a journalist long enough to recognize when things weren't as simple as they seemed.

A man passed by—broad-shouldered, clean-cut, dressed like a guest but moving like a soldier. His head turned, eyes scanning. Not looking for someone, but watching everyone.

Another man lingered by the stone column near the door, phone in hand, sunglasses fixed. He hadn't shifted in ten minutes, except for his head, which was always moving. Unnoticeable to most, but to her, clearly placed.

Danika's gaze swept the porch. The crowd had changed—faces sharper, movements more deliberate. The carefree couples with lemonade and frisbees were gone. In their place: delegates in tailored suits, entourages with practiced smiles, aides whispering into earpieces.

The resort hadn't advertised the peace conference, but everyone who needed to know did. And for the first time since arriving, Danika felt the weight of it. She was no longer here just to chase a corruption lead or trace her great-grandmother's story. She was here to uncover whatever force was moving beneath it all.

Danika shifted against the railing, noticing all of the changes. Something deep, barely tangible, had shifted. The mountain's rhythm felt off. Tension simmered beneath the surface.

Her heart gave a single, sharp kick at the thought of what lay ahead—and the uncertainty rising with it. Just then, her phone buzzed in her pocket, making her jump. Pulling it out, she glanced at the short text: *What's your location?*

A smile tugged at her lips. Short. Direct. She didn't need to see the name to know it was from Cole.

She started walking, pausing beneath the stone archway to type her reply. Unusual for him to text. Had he found something on his end? She'd read a few more letters but found nothing more than vague memories and sentimental phrases. Nothing useful.

Her pulse quickened as she moved again after receiving his quick response. He was apparently moving toward her. Coming from the far side of the lake.

She spotted him when he was still some distance away—a casual tee, jeans, and a ball cap pulled low over his brow. Danika did a double-take. She'd never seen Cole in a cap or jeans before, and something about the look made him seem younger, more approachable... more disarming.

The casual look jarred her until she remembered it was Sunday. Cole's duties were probably lighter today, though she knew he was never really off the clock.

Danika squinted, trying to see past the steel in his demeanor, to understand what drew people to him. It couldn't just be the blue eyes or rugged looks—though those didn't hurt. No, there was something deeper. The way he moved: steady, deliberate, unshakable. A quiet strength that didn't need to be announced. Confidence that spoke louder than words ever could.

Still some distance away, Cole slowed near a woman clearly struggling to manage three small children on her own. Her flowing, embroidered garments and headscarf suggested she was part of the international delegation—likely the wife of a visiting dignitary. One of the children, a little boy with flushed cheeks and wet lashes, cried loudly about a stone in his shoe, his voice carrying across the lake... and far beyond.

Others passed with polite smiles or sympathetic glances, but Cole veered off the path and crouched beside the boy. After a brief word with the mother, he dropped to one knee, offering his leg as a seat. With quiet ease, he helped the child settle, untied the shoe, and shook out the pebble. Then, with surprising patience, he slipped the shoe back on and opened his arms for a hug the child eagerly wanted to give him. The sister demanded one too, and he scooped her up before giving the youngest—a mere toddler—an exaggerated high-five.

A moment later, he set the girl down, nodded politely to the mother, and continued walking—as though it were all just part of his daily rhythm.

Danika tilted her head, unsettled in a way she couldn't quite explain. She was used to seeing him detached and guarded—the kind of man who held his cards close and kept his thoughts closer. But this... this quiet tenderness was unexpected.

It didn't lessen his strength, though. It deepened it.

Continuing to the bridge, Danika watched Cole do the same from the opposite side. He still hadn't seen her, but he suddenly stopped and tilted his head toward Parlor Porch, where musicians were warming up. The song they played was one of those timeless tunes that doesn't need to be loud to command attention. The chorus swelled just then, slow and familiar, threading the air between them.

Danika slowed too, watching him. He wasn't scanning the horizon, wasn't calculating the intentions of people nearby like he usually did. He was just... still, his gaze focused on something distant. Whatever he was hearing, it had pulled him somewhere far away.

She followed his gaze to see if there was something worthy of his focus—a suspicious conversation, some hidden threat. But all she saw were the gentle rhythms of a warm afternoon. People with maps in their hands looking for a trail. A small group gathered around the fire pit, the low hum of conversation rising and falling like waves.

Nothing out of the ordinary.

Except him. Standing there, as if the moment meant something.

The music drifted toward its final chords as Danika drew closer. "Are you okay?"

Cole didn't blink. Didn't move. His jaw clenched, and for a moment, Danika thought he might not answer. But then, his voice came, rough and distant, like he was trying to push something back.

"Yeah. Haven't heard this song for a long time, that's all."

He started walking again, and Danika fell into step beside him, matching his pace.

"Me either," she said. "I remember it from back in my early reporting days." She let out a soft laugh—partly as a way to lighten the moment, and partly to chip away at the wall he kept so carefully intact. "There was a time they played it non-stop. Had to be like ten years ago."

Cole's gaze didn't waver from the path ahead. "It was eight."

His words hit sharp, precise. Like the date was etched into him.

It wasn't a memory. It was a scar.

"Long days and late nights, running on nothing but caffeine," Danika said. "That's what it reminds me of." She walked a few steps. "How about you?"

His hand seemed to reflexively drop to his thigh, and a muscle ticked in his jaw before he answered.

"Funny how songs take you back," he said without answering her question.

His tone implied there was nothing funny about it.

For the briefest moment, something flickered in his eyes—heavy, unfinished—but it vanished as quickly as it came, leaving behind a gaze as still and unreadable as deep water.

If she'd thought he was going to reveal a crack in his armor, she was wrong. It was already sealed shut.

Danika didn't push. She knew the difference between wanting answers and respecting silence. Some truths needed time, not questions.

"What did you want to tell me?" she asked, gently shifting the weight of the moment. "Did you find something new?"

Forty-Two

"OH, YEAH," HE SAID as they headed back toward the Mountain House. "You have time to walk up to Eagle Cliff?"

"Right now?" Danika questioned, wondering why he hadn't texted her earlier and just told her to meet him there.

"Sure. It works for me." He placed his hand on the small of her back and guided her up the porch and through a throng of guests gathered in clusters around the rocking chairs. "You good cutting over Pine Bluff? Probably won't be as busy."

As they wove through the crowded porch, Danika noticed how many of the guests cleared the path as they moved. Dignitaries and luminaries alike acknowledged Cole with a polite nod or subtle smile, giving him both respect and distance.

"Everyone seems to know you," she said.

"They know of me," he replied without looking at her, his tone unreadable.

Danika wasn't sure if he meant his current role or something buried in his past. Whatever it was, his presence carried weight, creating an invisible current that made people take notice.

As they passed a cluster of distinguished men near the far wall, one paused mid-sentence and gave Cole a not-so-subtle nod—quiet, deliberate, unmistakably respectful. The brief interaction hinted at unfinished business.

"Who was that?" she asked once they were clear.

The man stood out to her, not for his suit or polished smile, but for the way others seemed to be paying attention to his words. Not quite admiration. Something more measured. Respect edged with caution, maybe.

Cole glanced back at her as if to see whether or not she was kidding. "Miles Hutton."

"Who's Miles Hutton?"

Cole, who had walked a few steps ahead, stopped and turned. "You serious?"

She shrugged. "Should I know him?"

"He's one of the most powerful men in Hollywood," he said. "Media, too. Movie studios, networks, streaming—he's got fingers in all of it."

"Oh-h-h. That makes sense now."

"What makes sense?"

"I saw him talking to Dalton Rivers earlier."

"Now there's a name I haven't heard in a while," Cole mused. "I haven't seen him for years."

"You mean, on screen? Or in person?"

"In person. He's been coming here for decades."

"Like, clear back when you worked here?"

That caused Cole to stop so abruptly, she almost ran into the back of him. "How did you know I worked here?"

Danika swallowed hard, realizing she'd just divulged too much. "Peggy mentioned it."

"Figures." He gazed down at her, blue eyes turning stormy. "What else did she tell you?"

"Nothing."

"*Sure.*" He turned and started walking again.

"No, she didn't. Really. And she didn't mention you by name. She was talking about someone she worked with, and I put two and two together; that's all.

"Oh, so you *assumed* she was talking about me," he said, looking back at her, one brow lifted. He let that settle a moment, then shook his head and mumbled something about journalists that she couldn't quite hear.

"Okay, you got me there." Danika accepted the criticism because she didn't want to get Peggy in trouble. She trotted a few steps to catch up. "So Dalton was a regular here?"

Cole nodded. "Back before he was famous." He appeared to think about it moment. "Or right about the time he was becoming famous, I'm not sure which. He'd spend weeks, sometimes the whole summer, if he wasn't shooting a movie."

Danika made a note of that. *Was it just a coincidence that he chose this place for his vacations? Or did it have something to do with Julian*?

"So what's the Miles guy doing here?" She quickened her pace to catch up. "Does he have something to do with the peace conference?"

"Of course," Cole said. "He's got connections everywhere... not just Hollywood."

"How?"

"Well, he's the son of a federal judge to start with. And then..." he looked down at her as if to gauge her reaction, "his father-in-law is Senator Wiley."

Danika stopped walking. "You've got to be kidding." She looked back toward the porch where she'd seen the man. "Talk about influence marrying money."

Cole nodded. "On the surface, it looks like a dangerous combination."

"Just on the surface?" Danika said. "He sure went out of his way to acknowledge you."

Cole stopped again, hands on his hips. "What's *that* supposed to mean?"

"Geez. You don't have to get all defensive." Danika held up her hands. "Just making an observation."

He nodded and started walking again. "Not that you need to know, but his people contacted my people, so to speak. He wants to talk to me."

"About what?"

"How would I know? I haven't met with him yet."

"Well, what do you think it's about?"

"Do you mean what do I *assume* it's about?" His tone sharpened as he looked down at her. "That's your job, not mine. I'll find out when I talk to him."

"Ouch," Danika said, absorbing the hit without flinching.

They walked in silence for a few minutes while Danika made a mental note to avoid the tall, sandy-haired man in the dark tailored suit. As their pace quickened and her respiration increased, she snapped back to the present.

"Why Eagle Cliff?" She asked as they started the incline and left the crowds behind. "Why can't you tell me what's going on? Did you find something?"

"Why do you ask so many questions?"

Danika groaned. "Why do you have to be so frustrating?"

Cole didn't bother to answer or even turn around. But he pulled something out of his back pocket and handed it to her. "Almost forgot. This is for you."

"What is this?"

She saw him shake his head and imagined him rolling his eyes, though she wasn't at a vantage point to see. If he answered, she didn't hear it.

Danika looked down at the laminated card with a lanyard: her credentials. Her gaze fell on the bright green bar and the words ALL ACCESS written across the top.

"Wow. Thanks." She clipped the pass onto her belt and felt heat rise in her cheeks as she caught back up with him. He was giving her free rein, despite the high stakes. "I appreciate this, Cole."

That made him glance over at her. "Don't make me regret, okay?"

"How would I do that?" She meant it as a joke, but Cole didn't smile.

He stopped and turned to face her. "I'll tell you how," he said, clicking off the ways on his fingers as he talked. "Ignore basic safety protocols. Wander into places you don't belong. Be impulsive. Rash. Reckless..."

Danika lifted an eyebrow. "You forgot stubborn and hard-headed."

She watched his eyes lift heavenward for just a heartbeat before he spoke. "I didn't think I had to state the obvious."

"Very funny," she said at his quick comeback.

He gave a curt nod and started walking again, picking up his pace so she had to struggle to keep up, let alone talk.

She wondered if that was the point.

They wound up the carriage road until the trees parted and the view opened wide. Forested hills stretched to the horizon like a green ocean, mountain peaks rising beyond. It was breathtaking, yet Danika barely noticed, her mind tangled in new questions.

When Cole began to slow, she glanced up at his profile, hoping to read something in his expression. He stared straight ahead, calm and steady, as if untouched by the world's chaos. Her grandmother would have called him "dashing." The thought made her smile.

"What's so funny?" Cole asked, his voice suddenly close enough to startle her.

"Oh, nothing." Danika looked away, focusing on the distance, trying to shake off the unexpected sense of connection that flickered through her.

"Let's stop here." Cole turned, gazing out over the landscape.

"I thought we were going to Eagle Cliff?"

"This is close enough." Cole reached into his shirt pocket and pulled out something, which he thrust in her direction.

"What's this?" Danika stared at the old black and white photo. Its edges were curled, and the paper had yellowed.

"It's a photograph."

Danika rolled her eyes. "I can see that."

"Just look," Cole said, his voice quieter now.

As Danika studied the photo, her pulse quickened instinctively, before reason had a chance to catch up. The image was faded, but unmistakable: a poised woman in early 20th-century riding attire, holding the reins of a horse. Beside her stood a man, similarly dressed, with another horse.

Danika drew the photo closer, heart thudding. It was like looking into a mirror—not just of her face, but of something older, deeper. A reflection of her own history staring back.

"Abigail Prescott?" She looked up at Cole and then back down at her great-grandmother's eyes staring at her from across a century, radiant with youthful happiness.

"You definitely have her eyes," he said. "And her hair."

Danika looked again at the photo—at those large, doe-like brown eyes that mirrored her own, and the wisps of blond hair escaping from the thick braid down her great-grandmother's back. The resemblance was subtle, but undeniable—like an echo carried through time.

"Where did you get it? I've been looking..."

"I told Nadine to keep her eyes open for anything related to these two names. It was misfiled with clippings from the 1970s."

Danika's knees buckled, and she sank onto the bench behind her, hands trembling as they clutched the fragile photograph. Her gaze shifted to the young man beside Abigail. His rolled-up sleeves revealed strong, veined forearms; his vest was neatly buttoned. But it was his expression that held her, marked with quiet strength and passion.

She focused on his eyes: sharp, steady, startling in their intensity. Even in black and white, they cut through the image with a clarity that felt alive. She imagined them blue—stormy, unblinking, memorable.

Danika could see why her great-grandmother had been drawn to him. There was something in that gaze—firm, unwavering, but laced with a gentleness that made you want to look twice.

"This is Noah?" she asked, her voice barely audible.

He was a stalwart figure, his forearms powerfully built, a reflection of his work as a carpenter, no doubt. He seemed to have an aura of quiet authority about him.

"Turn it over," Cole said, sitting beside her.

Danika flipped the photograph over, her fingers brushing over the faint pencil marks on the back. The names were scrawled in delicate script: Miss Abigail Prescott and Noah Morrison, riding the trails. 1907.

A hot pressure built behind her eyes, causing the edges of the photograph to soften into a blur.

Cole spoke softly, as though not to break the moment. "Look at the background."

Blinking back tears, Danika refocused on the image. For the first time, she noticed the setting: a rocky outcrop overlooking a vast expanse of hills and valleys. Her breath caught as recognition dawned. She stood and turned around, staring out over the exact same landscape. She picked out rocks in the distance and looked back at the photograph to compare.

"They were here," she murmured, glancing around. "They stood right *here*."

It wasn't just the beauty of the view that struck her. Something else stirred. A flicker of life lingering just at the edge of her awareness, like a shadow she couldn't quite see.

Cole nodded, his gaze distant, as if he could see the echoes of the past as well. "Funny how time works, isn't it? More than a hundred years later, and here we are, in the same place."

Danika traced the faces in the photograph. Abigail looked so alive. Eyes bright, lips curled in the soft shadow of a smile. What had she been thinking in that moment?

Just below the names, something faint caught her eye, nearly lost to time. She tilted the photo, squinting until the words slowly came into focus:

Not all things lost are truly gone.

She ran her fingers over the inscription, wishing that touch alone could draw out its meaning. "Did you see this?" she asked, holding it out to Cole as they sat down on the bench.

Cole studied the inscription, his expression thoughtful. "No," he admitted. "I wonder if it was referring to their relationship. Or something else?"

"Was she telling him goodbye, do you think? But letting him know she still cared for him?"

"Or maybe it has a double-meaning," Cole said. "One that she knew he would understand."

Danika nodded, staring at the photograph again. "It seems so strange that I never knew about him," she said, her voice cracking. "My grandmother never mentioned him. Not once."

"Maybe she didn't know about him either," Cole said gently. "Maybe it was a part of her mother's story that was never told."

The wind picked up, rustling the trees around them. Danika closed her eyes, imagining Abigail and Noah standing on this very spot, their laughter carried away on a breeze like this one. She wondered if they'd felt the significance of the moment, if they'd known how fleeting it was.

It served as a reminder to her how easily things slip away. Days. Chances. People.

For a long moment, they sat in silence, the photograph resting between them like a bridge to the past.

"I feel like she's trying to tell me something." Danika blinked back the moisture returning to her eyes. "Me being here. The pact. It's like it's all connected somehow." She brought the photograph to her heart before looking up at Cole. "Can I have it?"

He nodded. "Nadine scanned it and printed a hard copy for the files and archived the digital one for anyone who's looking in the future."

"Wow." Danika hadn't really thought it was something she could keep.

"Remind me to dig up a frame for you to protect it until you get home," Cole said.

Danika blinked, eyes fixed on the photograph. "I can't thank you enough for this."

Cole stood and rubbed the back of his neck like he wasn't sure what to do with his hands. "It wasn't me," he muttered. "Nadine found it. I was just the messenger."

He didn't meet her eyes. His stance was guarded, as if emotions like these were a terrain he didn't know how to cross—and didn't entirely trust. It was clear he wanted to retreat, to put distance between himself and whatever might happen next.

Danika stood and, before she could second-guess herself, stepped forward and wrapped her arms around him in a quick, awkward hug.

His body tensed, just for a breath, before reluctantly accepting her gesture. Not fully. Not enthusiastically. But enough to say he understood.

She pulled back quickly, brushing her hair behind her ear, suddenly unsure. Sorry," she mumbled. "I just... You know... Thanks."

He lifted the ball cap off his head for half a second, then put it back on. "You ready to head back?"

Danika nodded and started back down the path.

He didn't offer comfort in the usual way. No soothing words. No hand-holding. No attempt to fix what couldn't be fixed. But there was something in his quiet presence, in the way he walked beside her without trying to fill the silence, that steadied her more than anything else could have.

It wasn't polished or perfect. It was real.

And somehow, that was exactly what she needed.

Forty-Three

DANIKA SAT CURLED ON the sofa in old sweatpants and an oversized sweatshirt, her damp hair still wrapped in a towel. She'd only meant to check her email—but dusk had settled in, and now the soft glow of her laptop was the room's only light, interrupted occasionally by flashes of distant lightning.

She hadn't meant to go digging.

But after seeing Cole's reaction to that song, she knew something had happened. Something big. Armed with a timeframe, her investigative drive snapped into gear.

It didn't take long to uncover a vague headline, a fleeting reference to a failed extraction, and a heroic attempt to save lives. No photos. Just a name in a poorly scanned document:

Captain Coleman J. McCain—Awarded Silver Star for actions during Operation Echelon.

She kept clicking through archived reports and newspaper clippings, looking for more. The classified files she couldn't access all pointed to something bigger than a mission-gone-wrong or unfortunate "cloud of war" event.

She keyed in a fresh search using "Operation Echelon" as a term, and the screen exploded with headlines.

"Senator Calls for Emergency Defense Spending Following Tragic Ambush."

The article painted the operation as a sobering example of under-preparedness, quoting Senator Wiley directly: "These brave men were let down by red tape and outdated protocols. We must act now to prevent another tragedy."

A cold, hollow feeling opened inside her, the words on the screen blurring as a sharp, painful pulse began to beat behind her eyes. She pivoted again, changing her input to dig deeper into archived government documents. She wasn't sure what she was looking for—until she found it.

Just three words, but they were so shocking, she squeezed her temples as if to stop a headache before it began.

The Monarch Alliance.

It was buried in a redacted memo tied to a congressional briefing, under a file called "support contacts."

From there, everything unraveled. Julian DuBois, operating under Senator Wiley's clearance, had been embedded as a so-called peace liaison. But Danika knew Monarch hadn't stepped in to manage the chaos; they'd set it in motion.

The final after-action report confirmed what she was beginning to fear:

...Dual-stream intelligence was leaked to opposition forces by non-governmental diplomatic channels.

Not giving up, she continued to search, following every lead she could, no matter how insignificant it seemed. Somehow she arrived on a page marked "*Classified.*"

Most of the page was blacked out, or the documents listed had no link... except for one. It had no title. Just a string of numbers and a classification stamp: *Internal Use Only***.**

Her finger hovered over the trackpad, a tremor running through her hand as every internal alarm screamed: Caution. Danger. Don't.

She swallowed hard as fear battled with a growing sense of curiosity. She wasn't sure she wanted to know what it held. But she also knew she couldn't walk away.

A plant? A trap? Or an important document that she needed to see?

She held her breath. And clicked.

It read:

> *Internal Memo: Be advised that the Congressional Inquiry into the communication breakdown in Operation Echelon has been officially terminated per Senator Sebastian Wiley, Chair of the Subcommittee on Foreign Intelligence Accountability, citing "insufficient evidence to warrant further proceedings."*

A jolt, familiar and sharp, shot through her. It wasn't just adrenaline; it was the anger of someone staring at a terrible, shocking truth. Two men had died. Cole had nearly lost his life—and one senator had the power to erase it all.

The report brought to mind a sentence from one of Senator Wiley's speeches. "*Tragedy is the most effective fuel for policy change.*"

He'd framed it as funding for a natural disaster, but now she knew better. Cole's unit had been sent in under orders that anticipated casualties. Their sacrifice had never been about saving lives—it had been about profit. About power.

Wiley had secured an increase in emergency defense spending as a direct result of the ambush.

Danika drew a shaky breath, knowing that a complicit media had amplified the lie and buried the truth beneath headlines and spin.

She pressed the heel of her hand to her forehead, her breath shallow, her pulse loud in her ears. Then a sudden chime snapped her back—an alert blinking in the corner of her screen. She almost ignored it—until she read the header:

Access Limit: Secure Press Portal Credential Expiry

She clicked.

> *Notice: This secure database is only accessible to individuals holding current U.S. Government press credentials. Your temporary access, granted by [REDACTED], will expire at 1900 hours (7:00 PM ET),*
>
> *Please ensure all necessary downloads or screenshots are completed before expiration. Access cannot be reinstated without reauthorization.*

Danika glanced at the time in the bottom-right corner of her screen: 6:55 p.m.

"*Crap.*"

Her fingers flew across the keyboard, one hand grabbing her phone to snap photos while the other frantically clicked to download links. Most files returned the same unyielding message: *Not for Download*.

Others spun endlessly, the progress bars crawling like molasses.

She checked the first few photos on her phone—;blurry. She was shaking too much. Rushing too much. She took a deep breath and tried again. Deep breath. Steady. Focus. *Go slow to go fast*.

The cursor blinked. The screen dimmed for a second: 6:59 p.m.

A new warning flashed in red across the top of the screen.

Final Notice: Session Terminating. All unsaved progress will be lost.

She lunged to copy one last file, but the download stalled at 42%.

The screen flickered—and went dark.

A new message flashed.

ACCESS DENIED: This portal is restricted to verified users with active government press credentials.

Danika stared at the blank screen, the only light now coming from her phone. Her breath caught in her throat.

Had she gotten enough?

Or had the truth just vanished in the span of a heartbeat?

She sat back, still trembling from both adrenaline and fear, when a knock on the door made her jump.

Danika gathered herself up and turned the handle.

"I warned you about opening the door like that." Cole's gaze flicked over her attire, starting with the towel on her head and ending with her sweatpants and bare feet. Then his eyes went to the room beyond. "Why are you sitting in the dark?" He stepped inside. "Are you okay?"

Danika just nodded at first, unsure if she could talk. She cleared her throat. "I just found something."

She hadn't planned to tell him—not until she'd figured out *how*. But now, it didn't feel like a choice.

"About the pact?" His brows lifted, hopeful, wary. "What is it?"

"Not exactly." Danika walked over to her computer. "Have a seat." She nodded toward the couch as he dropped a folder onto the coffee table.

"Can I turn on the lights first?" He didn't wait for an answer, but walked over to the wall and hit the switch, causing Danika to blink at the sudden brightness.

"Okay," he said, sitting down. "What'd you find?"

"It's about Julian." Danika hesitated. "Are you sure you want to read it?"

He indicated by a motion of his head that he did, so she pulled up one of the files she was able to download and put the laptop on the coffee table in front of him. "Start with my phone," she said, tapping through to the photos. "I'm going to try to tame my hair. I'll be right back."

At the bedroom door she paused, watching Cole's face. The shift in him was obvious the moment he started reading. One blink. Then his eyes narrowed, jaw tightening as he took in the words. Whatever he'd expected—this wasn't it.

She stepped into the bedroom, pulled a brush through her hair, then gave up and tied it back with a bandana. When she returned, Cole was locked on the laptop screen, expression carved in stone.

"How did you find this?" he asked, without looking up, his dark eyes reflecting the tortured dullness of disbelief.

"Lots of digging. They didn't make it easy."

He placed the computer on the coffee table and put his elbows on his knees as he squeezed his temples.

"We all knew there was more to it," he murmured. "We weren't just unlucky. We were bait. But I never imagined—" His jaw tightened. "*Julian.*"

Danika didn't know what to say, so she just sat down beside him.

"Julian ran both sides," he said, staring vacantly at the fireplace as he talked, seemingly needing to say the words out loud to make it make sense. "He acted in a peacekeeping capacity with a high-level security clearance to gain access, then funneled intel to the opposition."

"So it would be sure to end in tragedy," Danika finished for him. "So the press would eat it up. So Senator Wiley could push for more funding. More contracts. More power."

"He didn't just betray us," Cole said in a tone that implied both disbelief and disdain. "He *used* us."

For a long moment, neither of them spoke. The room was quiet except for the rain now spitting faintly against the windows.

Danika had no words of comfort. No inspiration to impart. She was sitting beside a man who'd lost men. Who'd been wounded. And worst of all… betrayed.

She caught the hard set of Cole's jaw, his gaze locked on the far wall. His eyes were fearless—ruthlessly focused—processing data she had no access to. She saw no flicker of doubt, no room for second-guessing. Just an unshakable resolve that made him dangerous to anyone who stood in his way.

And yet, beneath all that steel, she sensed something else. A weight he carried alone, and maybe didn't know how to put down.

It almost made her pity Julian DuBois.

Because no matter how much money and power Julian wielded, he was facing something he couldn't buy, manipulate, or bend to his will.

Coleman J. McCain.

Forty-Four

"LOOKS LIKE YOU FOUND something too." Danika nodded toward the folder on the coffee table.

Cole slid it toward her. "Yeah. I got my hands on the agenda."

Danika opened it, already sensing the weight it carried:

"World Summit on Peace and Reconciliation– Finalized Agenda and Policy Recommendations."

Her eyes scanned the polished introduction and then moved down to the bullet points. She wrinkled her brow. "Could their language be any more vague?"

"Keep reading," Cole said. "Part of the agreement they're going to sign is on page five."

She flipped through and stiffened, her fingers tightening around the paper.

"If I'm reading this right," she said, "this consolidates control of the funding network into the hands of private contractors and shell NGOs." Danika leaned her head over the paperwork, engrossed in understanding the meaning of the words written in governmental language.

"That's what I got out of it, too," Cole said.

Danika tapped her finger on a paragraph. "Right here, it explicitly says these organizations will control, not only where aid goes, but which companies get the logistics and rebuilding contracts."

Cole's phone buzzed. He glanced at the screen, then frowned.

"Anything wrong?"

"Probably not. My guys just flagged some unknowns with diplomatic badges. They'll keep me updated."

He stuck his phone back in his pocket and pointed to a paragraph labeled Strategic Preparedness and Stabilization Response. "Read this part. Slowly."

Danika read it aloud.

"Proceed with readiness coordination for prioritized response to infrastructure disturbances, ensuring seamless transition to centralized allocation systems."

She looked up. "It seems like a contingency plan. Standard boilerplate—"

"No," he cut in, tapping the section. "It doesn't say if something happens. Look at the phrasing—'proceed with.' Not discuss. Not propose. It's already in motion."

Danika nodded. It wasn't a recommendation; it was a directive—quiet, discreet, but unmistakable. She scanned the paragraph again. "I see your point. It's like they're preauthorizing a response for a disaster that hasn't happened yet."

Cole nodded slowly. "But one they know will. Keep reading."

Danika brought the document closer. "*Proper positioning is essential to ensure swift transition into stabilization and control mode upon trigger of a civil disturbance.*"

She looked up at Cole. "It doesn't sound like they're just preparing for chaos."

"They're helping orchestrate it." He nodded. "Exactly what they did to my guys. Create a crisis so they can profit from the response. No matter the cost."

Another line caught Danka's attention, and she read it out loud. *"Funding will be distributed via compartmentalized operational accounts to ensure adaptive responsiveness."* She looked at Cole. "That means..."

"There's no way anyone will know where the money is coming from or going."

Danika absently twirled a strand of hair as she stared at the document. She noticed the footnote for the first time: "*In accordance with Monarch Advisory Panel recommendations*."

Her hand dropped to her lap as she stared into space as the significance of the words wrapped around her.

Cole tapped her on the knee to get her attention. "What are you thinking?"

Danika leaned back on the couch and exhaled slowly. "I'm thinking about what Senator Wiley can do with a signed document like this," she said in a low, serious voice. "It will be official. Endorsed by leaders from a dozen countries. It's the blueprint for what's next."

"And we both know what that means," Cole said. "Massive policy shifts that will change the world."

Danika stood and began to pace. "But this is a complete contradiction." She pointed to the letters on the coffee table. "Noah writes about his deeply rooted moral convictions to build a foundation of peace. They're weaponizing it for control."

"Which is why the original pact matters now more than ever," Cole said. "If we can prove what it really said—if we can show what they're *replacing*—we might still stop this."

"If we don't, it will be truth versus theater."

"War versus peace," Cole said as he looked over at her.

"And we're running out of time."

Cole leaned forward, rubbing his temples. "What if there are clues somewhere else? Not just in the letters?"

"Like where?"

"I don't know, newspaper clippings maybe?" Cole said. "It seems like someone is finding clues that we're not. There must be other sources out there that we haven't thought about."

"You're probably right, but we're not even done with the letters yet." Danika shook her head. "How will we have time to scan years of clippings?" Then she clicked her fingers in the air. "Oh, wait."

She picked up her phone and began scrolling. "Nadine did give me a couple of clippings she thought might be helpful. I took photos because I didn't have time to read them."

She held the phone so Cole could see. "Like this one from 1935. I just skipped over it."

She started to bring the phone back toward her, but he pulled it back. "Wait a minute." His eyes scanned the article. "It's an editorial in the Hudson Sentinel called "*On the Edges of Peace*."

"What does that have to do with the Monarch Alliance?"

Cole took the phone and kept reading. "It seems to be praising the early peace initiatives. The author lauds the Monarch Alliance's diplomacy, their vision of a world guided by stability rather than conflict."

"But..." His eyes kept moving. "*Whoa*."

"What?"

Cole leaned toward her shoulder to shoulder and tilted the phone so they could both read the words at the same time.

> *But not all who preach peace do so with clean hands. Whispers are suggesting that diplomacy alone no longer satisfies the*

stewards of the Monarch Alliance. Influence, not consensus, has become the true currency of peace.

She looked up at Cole. "You're right. This is something."

They looked back at the phone simultaneously and continued to read:

Among those shaping this shadow network are names long respected in international circles, most notably, the DuBois family, whose wealth was built not on crops or commerce, but on cannons and cartridges.

"Julian's family didn't just support Monarch." Danika said the words slowly, digesting them. "They helped build it?"

"With arms money?" Cole tilted his head. "Generations deep?"

Whether this moment marks the dawn of a more unified world—or the quiet rise of a private empire—remains to be seen.

Danika looked up slowly. "Did you know the DuBois family got their money through arms dealing in the early twentieth century?"

"No," Cole said, his voice just as incredulous as hers.

Danika brought her phone back up and did a quick search of "*DuBois arms dealers*."

All that came up were stories about gunsmiths in Du Bois, Pa.

"So Julian—or someone—scrubbed the web so that no articles appear in searches about where his family's wealth originated."

Cole rubbed his chin. "Not that hard to do when you're shelling money out to the tech giants."

"The hypocrisy is staggering," Danika said. "Julian offering to work for peace is like a fox offering to guard the henhouse."

"Corruption is like a cancer." Cole leaned back on the couch, arms crossed. "For some of the early believers, shaping policy wasn't enough. They thought they were entitled to shape the course of the world."

"This gives us a clue of when the transformation began, and who began it," Danika said, the disbelief evident in her voice. "The family of Julian DuBois."

She stood and began to pace. "The people gathering for this conference, whether they know it or not, are tangled in something that has nothing to do with peace."

"Reshaping the world under the guise of global stewardship doesn't result in harmony," Cole said. "This editorial shows that the shift—moving from unity to control—started in the 30s."

"Strategic dominance through manipulation," Danika said, sinking onto the couch. "Not war and peace, but engineered chaos. Eroding sovereignty one crisis at a time." She looked back down at the page, her voice barely above a whisper. "The original Monarch pact was a promise to protect peace—not profit from its collapse."

Cole stood and moved to the window, scanning the dark horizon beyond the trees. "If we don't find it, if we can't prove what they're trying to erase, they'll rewrite everything."

"And not just the future." He turned back to her. "They've already proven they can rewrite the past, too."

Danika laughed nervously. "Well, that's comforting."

Cole's jaw tightened. "They'll stop at nothing to see this through, and anyone who gets too close to the truth won't be safe." His blue eyes settled on her—steady, unblinking, leaving no doubt who he meant.

Danika nodded, her voice calm, laced with a confidence she didn't quite feel. "Stopping now isn't an option."

She knew time wasn't on their side.

But if the pact was out there, they were the ones who needed to find it.

Forty-Five

"ARE YOU UP FOR a marathon night?" Cole's voice was low, steady, but his eyes burned with purpose.

Danika didn't need to ask what he meant. They needed to finish reading the letters—tonight. Time was running out.

"I'll make some coffee," she said, already turning toward the kitchen. "You've been going non-stop. Are you sure you're up to it?"

"I got some sleep last night."

Danika shook her head, not knowing if that meant fifteen minutes or four hours. With Cole, it was hard to tell. He ran on something deeper than caffeine—drive, grit, duty.

She let out a slow breath and rubbed her temples. They were close, so close, but something was missing. Some small detail that would tie everything together.

Cole settled onto the couch, tablet in hand, already flipping through his notes."There are still too many possibilities," he murmured.

"We've ruled a few out," Danika said, returning a few minutes later and placing two mugs on the table. "The stone summerhouse was just a place for passing notes, I think."

"I agree," Cole said, lifting the mug. "If we had more time, I'd take another look, but it's too exposed. I doubt he'd leave anything that important out there."

They moved methodically through the list, reluctantly crossing off the cave under the bridge and the antiques that lined the hallways, mostly because they didn't have time to look.

"Keep going." Danika leaned forward and picked up her mug. "What's next?"

"Books."

She took a sip of coffee and squeezed her temples. "That's a hard one. Noah talks a lot about reading poetry. Is that a clue? Could he have hollowed out a book and put the pact inside?"

"If it is, we need a lot more time than we have," Cole said. "There are old books everywhere. Main library. The Smiley library. And I don't know how many old bookcases there are in the parlors."

"The little card in the Smiley library says Albert had 8,000 volumes—"

"Okay, so if we had about 800 years to look..." Cole left the sentence hanging as he looked over at Danika.

She pursed her lips as she thought. "I'm going to go with my gut."

"Which says?" Cole's blue eyes studied her intently.

"Which says the pact would be too big to stick between the pages of a book." She paused and bit the inside of her cheek as she thought about it. "And I don't think Noah would destroy a book by hollowing it out."

Cole nodded. "That sounds logical to me." He began to place another check.

"Then again..." Danika put her hand on his to stop him. "I'm not sure we can discount books altogether. The Smiley library has a lot of books about peace. Maybe there's another clue hiding in there? A passage? A note?"

"They have 'Peace' in their title?"

Danika nodded. "I wrote them down. I have a list."

Cole swapped his checkmark for a star. "Okay. Flagged, but low on the list."

"Let's keep going and prioritize from there," Danika suggested.

Cole crossed out the next line. "We have to hope that it isn't somewhere on the property outside. If it's under a boulder somewhere, it may never be found."

"Agreed," Danika said. "But I feel like Noah really was intentional with his clues. He seemed to somehow know the pact wasn't going to be revealed in his lifetime, but he had faith that it would be found when the time was right."

Cole looked up. "The time is right. It's up to us. We need to find it."

She leaned in again, her shoulder touching his briefly, and saw the last thing on his list: *Clocks*.

"That's a strong clue, but there are too many of them. We have to narrow it down."

"Let's keep reading the letters," Cole said. "Maybe something will jump out."

As Danika placed the next pile of letters on the table, her eyes landed on the bag holding the brooch. "Guess I'll use this as my good luck charm," she said, sliding it into her hand and pinning it to her oversized sweatshirt.

He gave a half-smile. "Suits you perfectly."

"What's that supposed to mean?" She wasn't sure if he was being sincere or sarcastic.

He shrugged, leaning back. "Not everyone can pull off *weekend casual and heirloom elegant* at the same time."

Danika glanced down at her outfit and let out a quiet laugh, feeling her cheeks flush with heat. She couldn't remember ever being this dressed down in front of a man before—let alone one she'd met less than three weeks ago. "Yep," she said, "that's me, a fashion trendsetter."

They went back to work, the hours stretching into silence as they pored over faded ink and fragile pages. Each letter added a brushstroke to the picture, but the final image remained elusive.

Then, just as the rhythm began to lull, a single line caught Danika's eye. Her hand stilled. The paper trembled between her fingers.

Cole looked up. "What? Did you find something important?"

"Probably not important. Just sad," she murmured, her voice tight. She handed the letter over.

> *There are days I still can't believe you write to me, but I fear even these letters defy your father's wishes. I believe he suspects more than casual conversation between us. Perhaps he wonders why a man with calloused hands dares to talk with his daughter.*

When Cole handed it back, Danika set the letter down—carefully, reverently—like an artifact from a sacred past. A century ago, love had to sneak through back doors, hidden by duty and divided by class. Now, thankfully, those lines had blurred.

But this was the cost of a truth buried by power.

A story she knew all too well.

She blinked hard and forced herself to focus.

Cole passed her another letter. "This one was written right before the conference."

Danika scanned the brief message.

> *I regret that I haven't found a quiet hour to see you. My days are consumed by preparations and long meetings with diplomats and officials. The work is weighty, and though I carry it*

> *willingly, I miss the ease of your company more than I can say. Please know that my absence is not neglect, but necessity.*

"It proves Noah was part of the inner circle," she said, eyes burning.

Cole nodded while reading another letter. "Here, read this one, too."

> *You ask if we have made progress, and I can tell you that our actions promote peace, and peace leads to success for all. Many are pledging to withhold arms and allegiance from those who pursue war for profit... to stand with one voice in pursuit of universal brotherhood.*

Danika exhaled sharply. "They weren't just *talking* about peace. They were trying to end the machinery of war before it began."

"The complete opposite of what they're about to vote on." Cole's jaw tightened. "If that pact surfaces now, it could expose the whole thing."

"That's putting it mildly," Danika muttered. "It would blow open decades of profiteering. Trigger a chain reaction they couldn't contain." She looked up at him. "And Julian knows it."

Danika picked up the next letter and leaned back, pausing as she noticed Cole reading his own—lips moving, eyes locked on the page.

"You find something?" she asked when he appeared to have finished.

"Yes and no," he said, handing her the letter. "What do you think? Read the last paragraph."

> *I have wrestled with my conscience more in these last weeks than I ever thought a man could. Doing what is right is often unclear, and choosing the proper path rarely comes without cost.*

"It's hard to say what he's talking about," Danika said, glancing back at the letter she held in her hand. "But this one's on the same subject." Her gaze drifted up to the date. "Written well after the conference, though."

I can't help but ponder, even amidst the echoes of laughter and hushed conversations that fill the grand parlor, if I have done the right thing. Only you know of the secret of which I speak... You and the 'soul of honor' who has watched history unfold and witnessed the burying of secrets.

Cole's gaze lifted and met hers, his eyes burning a deep, icy blue. "Soul of honor? That's the first time I've seen that reference."

Danika sensed that the pieces mattered. She just didn't know how they fit. "If we only knew what he meant," she said, her voice tight with exasperation. "It's all there—I can feel it—but it still doesn't make sense."

Cole leaned back, studying the floor as if the answer might be there. "Sometimes things don't make sense until you stop forcing them to."

They read in silence for a while, the quiet broken only by the soft rustle of paper and the occasional creak of the chair.

"This is interesting," Danika said, interrupting the quiet. She leaned in, her shoulder touching his, and tilted the page toward him.

My dearest Abigail—I scarcely feel right accepting something so fine as the pocket watch—it is far too extravagant for a man like me. And yet, I find myself unwilling to part with it. There is comfort in its weight and something timeless in the way it draws my thoughts to you. It is more than a timepiece. It is a keeper of truth. And it is worth more than all the treasures of the earth to me.

"A pocket watch?" Cole's brow furrowed. "And he calls it a keeper of truth."

Danika blinked to clear her blurry vision. "It's like we're being handed puzzle pieces, but the one thing we need is always just out of reach."

Cole took the letter and read the next sentence out loud: *"The inscription you chose says what I could not about the key to peace."*

"Now that sounds like an absolutely amazing, magnificent, wonderful clue," Danika said, sarcasm dripping from her voice. "Except for one small thing."

"Yeah," Cole agreed. "We don't have the pocket watch."

"It's so disappointing." She placed her head in her hands. "It's like we're being taunted. Great clues that provide no answers."

Cole nodded. "We're always so close, and yet so far away."

Forty-Six

For the next hour, silence settled over the room—thick, undisturbed, and filled with quiet purpose. No words passed between them, only the delicate crackle of brittle paper and the faint scent of time as each letter was carefully unfolded. Now and then, the scratch of a pencil broke the stillness, quick and sharp as notes were jotted on the yellowed legal pad between them.

The once-daunting pile of letters had dwindled, but not its weight. Each fragile page carried a chance. One phrase, one tiny detail could change everything.

That's what kept them reaching, kept them reading, kept them digging for what had been hidden by time or by intent.

Danika sighed as she picked up the next letter, hoping it would provide a better clue.

January 10, 1909
Your words struck me in a way no hammer or storm ever could. Just four words, yet the impact is dreadful. Europe in the Spring.

A jolt of pain passed through Danika, uninvited and sudden, as if Noah's long-ago heartbreak had reached through time and touched her. She continued reading.

It reminded me of something out of one of the books you used to read aloud by the lake, the tragic kind with carriages and castles and a story that ends far too neatly—and way too soon.

I know your father believes he's doing what's best—that distance will erase what's grown between us. But I also know what's true.

Distance may take your footsteps from Mohonk, but it cannot take your voice from my memory, or your kindness from the worn places in my heart. I will carry the sound of your laughter into every quiet morning.

Write, if you can. And if not... I will still be waiting.

With all the affection that one heart can hold for another -
Noah

Danika felt a tear slide down her cheek and quickly swiped it away. She was not going to cry. Not in front of the man sitting two feet away from her.

"What's wrong?" Cole's voice broke the silence.

"Nothing." Her voice cracked. She grabbed the next letter.

When you told me you would not be returning this spring, it felt as though the breath had left the mountain itself. Mohonk will bloom without you, but it will not feel alive.

In hindsight, I remember the heaviness of the day you left, how the clouds sobbed as you drove away. Had I known our last goodbye was truly the last, I would have held your gaze a moment longer, said more than I did—or perhaps said nothing at all and let the silence speak for us.

I am grateful for the memories that remain vivid and real, even when watered by tears. But if only I had known...

She lowered the letter to her lap and closed her eyes.

"Did you find something important?" Cole's voice made her bring the letter back up. "No, just resting my eyes a minute." She hurriedly bowed her head over the page, blinking away the blur caused by moisture.

I understand your father wishes to find you a suitable husband. I'm not sure he ever will. No man is worthy—certainly not a man like me.

"You okay?" Cole leaned closer. "You look like you're going to get sick."

Danika didn't answer. Her eyes clung to the page, though the words were practically unreadable through the haze of tears.

But if you are to be given to another, I hope—selfishly—that he never knows you as I did. Not in those still, unguarded moments when the world fell away—as if we had known each other long before this life and would find each other again in the next.

That is the part I will carry. And the part I pray no one else ever truly understands.

Danika stopped again and squeezed her temples, hoping the letter would end on a happy note.

"What is wrong with you?" Cole's voice was gentle now, full of concern. "Do you need a break?"

Danika shook her head and slid from the couch to sit on the floor so Cole couldn't see her face as she read. She placed the letter flat on the coffee table to keep it from shaking, and bent over it as the words slowly came into focus.

We once believed some souls find each other again and again, that our destinies were written in the stars before we ever drew breath. Over time, we discovered that even when love is hidden, it endures—tucked where only the heart might look. If this is the cost of knowing you, I'll pay it in silence. I have built things meant to last and guarded that which needed keeping. Yet nothing I have held in these hands has ever meant more to me than you.

Cole's voice brought her back to the present. "Only a handful left. We need to find something soon."

Danika swallowed the lump in her throat and looked at the pile, her heart sinking. She replaced the letter she'd been reading and reached for another.

This wasn't the ending she had hoped for. Abigail and Noah hadn't drifted apart. They'd been torn from one another by forces beyond their control. Their parting hadn't been a decision—it had been a sentence.

And now, even after all these years, Noah's voice still lingered. In ink. In silence. In the ache between lines.

It was as if he'd been waiting all this time for someone to finally listen.

Of course, she had always known it had all ended somehow. Her great-grandfather was not Noah Morrison.

But now that she had come to know Noah—not just his name, but his heart—it struck her with a sharp, hollow pain. Like mourning someone you never truly had, but somehow lost just the same.

It was history. It was fate.

But it didn't make it hurt any less.

She glanced around the room that had once felt so grand and open. Now the walls seemed to close in, suffocating her. She wanted to read the next letter, and yet she didn't.

Swallowing hard, she nerved herself to pick it up.

> *You cannot imagine with what eagerness I tore open your last letter. Seeing your handwriting brought you to mind with such clarity that it nearly stole the breath from my lungs.*
>
> *In response to the matter left unfinished at Mohonk, let your God and conscience guide you. I will take the secret to my grave, believing the truth is not ours to tell, but theirs to find when hearts are ready and the time appointed.*
>
> *At your request, I will stop my letters. But know that my silence is love, not disloyalty.*

Danika's eyes froze on the line: The truth is not ours to tell, but theirs to find.

Could it be about the pact?

She studied the words. They were simple, yet they seemed significant. It was hard to separate the serious and sentimental words from the possible clues.

"Looks like we're down to the last one."

Danika jumped at the sound of Cole's voice as he slid the letter toward her. "You do the honors."

She hurriedly brushed away a lingering tear and picked up the letter, glancing at the date. It was sent in 1919. Ten years after the last letter. She noticed immediately the scrawling nature of the handwriting. Though it resembled Noah's, it seemed to be written with a weak and shaky hand. It read:

My Dearest Abigail,

Forgive my handwriting and my boldness in sending you a note.

Something inside her shifted—painful, immediate—like a distant echo of what her great-grandmother must have felt reading the same lines.

As I watch the light filtering through the leaves in that golden way it does only at the end of summer, I am reminded of the quiet rhythm of the seasons and how it proves what we used to confide in each other—that life, in all its mystery, never truly ends, it only changes form. Even the barest tree in winter holds spring in its bones, just like your arrival at Mohonk each season revived me like birdsong returning to silent woods.

Danika paused and looked up, sucking in a deep, shaky inhalation of air, already seeing that this letter did not bring good news.

Over the years, I've often reflected on the mystery of love—how it moves unseen but shapes everything. True love is not bound by time. It endures.

A teardrop landed on the paper. She moved the paper to the right so the next one missed.

In that way, I feel nearer to thee now than ever—tethered not by presence, but by something eternal. Life, after all, is a circle, not a line.

Abigail, perhaps you have guessed... this is my way of saying that by the time you read this, I have stepped a little ahead of you on the path, and I will wait for you there.

Yours ever, Noah

Danika felt suddenly queasy and worried she really was going to get sick.

"You want a break?" Cole asked.

Danika stood, nodding. "Yeah. I need air."

She stumbled to her feet and stepped onto the balcony, the view swimming with the emotion in her eyes. Her great-grandmother had looked out over this same water. Same stars. Same ache.

A little while later, the screen door squeaked open behind her and closed with a gentle thud.

"Those are some heavy letters." Cole threw one arm around her like she was one of his buddies and gave her a quick side squeeze before placing his hands on the railing. "I know it must be hard to read about how it ended."

"I'm glad I know her story." She pinched her nose to stop any more tears from flowing and willed herself to keep her emotions in check. "I feel like she wanted me to know."

"Let's go over some of the re-reads and then call it a night," Cole suggested.

Danika nodded and turned to go back inside, her fingers drifting to the brooch. After reading the letters, it felt heavier somehow, as if history itself had been tucked inside it—carried across generations like a sealed message waiting to be read.

It had always felt like a keepsake. Tonight, it felt like a key.

As Cole held the door, she glanced back at the lake and the stars reflected on its surface, the same ones her great-grandmother must have seen. One star, low on the horizon, shimmered brighter than the rest—steadfast, unwavering.

Her throat tightened.

If that's you... Please, please, help us find the truth.

The wind stirred the trees, soft and whispering—almost like an answer.

Forty-Seven

Danika walked back into the room and gazed at the stack of letters sitting on the coffee table. They'd separated them all into three piles. One stack contained letters that both agreed had nothing of value. One was made up of letters that they both agreed needed to be re-read. And the last stack was a mishmash of letters that one of them thought might be important, but the other didn't.

The stack of re-reads seemed huge. Danika reached for the top letter in that pile, her eyes still misty, and brushed the hand of Cole, who was reaching at the same time. "Oh, sorry."

He picked up the top letter and handed it to her, then took the next letter. "This stack here is our best chance," he said. "Now that we've read them all, we have a clearer picture of what might be important."

Danika nodded, trying to share his optimism. He had a way of focusing on the potential for success, never the possibility of failure. Despite the lateness of the hour, his contagious enthusiasm rippled through her, giving her a much-needed boost of energy.

They dug into the pile, reading in silence for the most part, with Cole occasionally taking notes, and Danika sporadically picking up his notebook to scan his comments.

She let out an exasperated breath after re-reading one of the letters as her frustration mounted. Noah's words were poetic, but maddeningly vague. Phrases like *"time marking peace"* and *"the rhythm of hands turning steady"* danced on the edge of clarity, eluding her grasp.

"Why can't he just say what he means?" she muttered.

"Finding anything?" Cole glanced over at her curiously.

Danika sighed. "Noah loved his metaphors, didn't he?" She pointed to a line in the letter she was reading: *Time is the keeper now until the world is ready.*

"What in the heck does that mean?"

"It's like there are hints everywhere." Cole rubbed his chin, his brow furrowing. "But they just won't come into focus."

"His phrasing," Danika said, "it's careful. Almost like he didn't want to say too much."

"Exactly." Cole nodded. "It's subtle if you're just reading one letter. But when you put them all together, there's definitely a pattern." He paused. "Look at this one. It seems like he's definitely trying to convey something between the lines."

Danika leaned close and scanned the letter, then read the notes he pointed to. *The hours guard our words.* She raised an eyebrow.

"That takes us back to clocks, right?"

"Yes, but they're everywhere—hallways, dining rooms, even the library. It's part of the aesthetic."

Danika thought back to her initial exploration of the resort. She'd noticed the clocks, their antique faces framed in intricate wood carvings, but hadn't paid much attention. Now, the mention of time in Noah's letters seemed to take on new significance.

"Maybe he was talking about a specific clock, not just time in general."

"Possibly," Cole said. "But how do we narrow it down? Just about every clock in this place is an antique."

But it would make sense for it to be connected to the main parlor. The peace conferences were held there, and it's a place where he and Abigail met."

Cole flipped through the letters, trying to locate one that referred to the parlor. "Here's one," he said.

Danika leaned over and read:

> *I remember that brief evening in the parlor when the fire had dwindled to embers and shadows gathered in every corner. There is a curious comfort to that space—a sense that one is never entirely alone. The portraits seem to watch with quiet understanding, and one cannot help but feel the presence of the guardian of history, keeping silent vigil as the hours pass.*

"*Guardian of history*?" Danika shook his head. "In the *parlor*?"

"I know. Not really helpful," Cole said. "There's a parlor on every floor and on each end of the building. But since he mentioned the parlor with the two paintings, I think we need to take another look at that room."

Danika didn't respond right away. She slipped off the couch and lowered herself to the floor again, her movements slow, deliberate. Pressing her fingertips into her temples, she tried to quiet the pulsing ache that had settled behind her eyes like a storm building pressure.

Cole watched her. "You okay?"

She glanced up at his blue-eyed gaze. "Just a headache," she murmured. "Probably from staring at old handwriting too long."

"Give me your hand," he said.

"What?"

"Your hand." Cole reached down and picked up her hand, pressing his fingers into the soft web between her thumb and forefinger. His touch—firm, practiced—carried a gentleness that surprised her. Each motion sent a wave of relief through her nerves, loosening something inside her she hadn't realized was clenched.

Danika let out a slow breath, eyes drifting shut. For the first time all day, she felt herself begin to unwind.

Cole placed her hand gently on the coffee table. "Now scootch a little closer."

"This will help," he said when she hesitated. "Promise."

Danika reluctantly obeyed, inching toward him until his hands moved to each side of her neck, thumbs pressing and holding a single spot before working in slow, rhythmic circles.

"What are you doing?" She felt the soothing, calming effects wash over her, his touch so gentle it silenced thought itself.

"Heavenly Pillar," he said. "It's a pressure point for tension. Usually works on headaches."

Danika's limbs went limp and heavy, her body slack with unexpected ease. She wasn't just relaxing—she was unraveling. "Where'd you learn this?" she murmured, as her head slumped forward a little more.

No reply.

"You date a massage therapist or something?"

His hands stilled. "Did Peggy tell you that?"

She turned, dazed. "No. Just guessing." She blinked up at him. "Sorry. That was rude."

He shrugged it off. "Feeling better?"

She nodded as the room blurred at the edges. It wasn't just total relaxation, but more like surrender. A sense of being enveloped in a thick, syrupy haze... slowly slipping under.

"Yeah. Thanks." She moved back to her place and pulled the letter closer. "I'm going to read a little bit more." She placed her finger on the page to help follow along, willing herself to keep going. But the ink seemed to dissolve into the paper, and the paper to melt into the table.

"I think I'll rest my eyes a second," she mumbled, as she folded her arms on the table and laid her head down.

And then, everything faded to black.

Forty-Eight

When Danika opened her eyes, sunlight spilled across the room in warm, golden sheets. For a long moment, she lay still, barely breathing, as her eyes adjusted and her groggy mind stirred awake.

She was in bed, with the covers pulled up to her shoulders. She lifted the edge of the blanket and blinked at the sight of her wrinkled sweatshirt and sweatpants, still on. The bandana she'd tied around her head was half off, and her hair felt like a bird's nest.

Her last memory was sitting on the floor reading one of Noah's final letters. But even that felt distant now, like a dream she had wandered through.

As she pieced together the timeline, she remembered those hands, gentle but firm, kneading away the tension until her limbs felt weightless.

Then darkness. Lost time. A missing gap.

She turned her head toward the sun and blinked hard, trying to make sense of it—and then it came. Soft, like a whisper through fog.

Strong arms. The sensation of being lifted. Her head against a solid chest. The steady rhythm of a heartbeat. And warmth, that kind of warmth that settles not just in your skin, but in your bones.

Cole.

She sat up fast. Too fast. The room tilted sharply, then righted itself. Throwing off the covers, she padded barefoot across the room.

"Cole?" she called, her voice dry with sleep.

No answer.

She rounded the corner and found the room empty.

The letters had been stacked into tidy, careful piles on the table—far neater than she ever bothered with. On the counter, two mugs sat drying on a towel. Her gaze drifted, scanning for a note.

Nothing.

She grabbed her phone. No messages.

Sitting down on the couch, she pushed her hair out of her eyes and tried to remember the sequence of events. Had she fallen asleep and somehow awakened and walked into the bedroom? She looked down at her crumpled clothes. There was no way she would get into bed dressed like this.

Her hand moved to the butterfly brooch, still pinned where she'd put it. *Weekend casual and heirloom elegant.* His words floated back to her. So did the touch of humor she'd seen in his blue eyes when he'd said them. And then the magic touch of his hands on her neck.

The thought tripped a landslide of questions she wasn't prepared to answer.

She picked up her phone again, her finger hovering over his name. The message screen blinked back at her, empty and waiting. Should she send him a text?

No. He'd said he had meetings all day. Important ones. She didn't want to make a big deal out of something he probably thought was nothing.

What would she even say? *Thanks for the massage and carrying me to bed?* She cringed and tossed the phone onto the couch, staring straight ahead, seeing nothing.

She'd known Cole for... she counted back: two whole weeks.

So why did something so small leave her feeling so much?

Until now, she'd seen him through the lens of his position and authority—his quiet intensity, the way his eyes seemed to strip her bare without ever asking a question.

But this… this felt different.

Not softer. He was still all grit and precision. But there'd been something else in his touch. Not practiced. Not planned. Not even romantic. Just… human. Kind. Protective. She wasn't sure whether it comforted her. Or alarmed her.

Maybe a little of both.

She returned to the bedroom and splashed cold water on her face—cooling her skin but doing nothing for her puffy eyes or foggy mind.

I need to get moving. She yanked a brush through her tangled locks, wincing as it snagged again and again. Pig tails, it would be. Something to keep it out of her face.

The letters she'd read last night had given her Noah's voice—but not an ending.

What had happened? Did her great-grandmother ever get to see him again?

She couldn't leave Mohonk without knowing. She had to find more. Something concrete. Memories and fragments of affection weren't enough. She needed the truth.

Danika hid the letters in three different places around the suite—tucked, folded, protected. Then she grabbed her notepad and headed down to the archives one last time.

Hours later, she sat hunched at a wooden table, bleary-eyed and aching. The overhead light pooled dimly on the table, catching on the edges of brittle paper and faded ink. Her fingers throbbed from the hours of delicate sorting, but she didn't stop. She couldn't. She didn't even know what she was hoping to find anymore—just that there had to be more.

Each letter and every faded receipt felt like another dead end, another loose thread that refused to be tied. But she continued sorting, looking, searching.

Noah had said goodbye in his final letter. She needed to know why.

The search felt endless, but the obsession kept her moving. Somewhere buried in this quiet room was information about a man history had almost erased.

She slid aside a guest ledger and reached for the next pile of folders to see what they would reveal. Her pulse drummed with dull fatigue—another stack of receipts, reports, and hand-written records.

As she pulled the folders toward her, an envelope fell out from between the two on top.

She glanced at the front and read the notation scrawled across the front in pencil: "Gravestone Receipt."

I don't need to look at that. She started to set it aside.

But something made her stop. Instinct? Impulse? The journalistic compulsion to leave no stone unturned?

The paper was brittle and yellow, so she opened it carefully. Inside was a piece of paper. Crisp. Official. She unfolded it—and stopped breathing.

For a moment, the floor seemed to vanish beneath her. She braced her hands against the table, willing herself to stay upright. Her pulse thudded in her ears.

M. Whitlock & SonsMonument Carvers & StonecuttersChurch Street, New Paltz, N.Y.October 25, 1919

Received from Mrs. Abigail Prescott-Tipton the sum of $28.00 for one (1) headstone in natural granite for Noah Morrison.Paid in full.

Danika pressed a hand to her chest, her breath shallow. The love they'd shared hadn't faded with time or distance. It had endured.

Noah hadn't simply disappeared. He had died.

Abigail had never forgotten him. Even after leaving the mountain. Even after marrying another man.

The words of the receipt hit her painfully. Raw sorrow echoing through ink and time.

This was the cost of a truth silenced by power—a story she knew all too well.

... by the time you read this, I will have stepped a little ahead of you on the path, and I will wait for you there.

His words came back, heavy now with understanding—except for the *why*.

And *how*?

She did the math in her head. He would have been 32.

She went back to the envelope to see if there was more and found a folded note. Yellowed. Fragile. A newspaper clipping slipped from between the pages, but she barely noticed. Her gaze remained locked on the handwriting of the note—elegant and feminine, unmistakably Abigail's.

She touched the ink written by her great-grandmother. Tried to swallow, but found it difficult. She could feel the weight of her sorrow even before she read the words.

Enclosed is payment for the burial and a headstone for Noah Morrison. Please see that he is laid to rest with dignity. Let his headstone be of the earth—strong and enduring—so that those who pass may know his Faith was unshakeable and his wisdom profound. The inscription should be as noted on the following page.Sincerely, Abigail Prescott-Tipton

Danika turned the page, breath hitching.

Blank.

She searched the envelope again—nothing.

She was so close. So achingly close.

No inscription. No last words. Only silence.

She stared at the note, imagining Abigail's hand pressing into the page. Every word careful. Weighted. Final.

After taking a picture of the receipt and the letter, she turned her attention to the newspaper clipping on the table. A sob escaped her before she could stop it.

New Paltz, N.Y., Oct. 18, 1919 —

Noah Morrison, aged 32 years, of this village, was called home on the evening of the 16th instant, following an illness of pneumonia brought on by the prevailing influenza, commonly known as the "Spanish Flu."

A man of quiet spirit and humble bearing, Friend Morrison was long employed at the Mohonk Mountain House, where he was held in high esteem by both guests and proprietors. Endowed with rare skill of hand and a gentle disposition, his craftsmanship is of such quality that it shall continue to endure as a silent testament to his labor and love of honest work.

He is sorely missed by his sister, Gracie Livingston, of Newburgh, N.Y., and by many who knew his kind heart and steady ways.

Memorial services shall be held in keeping with the manner of Friends.

The words blurred as her eyes welled. Noah hadn't drifted from Abigail's life. He'd been taken by the pandemic. One man among countless others reduced to a number in history.

His death wasn't just the end of a correspondence, but of a life marked by unspoken devotion. And here, in her hands, was proof Abigail had never let him go.

The weight of it pressed hard against Danika's chest. Sadness twisted with anger. It wasn't fair that someone so good, so rooted in purpose, had been swept away without ceremony, his story nearly lost.

This had become so much more than a love story. Loss. Unfinished goodbyes. Memories kept alive. Danika's thumb brushed the delicate script on the receipt. Even after marriage, wealth, and travels across Europe, part of Abigail's heart had stayed here, on this mountain, with Noah.

When she returned the box, the archivist looked up. "Did you find what you were looking for?"

Danika nodded, her voice caught behind the weight in her throat. She stepped outside into the daylight, her steps slow.

She knew what she had to do next.

Forty-Nine

THE AFTERNOON SUN CAST a golden wash over the hills as Danika eased her Jeep down the gravel lane. Neat rows of tombstones in the Veterans Cemetery stretched on either side, flags lifting faintly in the breeze as if in salute. Then the landscape shifted—the uniform markers giving way to the older stones of the New Paltz Rural Cemetery.

She drove slowly and then came to an abrupt stop, staring in disbelief at the chaotic sea of stones in front of her. The sheer scale of the cemetery felt like a weight settling in her lungs.

Tombstones dotted the landscape in no particular order, many leaning at odd angles, shifted by time. The Veterans Cemetery she'd passed through was neat and orderly, its rows of white stones uniform and predictable. This place was nothing like that.

A few markers stood upright and proud, but most slouched or sank into the earth. Some were half-buried, their inscriptions worn smooth by weather and years. The effect was disorderly—almost overwhelming—as if the stones had scattered themselves without regard for those who might one day come searching.

It looked like a puzzle with too many pieces.

Danika put her foot back on the gas, moving slowly, eyes scanning the endless field of stone markers. It felt impossible—like searching for a single grain of sand on a beach. Where would she even start?

Her fingers tightened around the steering wheel. Many of the names on the stones she drove by were worn, nearly illegible. The ones she could make out were familiar from her visit to Huguenot Street—Deyo, Hasbrouck, Bevier, and of course, DuBois. Their history was etched into the land, just like Noah's. *But where was he*?

She swallowed her frustration. She hadn't come this far to leave empty-handed. She had to start somewhere.

Around the next bend, her heart sank again. The markers thinned and were even more widely spaced. Some stood alone in the grass, seemingly forgotten, wedged between the road and an encroaching tree line. One drew her gaze: a solitary, weathered slab, massive in presence, yet humble in its design.

Not Noah—but the word SMILEY etched into the stone sent her pulse racing. Perhaps he was close. Surely they would have laid him to rest near the family he'd been devoted to.

She shut off the Jeep and jumped out for a closer look. The tombstone, a large rough boulder, blended naturally with the landscape. Despite its simplicity, it radiated a quiet strength, as if marking someone who had mattered deeply to this place.

VIRGINIA and DANIEL SMILEY were etched into the stone. She knew the lineage—Mohonk still rested in Smiley hands, now tended by the fifth generation. Daniel, she remembered, was the grand-nephew of Albert, the resort's original owner. Her eyes scanned the clearing beyond.

No other markers. No sign of Noah.

Putting her hands on her hips, she turned in a circle. *Where are you, Noah?*

She sighed and began walking the rows, scanning each name. Forty-five minutes passed before her determination began to waver. Earlier, she'd been so sure—finding the tombstone receipt had felt like a sign. A lead. A promise.

But now, with shadows lengthening and the day slipping away, the cemetery felt like it was working against her, its secrets buried too deep to be found.

She kept walking, slower now, discouragement dragging at her steps. The stones blurred together, their inscriptions worn and unreadable. Her eyes burned. Her legs ached.

What if she'd already passed it?

And even worse... What if she was this close—and couldn't read the name?

She started back toward her Jeep, eyes still sweeping the stones. With one hand on the door handle, she paused for a final glance at the cemetery. Rows of markers stretched before her: silent, indifferent, refusing to give up their secret.

Maybe she wasn't meant to find him.

Her fingers curled around the handle. She gave it a sharp tug and climbed in, blinking back tears as she turned the key, bringing the engine to life.

Just as she reached for the gearshift, movement flickered at the edge of her vision.

A doe, startled by the sound, bounded across the path in front of her. Danika watched its graceful movements as it darted toward the tree line, white tail raised like a flag before vanishing into the woods.

Even in the midst of all this forgotten stone, life goes on.

Danika's gaze lingered, drawn by the quiet beauty of the moment.

And that's when she saw it.

At the edge of the woods where the doe had vanished, a single stone peeked out from tall grass. Not a proper tombstone, but a rough, unpolished slab of granite, leaning slightly, its surface darkened with moss. It lay deep in shadow in the tree line—yet its face caught the low afternoon light like a flame.

Danika's pulse jumped. She killed the engine and jumped from the Jeep, reminding herself not to hope. Her steps quickened anyway, sneakers whispering through the untamed grass as she crossed the narrow stretch of earth, partially reclaimed by time and wilderness.

Dropping to her knees despite the damp ground, she brushed aside the creeping vines and tangled grass. Nature had nearly erased the engraving, but something remained. The lettering was simple and unembellished, carved directly into the rock. She traced it with her fingers. Cold and final.

N-O-A-H.

Moss and lichen clung to the stone, obscuring the last name—but she knew. Blinking through sudden tears, Danika cleared more dirt with slow, deliberate strokes.

Beneath his name, the words emerged:

A Craftsman of Peace

Abigail had chosen those four words. A craftsman, yes, but Danika knew the deeper truth. He hadn't just carved wood. He had shaped something far greater by guarding the pact.

And Abigail had guarded his memory.

A tremor started in Danika's hands, a deep shuddering grief welling from a place so old it felt like it belonged to Abigail herself. This was Noah—the man whose letters spoke of a devotion so steady it had survived them both.

Her great-grandmother had never gotten to say goodbye; had borne a lifetime of silent sacrifice. Something twisted in Danika's chest, a key turning, unlocking an ache she hadn't known was there.

She ran her fingertips across the inscription, tracing a simple tribute to a man who lived without fanfare but left a mark all the same. Noah had written to Abigail in a way that echoed across time, and now Danika felt the truth of it settle into her bones.

Noah hadn't been wealthy. He didn't possess power or clout. But he had worked with his hands, carved beauty from wood and stone, and left behind something more enduring: a humble legacy.

She sat back, eyes still fixed on the stone, when something else caught her attention. A line, nearly erased by weather and time.

Heart pounding, she tore away the grass, yanking it by the roots. Her breath hitched as another inscription came into view:

Ashes to ashes, dust to dust—Time holds the secret once kept by us.

A single sob broke loose before she could stop it. It was as if Noah and Abigail had left a message—not for each other.

But maybe, for *her*.

Danika leaned in, her forehead nearly touching the stone as grief overtook her. It wasn't just for Noah—or even for her great-grandmother. It was for the loss of something timeless, sacred. Something buried away from the world, known only to the two of them.

As tears blurred her vision, a gentle hand touched her shoulder, startling her from her thoughts.

"Sorry," came a low, familiar voice.

She looked up to find Cole kneeling beside her, his presence anchoring her in the storm of emotion. His face held no questions, only quiet understanding—as if he, too, could feel the magnitude of what she'd uncovered.

"You found it," he said softly.

Danika nodded, unable to speak, her gaze fixed on Noah's name.

Cole crouched lower to read the inscription. He nodded once, silent.

Danika looked over at him questioningly. "How did you know I was…?"

"I ran into Nadine. She told me you found an obit. I figured you'd want to see it for yourself."

As they started to rise, Cole grimaced, yet still grasped Danika's hand to help her up.

"Are you okay?" he asked, reaching out and gently brushing away a stray tear from her cheek.

She drew a slow breath, but emotion surged sharp and sudden—not only for the past, but for something sacred never allowed into the light. Another tear slipped free before she could blink it back.

Cole seemed to sense what she needed and drew her into his arms. She hadn't planned to let him see this side of her, the vulnerable part she guarded so carefully. Yet his embrace didn't weaken her—it steadied her. He was all strength and quiet understanding, both storm and shelter, and in his arms, the ground beneath her felt solid again.

Fifty

THE LAST STREAKS OF sunset had vanished, leaving the forest trails around Mohonk Lake cloaked in deep, inky twilight. Danika moved briskly, eyes scanning the uneven path. The soft slap of water against the shoreline mingled with the steady crunch of her steps over rock and gravel.

She should have left Eagle Cliff earlier, especially after realizing she'd forgotten her flashlight, but she hadn't been ready to move on. Not after finding Noah's grave. She'd lingered on the overlook, needing a moment to breathe, to take in the blaze of crimson sky as the sun dipped behind the mountains like a final bow.

There had been something about it—something reverent, like a quiet acknowledgment of everything uncovered.

Now, with night closing in, shadows pooled in every dip and hollow, turning the trail into a twisting maze. She scanned the darkness for familiar shapes, certain she had to be close to The Twins summerhouse by the lake.

But where was it? She rounded a bend—and froze.

A tall figure stood just off the path, still and silent.

Her pulse jumped, and her footsteps slowed to a halt, just as the figure shifted, revealing a small dot of red light from a security radio.

Cole.

The relief came first, then curiosity. He stood in the crook of a wooden fence by the trail, his head tilted downward as he spoke into the mic clipped to his collar. His voice was low, smooth, the kind of tone meant to relay information without drawing attention. The shadows obscured most of his face, but when he looked up and saw her, she could tell he recognized her instantly.

"What are you doing out here?" His voice was edged with that familiar blend of concern and quiet reprimand, the same tone he had used the day he figured out she had checked into the resort under a different name.

"I was at Eagle Cliff watching the sunset," she said, gesturing vaguely behind her. "And, um, it gets dark fast around here."

'That's usually what happens when the sun goes down." He glanced down at her empty hands. "And you don't have a flashlight?"

The way he said the words made her feel slightly foolish, even though his tone wasn't patronizing...

Well, maybe it was a little.

"I thought I'd just use my phone," she defended. "...B-b-ut the battery died."

"Why didn't you stick to the main trail?"

Now Danika felt doubly stupid. "I meant to leave a little earlier, but I..." She didn't bother finishing her sentence when she saw the look on his face.

"This one is treacherous in the dark," he said, his jaw tightening, a clear indication he wanted to lecture her about safety. Instead, he exhaled, shaking his head as he pulled a small flashlight from his pocket and flicked it on.

The Cole who had comforted her in the cemetery just a few hours ago was nowhere in sight; in his place stood the other version—calm, commanding, all business, with eyes that missed nothing.

"Come on," he said, stepping beside her. "I'll walk you back."

***

They walked in silence at first, the beam of his flashlight cutting through the darkness. The night was cool and still, the scent of damp earth and pine filling the air. The resort was just a short distance away, but the rock-filled path made it feel longer, the uneven terrain requiring careful foot placement.

When Danika stumbled over a hidden rock, she hardly had time to react before Cole's hand closed around hers, steady and sure. Her breath caught, more from the swiftness of his save than the stumble itself. His fingers curled around hers with unyielding strength, grounding her in its firm protective grasp.

“You good?” he asked, his voice softer now.

She nodded, but she didn’t let go right away. Neither did he.

They continued like that—his hand holding hers, guiding her over the rocks through the darkness, pointing out obstacles as they appeared.

The conversation, when it came, was unhurried, their voices blending with the occasional rustle of the wind through the trees.

"You always walk around the lake and rescue damsels in distress after dark?" she asked lightly.

“Just the ones I find wandering on dangerous paths without a flashlight.”

She laughed softly, shaking her head that he had scolded with humor. “I’ll take that as a personal reprimand.”

He didn’t answer, and the silence nudged her into explaining.

“I did have it by the door. I just walked out without it. And then I thought I could get all the way back before it got completely dark.” Danika knew she was rambling, but for some reason couldn’t stop.

"All's well that ends well," he said. "Just watch your step."

When they reached the small wooden footbridge near the resort, Cole's grip on her hand tightened just a fraction before he let go and motioned for her to go first across the narrow bridge.

Danika slowed when they got to the middle of the wooden structure, drawn by the reflection shimmering across the surface of the water. A full moon had just breached the nearby cliffs, its golden light stretching in a perfect ribbon across the glassy lake.

She turned and leaned over the railing, breathing in the timeless beauty, thinking about all its hidden secrets.

Cole stopped just behind her. She could feel his presence there—solid, steady—close enough that she could sense his warmth against her back.

"Looks like you have perfect timing," he said, staring at the giant orb rising behind Sky Top Tower.

"Yes, perfect timing. A sunset and a full moon all in one evening. It really did all work out, didn't it?"

Just as Danika spoke, a breeze drifted across the water, sending a slight chill down her spine. She shivered involuntarily, not even realizing it until she felt Cole move behind her.

Without a word, he slipped off his jacket and draped it over her shoulders. "Looks like you forgot something else, too," he said. The weight of the fabric settled over her—solid, grounding, wrapping around her like a protective embrace.

"Thank you, but I'm okay," she turned. "We're almost there."

"Keep it for now," he said in a tone that removed any room for argument.

Danika pulled the jacket closer, her fingers brushing over the fabric. "Thanks," she said, her voice quieter now.

Footsteps echoed on the wooden planks as another couple approached, talking in low tones as they moved toward them.

Cole stepped closer behind her, shifting just enough to allow the couple space to pass behind them.

The warmth of him settled against her back.

For just a second, she thought about leaning into him—not much, just enough to feel the quiet strength of him there, the solid presence that made the problems she faced and the answers she sought seem less intimidating.

He didn't step away immediately, and as they stared out into the night, she felt the space between them narrowing in ways that had nothing to do with proximity.

Danika exhaled. "Thanks again for the jacket." She paused a moment and tilted her head back to look up at him. "You must be really tired."

He looked down, his blue eyes curious. "Why do you say that?"

"Because you're not usually this nice."

That made him smile, but only for a heartbeat. "Don't get used to it," was the simple response.

The glint of humor was just enough to make her think for a second that he might reach for her hand again. But instead he exhaled slowly, stepped back, and straightened his stance.

The moment slipped away, and the space between them returned, wider now; laced with a chill that hadn't been there before.

"You're good from here, right?" He nodded toward the light of the hotel that lit the path.

Danika nodded. "Yes. The moon is bright enough now to light my way." She turned around quickly to catch him. "But here's your coat."

Cole was already walking away. He just waved his hand in the air. "I'll get it tomorrow."

He disappeared from view, yet something about him lingered—a presence, a pull, a whisper she couldn't quite catch. It stayed with her, a quiet echo reminding her that Cole was the kind of man you could lean on—but never quite hold.

Fifty-One

DANIKA MADE HER WAY to the dining room for breakfast, pausing at the ornate mirror in the hallway—one of those gilded relics you only see in century-old hotels.

Every time she passed by, it made her think about the affluent women who'd paused here to smooth their skirts, or the dignified men who gave their ties a final tug before strolling into breakfast. A thousand small rituals of vanity and tradition lingered in the glass like the faintest of ghosts.

Today, though, something behind her caught her eye. Something coming up behind her.

She turned quickly.

"Julian," she said in a calm tone, successfully masking her emotions.

He looked surprised at first, as if wondering how she had known he was there, but he recovered quickly, lifting both hands in mock surrender. "No, I'm not stalking you. Just trying to catch up. I need to talk to you."

He motioned toward the small parlor off the hall and, without waiting for her reply, led the way. Danika followed warily.

"I hope the new security measures aren't proving too inconvenient," he said, offering a smooth smile as he gestured toward the couch for her to sit.

"Everything's been running smoothly as far as I can see." She answered his question without sitting.

"Good. That's what I like to hear."

Danika smiled politely, sensing something more beneath the surface. "Is there a reason you wanted to talk to me?" She glanced over her shoulder toward the dining room to show her impatience.

"Oh, yes, I won't keep you," he said. "I wanted to make sure you knew about the opening night gala." He leaned forward. "You've heard about it, of course... through your affiliation with GEM-Co?"

Danika stilled. The mention was deliberate. He wanted her to know that he knew.

"I have," she said, coolly.

"Well, I wanted to make sure you planned to attend."

Danika blinked. "Why?"

"Why?" He laughed. "It's a chance for our guests to mingle, get to know each other... feel comfortable in their surroundings."

"I thought it was more for the power players... for networking." Danika tried to find a way out. "I wouldn't feel comfortable—"

"Not true," Julian interrupted. "You're the perfect guest for the gala. You'd bring a fresh perspective, an authenticity."

He spoke with warmth, inviting trust, but Danika knew him well enough to be indifferent to his kind gestures. "Sorry, but I don't move in diplomatic circles," she said. "It's way out of my league."

Julian waved off her objection. "That's precisely why you're perfect. People feel more relaxed around someone who doesn't come with an agenda."

When Danika remained silent, he spoke again.

"*Trust me,* you'll be doing more than you realize simply by being there."

Those words made Danika even more cynical. *What does that mean? Am I being paranoid, thinking everything he says has a double meaning?*

Julian apparently took her hesitation for something else. He leaned in and spoke in a hushed tone. "If it's because you have nothing to wear, I can send someone into town. My assistant is making a list."

Danika smiled. "No, I brought a formal dress just in case something came up, but—"

Julian clapped his hands together. "A woman who plans for the unexpected—my favorite kind—and so rare these days."

Before she could reiterate that she did not plan to attend, he looked over her left shoulder. "Ah. Just the man I was hoping to see."

Danika turned to find Cole pushing through the side door from the porch, eyes on his phone. When he looked up and saw them, his surprise was unguarded—and gone in a blink.

"Danika and I were just talking about the gala," Julian said. "I'd like you to attend as well."

Cole's gaze flicked to Danika and then to Julian with a mixture of curiosity and confusion. "That's not possible. I'll be busy with—."

"That's what I—" Danika started to say, but Julian interrupted them both.

"Cole, your dedication to internal security has been noted, but I'll need your eyes on the main event."

Danika's heart jumped. That was no offhand remark. Julian wasn't offering an invitation. He was giving a summons.

"My team is already assigned for the gala." Cole's posture stiffened. "They know what they're doing."

"Yes, of course." Julian continued, undeterred. "But what better way to observe the crowd than from within? You'll have access to conversations, body language, subtle cues that no camera or guard stationed at a doorway could detect."

Cole folded his arms, clearly unconvinced. For just a heartbeat, his gaze met Danika's with a look that steadied and soothed her.

Julian responded by clapping a friendly hand on Cole's shoulder as if they were old buddies. Danika couldn't imagine the self-control it took for Cole to hide his repugnance, but his eyes betrayed no emotion.

"You've been invaluable so far, Cole. You've kept the security operation running smoothly." Julian lay on the praise. "But the gala night is about more than logistics. It's about understanding the dynamics in play. No one is better suited for that than you."

Cole's jaw tightened, his mind clearly weighing the options. "And the rest of the team?"

"They'll be positioned as planned," Julian assured him. "Your presence at the gala adds another layer of protection. People notice these things."

"I'll send Bart."

"No." Julian's voice was firm, the casual, friendly tone gone. "You're the one the delegates recognize. And anyway, no one reads a crowd better than you." Julian's gaze flicked up to the determined set of Cole's jaw. "Don't make me pull rank on you. If you remember, I did hire you for this position."

His tone shifted in an instant, turning light and easy. "It's just a fun get-together. Two hours, tops. And Danika's already agreed to come." He glanced her way and had the audacity to wink.

"No, Julian. I didn't say—"

"I can't wait to see you both at the gala." Julian turned to go, but not before casting a final look over his shoulder—a long, assessing stare that settled over them with the quiet gravity of a threat.

"What just happened?" Danika shook her head when he'd disappeared.

"I'm not sure." Cole stood with his hands on his hips. "He's playing some sort of game and we're invited." He stared blankly over her shoulder. "To tell you the truth, it might be the best way to see what he's up to."

That wasn't what Danika expected. She gazed up at him, trying to read his face. "So when you pushed back, it was just because you knew he was expecting that? You actually wanted the invite?"

Cole's lips curled up into a crooked smile as he brought his gaze back down to her. "Maybe." He lifted his mic and said, "10-4," then met her gaze again.

"If we don't go, it will look more suspicious than if we do. Make an appearance. Keep your eyes open. Play along."

"I'd rather get my teeth pulled—and be in bed by nine."

"Change of plans." His eyes drilled into hers. Now's not the time to throw in the towel. Remember the goal."

She arched a brow. "So the goal is to get dressed up and act like them?"

"No." His gaze locked on hers, steady and unblinking. "The goal is to look like we're having fun while we figure out Julian's game plan."

Danika nodded. "Easy as can be. And maybe we'll get lucky and find some answers.

"Hope isn't a game plan." He leaned in, his voice low, eyes never leaving hers. "Just trust me, and be there."

For a moment, the air between them seemed to tighten. Then he glanced at his watch, broke the connection, and walked away.

Fifty-Two

Danika sat on the deep-cushioned couch in the Winter Lounge, her eyes locked on the low flames in the fireplace. Words, clues, fragments of riddles spun in her mind, colliding too quickly for her to grasp. Every time one thought landed, another chased it away.

A figure passed by the doorway in front of the Central Stairs and then backed up. It was Cole.

"You okay?" he asked, stepping into the room. "You look like you're in a trance."

"Just thinking."

He nodded. "Let me know if anything clicks. I'll be—" He stopped, his attention drawn to something over her shoulder.

Danika turned her head to follow his gaze, instinctively sensing danger. Not in a million years did she expect what she saw.

"Senator," Cole said, a hint of caution in his tone.

"McCain." Wiley offered a curt nod to Cole, then focused his attention on Danika. "This must be the famous journalist I've been hearing about." He sauntered into the room. "I've read your name, but never had the pleasure." He extended a pudgy hand.

Danika blinked, staring at it without moving.

A nerve in Wiley's cheek twitched as he withdrew his hand, though his voice remained calm. "She's charming," he said to Cole. "You might want to remind her who she's dealing with."

"I have the feeling she's well versed on the matter," Cole said dryly.

The calm, steady tone of Cole's voice anchored Danika, even as the room seemed to tilt and then spin.

Wiley gave a barely noticeable nod to some unseen person. Within seconds, dark-suited men materialized at each of the three entrances, positioning themselves wordlessly. Danika's stomach turned as the exits were silently blocked.

Then he reached into his coat and pulled out a folded document. "For the record, I was trying to be nice," he said, his tone thick with condescension. "I think you're going to regret not playing along."

"Playing along with what?" Danika was surprised that her voice sounded steady and defiant, because that's not what she was feeling on the inside. "Corruption? Manipulation?"

Wiley's expression hardened. "Don't get sassy with me, young lady," he said. "I'm going to be blunt. You're not going to undo what I've spent a career building. You may as well get that out of your mind."

"What you've built is a machine made of lies."

He tilted his head, amused. "So young. So moral. My grandfather believed in fairy tales, too. Died broke, believing truth mattered. My father taught me better. Power is what survives."

Cole took a step forward, squaring off. "What exactly do you want, Seb?"

Wiley's eyes narrowed at the use of his first name instead of his title. "Well, I thought I'd give Miss Vaughn a chance—"

"A chance at what?" Cole interrupted.

Wiley turned to Danika. "You're smart. Tenacious. I can use someone like you on my team." He leaned down a little closer. "Why waste your life fighting a war you can't win when you could be at the helm of the narrative?"

Danika's breath caught, her anger simmering just below the surface, ready to blow.

"This is how it works," Wiley continued. "Your truth is a story. My truth is the law. There's still time to pick the winning side."

"The winning side is with the truth," Danika said. "The real truth. Not *your* version."

He chuckled. "The only problem is," he said, pinning her down with his gaze, "you haven't found it."

The words hung, heavy and intentional, just like they were supposed to.

"You're still chasing ghosts," he said, strolling toward the fireplace. "That original pact? Gone. Maybe it never existed. And if it did, who cares? You have nothing to prove it. And without it, it's just your word versus mine. Guess who wins that one?"

"You should be behind bars," Danika said.

He chuckled. "You're bold, I'll give you that. But I know something you don't."

"What's that?" Cole asked.

"You're out of time." Wiley tapped his watch. "The delegates are meeting on Thursday, and the new pact is getting signed on Friday. Once that happens, it's law. Cemented. Immutable. We'll leverage it for the next century." He smoothed his tie, admiring himself in the brass face of an antique clock. "And the best part? No one will know the difference."

"Not if we can help it." Danika said the words forcefully, but inside, she was not so sure.

"I hate to be the one to break it to you, but even if your supposed pact is found, it's nothing but a relic of a bygone era, irrelevant to modern geopolitics."

"Is that what the lobbyists you hired are pushing to the media?" Danika asked. "To sow doubt in advance... just in case?"

"Ahh, looks like you know me too well." He smiled, taking her words as praise. "But it's not a theory that's hard to sell. The world is too complex now for such naïve ideals."

"I guess we'll just have to see about that." Danika crossed her arms to show a boldness and confidence she in no way felt.

"Yes, I guess we'll see." Wiley laughed as if at a private joke. "Will the masses believe *me* when I tell them it's outdated and useless. Or *you*?"

He leaned forward and shook his finger at her. "Let me explain how truth works. Without evidence, it's just a myth. A story. And I already wrote the ending to the one the world is going to see."

He straightened back up and glanced at Cole before giving a soft, indulgent chuckle. "Because I like you two so much, I'm going to be nice and warn you instead of letting it come as a surprise." He paused as if waiting for one of them to question the statement. When they both stared at him stone-faced, he continued. "I've already got the press releases queued, the talking points distributed. The delegates will sign the new doctrine because the world wants peace."

"But that's not what they're going to get." Danika's mouth went dry. "You're a fraud," she said, barely above a whisper.

That made him laugh. "I've been called worse."

He took a step toward Danika, his voice low, confident, unshaken. "You can try to expose me, but by the time you do, the story will already be written. The new pact will be policy. And you? You'll look like the ones trying to tear it all down."

Danika jerked her gaze over to meet his. "What does *that* mean?"

"It means... things might get personal."

Danika didn't ask what he meant by that because she didn't want to know. But Senator Wiley decided to explain it to her anyway.

"When the legacy media tells the story I want told, you'll be too busy defending yourself to stop a single thing." He waved his finger in her face again. "Those searches you did where you came across classified documents? Remember? It's all documented, and it's not going to look good when it becomes a headline."

Danika froze.

"You planted documents with the hope she'd find them?" Cole stepped forward and spoke with a tone of disbelief.

Wiley's smile returned, tighter now. "Maybe? Who's to say? Maybe I laid the groundwork to raise doubt. Maybe not. No one will ever know for sure, will they?"

"They will if I have anything to say about it." Cole's stance was firm as he crossed his arms.

"Really?" That brought a look of contentment to Wiley's face. "Because I'd keep an eye on your email, if I were you. Word is the DOJ's internal affairs division has a few questions. Something about your communications during this summit. Surveillance. Misuse of government systems."

He grinned. "Sounds bad for someone like you."

"You're framing us," Danika whispered.

"No. That's not it at all." His gaze glided from one to the other. "I'm *re-framing* you the way I want you to be seen. And in my world, that's all it takes."

Wiley gave a subtle nod. His men stepped aside. "Enjoy your scavenger hunt," he said. "And remember, this isn't about beating *me*. It's about beating the clock."

He tapped his watch again. "Tick-tock."

When he disappeared into the hallway, the silence that followed wasn't relief.

Danika exhaled shakily. "So… no pressure."

Cole's face remained unreadable. "He's bluffing."

But she wasn't sure. Not after that last look. It was too composed. Too final.

Her voice was barely audible. "What if he's not?"

And what if there really is no pact, she thought to herself, starting to second-guess all the progress they'd made.

They had known time was running out. But now it felt like time itself was the enemy.

And they were already behind.

Fifty-Three

THE APPEARANCE OF SENATOR Wiley and the subsequent conversation gave a new sense of urgency to Danika and Cole. Despite his already-long days, he stopped by her room to take another look and try to figure out what they had missed.

The tension of their exchange with the senator lingered, but in the hush of the room, it gave way to something steadier, more deliberate. The scattered papers and faded ink seemed to beckon, pulling them back into the search. The significance of the letters settled over them both like an unspoken promise.

"Let's go over some possible scenarios here," Cole said. "You found that clipping that said most of the attendees in 1906 were in favor of signing a document, but the ones against apparently had enough power to sway opinions."

Danika nodded. "Massive global changes were taking place, so the stakes were high." She leaned back on the couch. "So, what if the pact was signed, but by the next day, there was so much pressure or so many threats that they held that secret vote to nullify it. The vote is recorded as part of the minutes. We just don't know what it was about."

“That’s plausible,” Cole said. “Or, the dissenters tried to burn the signed document when it passed, and since everyone at the conference assumed the pact was destroyed in the fire, they voted to keep it quiet rather than tell the world it was signed.”

He glanced over at her to get her reaction. “Having your name attached to a bold statement like that for no reason would be dangerous. And telling the world that a peace document had been signed but was destroyed in a fire wouldn’t exactly be a positive sign for the unity movement.”

“Which was already on shaky legs.” Danika nodded, amazed at how his mind worked. “That makes even more sense. When the larger powers declined to support it, and possibly destroyed it, the rest of the attendees decided to erase it from the record rather than face humiliation.”

“But how does Noah fit in?” Cole squeezed his temples as if that would help him come up with the answers. “I guess he could have heard rumblings that it was going to be destroyed—or he just believed in it so strongly that he hid it, hoping that one day it would come to light.”

“But it never did in his lifetime,” Danika said sadly.

“Right. Political winds shifted after the conference, and the entire world was on the brink of change. World War I was underway when Noah died.” Cole stared vacantly out the window. “Revealing the existence of the pact could have triggered a diplomatic crisis and retaliation at that point. Noah was a religious man and believed it would come to light at the right time.”

Cole exhaled sharply. "We’re still missing something."

"Yeah, no kidding." Danika stretched her legs out and leaned back into the plush armchair. "It has to be here somewhere. Something we haven’t put together yet."

She glanced up at Cole, his expression pensive, brow furrowed, the familiar look of a man reaching for a puzzle piece just beyond his grasp.

"We should go over everything we know—again," he said.

Danika groaned but reached for her notes. "Fine. Let's start with what we do know."

She ran her finger down the scribbled page. "Noah Morrison was a carpenter and very close to the Smileys. He met my great-grandmother and formed a bond with her despite their difference in status. He wrote letters that provide hints, but his wording is veiled... obscure."

Cole nodded, motioning for her to continue.

"Some of the letters suggest something about time—"

"Darn it!" Cole interrupted her, his unusual outburst alarming.

"What's wrong?" Danika looked over as he scrolled through his phone.

"Sorry. I just remembered something that came across my desk."

He sat down on the couch, and Danika sat down beside him. "What is it?"

"Clocks."

"What about clocks?" she asked.

"I received notification that permission has been granted for a restoration crew to pick up several of Mohonk's older clocks."

"When?"

"It hit my in-box late yesterday evening." He tapped to open the email. "The details are vague. It says, 'routine rehabilitation of historic artifacts.'"

"Authorized by who?"

His gaze met hers. "Julian."

"When is the pickup scheduled?"

He glanced back at his phone. "Thirty-six hours from now."

"The opening day of the conference." Danika exhaled as she said the words. "We can't let him do that!"

"There's not a lot we can do, I'm afraid." Cole sighed deeply. "I already looked into it since it's something that should have come through me for clearance. Julian made a major donation to the retreat under the pretense of restoring the clocks, and the higher-ups already approved it—with gratitude."

"And it's just the older clocks?"

Cole just nodded. "I guess he thinks something's there. He just doesn't know which one."

"Neither do we." Danika started biting a fingernail.

"We still have about thirty-six hours."

Danika stood and began pacing. "We need to act fast. The clock is ticking." She stopped and turned toward Cole. "Pardon the pun."

As they began to plan their next move, the urgency of the race against Julian pressed heavily on them both. If their theory was right, a clock could be the key to unraveling a mystery that could alter the course of the peace conference and expose the truth behind Mohonk's storied past.

Cole's jaw tightened. "And if Julian knows something, it means we're running out of time."

The irony of that statement wasn't lost on her. "What if we're looking at this all wrong?"

"What do you mean?" He tilted his head and crossed his arms.

"The clues aren't for Abigail to find the pact, but seem to be just reminding her of where it's hidden," she said. "He infers a couple of times that she knows where it is."

Cole's eyes narrowed. "Agreed."

Danika went over to the coffee table and flipped through the stack of letters.

"Like this one." She stopped and sat down on the couch, and Cole joined her, leaning in to read the letter she held.

You ask if we should ever speak of what was entrusted to us. I believe the answer is no, not yet. This truth is not ours to tell. By His hand, it shall be found at the right Time, by those with eyes to see.

“I remember that one because ‘time’ is capitalized.” Cole nodded as he stared at the letter. “Another reminder for her?”

She nodded. “It takes us back to clocks. Now all we need to figure out is *which one?*

Fifty-Four

Danika stood in the bathroom, brushing her hair with quick, efficient strokes, debating how to style it for the gala. Soft waves? A relaxed bun? After some deliberation, she settled on a French braid—tedious to weave, but sure to hold through the evening.

When she finally tied it off and met her reflection, she was surprised by her own handiwork. The style looked elegant—sophisticated, even. She turned her head, inspecting the braid from both sides. Striking in its simplicity, yet stylish enough to be fashionable.

She took a deep breath and crossed the room to the closet. Time to get dressed.

Danika hadn't expected to need a formal dress on this trip—at least, not for anything like this. But instincts born from years of unpredictability had served her well. When you planned to stay a month in a place like Mohonk, you packed for every possibility. Even galas.

As she unzipped the bag, the black fabric spilled out. It wasn't extravagant, but it *was* elegant—a floor-length gown that was sophisticated without being flashy.

Getting into it, however, proved more difficult than she remembered. Danika twisted awkwardly, arms straining to catch the zipper at her back.

After a few failed attempts and a muttered curse, she finally managed to work it upward. Hardly graceful, but effective.

The flowing fabric settled over her then and she remembered why she'd chosen it: not just for how it looked, but for how it made her feel. It was actually comfortable.

Stepping toward the mirror, she took in the full effect. The vintage pearl necklace, packed on a whim, added a final touch of refinement.

A woman out of place, maybe, but at least she looked the part.

Now came the harder task: believing it. Gowns and glittering jewelry weren't her world. She was more at home in jeans and dusty archives than in an opulent room full of polished strangers.

A memory stirred—gentle as a breeze lifting a curtain. Sometimes the most courageous thing you can do is admit you don't know what you're doing… and try anyway.

Her grandmother's voice. Abigail's daughter.

Danika blinked as her eyes stung unexpectedly. She let out a slow breath, stepped into her black heels, and smoothed the front of her gown.

"Here goes nothing," she whispered.

And with quiet resolve, she opened the door to her room and set off for the gala.

***

The dining room shimmered with quiet grandeur, candlelight glinting off the silverware as a quartet coaxed a delicate tune from their instruments. The tall windows framed the setting sun on the mountains beyond, giving a reddish glow to the linen-draped tables and their centerpieces of fresh flowers.

Guests moved through the room with a kind of quiet elegance—royalty, dignitaries, and stylishly dressed officials exchanging nods and pleasantries in a dozen different languages. There were robes and crowns and formal attire from cultures all over the world. Laughter rose here and there, buffered by the soft clink of champagne flutes and the rustle of expensive fabric.

Danika hovered just inside the entrance, trying to nerve herself to take a few more steps. She scanned the room with forced calm, trying to mask the unease. The dress was quite comfortable, but her shoes were not.

My feet are killing me already.

Everyone here looked perfectly at home, born into this rarefied world where small talk could shape treaties and a smile could signal more than affection. The hypocrisy of it all—diplomacy dressed as decadence—made her a little nauseous.

"If you're looking for an escape hatch, there isn't one." The words were spoken just behind her and were obviously meant for her ears only.

She turned, heart skipping at the timbre of the voice even before she saw the figure. "Don't sneak up on me like that."

"That's my job," Cole said, eyes scanning the room as if looking for threats—or a reason to bolt himself.

Danika's gaze dropped and took in the black tailored suit that hugged his frame with understated perfection. She'd thought he couldn't look any better than he did in a pair of worn jeans—but clearly, she'd underestimated the power of a well-fitting tux.

Taking a deep, shaky breath to calm her nerves, Danika ran her hand down her gown, trying to smooth away her anxiety.

Cole's expression softened. "You have nothing to worry about. You look great."

His words startled her. "I don't feel great, but I appreciate the attempt at a compliment."

He tilted his head, his eyes steady on hers. "It wasn't an attempt."

The look in his eyes was intense, but still, Danika couldn't read them. Did he mean he hadn't been *trying* to compliment her? Or that he had?

He didn't give her time to analyze it. "You can't stand in the doorway all night." Cole put his hand on the small of her back and guided her through the crowd toward a tall table by the windows.

"You have no idea how much I hate gatherings like this," Danika said under her breath as they walked.

"Pretty sure I do, actually," he replied.

As a server passed by with a tray of champagne, Cole grabbed two glasses, handing one to her.

"Here," he said, his tone casual again. "Might make this whole thing a little easier."

A cold beer would be better." Danika lifted the delicate glass, watching the bubbles rise before her gaze drifted to Cole. His expression told her the words stirred memories of that night on the balcony. Good ones. The kind you don't talk about, but never really forget.

Just then, a ripple swept through the crowd, subtle but unmistakable, like wind slicing through tall grass before a storm. Danika turned, her gaze pulled to the grand entrance as heads pivoted and murmurs spread like static.

Oh, boy," she said, a little louder than intended. She resisted the urge to reach for her champagne and take a big gulp.

Beside her, she felt—rather than saw—Cole stiffen. Tension radiated off him. Alert. Guarded. The energy in the room had definitely shifted.

And so had Cole.

Fifty-Five

Peggy stood framed in the doorway, radiant in a form-fitting emerald gown that shimmered like starlight. The jeweled fabric caught each glimmer, tracing her curves in a way that drew every glance without effort. Her arm rested lightly through Julian's, her posture elegant, her smile bright with what seemed like genuine exuberance.

"When she said he invited her to dinner," Danika murmured, "I didn't know she meant *this* one."

Cole's head tilted as he looked down at her. "She told you about that?"

"We ran into each other. She was upset you told her not to go."

Cole didn't respond right away. His eyes stayed locked on the pair as they wove through the gathering, nodding and smiling like a couple in a glossy magazine spread.

"You know darn well he's up to something," he said, voice low and flat.

Danika hesitated. "Maybe. Or maybe we're just too cynical. She looks like she's enjoying herself. She deserves that."

Julian grabbed two glasses off a tray and, after handing one to Peggy, raised his own in a toast, smiling with the easy confidence of a man in control.

Cole's jaw flexed, but he didn't look away. His gaze tracked Peggy across the room with a quiet intensity—protective, yes, but layered with something harder to name. It could have been jealousy. Or guilt. Or perhaps regret?

Or maybe it was just the frustration of watching someone you care about drift too close to something dangerous.

Danika watched him out of the corner of her eye. His expression didn't shift, but his hand moved to his collar, tugging it absently. Tension radiated off him in waves.

He glanced at his watch.

"We've only been here twenty minutes," Danika said, beating him to the punch. She'd just checked the time herself.

"I'm trying to make it to ninety," he muttered, tugging again at his collar like it had shrunk in the last five seconds. "This is a waste of time."

Danika started to say, "That's what I was trying to tell you," but stopped herself. He had enough to worry about. Instead, she kept her voice light as a way to take his mind off Peggy. "We could play, '*What's That Person Doing Here*'?"

"Never heard of it," Cole said.

She tilted her head toward two men in the far corner, deep in conversation. "I'll go first. You see the guy on the left? Definitely a lobbyist trying to sway the other guy to support the new agenda."

Cole followed her gaze. "Close. But he's actually a financier who bankrolls campaigns. My guess is he's trying to bribe the other guy into spreading disinformation to divide the delegates."

Danika sighed. "No fair. You already know who everyone is."

"This game was your idea." He shrugged. "I'm just playing along."

She scanned the room again until her gaze fell on a woman in a sleek blue dress speaking to a silver-haired man. "Okay, those two. She looks like an ambassador. I'm thinking she's here for the right reasons—peace, diplomacy."

Cole gave a soft laugh. "You're not very good at this game."

"Who is she?" Danika forced herself to look in a different direction. She had to conquer her involuntary reactions to this man when he smiled.

He lifted his glass to his lips before answering, but brought it down without drinking. "Artifact hunter from Europe."

"Artifact hunter?" Danika blinked. "That's a thing?"

"Yep. They're hired by private collectors and underground antique dealers to track down rare items."

"Don't tell me she's here looking for the pact." Danika's tone indicated disbelief.

"Definitely. She's active on forums that track every whisper about it."

"There are forums for that?" Her gaze shifted from Cole to the woman.

"You don't get out much, do you?"

"Not into your world, no." She shook her head.

He shrugged. "The mystery behind the pact inflates the value. Some dealers think it's worth tens of millions."

"So we're not just up against politicians and NGO's who are looking for the pact. We're up against treasure hunters, too?"

"Welcome to the summit."

Danika glanced up at him, a quiet awe settling in. While she'd been busy chasing single strands, Cole had a grasp on the entire web. He saw things most people didn't realize were there. And somehow, without ever needing to prove it, he made her feel safer just by standing beside her.

"Would you like a fresh glass, miss?" A waiter interrupted Danika's thoughts as he nodded toward her still-full glass of champagne.

"No, I'm fine, thank you."

Cole waved him away as well. "I'm good."

Danika leaned toward Cole, eyes on a woman to his right engaged in an animated conversation with a rotund gentleman sporting a chest full of medals. “Okay, last one,” Danika said, “so I can redeem myself. That guy she's talking to—he's either a diplomat or he plays one on TV.”

She put her hand over her mouth to cover her smile. His so-called uniform, with the chest full of colorful ribbons, made him look like a caricature from a satirical sitcom.

But Cole didn’t smile. Not this time.

He set his champagne glass down with a soft clink. “That’s General Voss. Retired. Or that’s what his ID badge says.”

Danika straightened. “Military? For real?”

Cole shrugged. “It’s an appointed position in some countries.” He nodded toward the woman. “She sits on the board of an arms logistics firm based out of Luxembourg. One of the 'philanthropic sponsors' of this event.”

Danika’s throat tightened. “So much for peace.”

Cole's voice dropped to a near whisper. “I could point out at least one person at every table tied to intelligence, defense contracts, resource negotiation, or global media.”

“But, it’s a *peace* summit,” Danika said in a soft voice, “for global unity and harmony.”

“We both know Julian didn’t bring people here to make peace. He brought them here to see who’s still loyal and who can be bought.”

“Well, Julian sure knows how to put on a good show,” Danika said, looking around.

Cole nodded. “This is the part that’s for public consumption. The real conference is happening tomorrow behind closed doors.”

“I don’t agree with it, but it’s actually a pretty solid plan,” Danika said.

Cole’s eyes, steely and calm, met hers. “Yep. Nothing masks deception like the hope for peace.”

A glance around the room painted a perfect portrait of goodwill—delegates from every continent, soft music from a string quartet, champagne flutes raised beneath glittering overhead light fixtures. Languages mingled like the laughter, light and effortless. But beneath the polished veneer, one thing was conspicuously absent: the true aim of the man who brought them all here.

Danika gestured toward the appetizer table. "You'd better fuel up while you're here. Sounds like you'll need the energy."

"I'll grab coffee in the office," he said.

"You call that stuff in your office, *coffee*? Is that what keeps you going?"

"These days, yeah."

"Well," she said, swirling the champagne around in her glass, but not drinking it, "don't think you're sneaking out without me. If you disappear, I'm right behind you."

"You mean you're not enjoying yourself?" he asked with mock astonishment.

She smiled. "Let's just say, I'm enjoying the company. Not the event."

Cole's lips twitched into the ghost of a grin. "Now you're talking like a smooth politician. I think you've been hanging out with the wrong people."

He took a small sip of his drink and grimaced. "That's terrible."

"I know." Danika lifted her drink and stared at it. "Where I come from, they'd give you a choice: beer, wine, moonshine..."

Cole fixed his gaze on her and tilted his head inquisitively. "Where do you come from anyway?"

"Virginia."

Something flashed in his eyes. "Really? Where?"

"It's a small town. You've never heard of it." She turned to scan the crowd, thinking the conversation was over.

"Try me." He touched her arm to bring her attention back to the conversation.

She laughed and turned back. "Really? Okay. Lucketts."

She studied his face to see if he recognized the town, but he didn't answer right away. Instead, he squinted over her shoulder, focused on something on the far end of the dining room. "Ten-Four. I'm on it," he said into the mic on his lapel.

"Give me two minutes," he said quietly. "I need to check something quick."

Danika turned, watching him disappear into the blur of tuxedos and champagne flutes. The moment hung strangely unfinished—like a sentence cut off mid-thought.

She stood there awkwardly, hands idle, gaze fixed on the space where he'd been. No one noticed, of course, but she was suddenly unsure where to look or what to do. The laughter and clinking glasses around her only sharpened the silence he'd left behind.

Seeking a reset, Danika slipped through the crowd, past glittering gowns and polished shoes. She exhaled in relief at the quiet hallway beyond the dining room. Sunset Porch—and the lure of fresh air—waited ahead.

Fifty-Six

THE MOMENT THE NIGHT air brushed her skin, something in Danika let go. She stepped onto the Sunset Porch, leaving behind the clink of glasses and the careful rhythm of conversation. Out here, the air was cool and unfiltered—carrying no expectations, no eyes watching. Just space. Just quiet. And for the first time all evening, she could breathe.

Other than a group of people at the far end of the porch, this end was empty. Except for one man.

Dalton Rivers stood alone in the shadows, leaning against the railing in an unbuttoned tux, bow tie still undone. He looked elegant and undone at the same time, like a model on a magazine cover that had tattered pages.

She wasn't sure what to make of him. Elusive yet present. Withdrawn yet perceptive. He was a man who had spent his life being watched, but there was something different about him here. Like he wasn't just hiding from the world, but searching for something himself.

Danika didn't know if he was intentionally ignoring her or just hadn't noticed her yet. They hadn't spoken since their last disastrous interaction, and based on his silence and somberness, Danika had little hope for a reconciliation.

She noticed him glance toward her, as if her own thoughts had disturbed his. Still, he made no move to start a conversation—so she did.

"I'm sorry about the other night," she said, sliding into one of the rocking chairs near him. "I really did just stumble across the information about the film's backlash, not on purpose. I didn't mean anything by it."

He was silent for so long she was afraid he wasn't going to answer. "I'm a little touchy on the subject," he said. "Probably overreacted." He turned and sat on the rail he'd been leaning on, arms crossed, head cocked to the side as he studied her.

That statement only created more questions in Danika's mind. "Touchy over the media's reaction to a movie?" she asked. "Don't you get used to that?"

"Not in this case," he said. "Touchy because they only told half the story."

He paused as if he wasn't sure of the necessity of saying more, then continued. "They rewrote the script the night before shooting the final scene, or at least that's what they told me. Turned what was supposed to be a closing scene into a political firestorm. I was blindsided."

She narrowed her gaze. "And you couldn't say anything?"

"I could. And I did."

"And?" Danika questioned.

"They gave me two choices. Get blacklisted from the industry for breaking my contract at the last minute. Or complete the film."

He stared at the wall over her shoulder. "Getting blacklisted seemed like the end of the world to me at the time, so I completed the film. I kept my name on the rosters and became the poster child for an agenda I never agreed to." He sighed heavily. "And, in some quarters, continue to be the face of it."

Danika heard the tightness in his voice. Regret, maybe even shame. "So you ended up leaving, but on your own terms."

He nodded. "Should have done it years earlier."

Danika could hear the pain in his voice.

Dalton exhaled again as he reached into his pocket. The faint click of metal caught Danika's attention. She turned her head just in time to see him flick open a watch—old and well-worn, its silver casing catching the dim light on the porch.

He checked the time with practiced ease before slipping it back into his pocket.

She sat up a little. "That's beautiful," she said.

Dalton glanced over, lifting a brow at the sudden interest. "This old thing?" He gave a half-smile as he pulled it out of his pocket again. "Had it so long, I tend to forget it's not something people see every day anymore."

Danika reached out before she could stop herself. "May I?"

Dalton hesitated, just for a fraction of a second, before leaning forward and placing it in her hand. The metal was warm from his touch. It was heavier than she expected, the kind of weight that suggested something built to last.

Danika stared at the silver case that gleamed when it caught the light. An intricate pattern of swirling vines and delicate flourishes adorned its surface, common for the Victorian era.

At the center of the design, something else appeared to have been etched—a monogram perhaps? She brought the watch closer and tilted it to the left and right, hoping to decipher the long-lost initials.

When she held it at just the right angle, something locked into place—like a thread had been pulled tight across a century.

"You should have seen that when it wasn't so worn," Dalton said, apparently noticing her look of shock. "The wings seemed to shimmer and almost move in the right light.

Danika tried to ignore the sense of disbelief. She brought the watch up to her eyes again, the outline of a butterfly more distinct now. Was this just a coincidence?

Dalton's expression shifted at her reaction, his easy demeanor giving way to something more observant, more alert.

"What?" he asked, his voice low. "Is something wrong with it?"

Danika swallowed, struggling to keep her composure.

"No." She tried to make her voice sound casual. "It's just so beautiful. Where did you get it?" She tried to keep her hands from trembling, but the watch seemed to pulse against her fingertips, as if trying to tell her what it remembered.

Dalton studied her for a long moment before pushing himself off the railing and taking a seat in the chair beside her. "An antique store." He turned his head to look at her. "Right down the road in New Paltz, actually."

"What a find." Danika tried to keep her voice steady. "Recently?"

Dalton laughed. "No. More like about twenty years ago." He tilted his head. "At least. Maybe closer to twenty-five. I think it was the first time they brought me here."

"Brought you here?" Danika wrinkled her brow.

"Yeah. Wined and dined me. Told me how great I was. I thought I was pretty big stuff back then." He sighed and began to rock. "A long time ago."

Danika nodded and went back to examining the watch. "Such a treasure. Did you get any information about its past owners?"

She waited breathlessly for the answer, even though she doubted he could provide any useful information.

"Oh my." He stopped rocking and squeezed his temples. "They did tell me the owner's name, but I don't remember it now."

Danika's heart fell.

"But I do remember they said he was a Quaker."

"Excuse me?" Danika tried not to sound too stunned. "Did you say a Quaker?"

Dalton leaned forward and eyed her curiously. "Yes. As I recall, the owner passed away, and it went to a sister, and when she died, it ended up at the antique store. Why do you ask?"

"Oh, no reason." Danika scrambled for words. "I mean, I-I guess it's just curious that a Quaker would own such a beautiful watch."

Dalton chuckled. "I always wondered the same thing, but that's what they told me."

"It's nice to have something with so much history." Danika stared at the timepiece in her hand, her mind wandering to Noah. "If the antique store knew who the owner was, then I guess it was from a local."

"I have it written down somewhere," Dalton said. "I've been meaning to ask Mrs. Winslow if she remembers anything about it."

"Mrs. Winslow?"

He glanced over at her. "Yes. You know her?" He chuckled under his breath. "Silly question. Everyone knows her. Anyway, Bill, her late husband, and I were talking about the good old days one night... a long time ago. And he told me about it."

He rocked for a few moments, obviously lost in thought. "I was working on an old movie at the time, and I thought a pocket watch would be a cool thing to have to stay in character." He sighed and leaned back in his chair. "Had it ever since."

Danika shook her head as if that would help clear it. "How did Bill know about it?"

"He's the one who sold it to the antique store." Dalton looked over at her. "The sister of the Quaker who died was his great aunt or something, and he had no use for it. But once he saw my interest, he wanted it to go to a good home."

Danika closed her eyes as more of the threads of the story began to weave together.

"It was a Bible name. I remember that much." Dalton interrupted her thoughts with another memory. "Joshua, maybe?" He sat back in his chair and rocked a few times. "No. That's not right." He shook his head. "Sorry. My memory isn't what it used to be."

Danika tried not to sound too eager. "A Bible name, you say. Let me think." She paused, almost afraid to say the name. "Noah?"

Dalton snapped his fingers and leaned forward. "Noah. Yes, I think that's it." He looked over at her curiously, a smile playing on his lips. "Was that just a lucky guess?"

"Yes." Danika lied. "Just one of the few religious names I could think of."

Dalton stared at the watch in her hand. "I know it's old, but it's something I couldn't live without at this point." He glanced back over at her. "And it makes for an interesting conversation when kids see me using it to tell the time instead of a cell phone."

Danika laughed. "I bet." She raised her eyes to meet his. "Do you mind if I open it?"

"Not at all," he answered, motioning with his hand. "Go right ahead."

With trembling hands, Danika pressed her thumb against the small latch of the watch, and with a soft click, the cover sprang open.

Beneath it, the watch face was a masterpiece of craftsmanship. Delicate sweeping hands pointed to elegant Roman numerals to mark the passage of time. The glass crystal, though slightly scratched, still allowed a clear view, capturing the slow, steady tick of the watch's heart.

"It's exquisite," Danika said under her breath. She glanced over at Dalton. "Have you seen any engravings anywhere?"

Before she had even finished the sentence, she saw the etching along the bottom of the watch, its delicate script visible when held a certain way in the light. She squinted, trying to read the words.

"It says, *Regal wings hold the key to peace."* Dalton noticed her trying to read the well-worn engraving and recited the words for her.

"What does that mean?" Danika looked over at Dalton with hopeful eyes.

"I have no idea. I've always thought maybe it's connected to the butterfly on the front. You know, regal wings."

A shiver ran through Danika as the realization hit her. *Regal, like a Monarch or a King. Regal Wings.* It was just like Noah to speak in riddles. But this wasn't written by Noah. It would have been written by her great-grandmother and *given* to Noah.

Danika tried to remember the wording of his letter Noah had written, thanking her for the beautiful pocket watch and the inscription. She hadn't spent much time thinking about it because they didn't have the watch.

She closed her eyes as she held it in her hand and felt its weight—not just in silver, but in the love and longing that had been carried within it for all these years.

Should she tell Dalton?

She swallowed hard and stared at the watch again. No, not yet. There were too many unanswered questions. Like, why was he here? For the conference?

And anyway, she wouldn't even know where to start.

Danika forced herself to smile. "Well, it sure is beautiful." She leaned toward Dalton to hand him the watch. "They don't make them like this anymore."

Dalton accepted it without breaking eye contact. For the first time since she met him, she saw something flicker in his expression—an unspoken question, as if he wanted to trust her, but wasn't quite sure.

She decided to take a chance because, well, she really had nothing to lose.

"You know how you told me that finding the wrong thing at the right time isn't luck. It's strategy?"

He nodded. "Yeah. Sorry about that. I'm not usually that brutally honest and harsh."

"No, that's okay." Danika cleared her throat. "But don't you think that finding the right thing at the wrong time might be a strategy too?"

"What are you trying to say?" He tilted his head.

Danika met his gaze. "Why would Julian tell you I'm a journalist? It's almost like he's been watching. And wanted to make sure you stopped talking to me."

Dalton leaned in, eyes steady on hers. He let out a quiet breath and leaned back again, the chair creaking beneath him. "You've got a point."

A swell of music drifted through the porch doors just then—violins and laughter mingling in the air—causing her heart to jolt. She'd been out here longer than she meant to.

"Oh, I need to get back inside," she said. "You're attending, right?"

He frowned. "I'm not dressed like this for my health." He turned away and stared at the dark sky. "Pretending doesn't come as easily as it used to."

"Well, for the record, you look great."

He turned, a look of surprise lighting his face. "I'm only half dressed."

Danika nodded. "I know. Reminds me of that poster you did—the one with the expensive bourbon and the don't mess-with-me stare."

As soon as the words left her mouth, Danika felt a flush rise. Too much. Too familiar. She cleared her throat and stepped back. "Anyway, I'll see ya."

Something shifted in Dalton's expression—a flicker of recognition, as if he was starting to see her as an ally instead of a threat. He watched her a second longer than necessary, then gave a slight nod, as if filing it away for later.

Fifty-Seven

DANIKA HAD ONLY JUST stepped back into the dining room when she spotted Cole rejoining the crowd as well, his expression unreadable.

He crossed the room quickly, weaving through clusters of guests with ease—looking like he belonged, yet it was clear he stood apart. It wasn't just the tuxedo, but the way he carried himself. Like a man with nothing to prove.

When he reached her, he didn't speak right away. Just gave a slight nod, as if to say *I'm back.*

"You'll never believe what I just held in my hand," Danika said.

Cole raised his eyebrows and leaned in close. "Really? Because you'll never believe what I just found."

Before they could converse any further, a familiar voice chimed in behind them.

"Hey, guys! I didn't know you were coming to this."

Danika straightened and threw an arm around Peggy. "Girl, you look stunning."

"So do you," she said before turning her attention to Cole. She eyed him warily, uncertain of his reaction to her presence. "I don't think I've ever seen you in a tux, Cole. You look like you fit right in."

"*Sure* I do." He bent down a little and looked straight into her eyes. "You know I can tell when you're lying, right?"

She laughed. "I'm not lying. He looks great, doesn't he, Danika?"

Danika wanted to say he looked pretty good in anything, but just nodded.

"Where's your date?" Cole's head, as usual, was on a swivel.

"He's not my date exactly," Peggy tried to defend herself.

"You came with him, right?"

"Yes, I came with him," Peggy said. "He's right over there talking to some gentlemen I don't know. I thought I'd come over and say hello while they're discussing politics."

"Is that what they're discussing?" Cole leaned in a little, obviously wanting more information.

Peggy shrugged. "I have no idea. When they start talking about deals and summits, it's all Greek to me." She flashed them both a smile.

Cole nodded calmly as if no longer interested, but his eyes scanned and rescanned the room until they settled on Julian standing with his hand on another man's shoulder. It didn't look like a friendly gesture, but more like a power move.

"Is something wrong?" Peggy stared up at him.

"No." His gaze flicked over to Danika for just a heartbeat. "Everything's fine."

Peggy turned and waved at someone across the room. "Well, maybe I'll see you guys later. Make sure you stop by our table and say hello to Julian. Okay?"

Danika successfully avoided rolling her eyes and even managed a smile and a nod. "Of course."

As soon as Peggy stepped away, Cole pulled out his phone and sent a text.

Danika's gaze drifted around the room where everyone seemed perfectly at ease, laughing and chatting, their movements as graceful as the waltz playing in the background. But she couldn't shake the growing sense that something was off.

Cole appeared just as unsettled. He hadn't spoken in the last few minutes, but his posture—the slight tension in his shoulders, the alertness—told her he was seeing something she wasn't.

Danika was just about to ask him what he'd found when he lifted his mic to his lips. "Go ahead. What do you have?"

Danika watched as his expression shifted, his brow furrowing. He turned slightly away, the noise of the room making it hard to catch his words. But the tone—short, clipped—spoke volumes.

Danika straightened, her attention fully on him now.

Cole's eyes swept the room with the casual rhythm of habit, but Danika recognized the slight narrowing of his gaze. He wasn't admiring the fashions or furnishings. He was concentrating on specific security points.

Shifting his stance, he lifted a hand to the discreet mic clipped beneath his collar.

"Taggert, do you have eyes on Julian's detail?" he murmured, barely moving his lips. A pause and then, "You checked the exterior angles?"

He raised his head, eyes half-closed, as if squinting to see what lay ahead, just out of view. "Ten-four."

"What's going on?" Danika asked, lowering her champagne glass.

"Julian's entire security team is gone," Cole said, his voice low but tense.

"Gone where?"

His eyes revealed a hint of warning, though his voice remained calm. "That's the problem. They're not at their assigned posts. And they're not on any of the camera feeds."

Danika followed his gaze across the dining room—lavish decor, flowing gowns, champagne, music, and laughter. On the surface, it was a flawless evening. But now that he'd said it, she saw it too: the absence.

"I thought I saw one of his guys by the door a little while ago," Danika said. "At least it was a man I've always seen hanging around Julian."

Cole's jaw tensed. "They were definitely in place. I saw them fifteen minutes ago—one by the kitchen, two near the entrance. Right where I placed them."

Danika frowned. "Where you placed them?"

He nodded. "I spent an hour walking them through this room yesterday. Entry points, crowd flow, blind zones. I gave them contingency plans for two different breach scenarios."

Her brow furrowed. "So where did they go?"

Cole's gaze scanned the dining room again. The guests were laughing and posing for photos in front of a floral arch with the flags from the different nations represented at the peace conference. Nothing about it looked wrong.

Which only made it worse.

"It's almost like they left when Julian entered," Cole said, thinking back. "Like that was the trigger."

Danika looked at him, stunned. "That doesn't make sense. Why leave when the person they're assigned to protect just arrived?"

Cole didn't answer right away. She saw the shift in his expression, a flicker of realization behind his steady exterior. "They know all of the security protocols for this room. They know where my men are, and they know what our focus is."

A chill laced down Danika's spine. The string quartet played on, unaware.

They stood in silence, their eyes roving over the glittering crowd. Servers wove through the tables with trays of drinks and hors d'oeuvres. Guests mingled and laughed. Everything seemed perfect.

Yet everything was undeniably wrong.

Their eyes met as they seemed to come to the same conclusion at the same time.

"So Julian went to all this trouble to host a gala of this scale—only to have his security detail vanish almost as soon as it began," Cole said.

"And he made sure we both attended," Danika added.

For a beat, the room seemed to spin, the glittering lights and elegant guests receding into the background. The music and chatter all faded into a dull hum, leaving only the sharp focus of the trick Julian has pulled.

"His men are looking for the pact," Cole said. "And they made sure the right eyes are looking the wrong way."

Cole paused a moment as another transmission came into his ear, which he repeated to Danika. "Lake Lounge cameras showed movement eight minutes ago. That sector's footage has been on partial blackout since 7:25."

They didn't speak again. They didn't need to. Cole's hand found her arm, firm but calm, as they drifted toward the exit, trying not to draw attention.

Outwardly, they appeared composed, like a couple who'd decided they wanted some peace and quiet... alone.

But inside, they knew, the real race had begun.

Fifty-Eight

THE ECHO OF LAUGHTER and clinking glass from the gala still lingered in her ears as Danika unlocked the door to her room, leaving the glittering illusion of peace behind them.

She kicked off her heels as she walked and headed to the satchel of letters and notes, sliding the clasp from her hair as she sat down.

"This is everything." Cole spread the collection of notes, diagrams, and photocopies across the desk. "Every clue, every connection we've pieced together so far."

A flash lit the room to punctuate his statement, followed by a low growl that started as a gentle rumble and ended with an earsplitting bang. Both Danika and Cole's heads turned to the windows.

"You order a storm as a contingency plan?" Danika asked.

"Just to keep things interesting," he said without missing a beat.

He paced, tossing his jacket over a chair and loosening his tie as he walked. Now and then, he would speak into his mic, reminding Danika that there was an entire conversation going on in his ear at the same time he was reading.

She leaned forward, eyes sweeping over the scattered notes—dates, names, phrases, locations—everything they'd uncovered about the pact and where it might be hidden. As she studied the mess of paper, her fingers moved impulsively to her hair, separating the elegant French braid she'd worn for the gala. The polished style wasn't meant for long hours and deep thinking. Loosened, it felt like shedding a layer of discomfort.

Staring at the documents, she thought back over the last two weeks—at the mysteries, the clues, and the trail that seemed to beckon her forward into a past waiting to be remembered. But even with everything laid out in front of her, the full picture remained just out of reach.

They didn't speak. They didn't need to. They both knew they were running out of time. Danika felt it in the air—electric with urgency and thick with fear and adrenaline.

She groaned with frustration at the lack of progress and dropped her head forward, massaging her sore neck before flinging her hair back with a sharp toss. Then she turned back to the pile of papers, rifling through them with renewed focus.

Out of the corner of her eye, she noticed Cole staring at her.

She glanced over. "What?"

He blinked, snapping out of a thought. "I just—" He hesitated before giving a small shrug. "I've never seen you with your hair down."

She reached up, smoothing the waves that cascaded over her shoulders and down her back. "Oh. Yeah. I'm sure it's a mess." She ran her fingers through it, trying to tame the waves left by the braids.

His gaze lingered a moment longer than necessary before he stood and began pacing, fingers gripping a letter as though trying to hold onto the connection it offered. He paused a moment, leaning over the back of an armchair, and read aloud.

"*A thing shaped by care will outlast its maker, just as the truths we hold dear will outlive the voices that tried to silence them.*" He looked over at her. "This was written in his letter about the brooch, but I think he's talking about the pact."

Danika nodded. "I agree."

"*The rhythm of peace is measured not in words but in time*," he murmured, seeming to concentrate on each word. "*Remember the fireplace where we shared more than a stolen glance...*"

Danika exhaled, her brow furrowed. "We've concentrated on clocks and never considered the fireplaces." She glanced over the top of the letter she was holding. "He does mention fireplaces more than once."

Cole looked up, his eyes filled with a vivid intensity. "Do you know how many fireplaces there are in this building?"

"Yes, literally hundreds," Danika said. "But we could narrow it down to the parlors."

Cole sat down and put his elbows on his knees. "If we narrowed it down to just Lake Lounge, including Albert's office, and the Parlor, that would be five," Cole said.

"Five?"

"There are two in both of the big parlors, plus one in Albert's office."

Danika nodded, recalling now the fireplaces in the corner of the room. "And they are massive. Some of the mantels are over my head." She stared at the wall, deep in thought. "But Lake Lounge and Albert's office seem to be the rooms Julian is focused on."

Cole shook his head, sighing. "It sounds poetic, but it's vague. If Noah was leaving clues, he didn't make them obvious."

She tapped the letter again, her frustration mounting. "Read the rest of the sentence in that letter, though. It says, "*where the heart of Mohonk beats in steady rhythm with time.*"

Then, her finger slid down the list of notes and settled on one they had questioned. Searching through the stack by date, she pulled the letter and began reading the delicate script. "*The measure of peace is not in time, but in truth.*"

"We have to make a decision and go with it," Cole said, interrupting her. "We have to act. Tonight. *Now.*"

"Okay." Danika paced and groaned. "Noah wasn't a politician. He was a craftsman. His mind wouldn't work like the others. He'd think in terms of objects. Things meant to last."

"So what are you thinking?"

"The rhythm of peace. Time. A clock."

He nodded. "I agree."

"The most logical one would be the parlor where he and Abigail spent time. It was also where the conferences were held, so it would be hidden in plain sight."

"And it's the parlor with the portraits of Albert and Eliza, which he directly referenced as a meeting place."

Danika leaned forward and excitedly put her hand on Cole's knee as another thought came into her mind. "He talks about that parlor a lot. Maybe that's the place where they exchanged letters the last few years of their relationship. They were looking for someplace closer, more convenient—"

She stopped in mid-sentence and removed her hand when she saw Cole glance down and stare at it.

"That would be just like Noah to hide it right under their noses," Cole said, smoothly. "And that clock's been there since 1904."

Danika did a double-take. "How would you know something random like that?"

He pulled his phone out of his pocket and scrolled through some photos as she watched. He enlarged one and handed it to her. "I took some photos a few days ago of objects on our list. The bronze plaque is hard to read."

He enlarged it a little more and read:

Presented to Mr. & Mrs. Albert K. Smiley by the Tenth Lake Mohonk Conference on International Arbitration. June 1-3, 1904. In grateful recognition of their devoted services to the cause of universal brotherhood and peace.

"Back up a minute." Danika pointed to Cole's phone. "Pull up that wide-angle photo of the clock."

He scrolled through and handed it to her. "What are we looking for?"

She zoomed in, then turned the screen toward him. "The bust. Chief Saconaquado. It stands next to the grandfather clock."

Cole leaned in, squinting. "I've seen it so often, it just seems to be a part of the room."

Danika sifted through the pile of letters. "I'm just now putting two and two together." She pulled out a worn page and handed it to him.

> *In moments of weakness, I return again and again to one image: the soul of honor. Not a man of my blood, nor of my faith, but one whose story has long been told.*

She paused as Cole read, letting the words sink in. "I remember reading that letter, but it didn't really make any sense to me," he said.

"Do you have any other photos that include the bust?"

Cole swiped through his camera roll and stopped to enlarge the screen. "The plaque says the bust was donated in 1888—gifted to Albert and Eliza by attendees of the Lake Mohonk Conference of Friends of the Indians."

Cole returned to the letter and read it out loud.

> *I have drawn strength from his example more times than I can name, which is why I placed my trust in him once more—to keep watch. He will stand guard over what should not be destroyed, and protect what must one day be found.*

"The 'soul of honor' he's talking about is Chief Saconaquado," Danika said.

"He watches over the grandfather clock."

"It's there. It's got to be!" Danika headed for the door, but Cole stopped her.

"Wait."

She turned, her hair swinging out behind her, long and loose.

"It won't do any good to go down there," he said, "and we'll just cause suspicion."

"What do you mean?"

"He talks about a key. We haven't found it yet."

Danika sat down and put her face in her hands. "Why do you always have to think ahead?"

"This is solvable." Cole still wore a determined look on his face. "We can do this."

"Always the optimist," Danika murmured, as she coiled her hair into a knot and stuck a clip and hair pin through it.

"When I took this photo, I looked at the clock pretty closely," he said.

"And?"

"I found two holes in the base. Not like a keyhole exactly. But I couldn't tell why they were there."

"You're saying it doesn't look like a keyhole, but you think that's what it might be?"

"Not getting my hopes up, but I don't see why else they would be there." Cole spoke as if undeterred by the fact they didn't have a key. "Remember the letter where Noah thanked Abigail for the pocket watch?"

"Kind of?" She looked up, her mind running through the words of hundreds of letters.

It said, *"You have seen the truth in the piece I gave you."*

Danika began to pace, the wheels in her mind spinning, grasping, until at last they clicked on a memory.

She spun around and almost screamed the words. "Oh, I forgot to tell you!"

"Forgot to tell me what?"

"I ran into Dalton on the porch when you stepped out." She ran out of breath and gasped for air, unable to continue.

"Slow down," Cole commanded, holding onto both of her arms. "You ran into Dalton *and*...?"

"And he had a pocket watch."

"*The* pocket watch?" He bent down and looked directly into her eyes. "Did it have an inscription? What did it say?"

"It said..." Danika had to close her eyes and take a deep breath before she could remember the exact phrasing. "It said, *'Regal wings hold the key to peace.'*"

"Regal wings," Cole repeated under his breath.

"Dalton thought it might have something to do with being regal. Or royalty."

"Or regal, as in Monarch?" Cole slowly lifted his head.

"Regal wings," he repeated as they both began to pace. They moved in opposite directions, crisscrossing the room, until they both stopped at the same moment, eyes locking.

"The brooch," they said in unison.

"He crafted it with his own two hands." Danika grabbed his arm. He said it's a gift that *holds the secret to history itself.*"

Cole's expression shifted from uncertainty to understanding at the same time as hers did.

"Get it." He grabbed his jacket and headed for the door, glancing over his shoulder. "I'll meet you in the parlor. Don't take the elevator. Don't talk to anyone. And bring a flashlight."

And then he was gone.

Fifty-Nine

Danika grabbed the brooch and looked around frantically for her flashlight. *Why in the world did she need a flashlight?* When her eyes spotted the yellow shaft on the mantel, she grabbed it and took off down the hall, racing as fast as her tight-fitting gown would allow.

All of the clues and the eye-wearying reading over the past two weeks had come to this moment. Did the pact exist? And if it did, who would find it first?

If Julian did, the widespread ramifications could result in hundreds of thousands of deaths over a span of years. The weight of that thought almost crippled her.

She'd made it to the third floor on the slate stairs when lightning flashed outside, followed by a loud clap of thunder.

Then sudden darkness.

She only paused a moment to turn on the flashlight, but a smile lifted. *Cole.* He'd somehow timed the outage with split-second precision to the thunder clap.

She was beginning to think he had powers beyond the scope of the head of security.

The sound of muffled voices brought her back to the task at hand. Probably Julian's team, one floor below, reacting to the power outage while searching for the document. Whatever emergency Cole had orchestrated to occupy them seemed to be working, but Danika knew they had only minutes to find what they were looking for and return to the gala.

When she reached the parlor door, she found it slightly ajar. Slipping inside, she pushed it closed and swept the room with her flashlight beam. Cole was crouched beside the tall grandfather clock, examining it intently.

"You made it," he said without looking up, his voice low and steady.

Danika held up the flashlight, the beam steady in her trembling hand. "You could have warned me about the lights."

"I did. I told you to bring a flashlight."

Danika shook her head and glanced around at the utter darkness. "I mean, you went all the way—emergency lighting and everything."

"That's how I operate," Cole said calmly. "All or nothing."

Turning her attention back to the task at hand, Danika focused her light, first on the bust of Chief Saconaquado, and then on the clock. She had to admit the electrical outage was a brilliant move that would buy them some time. Julian and all of his associates would be needed in the dining room to help with the guests.

"Nice touch with the timing of the outage, by the way," Danika whispered.

Cole was already concentrating on the clock, but gave a short answer. "Thanks."

She tried to quell her racing heart and anxious nerves by talking in a hushed whisper. "Don't tell anyone I said so, but I'm kind of *impressed*."

"Really?" He stopped and turned toward her. "Then you'd be surprised by the other superpowers I have."

Danika felt her cheeks grow warm and wondered if this was one of them. Maybe he'd been taught in the military how to deliver light-hearted comments in the middle of a life-or-death mission to calm nerves, lower heart rates, and sharpen the focus of the panicked people around him.

What kind of man would act as casually as a plumber inspecting a leak, when he was really hunting a hidden pact that could alter the course of global politics for generations to come?

As for her, she could barely breathe.

"Here." Danika stepped closer, pulling the brooch from her pocket and holding it out to him. "Now, please tell me this isn't just some wild guess."

Cole took the brooch from her with deliberate care, his flashlight beam flickering over its intricate design—the butterfly wings delicate yet strong, the craftsmanship exquisite.

"Here are the holes I found the other day," he whispered, pointing to a small, oddly shaped opening near the base under the clock's glass side panel.

Danika pulled her gown up high enough to crouch beside him, aiming her flashlight where he pointed. He was right. It just looked like two small holes, not something you would notice if you weren't looking for it—and definitely not a keyhole.

"It's a long shot," he admitted, angling the brooch so the butterfly wings caught the faint glow of the flashlight. "But *regal wings hold the key* is too specific to ignore."

He pressed lightly on the base of the brooch, testing its construction. When nothing happened, he examined the wings more closely. "The wings and the antennas move a little," he muttered, his fingers deftly exploring the mechanism.

"I noticed that, but just thought it was the way Noah made it."

Danika leaned closer, her breath catching as Cole applied more gentle pressure to the wings. Did you ever try squeezing them together like this?"

She held her breath. Waiting.

Nothing happened.

"I can feel it giving," Cole said, "but it won't quite—"

He pressed harder, grimacing at the effort. And then they both heard a soft, but unmistakable, *click*.

"Something moved," Danika whispered.

Cole nodded. The wings had indeed moved, revealing two small, protruding pegs where the brooch's delicate design had hidden them.

Speechless and disbelieving, Danika grabbed Cole's arm, not realizing that her fingernails were sinking into his flesh.

"You need to let go of my arm, Dani," he said calmly, before leaning down toward the holes. "Concentrate. Focus. Shine your light down here."

Cole turned the brooch in his hand, aligning the pegs with the holes in the clock. He hesitated for just a moment before inserting it.

For a breathless second, nothing happened. Then, she heard another soft click.

Danika exhaled a shaky breath and squeezed his shoulder. "It worked."

Cole didn't respond immediately. He worked on prying open a door that had not been tested for more than one hundred years.

"It's stuck," he said. "It wiggles a little, but I can't get it to budge."

Danika looked around wildly, then removed the hairpin from her head, sending some of her hair tumbling down her back again. "Does this help?"

Cole took the pin and jammed it into the narrow groove between the door and the clock. He stuck it in the top and got that to move, but when he stuck it in the bottom, the top got tight again.

"We're running out of time," Danika whispered. "How long will the lights stay out?"

"Till I tell them to come back on," Cole said, concentrating on the door. "But the longer they're off, the more suspicious Julian will become."

He hesitated, then glanced back at her. "Let me borrow one of those fingernails that just drew blood on my arm."

Before she could react, he caught her hand and tugged her down under him.

"Wait—hang on." Danika hiked her gown up even higher over her hips. "I'm wearing a freaking evening gown, in case you didn't notice."

Unfazed, he shifted her into position beneath him, bracing himself over her with both hands. "Oh, I noticed," he said, as he pushed away the excess, getting his hand tangled in the spill of fabric and grumbling under his breath.

"Can you get your nail in there to pry from this side while I work the other?"

Danika exhaled as his weight pushed down on her. She found the tiny crevice and stuck her nail in the gap as far as she could. "It's moving a little," she said, gasping for breath now. "Wait. I can get my finger in a little bit more now."

"Turn your flashlight off. Quick." Cole's voice was calm but carried an edge of urgency. "They're on the move again."

Danika fumbled with the switch. Wedged under Cole against the clock with only one hand free, it felt like eternity. Finally, the room went dark.

Seconds later, footsteps approached. One seemed to be coming up the steps, and one from down the hall.

Danika held her breath as they paused just outside the door.

"Did you find the source yet?"

"No. We're in contact with the house security team. They're trying to figure it out. They think it's a lightning strike."

"Pretty suspicious if you ask me," one of them said.

"Keep moving and keep your eyes open," the other said before their footsteps receded.

Danika's eyes were shut tight, her focus razor-sharp. Even in total darkness, she kept working—pressing her fingernail into the narrow seam of the hidden compartment, prying and wiggling despite the sharp sting that shot through her finger. It felt like her nail might tear completely off, but she didn't stop.

"On the count of three," Cole whispered. "Give it everything you've got."

"One... two... *three.*"

Gritting her teeth, Danika drove her nail into the crack with all her strength. For a heartbeat, nothing happened—then a faint click broke the silence, and the panel popped open.

They both froze until Danika withdrew her hand and shook it. "*Owww,*" she whined. "That *hurt.*"

"Should I call an ambulance?"

Danika wiggled her way out from between his arms so he could reach into the compartment. "I guess I'll live," she said, leaning down, her head right next to his, her entire body shaking with anticipation as he reached into the compartment.

"Is there something there?" she whispered, her voice trembling with expectation.

"Yes." Cole paused, taking a deep breath as if to add to the suspense. "Cobwebs."

Danika reacted by conking him on the shoulder with her flashlight and then shining the light on his hand as he withdrew a small bundle wrapped in aged, faded cloth.

Before they could inspect it, heavy footsteps reached their ears, moving fast from the floor below them.

Without a word, they both switched off their flashlights. At the same time, Cole grabbed her, pulling her back into the shadows between the clock and the fireplace, completely shielding her body with his.

"It's dark in there," someone said.

"Check it anyway," came the reply. "Julian's flipping out."

The quiet was cut clean as the door eased open, deliberate and cold like the sinister cracking of ice on a frozen lake.

Danika concentrated on the steady rhythm of Cole's heartbeat against her cheek—strong, calm, steady, unshakable.

But when the flashlight beam swept into the room, she shut her eyes tight, pretending that would make her invisible.

The light passed once; then swung back.

She didn't move. She couldn't. Cole's arm around her was iron-solid, steadying her as her pulse thundered in her ears—so loudly, she was certain it would give them away.

The beam lingered on the clock—merciless, precise, unforgiving. One second. Then two. It swept the clock slowly from top to bottom.

Then, bottom to top.

Danika braced, waiting for it to scan left to right—straight onto them—but it didn't come.

"Told you," one of the men muttered. "That's the clock we're supposed to pick up tomorrow, but there's nothing here."

The door slid shut.

The footsteps faded.

Danika exhaled, only then realizing how tightly she'd clung to Cole. Without his arm around her, she might have passed out.

"You okay?" Cole whispered, his breath gentle against her temple.

Danika nodded as Noah's words returned like a whisper through the darkness—words she'd never dared to believe until now:

"Trust that God will reveal in His good Time the truth that not all things lost are truly gone, and not all things hidden are beyond your reach."

Sixty

"Now what?" Danika whispered, her brain running on equal parts adrenaline and fear, thoughts colliding faster than she could catch them. "Where do we hide it?"

"I could take it to my office and post a guard," Cole said, already thinking ahead.

He paused. "No—that won't work. There are security feeds trained on the hallway. Julian would have access to them. He'd know the moment we stepped through the door."

Danika shook her head. "Then it can't be your office. And I don't trust anyone else to have access anyway. Julian's grip on this place runs too deep."

She hesitated, then added, "Let's put it in my room."

Cole exhaled, weighing the risks. "That's not safe either. He's already used a master key to get in once. And with the power out, your door magnet won't hold."

Danika's mind raced. Then her eyes sharpened. "There's a place. In my room. I thought about hiding the letters there earlier. If we move quickly, it could work."

Cole studied her for a beat. "You're sure?"

"I'm sure. But we'll need tape," she said. "And we should make an appearance in the dining room. If we vanish, it'll raise flags."

"I was thinking the same thing," he said. "And we don't have long. If Julian finds out the pact is in play, he won't sit quietly."

He started moving. "I'll grab the tape. Don't stop for anyone. Don't open the door for anyone but me. I'll knock twice and then twice more. Go!"

Danika clicked on her flashlight and moved toward the door. Once Cole slid it open, she took off as fast as her gown would allow through the dark hall and up the stairs. She didn't meet anyone and hadn't expected to, considering the darkness.

When she got inside, she snapped off her flashlight and waited for Cole in complete darkness. She breathed a sigh of relief when she heard footsteps and started moving toward the door in the darkness. She heard one, two, three knocks and placed her hand on the doorknob. She was getting ready to open it when she remembered Cole had said two knocks and two knocks. She held her breath.

"Danika, are you in there?" The voice sounded frustrated.

It was Julian.

He knocked again. This time louder. More serious. More threatening. Like he was using his fist.

She held her breath, petrified. Did he have a master key card on him? Without the magnetic lock, he could walk right in. Surely he could hear her beating heart through the door.

She waited. Terrified. Trembling with fear.

Breathe, she told herself. *Just breathe.*

He pounded on the door again, even harder, like he was trying to break it down, then muttered something under his breath she couldn't make out.

Danika exhaled—slow, shaky. Maybe he was giving up.

She strained to hear his footsteps retreat, but none came.

Pure overwhelming panic gripped her again. *What is he doing? Searching for a key? Calling someone?*

She backed away from the door, inch by inch, careful not to trip in the darkness. If she could make it to the bedroom, maybe she could hide.

But does that door even lock? She'd never checked.

Suddenly, the latch jiggled. He was trying again.

She froze, too afraid to move.

Then more silence—followed by Julian's voice, muffled and low. "She's not here. I don't have the master key on me. I'm on my way back."

Be careful, Cole, she thought, heart still racing. Don't run into him.

Finally, after what felt like forever, his footsteps faded.

And not long after came a—

Knock. Knock.

Knock. Knock.

She bolted for the door.

"Julian was here," she whispered.

"I noticed," Cole said. "He's suspecting us. We need to get back down there and pretend we were never gone."

"Here," he said, hitting her in the arm in the dark. "Put this in your lockbox."

Danika reached out and felt the small bundle of papers. "What is it?" she whispered.

"Just a bunch of papers. If they break into your lockbox, maybe it will get them to move on."

Before she moved toward the lockbox, Danika grabbed Cole's hand and led him to the fireplace as he clicked on his small penlight. "Feel this lip?" She guided his fingers along the mantel. Even in the dim light, she saw Cole's smile.

"Perfect." He removed the historic document from inside his tux and a plastic bag from his pocket, sliding the bundle in. Then he securely attached the papers to the lip of the mantel with tape he pulled out of his pocket. Intruders could tear this room apart, but they would never see this hiding spot.

Danika used her light only when necessary to stash the papers he'd given her into the lockbox. Then she returned to his side, twisting her hair back up into a bun and securing it with a hair clip.

"Hurry. We need to go. We're running out of time."

Danika left her flashlight in the room and followed the small light of Cole's key chain. They didn't speak as they raced down the hall. Only when they could see the dim glow of temporary lighting in the dining room did Cole speak.

"Pretend you were in the ladies' room, okay? You stayed there because you didn't know what was happening." He released her arm and disappeared down the hall before she could respond.

Danika took a breath and steadied herself, stepping into the dim glow cast by an assorted arrangement of emergency solar lights. She barely made it to the door before she saw movement ahead.

A flashlight beam cut through the darkness and hit her full in the face.

"Danika? Is that you?"

"Julian!" She stepped forward, catching his arm. "What's going on? Why did the lights go out? Was it a lightning strike?"

She kept her voice high and anxious, praying he wouldn't look down and notice she was barefoot. In her haste to return, she'd forgotten to put her shoes back on.

Julian's brow furrowed, but he didn't seem surprised to see her. "We're not sure yet. I told everyone to stay in the dining room. We've placed emergency lighting in there."

"I was in the restroom—"

"I cleared this restroom more than fifteen minutes ago," he interrupted, his voice sharp now. He angled his flashlight toward her. "I was looking for you."

An anxious pulse hammered at the base of Danika's throat. "N-no... not this one," she stammered. "This one was crowded. I went to the one farther down the hall. I got turned around when the lights went out. It was pitch black—I thought it was safer to stay put."

She knew it sounded flimsy, but the way her voice trembled added some authenticity. "It was terrifying."

Just then, the lights flickered and snapped back on. A collective murmur of relief rippled through the building. Laughter and low voices began to rise again, like tension slowly evaporating.

Julian lowered the flashlight and gave her a long, unreadable look. "That was... interesting." His gaze narrowed. "Did you change your hairstyle while you were in the restroom?"

Danika flushed. She lifted a hand to her hair. "I—I wasn't used to the way I had it, so I took it down. I was trying to fix it when the lights went out." She gave a small, sheepish smile. "I hope I don't look too much like I crawled out of a closet."

Julian didn't smile back. His eyes drifted toward the dining room doors, where Cole was now helping an older woman into a chair. Julian's jaw ticked once before he turned back.

"I'm surprised you didn't text Cole for help," he said. "You two looked... quite cozy earlier."

Danika didn't miss a beat. "I did. He told me to stay where I was. He was busy trying to help guests and figure out what was going on."

Julian gave a slow nod, but his expression stayed unreadable. "Yes, I need to ask him about what was going on, too. He should have had a contingency plan for something like this."

"I guess he must have," Danika said. "The outage lasted less than thirty minutes. Everyone seems fine."

He eyed her thoughtfully. "Yes, I guess you're right. Let's get back inside before people start to drift."

He turned without waiting and strode toward the dining room, already slipping back into the role of host. As they entered, he raised his voice with practiced ease.

"Ladies and gentlemen—thank you for your patience. Power has been restored, and there's no further concern. Please, help yourselves to food and drink, and enjoy the evening."

The quartet picked up right where they'd left off, the same melody floating through the air as if nothing had happened.

Danika slipped into a seat at a nearby table, her nerves vibrating beneath the surface. When she caught a glimpse of her ragged, broken nail, she lowered her hands discreetly to her lap.

They were back in place. For now.

But she could feel it in her gut: Julian hadn't bought a word of it.

If that were true, the real show was just beginning.

Sixty-One

Danika sat alone, acutely aware she needed to make a move before anyone, especially Julian, noticed she wasn't wearing shoes. Around her, the mood had shifted back to celebratory. Laughter returned. The low hum of conversation rose again, treating the blackout like nothing more than a charming inconvenience.

She let her gaze drift across the room and found Cole.

He stood near a table of dignitaries, shaking hands, smiling at something someone said. He appeared completely relaxed and composed as though nothing out of the ordinary had happened.

Like he wasn't hiding the most dangerous secret in the room.

Danika knew it was an act—smoke and mirrors for Julian's benefit—but it still impressed her. The ease with which he slipped into a role, the composure he carried while everything around them teetered on the edge of collapse, was striking.

Seeming to sense her gaze, he glanced up, and their eyes met. No signal. No words. But he passed a message with his eyes.

Go.

Danika rose, casually adjusting her gown to sweep over her bare toes. Every movement was controlled. Measured. She walked at a calm pace toward the door, resisting the urge to glance back. She was being watched—if not directly, then certainly on video. The last thing she could afford was to look like she was fleeing.

Somehow she made it back to her suite without incident, but the moment the door clicked shut behind her, her composure cracked.

A tremor moved through her as if her body finally registered the danger they'd skirted. Her hands shook. Her breath came fast and shallow. Just knowing what was hidden inside this room made the air feel heavier, the walls closer.

She paced. Checked the hidden bundle once. Then again. And again. Her mind wouldn't stop spinning.

Is that really the best place? Should I move it? What if Julian comes here first? What if he already knows?

She sat on the edge of the bed, elbows on her knees, head in her hands. She couldn't think straight—too much adrenaline, too little sleep. Her nerves were shot. Her judgment clouded.

She had no idea how much time had passed before her phone chirped with a message from Cole: *Meet me in Cliff View Parlor...* ASAP.

Danika frowned. *That's strange. He usually calls it SecHQ.*

But the ASAP made her heart pound. Had something happened? Without thinking another thought, she slipped on her shoes and hurried down the hall.

***

Hopping clumsily down the short set of steps in her gown, Danika ran to the end of the hall and opened the door, wondering briefly why she hadn't been stopped by one of Cole's men.

Inside, Cole stood to her right, tux jacket unbuttoned, looking slightly disheveled and flanked by two men.

A tremor of fear tickled her spine at the atmosphere in the room, an instinctual fear, not reasoned.

"I came as fast as I could," she said to Cole, confused by his lack of greeting and emotion.

"I told you she would be here any minute." A voice from behind a desk jerked Danika's attention to the other side of the room.

Julian sat with his feet propped up, looking relaxed and in control.

"What's going on?" For the first time, Danika realized the two other men in the room weren't part of Cole's team.

"I got a text from you," she said, looking at him with a confused expression. He merely nodded toward Julian.

"Oh, I borrowed Cole's phone," he said, bringing his feet down to the floor with a loud thud. "That was from me." He lifted himself from the chair and walked toward her.

Danika's instinct was to turn and run, and that's what she started to do. But she'd hardly moved before being halted by an iron grip on her wrist.

"I want the pact." Julian's expression was calm, but his eyes were black—bottomless, unreadable. Something in them made her take another step back, despite his firm hold.

"Let her go." Cole's tone was commanding enough that Julian released his hold, but Danika noticed how the two men beside him appeared ready to step in—shoulders tense, eyes sharp, like they were just waiting for a signal from Julian to subdue Cole if needed.

Julian didn't look at them. He kept his gaze on her, a faint, unsettling smile tugging at the corner of his mouth.

Danika smoothed her gown and straightened. "What pact?" she asked, proud of the steady tone she managed. From the corner of her eye, she thought she saw Cole do a double-take at her composure.

Julian's mouth curved into something between amusement and contempt. "Now's not the time for games," he said. "You know what I'm talking about."

Danika gave a casual shrug, though her pulse had already quickened. "Enlighten me."

His smile vanished like a switch flipped. "The pact for peace. Signed in 1906. The one that could unravel everything my family has built for more than a century."

Her pulse kicked up another notch, but her face remained neutral.

He stepped closer, voice dropping. "My grandfather believed in all that stuff. Peace, harmony, the greater good. Noble ideas, sure. Just not the kind that survive in the real world."

"Really?" Danika fought the nausea crawling up her throat. "Why would you say that?"

"Because peace is a story people like to hear. Everyone knows you can't build an empire on harmony."

He let that hang in the air, taking a step back and adjusting his cuff as if the topic bored him now. "My father taught me that important lesson. He disagreed with his own father so much that he made sure everything he'd stood for was discredited."

"What do you mean?" Danika pretended she was unaware, but more pieces of the puzzle were clicking into place. Online references related to the peace pact all had the same wording:

Fabricated story. Historical hoax. Unsubstantiated legend.

Now she understood. Julian's own father had planted the original seed of doubt. From there it bloomed—through journalists, think tanks, paid influencers—until it became an accepted fact.

Fact by repetition. Truth by echo.

And now, instead of being an unprovable myth, the real thing had surfaced. And Julian was unraveling.

She kept her voice quiet. "And if the public knew the truth?"

Julian's gaze hardened. "Then everything my family built crumbles. Every deal. Every alliance. Every inch of control."

For a moment, his voice dipped into something almost calm. "It's remarkable how fragile truth can be, isn't it? Bury it deep enough, repeat the lie often enough, and eventually no one bothers to dig."

His eyes locked on hers—cold, unblinking. "Until *you*."

He sat down on the edge of the desk, drawing a breath as if to steady himself, a thin performance of control. "I know you found it. The security footage doesn't lie." His voice dropped. "And I know you stashed that worthless stack of papers in the safe as a decoy."

He grabbed the bundle from his desk and slammed it down with a crack, the sound echoing in the room like a gunshot. Danika flinched.

So, her room had been searched. And Julian had taken the bait.

Danika suppressed the urge to look at Cole, but mentally chalked up another win for him. It hadn't stopped this moment from happening.

But it had delayed it.

Julian exhaled, the false calm in his voice more terrifying than his anger.

"I know you're both smart enough to understand how much danger you're in."

He let the words hang. Danika felt the heaviness of them settle in the air like a curtain of dense fog.

"So here's my dilemma," he said, steepling his fingers. "Which one of you can I break first?"

Danika felt, rather than saw, Cole glance over at her.

Julian's gaze flicked to him.

"The way I see it, Cole's strong. The type that won't give up without a fight. But..."

He tapped a single finger on his cheek, slowly, deliberately. "He has a flaw."

Danika's pulse quickened. She didn't dare move. She hardly even breathed.

"He's virtuous," Julian said. "Selfless. The kind of man who would take a bullet for someone else."

Cole stood a little straighter, posture tightening like a spring. He knew where this was going.

Julian's eyes turned back to Danika. "Which is why you're here."

She shook her head, confused. "I don't understand."

Julian laughed—a sharp, humorless sound that made her skin crawl. He turned to Cole.

"Want to explain it to her?"

Cole looked away. "I'll pass."

Julian gave her a smile that never reached his eyes. "Here's how it works. If Cole doesn't give me the location of the pact... You pay the price."

The breath Danika had been holding slipped from her lungs in a silent gasp. The understanding landed hard.

Julian had found the perfect vulnerability: Cole's inherent goodness.

He was betting Cole wouldn't stand by and let someone else suffer—not when he could do something about it.

Not ever.

It was twisted. Calculated.

And it just might work.

Julian leaned forward, voice soft now. "Of course, you can save yourself the pain by telling me where it is. I'm extremely considerate that way."

Cole took a step forward, forcing Julian to shift his focus.

"That's enough," he said. "You've made your point."

Julian gave a small nod, but the smile didn't fade. "Have I?" He turned to Danika. "Are you ready to talk?"

Danika didn't hesitate. "I'll pass," she said, lifting her chin in defiance, mimicking the confidence she'd seen in Cole so many times. She wondered if he felt as poised as he looked... because she sure didn't.

In the breath it took to say the words, two men stepped forward, one on either side of her. The idea of trying to get away, which had flickered briefly in the back of her mind, vanished. They were too close. Too prepared.

Julian glanced at his watch, jaw tightening with impatience. "We're wasting precious time," he muttered, pulling out his phone and tapping quickly.

The sudden stillness in the room only made the storm in her head louder.

"I'll give you each one more chance," he said, voice cool but with a thread of heat smoldering just beneath it. "Tell me where the pact is."

His gaze moved from Cole to Danika and back again. No response. No reaction.

Julian smiled faintly and hit send before slipping the phone back into his pocket. "Danika is going to take a little trip with these gentlemen."

A tense silence filled the room. Danika didn't move, didn't blink—only listened to the pounding of her pulse, loud and relentless in her ears. Across the room, she sensed the shift in Cole. The air around him snapped taut, his focus razor-sharp, like a wire stretched to its breaking point.

And beneath the fear crawling up her spine, guilt twisted in her chest—a knowledge that she was responsible for the position she'd put him in.

Julian leaned back, as if this were simply a business meeting and not the prelude to something far darker. "Don't worry," he said to Cole, mock sympathy in his voice. "We won't hurt her. That is, as long as you cooperate."

Cole didn't speak.

But Danika saw it. The subtle shift in his jaw. The flicker in his eyes.

He was calculating his options.

Sixty-Two

Cole drew a deep breath, and his fingers curled into fists, causing a flicker of fear to stir in Danika's chest. The men beside him must have felt it too. They each grabbed an arm before he could move. But she could still feel the pent-up power simmering just beneath the surface.

She took a deep breath and turned to Julian. "There's only one problem with that plan." Danika's voice did not quiver, though her legs were trembling so much she was afraid she was going to fall.

"And what is that?"

"Cole doesn't know where the pact is hidden."

"Dani... *don't.*"

The gaze Cole shot her—both fierce and tender—was one she knew she'd never forget.

"What are you talking about?" Julian stood and walked toward her, stopping mere feet from her.

"You're right that we found the pact. And Cole hid it." Danika paused for effect. "But I took it and re-hid it." She swallowed and cleared her throat. "So Cole is of no use to you, and if you harm me, you'll never find the pact." She looked him in the eye. "Never."

She didn't dare look at Cole, but she could feel his surprise, sharp and silent.

"And you have another problem, Julian." Cole's voice was calm, almost casual, like he was commenting on the weather or the price of eggs.

Julian's gaze snapped to him, suspicion flaring. "What do you mean?"

"Everything said in this room is recorded."

A flicker of alarm crossed Julian's expression, but it was Danika who stiffened in shock. She turned to Cole, barely containing her surprise, verging on anger. He had never told her she was being recorded when she was in this room!

Julian's head whipped around, eyes scanning frantically, trying to spot the device. "I'll find it," he snarled, his voice laced with fury. "And I'll destroy it, even if I have to burn this whole room to the ground."

He stalked toward Cole, jabbing a finger in his face. "This isn't a problem I can't fix."

"Well," Cole said, "I hate to be the bearer of bad news, but you actually have an even bigger problem."

Julian's nostrils flared. "Stop talking! I'm in control. Not you. And I'm not leaving this room until I get what I want."

Cole sighed, opened his jacket, and pointed to the radio clipped to his belt. "My mic is open."

Julian froze as his gaze shifted to the radio. A second ticked by before understanding dawned in his eyes. He blinked. Once. Twice. Then his gaze flicked to the door. Droplets of sweat formed instantly on his forehead.

"My men are at the door." Cole's voice was unruffled, but had a threatening tone to it. "And they've already called for backup."

Danika's heart pounded as she looked at him and noticed the earpiece tucked discreetly in his ear. He hadn't just been listening to Julian. He'd been monitoring the entire security team the whole time. And he'd been stalling for as long as possible until his men were in place.

"I'd strongly advise your men to stand down," Cole added. "They're outnumbered. And outgunned."

As if on cue, the two men flanking Cole raised their hands and took a measured step back, already anticipating the firepower gathering beyond the door.

Julian, however, exploded into motion. With a sudden burst of rage, he pulled a knife from his pocket. "Tell me where the pact is—or I'll kill you!"

Danika took a moment to react, but Cole was already moving. With a swift, instinctive motion, he stepped in front of her—just as Julian lunged. Even though the knife appeared to make contact, Cole didn't stop. He seized Julian's wrist, twisting with practiced precision, wrenching the knife free. At that moment, the door burst open and his security team flooded in, weapons drawn.

The chaos lasted mere seconds. Julian was forced to the ground, his hands wrenched behind him, handcuffs clicking into place.

Danika struggled to breathe.

"You need a medic?" One of the men stopped in front of Cole, concern in his voice.

Cole shook his head. "Just a scratch."

Danika stared at the red blotch on his white shirt. "I think it's more than just a—"

She stopped mid-sentence when Cole's fingers wrapped around her wrist. His grip was firm, his touch warm despite the cold sweat on his skin.

"You good here then?" The voice of one of his men interrupted them.

"Yeah, we're fine." Cole's gaze never left Danika's face as he talked. "Do a sweep to make sure the guests are safe."

"Yes, sir."

As soon as the man stepped away, Cole pulled her closer and stared at her. "Don't ever do that again," he said, his voice rough. Raw.

"Do what?"

Cole's eyes—those clear, piercing blue eyes—held hers, a storm of emotion swirling in their depths. He placed both of his hands on her arms, his fingers tightening as he gave her a slight shake.

"Scare me like that," he said hoarsely, his face pale with emotion. "Don't ever do that again."

Her breath caught. "What are you talking about?"

"Telling Julian you moved the pact." His voice wavered as his hands tightened even more on her arms. "Why did you do that?"

Danika's heart squeezed painfully. She was about to answer when a movement in the doorway caught her eye, followed by the sound of a voice that sent a quake of fear shooting up her spine.

"Well, well, well."

Cole turned around in the blink of an eye and pushed Danika behind him again.

"Senator Wiley," Cole said. "Sorry, but this room is off limits to the general public."

Sixty-Three

Meanwhile...

Champagne glasses clinked like delicate wind chimes beneath the soft glow of the overhead lighting fixtures. The dining room pulsed with laughter and endless chatter, as if the power outage had never happened. With drinks flowing and nerves loosening, the blackout became a mere hiccup in the evening, erased by the opulence, power, and influence in the room.

Dalton Rivers walked into the dining room while tugging absently at his shirt cuff, a half-hearted attempt to settle the tension in his shoulders. He didn't want to be here. Too many polished smiles. Too many lies dressed in tuxedos. But he knew better than to skip out entirely. Julian expected him, and absence would be its own kind of message.

When the lights had gone out earlier, Dalton had allowed himself a sliver of hope that the evening would be called off. Maybe he could escape down to the lake, let the cold air clear his mind.

Unfortunately, the brief blackout had only added a sense of drama to the event, not derailed it entirely.

Now here he was—too wired to sleep, too wary to let his guard down.

He drifted toward one of the buffet tables, drawn by the knowledge that Julian would not let anyone go away hungry. His eyes were scanning the appetizers when a sudden movement caught him off guard. A woman in a sparkling green dress stepped abruptly into his path as she veered to avoid an oblivious man balancing an absurdly full plate of food.

Dalton reached out to steady her, and she grabbed his arm, sending an unexpected jolt of warmth through him.

"Oh—pardon me, miss," he said, managing a small, rueful smile. "Wasn't watching where I was going."

She gave a nervous laugh, one hand fluttering near her collarbone as if trying to hold herself together. Her gaze darted, restless and uncertain. Her smile was just a shade too uneasy.

"No, it's my fault," she said quickly. "I'm such a klutz."

Her voice trembled a bit, and Dalton regarded her more closely. She didn't look like someone who belonged in a place like this—too genuine, too raw around the edges to be around all this pretentiousness and pomposity.

She was beautiful in a way that didn't try too hard. No glitter. No gloss. Just the kind of natural ease that suggested she'd be more comfortable beneath a wide blue sky than crystal lights. And maybe that's why he couldn't look away.

There was something familiar about her—not only her face but her presence—like a forgotten song that stirs something the moment it plays again, making you wonder how you never missed it.

"Oh, you're Dalton Rivers, right?" she said, her voice brightening. "I thought I recognized you. I'm Peggy. I work here, so I've seen you around over the years."

She offered her hand. It was warm, soft, grounded in a way that made him pause.

He took it gently, returning her smile with one of his own. "Nice to meet you, Peggy. I remember you now, though I don't think you were dressed up quite so much last time I saw you."

Peggy laughed, and her uneasiness seemed to relax just enough to let something real shine through. "You're right. This isn't my usual attire."

As she nervously tucked a loose strand of hair behind her ear, Dalton noticed the faint flush that colored her cheeks, delicate and telling, like a flicker of vulnerability she hadn't meant to show.

He didn't press.

"Can I get you a drink?" he asked, nodding toward a waiter weaving past with a silver tray of flutes. "You look like you could use one."

She tilted her head, studying him, giving Dalton the impression she was going to decline. But then her shoulders eased, and a soft grin tugged at her lips.

"That sounds wonderful," she said, like she'd decided to enjoy herself instead of playing it safe.

He returned with two glasses of champagne and handed her one, noting how her eyes scanned the crowd—not with curiosity, but intent.

"You looking for someone?"

"Julian, actually," she said, her expression dimming into a frown. "He brought me, then vanished not long after the lights came back on. Charming, right?" She lifted her glass and looked at him over the rim with big, brown eyes that held him captive. "Not exactly a great confidence builder."

Dalton masked the flare of anger that tightened his jaw. Julian's gift for discarding people like empty glasses was unmatched. "Doesn't sound like much of a date," he said. "But that says more about him than you."

She gave a small shrug, a gesture obviously meant to downplay the sting. "It was nice to be invited. I got to dress up, pretend I belong here." Her voice was light, but it couldn't quite hide the undertow of disappointment.

Dalton offered a half-smile. "So you're one of those people who always find the silver lining. Eternal optimist?"

"Guilty as charged." She laughed, the sound bright and bubbling with warmth. Her eyes sparkled—not with champagne, but with something brighter. "That's what my best friend always says. Not a bad thing, right?"

Before he could answer, her clutch chirped. She slipped out a bright red phone, the screen casting a soft glow on her features.

"Speak of the devil," she said, her face brightening. "This text is from Julian."

Dalton watched her lips move silently as she reread the message. Then she looked up, blinking as if waking from a spell.

"He wants me to meet him later."

"Is he here?" Dalton's tone was casual, but his alertness kicked into high gear.

She shook her head, glancing at the screen again. "He's tied up in an unexpected meeting at the moment."

Dalton's jaw ticked.

"He says he'll be done by ten," she said, reading the text again. "And I should meet him at the footbridge by the lake."

Dalton checked his watch. "That's nearly an hour from now."

Peggy nodded, her fingers absentmindedly tucking the same stray strand of hair behind her ear. "That gives me enough time to fix my hair." She glanced at her reflection in the tall window beside them, smoothing a hand over the side of her head. "Poor Julian. I'm sure he has a million things on his plate. And you know how he is... so generous. So charming."

Dalton studied her face more closely now. He couldn't believe she would defend a man who had clearly abandoned her. She wasn't faking it—he could see that. She believed what she was saying. Or maybe she just *wanted* to believe it.

And that worried him.

"Yes," he said, his voice low. "I do know how Julian is."

The low hum in his ears that started when she read the message swelled into something sharper, more insistent. It pressed at him like a warning bell, vibrating through muscle and bone, shattering any pretense of calm.

"You're sure that message was from Julian?"

She looked surprised by the question, then smiled—wide, red-lipped, and beautiful in that effortless, trusting way that made his stomach twist. "Of course. Who else would it be from?"

She set her drink down long enough to slip her phone into her clutch, then picked the glass back up for one last sip, unaware of the knot forming in Dalton's chest.

He hesitated, shifting his weight, trying to stay grounded. He didn't want to come off as pushy. But he also didn't want to watch her walk straight into something she couldn't see.

"I'd be happy to tag along," he offered, keeping his voice light.

She studied him a moment, tilting her head as if unsure whether to be flattered or amused. "You mean like a bodyguard?"

He gave her a crooked grin. "Well, I have played one on TV."

That earned a warm, enchanting laugh, but it faded too fast.

"Thanks," she said, a gentle smile on her lips. "But I'll be fine."

She set her glass on the table for good this time and extended her hand. "It was really nice meeting you, Dalton. After all these years."

He took her hand and gave it a light squeeze, holding on for a second longer than necessary. "Likewise."

Then she turned and walked away, heels tapping a soft rhythm across the wood floor as the crowd seemed to part for her without noticing.

Dalton stood motionless, jaw tight, his ears still buzzing—not from champagne or noise, but from something sharper.

Instinct.

This was the part in the movie where the hero should make plans to swoop in just in time—cool, unshakeable, prepared for the save.

He exhaled, slow and steady, reminding himself he'd played this part dozens of times.

But this wasn't a movie—and he wasn't a real hero. Just an actor, reciting lines someone else had written.

And here, there would be no retakes. No director to yell cut if something went wrong.

As he watched her go, a hollow ache settled in his chest—familiar and unwelcome. It reminded him of a recurring nightmare where he showed up unprepared, the words gone from memory, the lights too bright.

Only this was worse.

Because this time, the scene hadn't even been written—and the script was up to him.

As a last resort, he scanned the room for that security guy—Cole. Professional. Sharp-eyed. Cool under pressure.

He'd know what to do.

But what could Dalton say?

Julian sent a text asking his date to meet him by the lake.

It sounded harmless. Silly, even.

Then again, it might not hurt to stop by the security office.

Because if he was being honest, improvisation had never been his strength.

Sixty-Four

Security HQ

Senator Wiley ignored Cole's comment and walked casually into the room. "I got a text from Julian and thought I'd stop by."

He adjusted the knot of his tuxedo tie with the kind of care that made Danika's stomach twist—slow, deliberate, theatrical. A man who knew exactly how much power he held.

Then, with a casual flick of his fingers, he gestured toward Cole's belt. "Do me a favor—turn off that radio."

Danika's heart sank as she watched Cole comply and heard the soft ping as the device powered down. It sounded louder than it should have—sharp and final, like a lifeline snapping.

Their only connection to the outside world and any hope of backup vanished into thin air.

"You couldn't leave it alone, could you?" Wiley walked toward them, his voice dropping to a more threatening tone.

"Leave what alone?" Cole's voice was calm, almost indifferent—unshaken by the senator's presence. The composure he exuded drew her in. She reached for him without thinking, her fingers curling into the fabric of his jacket like it might secure her to something solid.

"If you're talking about the corruption you've been pushing for the past thirty years," Cole continued evenly, "then yeah. You're right. I can't leave that alone."

Danika bit her lip and closed her eyes, bracing for the response.

Wiley swore under his breath. She heard the sharp click of his shoes as he stepped closer. When she opened her eyes, he was wagging a finger at Cole like a schoolmaster reprimanding a disobedient child.

"You—" He jabbed the air toward Cole. "And you," he snapped, turning the finger toward Danika, "have been a thorn in my side for the past two years."

He gave a bitter smile, one that didn't reach his eyes. "That ends today."

Cole shifted, straightening to his full height and crossing his arms—unmoved. "Really?" he asked. "And what are you planning to do about it?"

Wiley's response was wordless. He pulled his phone from his pocket and typed with surprising speed, for a man his age, fingers flying across the screen. Then he looked up, eyes gleaming.

"In a few minutes, a press release will hit every major media outlet in the country," he said. "It will state—on official Congressional letterhead—that the so-called pact discovered at Mohonk is a fake. A forgery."

Danika's voice cut through the tension from behind Cole. "No one's going to believe that."

Wiley turned his gaze on her and let out a dry, humorless laugh. "Coming from Senator Wiley? With the full weight of Congress behind it?" He raised his brows. "Of course they will."

The senator's look of satisfaction faltered at the sound of footsteps. He turned as a shadow appeared in the threshold.

Dalton Rivers stood casually in the doorway, dressed to kill in his perfectly tailored tuxedo, and appearing every inch the leading man. He leaned against the doorframe like he belonged there.

"Hope I'm not interrupting anything," he said, voice smooth, casual.

"You are," Wiley snapped. "This has nothing to do with you, Rivers."

Dalton's posture didn't change, but something sparked behind his eyes—a flicker of steel beneath the charm. Danika saw it. Determination. Resolve. The kind of steadfastness that only comes after years of regret. It was as if, in this moment, he'd decided to stop playing the role others had handed him—and finally write his own part.

"Strange," Dalton said lightly. "I have a feeling it has everything to do with me."

Wiley scoffed. "Whatever stunt you're planning, don't bother. This is well above your pay grade, Hollywood."

Dalton took a step forward, hands still in his pockets. "I'm sure it is. But after all these years, I think I've earned the right to turn down a script I don't like—and write a new one."

The tension crackled again, thick and stifling, like the moments before a summer storm breaks. "I wouldn't do that if I were you," Wiley said, voice low and dark. "You know the dirt I have on you."

Dalton smiled, a slow, knowing grin. "You mean the stories you made up? I'm not afraid of those anymore."

He pulled his phone from his pocket and turned it in his hand, thumb hovering over the screen.

"Especially not when I've got the real story."

With a single swipe, the room filled with the crackling hiss of a recorded conversation.

Wiley's voice boomed through the speaker—harsh, unmistakable.

"Don't test me, Julian. The vote will pass—so make sure the requests are packaged right. Once the signatures are in, no one will question the shift in allocation."

Danika's eyes darted to Wiley, catching the flicker of panic that crossed his face. It was fleeting—but it was real. A crack in the armor. A glimpse of the man behind the performance.

Wiley's voice came again, slick, calculated, and unmistakably smug.

"The funding is ready to go. The delegates want peace. That's what it will look *like they're getting. The rest of the world won't know the difference until it's too late."*

Dalton tapped the screen, silencing the audio. "There's more," he said, tilting his head toward Wiley. "But I think you get the picture."

Wiley's face flushed. "Where did you get that? It's not admissible in court!"

Dalton's voice remained even. "I was standing on the wooden bridge above the rock cave last night." His eyes locked on Wiley. "And you're right. This recording isn't admissible. I wasn't part of the conversation."

He turned to Danika, flashing a wry smile. "You'd be amazed at what people say when they think a movie star's too self-absorbed to listen. Turns out, I'm a better actor than most people thought."

Danika felt the breath rush from her lungs. The cave. That semi-secret hollow at Mohonk that Peggy had first told her about. It felt secluded the moment you stepped inside, yet voices still carried easily. The solitude was only an illusion.

Wiley held up a hand—not to surrender, but to bargain. "Wait," just as four of Cole's men surged past Dalton, fanning into the room with precision.

Dalton stepped aside, a flicker of something unreadable crossing his face. He looked like he wanted to talk to Cole, but checked his watch and backed away into the shadows.

Danika lost track of him after that.

"Everything okay in here?" one of Cole's men asked. "We lost contact with you."

Cole nodded, eyes never leaving Wiley. "Funny thing," he said dryly. "A radio that's suddenly shut off? It alerts my team faster than an SOS."

I wish I had known that, Danika thought to herself. Her knees nearly gave out from the rush of adrenaline, fear, and sudden relief.

Wiley's expression didn't flinch, even as two men began to escort him toward the door. For a moment, it was as if his mind refused to register what was happening. But Danika could feel it—the pressure building behind his silence like thunder in a cloud-choked sky.

And then, as predicted, the storm broke. As they got to the door, Wiley dug in his heels, twisting against the agents' hold.

"If you think this ends with me," he snarled, "you don't know anything about Monarch." His voice rose, his composure unraveling. "You don't understand what you're doing—what you're destroying!"

"Keep moving," the man on his left said, grabbing his arm.

"Everything I did was for the greater good!" Wiley yelled, half-turning, as they started through the doorway. "The average voter doesn't have the capacity to grasp what's at stake. We know what's best!"

His voice echoed off the walls before dissolving into silence.

Danika didn't speak at first. Neither did Cole.

When the last tremor of Wiley's rant faded, Cole turned to her, calm and composed as if nothing had happened. His voice was low but direct, like they were simply resuming an earlier conversation.

"Where did you re-hide the pact?" he asked. "And why?"

When she didn't answer, he lifted her chin with one finger, forcing her to meet his eyes. "Don't you trust me?"

Danika hesitated. "I didn't re-hide it."

He blinked. "What?"

"I only said that so he'd have no reason to keep you."

Cole stared at her, a slow blink betraying that her answer wasn't the one he'd expected.

There was a long silence between them before Danika spoke again.

"Since we're being honest," she said, "why didn't you tell me everything in this room was being recorded?"

Cole's jaw flexed. "Because it wasn't," he said. "I just told him that."

Another pause, and then without warning Cole pulled her into his arms. For one suspended moment, Danika let herself give in to the feelings she'd buried, finally acknowledging the attraction she hadn't admitted existed.

Cole exhaled long and slow, his forehead resting against hers. He didn't say anything, didn't push for her to say anything either. Because for now, this quiet, tentative surrender was enough. Nothing else mattered.

Not the pact.

Not the danger.

Not even the past that had brought them to this unexpected present.

Only this.

Only them.

—Until one of Cole's men entered the room. "Sir, we have a problem."

Cole straightened. "What is it?"

The man stepped in, eyes flicking between them. "Julian wanted me to tell you something. I didn't want to relay it over the radio."

Cole waited, his nerves going on high alert, even though he had no reason to believe anything could be wrong. Maybe Julian's cuffs were too tight, or he wanted something to eat before going to jail. "What is it?" he asked, exasperation evident in his tone.

The man cleared his throat. "He wanted me to tell you he's willing to negotiate."

Cole's voice sounded thunderous. "Negotiate? With me? Why would I even entertain that?"

The agent cleared his throat. "He said it had something to do with Peggy."

Sixty-Five

Cole made a sound—low and raw—the kind that made it clear his reaction wasn't just anger, but pain sharpened by fear. The muscles in his jaw twitched as he yanked his phone from his pocket and strode toward the door, already thumbing the contact button under Peggy's name.

He didn't wait, but talked into his mic as he listened to it ring. "Check the dining room for Peggy. Green gown..."

"Emerald green," Danika said quickly, hurrying to keep up. "With sequins."

"Emerald green. With sequins," Cole repeated, his voice clipped. "Pull the camera feed. At least thirty minutes back. Start from the service wing."

The phone rang in his ear—once, twice. He walked faster.

Third ring.

Fourth.

Fifth.

Voicemail. Peggy's recorded voice was far too calm—and happy—for what churned in his gut.

He hung up, redialed. Walked faster.

Same thing.

His stomach dropped like a stone into dark water.

Peggy never ignored his calls—never. Even if she was mad at him.

The air felt thicker now, as if the corridor itself was closing in on him. He passed two of his men near the service hallway—both straightening as he approached.

"Have you seen Peggy?" he asked, voice low, tight, dangerous.

They shook their heads. "Not since earlier. She's at the gala, right?"

"That's where she should be," he muttered.

He tried her again. Voicemail.

Shoving the phone back into his pocket, he didn't stop moving. His dress shoes hit the floor harder now, a rhythmic warning.

"Tagg," he said into his mic. "Start pulling guys out of the dining room. I want every available man sweeping the building. Every floor. Every hallway. Send two more to SecHQ to study camera feeds."

He turned a corner, eyes blazing.

"Bart—start questioning Julian. Don't bother being gentle."

He paused long enough for the impact of his next words to settle.

"And tell him I'm on my way."

The problem was that Cole didn't know where to start. Had no idea where to look. He hadn't had eyes on her for more than an hour. She could be anywhere by now.

And that terrified him more than anything else.

Why hadn't he checked on her sooner? Why hadn't he insisted she stay away from Julian? Why hadn't he seen it coming—that Julian would use her like he used everyone else?

His hands curled into fists as the guilt slammed into him like a second heartbeat.

"It's not your fault," Danika said, like she could hear the storm tearing through his thoughts.

But it was.

When he pushed into the dining room, his eyes swept the space, taking in the sea of glittering gowns and black tuxedos. The clink of glasses. The muted laughter. The surreal calm of a party still in motion.

Peggy should have been easy to spot. She always stood out at these events—not because she was flashy, but because she tried so hard. Always smiling too widely, eager to be liked by people who were sometimes too self-absorbed to care.

She was the kindest, most open-hearted woman he'd ever known—and one of the most vulnerable. Generous. Compassionate.

And too damn trusting.

Dear God, not Peggy, he prayed, swallowing the sudden rush of panic.

Then he stopped cold, his earpiece crackling to life.

"We may have found something on the footbridge," a voice said.

Cole's blood congealed, slow and heavy, like ice creeping through his veins.

"I'm on my way," he barked, already moving.

The stretch between the dining room and the footbridge disappeared in a blur of pounding steps and swinging doors. He slammed through the last exit so hard the frame shook, shoes thudding against the wood of the porch as he sprinted around the corner.

Flashlights darted over the planks of the bridge and along the water's edge. Shadows flickered. Men moved in tight formation, combing the area with urgency.

"What do we have?" Cole called out, breath short, voice tight.

One of the men straightened and held something up, hitting it with the beam of his flashlight so Cole could see.

"I found this at the edge," he said.

Cole stepped closer, squinting against the glare. It was an earring—small, delicate, and green. He didn't know for sure it was Peggy's, but his gut clenched as if it were.

He took a slow, steadying breath, willing the surge of panic to stay beneath the surface. Then, on impulse, he pulled out his phone again and pushed the contact button for her number.

After a few seconds, the garbled buzz of a ringtone pierced the silence.

Every head turned. Flashlights swung toward the sound, converging on the small red square in the weeds near the footbridge. Half-hidden. Still vibrating faintly.

Peggy's phone.

The glint of it in the water made something inside him drop. The ground around it told the rest of the story—trampled brush, scuffed earth. Signs of a struggle. Evidence that someone had fought hard not to disappear.

"Block this off," Cole said, his voice clipped and terse. He drew in a breath of the night air, fighting as the iron calm he depended on wavered. He forced the next words out through sheer will. "Set a perimeter."

He reached for his radio at the same time as the unmistakable echo of hurried footsteps rang across the porch behind them. Cole turned and looked up as Dalton Rivers appeared from the shadows of Lake View's wraparound veranda, moving at a fast pace while looking at his feet.

He slowed and glanced up when he noticed the sweep of lights and the cluster of men. Then his eyes landed on Cole.

"If you're looking for Peggy," he said, slightly breathless, "she's safe in my room."

Silence fell.

The words hovered, suspended in the dense air between them.

Dalton took another step forward. "She lost her phone down here during a struggle. She wanted to call you, to tell you she's okay."

Relief hit Cole so hard it almost knocked him off balance.

He took the flashlight from the hand of the man beside him and aimed it at Dalton's face. "You okay?"

Dalton raised a hand to his cheek and touched the swelling under his eye with a wince.

"I'll be fine," he said. "Turns out I don't move as fast as I used to."

Sixty-Six

3 DAYS LATER...

The rain had started as a whisper.

Dani hardly noticed it at first—the light patter of droplets against leaves, the faint shimmer collecting on the path ahead. She pulled up the hood of her light sweatshirt, more from instinct than discomfort, and kept walking.

The sun had been shining when she left the Mountain House, and the air still held its warmth. The shower would pass quickly—but its arrival transformed everything. Each blade of grass sparkled like it had been strung with diamonds, somehow catching light from a cloudy sky. Had nature always put on a show like this during a rain shower, and she was only noticing it *now*?

Maybe she was finally learning how to slow down.

Lifting her head, she tried to get her bearings, unsure how far she'd wandered. The soft chorus of peepers carried faintly through the trees—a familiar, rhythmic song that told her she was near the Lily Pond.

Her gaze returned to the path as thoughts from the last few days rose to the surface. She exhaled, still trying to make sense of the storm she'd passed through.

The World Summit on Peace and Reconciliation was now part of the past—another neatly packaged chapter in the history books. On the surface, the conference had been a success: rebranded, reorganized, and resolved with not even a ripple of scandal.

The press never got a glimpse of the fault lines beneath the surface.

And that was thanks mostly to Miles Hutton, Senator Wiley's son-in-law. He'd stepped in at the eleventh hour, leveraging his media empire and Wiley's political clout to shape the narrative. The same man who had once used those tools to elevate Wiley's agenda had helped rewrite the story before it could be twisted and distorted.

Danika had misjudged him, dismissing him as another entitled kingpin with polished shoes and inherited power. But Cole hadn't rushed to judgment. He'd waited. Watched. Met Miles with open dialogue instead of cynicism.

In the end, Miles had chosen a path she hadn't expected he would—one not paved for him, but one he carved out himself. A path toward redemption. Toward fixing what had been broken.

As for Wiley and Julian, the official story was carefully spun—health-related complications and a quiet withdrawal from public life. Graceful, dignified, controlled... giving them more latitude than they deserved, but she had faith justice would be served in the end.

And then there was Dalton Rivers.

The man who'd spent a career behind carefully crafted scripts had stepped forward with a role no one saw coming. During a surprise appearance, he'd publicly endorsed the recovered pact. One speech. No teleprompter. No costume. Just truth.

It had been his most honest performance, and somehow, the one that mattered the most. In the end, truth had managed to slip in through the cracks of an elaborate ruse. Quietly. And, she prayed, permanently.

A few minutes later, Danika rounded the bend in the trail and caught sight of the Lily Pond. Mist curled off the surface like ghostly fingers, drifting and rising in the rain-damp air. The trees stood in reverent silence, their reflections soft and blurred on the water. The entire world seemed hushed, like she'd wandered into a dream or some forgotten cathedral carved into the forest.

This had always been one of her favorite places—but today, it felt different. Sacred.

Her eyes scanned the picturesque scene, then landed on a solitary figure standing on the narrow footbridge.

Even from this distance, there was no mistaking him—tall, formidable, with a stance that radiated relaxed control. The work trousers were gone, replaced by faded jeans and a black T-shirt stretched taut across broad shoulders. He stood with his forearms resting on the wooden railing, head bowed as he stared into the water, seemingly indifferent to the raindrops slipping from the branches overhead.

Cole.

She slowed, not wanting to interrupt, not sure if she was ready to speak—or even breathe. She placed a hand lightly against her chest to keep her heart from breaking through.

He turned his head slightly as if he'd *felt* her presence rather than heard it. When their eyes met, something in her steadied. His gaze carried that same quiet strength she'd come to rely on—and a tenderness that unraveled her more than she wanted to admit.

"Sorry to interrupt," she said as she stepped closer, rainwater sliding from her hood. "I needed to get out for a little fresh air."

Cole opened his mouth to respond, but the sky chose that moment to crack wide open. The rain shifted from gentle to torrential in a single breath—like Heaven had tipped a bucket.

Without a word, he reached for her hand and pulled her the rest of the way across the bridge, guiding her beneath the sloping roof of the summerhouse. The shelter was little more than a frame with a roof, but it was enough to separate them from the sudden downpour.

"Pretty good timing for your walk," Cole said, running a hand through his wet hair, flinging droplets onto the floor with a slight shake of his head.

She caught the fleeting trace of a smile on his lips, at odds with the weariness in his eyes and the rough stubble casting shadows along his jaw.

"You mean because the summerhouse saved me from the rain?" she asked, blinking water from her lashes. "Or because you're here?"

His expression faltered then, the smile slipping into something quieter. Deeper.

"Maybe a little of both." He turned and stared out over the pond. The mist lifted again, swirling in fantastical shapes over the water. "I wrapped everything up about a half hour ago. Thought I'd clear my head before heading back."

Dani nodded and waited, giving him space to say more. But he didn't. He only looked at her, and for a long moment, silence filled the space between them—not uncomfortable, just waiting.

"How's Peggy?" she asked at last.

"Pretty shaken at first, but she bounced back." He paused. "She's always had a bit of a crush on Dalton, so it kind of worked out."

Danika let out a soft laugh. "That's so romantic! Her white knight showed up in the nick of time and swept her off to safety. It sounds like something out of a movie." She closed her eyes and sighed. "A true happy ending."

"I guess so," he murmured.

Danika glanced up at his sullen response. He looked tired. Worn. In addition to overseeing security, he'd been dealing with classified debriefings and meeting with members of Congress. This was the first time she had a chance to talk to him—or even see him—since the gala three days ago.

And now, standing here under a rain-soaked roof, she saw how much weight he still carried..

"I guess you're curious about the pact," he said, his voice low. Always knowing what she was thinking.

She nodded. "If you're allowed to talk about it."

"It was more explosive than we thought," he said, raking a hand through his damp hair. "An Official Declaration of Unified Peace. Signed by more than two dozen nations that wanted to create a formal alliance built on transparency."

Danika's eyes widened. She hadn't expected something that bold. "I can't imagine what that's doing to Washington right now. To have proof that peace was once the plan. That it was sabotaged over the years."

"It's rattling cages," Cole said. "It's a true blueprint for building a moral and strategic peacekeeping strategy."

"Including specific actions?" Danika asked, tilting her head, already suspecting the answer.

"Detailed ones," he said. "A ten-year roadmap for global disarmament. Full transparency for industrial contracts tied to arms manufacturing. Nothing vague. It was audacious—radical, even."

Danika let out a low breath. "No wonder Julian didn't want it found."

Cole's jaw tightened. "It also called for diplomatic solidarity. If one signer pursued war, the others were bound to withhold support and push for arbitration instead."

"Wow. They were decades... generations even ahead of their time," she whispered. "And it was almost lost forever."

"Yeah." He rubbed the back of his neck, then let his arm drop. "The State Department thinks some of the signers acted on their own without full approval from their governments."

"No wonder they were scared," Danika said. "Doing what they thought was right instead of what they were told. They must have second-guessed themselves the moment they signed."

"Exactly. But the Alliance anticipated problems, so they built in a delay. The pact wasn't meant to go public for a year, giving them time to settle enforcement strategies and diplomatic pathways behind the scenes."

A beat of silence passed between them, filled only by the quiet drum of rain against the summerhouse roof.

"Is there any indication who set the fire?" she asked.

He exhaled. "That'll take time. But the working theory is that the pact was signed and then sparked immediate outrage from dissidents."

"Enough that Noah feared for its safety?"

"Yes." Cole glanced out at the mist-shrouded pond. "He was trusted, and some of the objectors probably spoke too freely around him. Maybe even confided their plans to him."

Danika's gaze went distant. "So he had to decide whether to stay silent—or act."

"Which, for him, must have been its own kind of war," Cole said.

"To steal the pact and then hide it," Danika said. "That's a heavy burden. The moral weight alone—"

"He didn't do what was easy—he did what was right," Cole said. "Once the fire was assumed to have destroyed the document, the attendees voted to bury the entire affair, put it behind them like it never even happened."

Danika looked down, her fingers absently tracing a drop of water trailing along the summerhouse post. "When you think about the pressure they were under, it is understandable. They thought they were protecting the world from a truth it wasn't ready to face."

She drew in a long breath and let it out slowly, exhaling the weight of the last several days all at once. It was as if they hadn't just uncovered Abigail and Noah's legacy—they'd become part of it.

"I'm glad that part of it is over," she said softly.

Cole leaned back against the post, rain still dripping from the edges of the summerhouse roof. "Well, it's not really over."

She looked up. "What do you mean?"

"Congressional hearings. Investigations. Interrogations." He shrugged. "You're going to be busy."

Danika sighed. "Yeah, I figured I'd be getting a call."

"They want to talk to you now, believe me," he said. "I told them you were... on vacation."

She smiled and caught the glint of humor behind his otherwise tired expression—a flicker that turned his eyes an unexpectedly vivid shade of blue.

"Thanks," she said, a little breathless. "I appreciate that."

"You should probably get some extra security until then." Cole's tone turned serious again. "What you know is dangerous. There are still dozens of people involved who haven't been named. Yet."

"Know anyone who can help with that?" She looked up at him, smiling suggestively.

"Yeah," he said evenly. "I can give you some names."

Danika's smile disappeared, and she bit her cheek to keep from saying anything else.

"Oh, by the way..." He reached beneath his rain jacket and pulled out a clear evidence-style bag with a yellowed envelope inside. "I talked them into letting me take this. They're going to want it back."

"What is it?" she asked, her fingers brushing his as she accepted the bag. Her eyes narrowed as she examined it, then looked up at him.

"It's a letter. Found wrapped up with the pact, but the date suggests it was placed there later. Much later."

Danika stepped back and lowered herself onto the bench behind her, eyes still locked on the envelope.

The paper was brittle; the ink faded. It was addressed to *Noah Morrison, Mohonk Mountain House, dated 1919.* A red stamp read: *Undeliverable. Return to Sender.*

She turned the bag over, breath catching in her throat.

The handwriting was unmistakable. She'd seen it once before on a folded note to the stone carver—her great-grandmother's.

Danika swallowed hard and looked up at Cole. "Should I open it?" Her voice was barely above a whisper. "Something meant for Noah's eyes but that he never saw?"

Cole didn't answer right away, but then nodded. "She came back here at some point and hid it with the pact. That wasn't an accident. She wanted someone to read it."

He sat down beside her, close enough that their shoulders touched.

"The federal agents agreed you should be the first to read it."

Danika slipped the envelope from the bag with careful fingers, opening the flap slowly, reverently—preserving as much as she could of the worn paper.

Then she unfolded the letter, and together they began to read.

My dearest Noah,

You need never apologize for writing to me. Your words were a balm to my heart, and I pray you receive these in return—and know how earnestly I am lifting you in prayer.

You once told me that truth is not ours to speak, but the Lord's to reveal—when hearts are ready and the hour appointed. I have clung to that wisdom through every silent day, entrusting both this secret and my love for you to the Keeper of Time.

I do not know if you remain here, or if you've already returned to the God who so faithfully guided your steps. If your suffering on earth has ended, then mine, I fear, has only begun. I shall never know peace without you—but I believe, with all that I am, that someday the world will *know peace* because *of you.*

Until that day and that hour, I will carry you in my heart... and wait.

Yours forever - Abigail

Danika folded the letter with shaking hands, her throat too tight to speak. She returned it to the envelope, then slipped it back into the evidence bag.

"He didn't get it in time," she murmured, handing it to Cole without looking up. "He never saw her words."

Cole accepted it silently and tucked it into his jacket. Before he could speak, Danika rose to her feet, turned away—and broke. She buried her face in her hands, the sob rising like a wave she couldn't hold back.

Cole stepped forward, turned her gently, and wrapped his arms around her as the storm within her finally let loose.

It wasn't just the letter. It wasn't just Noah and Abigail.

It was everything.

"It's so sad," she choked out, her breath catching between sobs.

"But it has a happy ending," he said tenderly against her hair. "Everything they believed in—everything they trusted—came to pass. They were right."

Danika inhaled deeply to calm herself and turned toward the pond again, watching the mist curl over the water. "Sorry," she said, with a faint shake of her head. "I'm not usually this emotional."

Cole didn't answer right away. For a long moment they simply stood there, the rain soft around them, time stretching like the space between heartbeats.

The world hadn't changed—but something in it had shifted.

Sixty-Seven

"What now?" Cole's voice broke through her thoughts.

She half-turned her head. "What do you mean?"

You heading back to Virginia?"

She gave a slow nod. "Yeah. End of the week."

The words hung there, suspended in the mist and rain. Silence followed—thick with everything that hadn't been said.

Danika returned her attention to the pond beyond the open archway, placing her hand lightly on the damp railing. She didn't want to look at him; didn't want to focus on the thoughts running through her mind either.

In two days, she'd climb back in her Jeep and drive three hundred miles away from here. She hadn't let herself think about it until now. It was too heavy. Too final.

Staring straight down, she watched the rain strike the surface of the pond, each drop sending out gentle ripples—circles upon circles, coiling, merging, dissolving, beginning again. The lily pads floated in clustered stillness, their green leaves forming an artistic mosaic upon the water. And all the while, the sound of the downpour drummed against the roof of the summerhouse, drowning out the rest of the world.

"I've never seen the Lily Pond like this," she said, almost to herself. "In the rain and the mist, it looks like a different place. Same pond, same bridge... but everything's different."

She glanced back at Cole's silence and found him staring at her.

"Yes. Everything's different. That's for sure." His voice carried a quiet ache that caught her off guard. He drew a long breath, then let it out slowly, lips pressed tight as if holding something back—something heavy.

She turned all the way around and looked up at him inquisitively. "Do you mean everything's different since finding the pact?"

He shook his head, a faint crease forming between his brows. "No," he said, staring straight into her eyes. "Since *you*."

Danika's breath caught—but she didn't look away.

"I didn't plan on any of this," she said, her voice quiet, uncertain why the words came out at all. Maybe because they were the only truth she could grab hold of in that moment.

He stepped closer, not hurriedly, but like a man who had made a decision and was ready to face what came next. The guarded expression was gone. In its place was something honest. Something open.

"Neither did I."

They stood in silence as the chorus of peepers swelled around them, the air between them buzzing with possibility—gentle, yet electric. The rain noticeably softened to a steady hush against the roof, tapping lightly on the water that circled them. It was a sound both ancient and familiar. The kind of sound you don't just hear—you remember.

"Sorry." He shook his head, obviously struggling for words. "I'm not good at this."

"At what?" She reached for the solid strength of his arm, steadying herself as the question hung in the air.

"This," is all he said, reaching out and brushing a strand of hair from her face. His jaw tightened—like he was wrestling with something just beneath the surface.

"Me neither." Dani cleared her throat, knowing her voice would be unsteady. She had spent weeks pretending she didn't care—or perhaps not knowing how much she did. She had assumed that at the end of her stay she would walk away, that this whole experience was simply a chapter in her life she would close.

Strange how a packet of old letters had led her here—to this moment, this shelter, this quiet ache she still couldn't name.

And what now? she thought.

What comes after this kind of unraveling—when the story you thought you were writing turns into something you never meant to begin? She looked up at him, her heart thudding like it had something to say.

Maybe it did. But she wasn't sure she was ready to hear it.

And she was even less sure that *he* was.

Cole's eyes closed briefly, a flicker of exhaustion crossing his face—a man carrying too much weight, both visible and unseen. She felt a sudden urge to ease the moment, to give him room to breathe, even if she couldn't yet find the words to offer.

"What about you?" she asked. "You'll be heading home, I guess."

He nodded as if relieved for the change in topics. "Yeah. Back to Phantom Force. See what they have for me next."

She tilted her head, curious. "Where's that based anyway? I've never heard of it."

"Virginia."

Danika jerked her head back even farther. "*Virginia*? I thought you were from up here somewhere. You never told me that!"

"You never asked," he said with that maddening calm of his.

She hit him on the arm, playfully—but hard. "But you worked here when you were a teen—"

"I grew up here. When I left the service, I moved to Virginia. It's where most of my buddies are."

"Okay. Narrow it down a little. *Where* in Virginia?"

"It's small—not even a town," he said in a voice that made it sound inconsequential. "No one's ever heard of it." His gaze drifted past her, vacant, like the conversation had already ended.

"I know Virginia pretty well." She stared up at him. "Try me."

"Okay." He took a deep breath and then spoke in a low tone as if revealing classified information. "Aldie."

She stepped back, blinking. "You're joking, right?"

The look in his eyes—half amused, half uncertain—told her he wasn't.

"You've known all this time you live like... maybe twenty miles from me?"

He shrugged. "It never came up."

"It never came up?" Her voice lifted, incredulous. Don't you think that's something I would want to know?"

His brow furrowed with a look of transparent honesty that needed no interpretation. "To be honest," he said, "I wasn't sure."

Something in his voice—plainspoken, unguarded, raw—stopped her cold. For a moment, she just stood there, the silence filling in what words could not. Then she stepped forward, laid her cheek against the damp fabric of his shirt, and let herself breathe him in—steady, solid, real. This was a peace that had nothing to do with international negotiations or historical pacts.

His voice came soft, almost hesitant, like a whisper meant only for her. "So... just to be clear, are you okay with that?" He pulled back enough to see her face.

"Yes, Cole. I'm okay with that." Her heart slowed as a quiet calm settled into her bones—along with an unexpected feeling of certainty. All of the doubt and hesitation were behind her now. "Hopefully, I can afford the security services of Phantom Force," she added. "Since they're so close."

A slow, relaxed smile spread across his face. "Not sure about that. Round-the-clock protection is pretty pricey."

"I'd need the best, of course."

"That would be Colt or Blake," he responded without missing a beat.

"That's not what I heard," Danika recalled Peggy's mention of his reputation.

"On second thought, you're right," he said, contemplatively. "I'd better handle it myself. No sense putting someone else through the excruciating process of trying to figure you out."

"*Excruciating*?" She stared up at him, blinking innocently. "Really? And you think you have me figured out?"

"Not by a long shot," he answered honestly. "But that doesn't mean I don't want to keep trying."

Danika's fingers trembled as she grabbed a handful of his shirt, not from apprehension, but recognition. Recognition of everything unsaid, everything almost lost, everything now beginning to be found.

Cole drew her closer—gently, needfully—as if he, too, was done talking and not ready to let go. Their lips brushed, so light it might have been imagined. Not a kiss, but a question hanging in the silence. He didn't press or push—just waited, eyes searching hers, every muscle taut with the fear she might pull away, laugh it off, pretend it hadn't happened.

But she didn't.

She'd followed her great-grandmother's footsteps in search of truth, not knowing it would lead *here*...

To possibility—not closure.

To a beginning—not an ending.

And perhaps that was the promise whispered through time: that love, once rooted, doesn't disappear. It lingers—through war and peace, through memory and mist—waiting for the next soul to find it and make it flourish again.

The End

Do you want to see what happens to the characters?

Catch up with Danika and Cole 25 years later.

Request the Epilogue.

Aim your phone's camera at the QR code and it will show you a link or visit: https://landing.mailerlite.com/webforms/landing/o0t6a2

Need help? Email: writefromthepast [AT] yahoo.com.

Dear Reader,

Thank you for joining me on this beautiful, messy, magnificent adventure—my first mystery novel.

The seed for *The Monarch Alliance* was planted during my first visit to the iconic Mohonk Mountain House as a travel blogger. I've stayed in countless historic inns, resorts, and hotels, but this one didn't just welcome me—it seized me, held me captive, and refused to let go.

Like all of my stories, this one began with a nudge. Not a lightning bolt or a grand epiphany—just a fleeting thought that flickered, faded, and then returned with irritating persistence. When it continued to linger, I found myself asking, *"Is this something I'm meant to do?"*

When the gentle nudge turned into a full-on push, there was no turning back. The writing became an obligation—a calling I couldn't ignore.

So you'd think that if a *higher power* wanted you to write a book, the plot and characters would flow with ease... right?

Wrong. The words *easy* and *effortless* have no place anywhere near this novel. My writing process is, to put it mildly, unconventional. I don't write scenes in order. Instead, I snatch them as they drift into my mind—half-formed, out of sequence, and often completely nonsensical. Later, I gather those fragments and try to weave them into something that resembles a story.

Writing a mystery novel that way means I planted clues without having the faintest idea what they meant. It also resulted in writing—and throwing away—more scenes than I care to admit.

I finally learned to let my characters run the investigation and wait for them to explain to me what the heck was going on.

If you've read any of my other novels, you know that time and history have a way of slipping into everything I write. I'm not sure why—only that the past seems determined to be heard.

And perhaps that makes sense. Time touches all of us equally—rich or poor, young or old—it moves forward, steady and relentless, carrying us onward whether we're ready or not.

Then again, there are moments I wonder if I'm truly writing these stories at all—or if they're just being told *through* me. Could it be that there are spirits from the past flitting around, wanting to be heard, and I was just the one who finally listened?

—*Jessica James*

Acknowledgements

Even though writing a book is a very solitary endeavor, no story is ever created alone. There are always people—some knowingly, some unknowingly—who help shape it along the way.

Truth be told, I would never have had the opportunity to visit Mohonk Mountain House if not for Darlene Fiske of the Fiske Group, a marketing firm that generously arranged a two-night stay to introduce me to the property. At the time, I believed I was simply researching and writing a travel feature on a historic mountaintop hotel—and so did she. I'll always be grateful for where this stay ultimately led me.

My deepest gratitude goes to Pril Smiley, a descendent of Mohonk's original owners. When I mentioned I was working on a novel, she not only read an early draft, but graciously performed a meticulous, line-by-line review to ensure historical and grammatical accuracy.

I'm also grateful to the entire Mohonk marketing team, who coordinated reservations and itineraries during my visits.

Special thanks to Nell Boucher, Mohonk's archivist, who sat with me during my first visit and patiently answered every question, sharing her deep knowledge of the property's remarkable history.

On the physical book creation side, a heartfelt shout-out to Lesia of *germancreative*, my cover designer, whose talent—and patience—never wavered through countless tweaks and multiple revisions.

And last, but certainly not least, my thanks to Glenn, who cooked dinners and washed dishes while I disappeared into the world of writing... then editing... and finally, laying out the novel itself.

I also want to apologize to anyone I've missed—especially my incredible early readers and everyone who's supported me since my very first book, *Shades of Gray*. There are too many of you to name, but your emails and messages throughout the years have meant more to me than you'll ever know.

This book may have been written over many long months of isolation, but it was made possible by many generous hands and open hearts. Thank you, all!

Fact or Fiction?

I remember the first time I saw Mohonk Mountain House rising above the trees like something from a fairytale or a dream. That was my first impression, but the more I learned about it, the more mysterious and intriguing it became.

Founded in 1869 by twin brothers Albert and Alfred Smiley, this Victorian mountaintop resort was envisioned as a peaceful retreat rooted in nature, simplicity, and moral purpose. The Smiley brothers, devout Quakers, believed strongly in quiet reflection, wholesome recreation, and the idea that natural beauty could restore both body and spirit.

Even in its earliest days, Mohonk was never merely a hotel. It became a gathering place for thinkers, reformers, and world leaders. Beginning in the 1890s, the Mohonk Conferences on International Arbitration brought diplomats, educators, and activists together to discuss peaceful resolutions to global conflict—decades before such ideas were widely embraced.

Architecturally, Mohonk evolved organically. Additions were made over decades rather than following a single grand plan, resulting in its distinctive silhouette of turrets, balconies, and sprawling wings. Many of the spaces guests walk through today—including the parlor where Danika sees the portraits—are very much as they were more than a century ago.

In *The Monarch Alliance*, real history serves as the backbone of the story—but fiction fills in the shadows. The hotel itself, its founding family, the peace conferences, and the mountain landscape—from Eagle Cliff and Sky Tower to the Lily Pond—are all there and part of the Mohonk experience.

What *is* fictional is the secret peace pact at the heart of the novel, the hidden correspondence tucked into unexpected places, and the idea that a small, private group continued the spirit of Mohonk's peace mission in secret long after the conferences ended.

The characters, their relationships, and the dangers they uncover are imagined—but they are intentionally woven into real moments and locations from Mohonk's past. The result is a story where readers can question the truth at every turn: *Did that really happen here?*

Sometimes the answer is yes. And sometimes, the answer is even more mysterious when an author imagines what *might* have been hidden in plain sight.

About the Author

Jessica James is the author of more than a dozen suspense, historical fiction, and military fiction novels ranging from the Revolutionary War to modern day. She is a four-time winner of the John Esten Cooke Award for Southern Fiction, and has won more than a dozen other literary awards, including a Readers' Favorite International Book Award and a Gold Medal from the Military Writers Society of America.

Her novels appeal to both men and women and are featured in library collections all over the United States including Harvard and the U.S. Naval Academy.

When not writing, Jessica loves to travel to the back roads of America and share hidden gems and historical destinations on her blog, Past Lane Travels.

WHAT READERS SAY

LACEWOOD: The past meets the present in this haunting read about the restoration of an abandoned mansion, and the secrets it reveals about a long-lost love.

"From start to finish, I loved reading Lacewood. It holds a special place in my heart and my bookshelf."

– NN Light's Book Heaven

PRESIDENTIAL ADVANTAGE: An unsuspecting First Lady must rely on a Secret Service agent to discover who can be trusted—and who will do anything to keep control.

"Ups and downs with twists and turns, and you won't believe who did it. Gripping, page turning and you will read it in one sitting."

– J from CNY

SHADES OF GRAY: A renowned Confederate officer discovers that the woman he promised his dying brother he would protect, is the Union spy he vowed to his men he would destroy.

"Rivals Gone with the Wind as my favorite novel of all time. I can think of no better way to describe it."

– Amazon Review

www.ingramcontent.com/pod-product-compliance
Lightning Source LLC
LaVergne TN
LVHW041057080826
845145LV00007B/1614

9781941020555